BAD OPTICS

ALSO BY JOSEPH HEYWOOD

Woods Cop Mysteries
Ice Hunter
Blue Wolf in Green Fire
Chasing a Blond Moon
Running Dark
Strike Dog
Death Roe
Shadow of the Wolf Tree
Force of Blood
Killing a Cold One
Buckular Dystrophy

Lute Bapcat Mysteries
Red Jacket
Mountains of the Misbegotten

General Fiction
Taxi Dancer
The Berkut
The Domino Conspiracy
The Snowfly

Short Stories
Hard Ground
Harder Ground

Nonfiction
Covered Waters: Tempests of a Nomadic Trouter

A Woods Cop Mystery

BAD OPTICS

JOSEPH HEYWOOD

Guilford, Connecticut

An imprint of The Rowman & Littlefield Publishing Group, Inc.
4501 Forbes Blvd., Ste. 200, Lanham, MD 20706

Distributed by NATIONAL BOOK NETWORK
800-462-6420

British Library Cataloguing in Publication Information available

Library of Congress Cataloging-in-Publication Data

Names: Heywood, Joseph, author.
Title: Bad optics / Joseph Heywood.
Description: Guilford, Connecticut : Lyons Press, [2018?] | Series: A woods
　cop mystery ; 11
Identifiers: LCCN 2017055813 (print) | LCCN 2017058752 (ebook) | ISBN
　9781493031047 (e-book) | ISBN 9781493031030 (hardcover : alk. paper)
Subjects: | GSAFD: Mystery fiction.
Classification: LCC PS3558.E92 (ebook) | LCC PS3558.E92 B33 2018 (print) |
　DDC 813/.54—dc23
LC record available at https://lccn.loc.gov/2017055813

Printed in the United States of America

For Lonnie, again, and always.

For Heather Stein, whose fight against cancer taught all of us the true meanings of resolve, toughness, and courage.

And for Jordan, Olivia, and Atley, whose whole lives lay ahead.

PART I: ALOQUOT

CHAPTER 1

Midwinter, 2009

HARVEY, MARQUETTE COUNTY

"Listen to me, kid, and do exactly what I tell you. Hop over the back seat and get my service revolver out of the holster. It's under the horse blanket. Be careful when you pull it out of the holster, then hand it up to me butt-first. Got it?"

"Yessir, butt-first."

"After you hand it to me, get under the horse blanket and stay there 'til I tell you different. Got it?"

"Yessir."

"Okay, go now."

Grady Service slithered over the seat, found the weapon, and passed it forward. "Curl up under the horse blanket and stay there, lessen you hear me tell youse different, okay?"

"Yessir." The boy crawled under the massive green wool coat, but kept a flap up with his right hand so he could hear.

"Marquette, dis is DNR Two Six. Dose fellas from over da Soo, I t'ink mebbe I got dose fellas right front of me, hey. Gray Stupidbegger, plates all mudded over. I'm just south Gwinn, M-35, headin' south t'ward Rock."

Stupidbegger. Grady could feel the tension in the clipped tone of the old man's voice, but still the old man had to make his dumb jokes. He always said Stupidbegger, never Studebaker.

"DNR Two Six, follow, but await backup, copy?"

"Yah, yah, Marquette, I hear. Dese jamokes ain't goin' nowheres now. I'm on dem."

"Two Six, Marquette, be advised you've got two of our deputies coming west, two Delta County units coming north, and a state unit in Rock right now, northbound."

"Got dat. Two Six," the conservation officer said as he grunted loudly and yelped, "Hold on back dere, kid. Dese knuckleheads goin' offen to da dirt but we right on dere butts like a tick on a dog's butt, and dis my house outen here inta dirt. All clay, dis road, and it startin' drizzle. Bad for dese fellas. Road gone be like pure snot in one minute, maybe less."

The car fishtailed wildly several times. The old man was chuckling as Grady braced himself to stop from sliding around on the back bench seat. "Hey Marquette, dis Two Six. Dat Stupidbegger, she just turn west on Rat River Spur, just before da big-ass hairpin break from north to east on M-35, copy?"

The car continued to fishtail, but less violently as his father got control, as the boy knew he would. Once the fishtailing stopped, they were hammered by deep ruts that grabbed the tires. He could hear the old man grunting as he willed the car along at high speed. "Kinda bumpy, kid, sorry, youse okay back dere?"

"I'm good," the boy said, the bumps making it difficult to talk.

"Marquette, copy Two Six. Be advised that unit Eight Four is now about one minute south of where you turned off. He should be right behind you now."

"Tell Eight Four dis clay like skatin' rink, tell 'em slow 'er down, I got dese guys good so let's not do no stupid drivin, hey. Dis road already messy and she gettin' worse."

"Copy, Two Six. Do not engage, copy?"

"Yah, yah, just dandy dere, Marquette." Grady Service's father said into his radio. Then, "Still okay back dere, kid?"

"I'm good," Grady managed.

"Attaboy. Listen me, dese birds jess slud offen from da road out into swamp muck. We gone try stop now, so hang on."

Grady grabbed hold of a metal brace on the bottom of the front seat and prepared to be thrown back against the seat back. He could feel the brakes locking and releasing as the old man pumped like crazy, but his father kept control and brought the car to a smooth stop. And it seemed that, even before they were stopped, the driver's door was open and the old man was out. Grady was alone. No sound but the Fury's engine, drizzle on the roof, the radio crackling nonsense, and, after a long few minutes, his old man's voice again.

"Kid, kid, your old man needs help. Come quick, kid!"

The old man needs help from me? Seriously, really? Head spinning, the boy threw off the heavy blanket, then swam over the front seat and out the open door into the black mud. His father had a man on the ground by the Studebaker, pinned down, the prisoner's right wrist cuffed to his right ankle. The prisoner was not fighting or resisting. There was blood on his face. It looked more black than red.

"C'mere, kid," Gibson "Gibby" Service told his son, his voice calm, not the least bit excited.

The old man held up his service revolver, a Colt .38 snubby that he kept in an ankle holster. Gibson had let his son shoot the short-barreled weapon for years, almost every day and sometimes even at night and in the snow so he could learn to shoot in all weather conditions.

"Hold dis piece on jamoke's head, kid. 'Is partner's run into da cedars down dere and I got go birddog 'im. Dis guy 'ere he even wiggle, shoot 'im. Left eye, like we always practice, okay?"

"Yes, sir, left eye."

The old man let loose a growly snarl of satisfaction and rapped the cuffed man with the back of his left fist, his service revolver in his right hand as he jumped up and surged toward the cedars. Gibson Service stopped and looked back. "Troopers gone be here right quick, Grady. Dey come, you give dat knucklehead to the troopers, tell 'em I fetch back pert quick dat udder jamoke, okay?"

"Okay," Grady said meekly, his mind racing, wondering, am I actually supposed to shoot this man? Or is the old man playing poker? He likes to put people on, does it to me all the time. But he said I'm in charge. With a *gun*. And a real prisoner, like a real cop. God.

The old man disappeared into the maze of white cedar and black spruce.

The handcuffed man said, "Listen, brat, I'm gonna kill your old man and then I'm gonna kill *you*."

Grady Service, age seven, pulled back the hammer on the snubby and released a single round right past the man's left ear. He shifted the barrel back to the man's left eye. The cuffed man slumped back, yipped, "Fuck," and had no more to say.

The troopers arrived with full music and ran to the boy and his prisoner, their weapons unholstered.

Grady calmly told them, "Dad's chasing the second guy. He says you guys take this jamoke and he'll bring back the other one real quick."

The troopers laughed.

The prisoner whined, "Sirs, this crazy-ass kid tried to shoot me."

One of the troopers said, "No he didn't. This is Grady, Gibby Service's kid. He wanted to shoot your sorry ass, you wouldn't be breathing now."

"This is a nightmare," the prisoner complained. "This damn U.P. You're all crazy people up here."

The deputy said, "Right, Grady?"

But Grady Service was thinking about something else that had just happened, something more significant. Grady. "My old man called me Grady," he told the deputy. Did I really hear that? I can't remember the last time. It almost never happens.

"*Grady!*" the deputy repeated. "You just shot a bullet right beside a man's head and all you can think about is what your old man calls you?"

Grady didn't reply. The old man must be nuts giving me a gun, he thought. Still, it had been "Grady," not the usual "hey kid."

Was there a numerical value assigned to earworms, and this *was* an earworm, not a dream, right? Or was it just that same damn dream? Yes, your old man called you Grady and you did fire a round past the guy's head. Jesus.

*****

Grady Service awoke in a heavy sweat, rubbed his eyes too hard, as if he were trying to push the memory back inside, hoping it would never escape, but knew too well that what he hoped for had no effect on his future.

"That dream again, hon?" Tuesday Friday asked.

"Pretty much," he mumbled.

"Your father caught the second suspect, right?"

But not in his dream. "Yah, caught 'im."

"And got a medal."

"Yah, a medal."

She said, "My sympathy is with that poor jerk on the ground, held prisoner by an armed seven-year-old. The Upper Peninsula runs on A.C. while the rest of the world runs on D.C. or whatever," she whispered sleepily. "Who the hell trains a seven-year-old child to shoot things, much less in the left eye only? *Would* you have shot that man?"

"Dunno," Grady said, but he did know, and knew with certainty. He hated the old man, but he would have done what he was told to do, especially after the old man had called him Grady.

"You do *know*," Friday said. "And I know, too. You would have followed the orders of the man you loathed. You would have shot that man."

"You weren't there. And I didn't shoot anyone."

"No, I wasn't there because I had a *normal* upbringing."

"It was family, you know, different, not duty, not family exactly, but something like both things—something you have to do."

"Duty? Listen to yourself, Grady Service. You feel a dedication to this state and its citizens which they *do not* reciprocate in the slightest. Almost everyone you talk to out in the woods thinks you're a wart on the ass of their progress and freedom. Do you understand that in the greater scheme of things, sense of duty or not, you *do not* count, and neither do I?"

"Doesn't matter," he whispered. She was wrong, he thought. You matter as long as you make yourself matter.

"Go back to sleep," she mumbled. "Please."

To what, the same damn dream? He'd had this one every night now for weeks, but never twice in a night. He got out of bed, stepped over Newf, their 130-pound Canary Island mastiff, and went to their son's bedroom.

The five-year-old boy was sleeping with his mouth open, as he always did. Shigun Friday. Not his son legally or biologically, but his son now and forever. The boy was about the same age he'd been when the old man started teaching him to shoot. Not much younger than when the old man gave him the loaded .38.

What the hell had the old man been thinking that day? Had he been drunk? Certainly he was hungover. Hungover was Gibby's normal condition. He was always drunk, drunk or hungover, these were his father's only two states. That morning they had been on their way to the Escanaba River around Cornell when they chanced upon the escapees. The old man had come back with the runner, as bloodied as his partner, but being dragged like a sack of freshly dug potatoes.

They remained with the Studebaker until a wrecker hauled it out of the muck and then continued on with their fishing expedition.

Grady hooked a big trout on a bedraggled fly of brown fluff that the old man had tied to his leader. He dragged the fish up onto the pea-gravel bar where it made him think of the cuffed prisoner. He was studying the fish when the old man shouted, "One fish don't make you no fisherman, kid. Get your butt back to work. We can't have no fish fry without no fish, and one ain't enough for the likes of us." Just like that, from kid up to Grady and back to kid, he thought. My lot in life.

Grady patted his boy's head and went back to bed, and the dream did not come again. How did little moments like this stay with you, and why? It was like a cancer or something. You couldn't get rid of it—even with so-called modern science.

CHAPTER 2

Midwinter, 2009

SLIPPERY CREEK CAMP

Grady Service's life was like a wet shroud draped over everything, the thing so clingy, tight, and heavy it was impossible for him to peel it off. Add to this a recent (and totally unanticipated) decision pushing his professional suspension to July 1.

The whole damn thing was a pain in the ass. And all his contacts in Lansing had suddenly seemed to have gone deaf and dumb, even his friend and ultimate boss, Chief Eddie Waco. No one could give him a full explanation for the suspension, no matter who he asked.

He kept telling himself that this was a preview of retirement, or death, which were the same thing. Nothing to do after decades of action, his ship now dead in the water, becalmed in a Sargasso Sea, perhaps permanently. Bad enough, but now the stupid recurring dreams and headaches were plaguing him—those sudden, blinding, and painful headaches, hurting beyond the reach of any known drugs or therapies. Endure. He knew he had to muscle his way through this crap, but it was not that easy, yet there was something deep down pushing him to keep fighting. For one of the rare times in his life, he had no idea how or whom to fight, much less what.

Limpy Allerdyce held the mottled, yellowed thing in two hands, like a supplicant to his master. "Dis take care dose headaches, Sonny. Youse betcha."

Service looked down. "A human *skull*?" What the hell is this old man's major malfunction?

"Yah sure, you betcha," Allerdyce said, thumping the bone with a knuckle.

"Whose skull?"

"Wah! How 'my 'pose know dat? Some dead Ind'in? Dunno."

"You know it's against the *law* to possess human body parts, right?"

The old man winced. "Dese bones ain't no real parts. Ain't got no meat on it, jes da olden head bone."

"From where?"

"Down in 'Skeeto."

"Where *exactly* . . . down in the Mosquito?"

"Have to show youse. Don't got no words for da place."

Switch directions. "OK, *when* did you find it?" Damn Allerdyce is as off the wall as Grady's father had been, but unlike his old man, Limpy was sober. Crazy maybe, but sober. It was a big step up over the old man.

"Wah! What da fuck dis, like Twinnydafuckin' Questions? Was wit' youse's old man in da way back."

"My *old man* knew about this . . . *thing*?"

"Yah sure, course, he know all sorts places got ole bones, but he don' pay no tension, hey."

The old man had been a legendary conservation officer and stumbling alcoholic—sometimes simultaneously—the latter fact in Service's mind canceling the former.

Allerdyce said, "Old bones, nobody give no two shits. Youse need take dis fella, use for pilla."

Service drew back in disgust. "I'm *not* sleeping on a man's *skull*."

"Youse sleep on own skull, hey, but youse's choice. Youse da one wit' da head-pounders."

"How do you know it's from a man?"

"Who else get seff killed out in da bush? Take look at bone dere, dat slicy t'ing dere, like knife, mebbe, tomahawk bonk on noggin, hey."

Service looked, examined the skull, and, after a while, asked, "Is it *clean*?" He took the human skull, and Allerdyce smiled like a dog with one side of its lip caught on its teeth, teeth which the old man no longer had.

What was it Treebone was always preaching? If nothing works, try something else.

He doubted his old friend would put a human skull under *his* head. But it wasn't Tree's head that was hurting. It was his, and he needed relief. So, a skull for a pillow?

Eddie Waco said that I should get a lawyer, Grady thought, but I'm not jumping into that cesspool. Okay, okay, I get it, I really do get it. You're right, I hear you loud and clear: I used an ex-felon as my partner for deer season.

I can understand that this might ruffle some feathers and bend a few noses, but look at the cases we made. Mea culpa, mea culpa, mea culpa; do results count for nothing in this job? They used to count for something.

And we broke no actual laws, at least none I know of. Okay, maybe I bent the intent of some laws over the letter of them, but not by that much. All they can do is question my judgment in the help I chose. There'd been no money exchanged, nothing. Almost thirty years in uniform, or was it over thirty? I no longer remember the numbers. And after all that shit, now *this* *pettiness*? Jesus H. Maybe a hair *over* thirty years—if I lump military, state police, and DNR law enforcement time together, which the pension folks will. Bastards down in Lansing know I can put in my papers for retirement any time I choose. Could it be that they're waiting for me to make the move and put in my papers? Is this what those assholes want? Why?

Which assholes? the voice in his head chided.

With Lansing's perpetual fog, you never knew. The place was dipped in the syrup of creative ambiguity, which enabled elected and appointed political hacks to slide in and out of issues and situations, encouraging them to delay decisions until they fermented, went away, or until they simply couldn't procrastinate anymore and had to face the risks and rewards of an actual decision. Here was the cardinal rule of politicos: Take no personal or professional risks, *ever*. Well, he thought angrily, fuck them! My scalp is a prize. I know that, and it's no surprise, but why this shelfing? Why now—after such an incredible deer season? Were these two things connected? Possibly. That voice in your head: You don't know diddly, Bub. Not enough to go on. Making a case is like cobbling together a statue from driftwood, trying first to find all the pieces and then getting them to fit together so they looked like something. A story and a case needed who, what, when, where, and why, and right now most of those factors were unanswered.

I've known Allerdyce my whole life. I can't remember when he wasn't just . . . well . . . here, or there, around, present. The old man had always insisted, "Limpy is half crazy, but he'll never quit on a real friend." Two questions lingered after the sloppy drunk's assessment. Which half of Allerdyce was crazy and what part, if any, defines a true friend? Life's always a river of bullshit, like after a fight at a hockey game, questions piling on the ice, which leaves some clueless striped shirt to make some sort of half-assed call based on partial information that amounted to a flawed impression.

By now you'd think I'd start to figure out some of this crap and begin to see some sort of big picture. But there are no miracles like that, no way. Reality and my own observations make it seem that most folks stumble through life, many of them just faking their way until they fall over dead. Not a comforting thought.

Man, you need an attitude check. Maybe the skull will clear your thoughts.

CHAPTER 3

Mosquito Wilderness Tract (MWT)

There was a hint of first light in the woods along the wilderness area's northern perimeter road when Service found some kind of media truck. What the hell? he thought. Damn media correspondents were everywhere, acting like endless variations of amateur hour. There's no common sense in these snot-nosed reporters these days, he thought, their hair slicked back like pimps, all of them on their high horses, preaching and prancing, blind to any other viewpoint, especially a cop's. Until they really need one.

Who the hell was out here, and why? Not that he had ever trusted the likes of them, but it wasn't always like this. For a long time, reporters seemed more like partners—at least the good ones did, the old pros who had learned the rules and hung with cops and learned their ways. The old pencils knew how to keep their eyes open and their yaps shut, and they didn't ink their personal opinions as news. But this was a new era and a new bunch, operating at full volume all the time, and they went on and on and on about this and that and things they didn't have a clue about and never would.

Seriously, Grady Service reminded himself, don't normal people look out a car-door window before opening the door and getting out? Don't women clutch their purses tighter when they see certain people who tickle some sort of inner warning system? Don't people cross the street to avoid an unsavory character, or watch the guy fumbling at the end of the bar and move away from him? *Everyone* profiles. It's a practical way to analyze and evaluate your situation and location, a question of safety and self-preservation, not some stupid political *ism*. All people have to weigh their safety and their chances, and act accordingly. People profile faces, clothes, voices, races, religious beliefs, accents, manners, vocabularies, shoes, jewelry, tattoos, hairstyle, you name it, anything noticeable to help cull good from bad.

As a trooper in Detroit, before moving over to the DNR, he'd seen city do-gooders profiling cops, and black folks profiling white folks, a human process that rolled along 24/7, then, now, and tomorrow. Situational awareness: This was a term that described how to stay safe and alive.

Get back to now, doofus, he told himself. Don't let your mind wander. That's how shit gets missed.

The truck seemed to be backed up to the trees, like it could go right or left when it pulled out. He used his binoculars to scan the silver Ford 350 two hundred yards in front of him. A decal on a door panel caught his eye: DRAZEL SISTERS L.L.C. SATELLITE SERVICES & EARTH SURVEYS. The name was painted in a bright red Old Englishy script on the doors, with a cartoon blue-and-green earth above the company name and eight small gold satellites, presumably global positioning system units.

Tuesday's voice in his mind from this morning echoed again. "Grady, honey. You don't have a *badge*. You're not on duty. You need to stay clear of the Mosquito. It's *not* your concern."

"Always been my concern, always will be," he'd countered. "First it was my old man's, now it's mine." His old man had guarded the area after World War II, and Grady had defended it ever since it was declared a wilderness area.

"You hated your father," his girlfriend reminded him. "You're hopeless," she concluded.

"I'm not *doing* anything, just *looking*," he told her.

"Right, stalkers sing the same stupid song," Tuesday said. She was a Michigan State Police homicide detective, covering all of the Upper Peninsula. "You don't have colleagues to cover it?"

"Nobody knows the Mosquito the way I do."

"And you believe that somehow they will magically and miraculously learn if you keep hovering and pushing them away?" She was seething.

"I'm neither hovering nor pushing," he said.

"*Men*," she hissed. "Like hell you're not! You and that crazy old man Allerdyce."

"That crazy old man has saved my life—at least twice."

"And shot you once and did seven years in Jackson for it. How do you even score *that* shit? Why *would* you?"

"It was on accident," he mumbled.

She squeaked. "*By* accident, not *on* accident; even your language skills are eroding because of that creature."

"You're too hard on him. He likes you. And the cat and dog love him."

"Cat and a dog, yeah, that speaks highly of *their* judgment. Good god, Grady Service. You really are hopeless. Are you going to be back here tonight or bunk out to camp?"

"Camp. I'm not great company these days."

"Fooled me," she had said, closing the front door behind her, and headed for work. He had bundled Shigun in his snowsuit and taken him out to the truck to drop him at Tuesday's sister's house. Allerdyce had already been riding shotgun, but got out to strap the boy into his car seat in back.

Stay focused, he thought, get back in this moment. This morning is gone, runway behind you. Gone, okay, no value to anyone.

There was a single person in the silver 350, in the driver's seat, a woman with a cigarette and a red coffee cup. He got out of his vehicle and walked up to the truck, where he stood silently by the window waiting for her to notice him. He knew he could announce himself, but better to see how she handles surprise.

She bucked visibly when she discovered his presence inches from her window. She slid the window down and hissed at him, "What the hell is *your* problem, dude!? What is *wrong* with you, creeping up on me like that?"

He said nothing, preferring to let unresponsive silence work its ambiguous magic.

"Seriously," she muttered. "Are you like lost or something?"

She glanced at her rearview mirror, then the passenger-side mirror. "How did you even *get* here?" she demanded, tugged up her brown Carhartt coat sleeve and looked at her wrist. What was it about startled people that invariably made them look at their watches? Some sort of weird wiring, some kind of biological default.

Again she asked, "*Really*, where did you *come* from?"

"My mum," he said. "And God. She's dead. He's not."

The woman's face flushed red, her neck too.

"It's okay," he said.

"What's okay?" she came back.

"Your being here," he told her.

She smirked, looking something between nervous and irritated. "You're telling me that it's all right for me to be here on state land? That's *rich*."

"*My* land," he said. "But it's okay. Just tell me why."

Her look changed from surprise to a flare of temper. "This is *state* land, not yours. Mosquito Wilderness Tract. There are signs. You *can* read, right?"

"Mine," he said, still grinning. "You think state land is yours?"

"Don't think it, know it."

"What's your name?" the woman asked. She looked late twenties, though age among the young was getting more difficult for him to determine.

"I don't care," he said. "One name is as good as another one."

"Jesus," she said.

"No, definitely *not* Jesus," he said quickly. "Have you got business out here?"

"My business is none of your business."

"It's my land, ergo, it's my business."

"This is so much bullshit!" she said, fumbling her way out of the truck and scurrying away from him, then stopping suddenly, turning back, and barking, "Stay," like he was a dog. "I've got work to do," she added.

"Okay. What work?"

"Go *away*," she said.

"My land. *What* work?"

The woman took a cell phone out of her pocket and walked down the snowy perimeter road. "I've got great ears," he called out to her. "I can hear owls breathe at night."

She stopped and looked back, and he said, "You're still in my range."

She scuttled even farther away.

Perfect. She ought to be right by Allerdyce's position now.

He watched her talking and gesturing, her voice coming up in little bursts of angry breath. The cell phone conversation was muted, but the pantomime was instructive to watch. Did humans think gesturing while on a phone call added meaning or clarity? This behavior had always puzzled him.

When she was done, she marched past him back to her truck, got in, turned it around, and raced away from the wilderness area.

Allerdyce tramped out of the snowy woods. "Dat blondie got mout' like swabby. Turnt my ears green she did."

"Could you hear what was said?"

"She not happy youse be 'ere. Udder voice tell 'he not posed ta be dis way.' Dis one, she describe youse. Udder, she say, 'Can't be him. He on da sheff, been putten outten da way.'"

"You heard those exact words?"

Allerdyce gave him his bobblehead nod. "Just told I did."

Is *he* me? Grady wondered. How could a stranger know about my suspension? "She say anything else?" he asked the old violator.

"Call youse mean old coot," Allerdyce chuckled happily. "We gone hike bush all day or go get some five-scar breakfast, hey?"

He was hungry too. "Got somewhere in mind?"

"Know place, she cooks real good. Make your ears water."

"Mouths water, not ears. We're just gonna drop in?"

"You hear her voice your ears water. Yah, we drop by, she likes t'ings quick like dat, s'prises, like lil honeybird she is."

"Sounds dubious."

Allerdyce looked him in the eye. "Dubious? He ain't president no more . . . and 'member, I seen her first."

God. "Got it. You saw her first."

"She's Yoopnique," Limpy said. "Youse betcha."

CHAPTER 4

McFarland Area

MARQUETTE COUNTY

The house was on County Road RE adjacent to a swamp and the meager, nearly invisible headwaters of the Rapid River, a couple of dozen sinewy miles south of Lake Michigan. As towns went, McFarland wasn't much of a place, more a post office than anything else. But when he found the location, he saw two manufactured housing units shoved together in the shape of a V, with a mud porch between and a bread truck–sized antenna in the open crotch of the buildings, the whole place hacked out of white cedars, which stood as natural barriers on three sides.

"This part of the SETI operation?" he asked Allerdyce. SETI was a government program tasked with searching for extraterrestrial life, which involved a series of quasi-government and public listening posts. Or it used to be. He wasn't even sure it existed anymore or if it itself was now quasi-governmental and not run directly by the government. This kind of free-lance information floated through his zone of awareness as he went about his life and popped into mind at odd times.

"Ain't no bloody Yeti," Limpy said. "What wrong youse's head, Sonny? Dat skull not workin' yet?"

"There's always hope."

The old man maneuvered himself behind Service and pushed him toward a door.

"Now what? You're sure this is all right?" Service asked the old man, who was hunched behind his right shoulder.

"Yah sure, she's a peach she is. *Hot* peach."

"Do you know anybody who's *not* a hot peach?"

Allerdyce frowned. "Why I do dat?"

"And we just drop in and she whips up breakfast, just like that? You're suspending my suspended disbelief."

"You ain't got no subpenders. Don't talk jabbershit, we need chow."

Grady Service *was* hungry. He knocked on the door and got no response.

"Go on in," Allerdyce whispered, pushing at his back. "S'okay."

"You're *sure* this is all right?"

"Yah. Go on."

The main door opened into a foyer with a door to the right and another to the left. Allerdyce pushed him toward the left door. Monty Hall, Service thought and fought off a grin. The door opened into a long hallway. No decorations on the walls, some kind of interlocking rubber blue mat down the center of the floor with a hard tile surface on either side.

Not much of a decorator, he thought as they entered an area filled with electronics, screens, drives, phones, antennae, wires curling everywhere like balls of snakes. When he looked up, he found the business end of a 1911 Colt .45 in his face, pointed up at his chin, not two inches away.

The woman holding the pistol said calmly, "I squeeze one off, you think it's got enough to plow through you and hit that worthless little beast trying to hide in your butt-shadow?"

"Probably not," Service said. "If you let that thing go at that angle, it'll just plow through my empty head, and if you lower your sights, I'm wearing a vest, which might bust some of my ribs, but won't go any further than that. You ask nice, I'll just step aside and give you a clear shot."

When Service tried to move, Allerdyce squeaked and clung to his back.

"Pity," the woman said. "How about you just scrunch sideways and I pop the little weasel in the back while he attempts to flee after an attempt to break into my house?"

"There's no need for all that effort," Service said, reaching back and plucking his companion to a place directly in front of him. "Here, he's all yours."

The old man slapped ineffectually at Service's grip before surrendering and sheepishly turning his gaze to the woman. "You sure lookin' real hot, Fellow."

The woman snorted. "Oh, I'm hot all right. Who gave you license to bang-bang a girl seven nights running, then disappear for going on a year?"

She was sixtyish, short of five feet tall, attractive. Silver hair in a female bowl-cut, clear nail polish, thin face, with the lean and sinewy feral look of a predator.

"Now youse know it weren't not like 'at," Allerdyce said defensively. "Been jes what, t'ree mont', Fellow? No shit, tree, four tops. I had go work deer season wit' Sonny 'ere. Ast 'im, ast 'im."

Service nodded and thought, Great, Lansing's all over my ass about Allerdyce, and now he's drawing some woman's wrath down on me.

"Deer season lasts a whole year now, does it? When did that change? I wrote down on the calendar when you were here last. Want to see?"

"No need," Allerdyce said. "I trust youse."

The woman laughed and shifted the pistol barrel to the old man's forehead. "Tell me why I shunt' pop one?"

"Cause 'stead of year, den she be forever," the old man said. "You want go forever widout no sweets?"

The woman said, "You badly overrate yourself, and for the record, months and years already seem like forever, but you know I'm not waiting on the likes of you, no way. You're not the only hobnail in this girl's boot."

"I aint' a'tall s'prised," Allerdyce said. "Any chance two wood ticks mebbe get us some special breakfast?"

"The big one there with you aint' no common wood tick. He's a game warden to the marrow: Grady Service. Everybody knows their game warden, you ignorant old man. You still downstate?" the woman asked Service.

"Not exactly."

"That's why I left Lansing," the woman said. "No direction anywhere but Mama Echo."

Service rubbed his face. Was this another weird dream? "Mama Echo?"

"The letters M and E equals me, or I, which is all people like that ever see. Not a person down there can spell or think another damn word."

He asked, "You were in Lansing?"

"Indeed, with a damn good consulting business, policy intelligence, twenty-two and a half employees. Say you're a legislator thinking about introducing a bill to make handguns legal for kids under three, your staff hires us to do the research and map out the ins and outs. If you like what we do, you take our report and recommendations to the Legislative Services Department to draft the actual bill. We then help LSD fine-tune and tweak the draft for you. Lucrative? Bet your ass. But Republicans, Democrats, Greenies, Socialists, they're all just rats on the rubbish pile, leaving a trail of turds wherever they go. I got tired of slipping on that junk. I branched out into academia, and now I work strictly for folks chasing PhDs. But that's my story. How shitty is your life that you have to hang with the likes of *that*?" she asked, pushing Allerdyce's shoulder with the pistol barrel.

"I haven't stooped to sleeping with him," Service said without thinking.

The woman had deep lines carved into the flesh on the outsides of her eyes and a slightly hawked nose. She looked tired. There was a long pause.

She laughed, finally pointed the Colt at the floor. "I like a man who can spit out what he thinks."

"I t'ink youse look fine," Allerdyce said, and the gun was immediately back at his head again.

"You are *not* included in that generalization, bucko." The woman looked up at Service. "You don't look like some silly-ass free-range locavomit foodie. You bring real appetite to a woman's table, do you?"

"I try."

The woman grinned. "I'm Fellow Marthesdottir, my family Icelandic in the way-back, bad-ass old Vikings. Funny thing, our genes kept shrinking till all that's left is pint-size me, last of the line, and likely going to stay so for the good of the world." The woman reached out and patted Allerdyce's face affectionately. "You've been missed."

"Me too," Allerdyce whimpered, and started into a room with Service right behind him. The room was a surprisingly large and astonishingly well-equipped kitchen, high-dollar cooking gear all the way.

"Here's your coffee," Marthesdottir said. She poured a cup, pulled out a chair, put the cup on the table in front of the chair, tapped Service's shoulder to let him know he should sit, took Allerdyce's hand, and said, "You come with me, Bub, and this ain't no request, it's an order." The couple walked back out the door they had all come in.

Service was alone for close to thirty minutes, wondering all the while how long he could nurse one cup of coffee. Not that long. Antsy, he made his way back to the room cluttered with electronics. It looked like the back warehouse at Radio Shack, or the NASA space center, whatever that was called these days. The lady said she was connected. To whom and why? He recognized a bank of external security monitors. Reality or paranoia? Hard to judge up here in the Yoop; so many people were sure they would make their last stand when the world came to its end, or Martians landed, or in the face of black holes, hordes of liberal gun-snatchers, anything. Conspiracists were a pain in the ass, and aplenty. This was the last redoubt of the self-proclaimed independent-thinking man, even those that had never had an original or clear thought in their lives.

The cameras seemed to be monitoring somewhere that didn't appear to be anything quite like this place. It seemed vaguely familiar, a grove of yellow birch and a grassy area. Definitely not any terrain near here.

Security cameras were not a surprise. Despite the bucolic setting and few people, the U.P. was no more crime-free than anywhere else. There was less of it in sheer numbers, yes, but less violent and less random? Not so much. In his experience up here, eight in ten households kept loaded weapons within reach and scattered all over their homes and camps. Calls for help were fine, but response times beyond towns were measured on the snail scale, worse than Detroit, not because of incompetence, but because of sheer and inconvenient geography. Places up here were scattered and peoples' homes not that concentrated. In sheer geography, it took time to get anywhere, even with your lights and sirens going. Up here people were largely on their own for most things, health and safety included, ergo guns were everywhere. He couldn't remember the last time a citizen had stopped a crime with a gun, but never mind that. The Second Amendment gave comfort to people.

Allerdyce and the woman returned, and both of them wore subdued smirks. "Bet your hunger's off the scale by now," their hostess said to Service, smiling.

"Mine is," Allerdyce volunteered.

"Shut up, you. I guess we all know about *your* appetites," the woman said and took eggs from the fridge and began cracking them on the edge of a metal bowl.

"I m-m-mean breakfast," the old man said, stammering slightly.

"Hard to know what the likes of you *ever* means," Marthesdottir shot back. "Got eggs, peach, and blueberry pancake batter made with wild berries frozen since last summer, good for all us old folks, with antioxidants and all that good stuff."

The words "all us old folks," made Service recoil, but he recovered. "Sounds good."

The woman smiled at him, turned to the fridge, moved the ingredients to a small counter, and began to whip up the promised breakfast for the drop-ins. Hospitality for visitors, expected or otherwise, wanted or not, was a long-established rule in the U.P. Serving food was a gesture of temporary peace, and expected even for your sworn, worst enemies.

Service tried to suppress a smile. Obviously the door opener here was Limpy, and the price of admission was something other than morning repast. How Allerdyce could have such an appeal to and hold on women was far beyond his ken, but it seemed real, never mind downright weird. Some things just were, and would and could never be explained in any rational terms. There was probably a picture of Limpy under the word "inexplicable" in the *Encyclopedia Britannica*.

Service watched Marthesdottir attacking her food as eagerly as his partner. Such a small and thin thing. How does she keep off the pounds?

Allerdyce was gumming his food loudly and obnoxiously. Service had never much thought about it, but the old man seemed to look the same now as the first moment he could remember him, which was decades ago. He never seemed to change and could go astonishingly long periods with no food at all, or sit down and pig out for hours on end. He was as feral and bingy as a wolf, feast or famine.

"Impressive electronics," Service remarked as they ate.

"My own backup generator, too," the woman said. "My clients expect product when *they* want it, not when I can get it to them."

"You've got quite the security system."

She nodded. "Voice and facial recognition software built in with all the latest technical marvels."

"You get a lot of unwanted visitors?"

"No, but a girl can't be too careful," Marthesdottir offered.

Allerdyce grunted some sort of ambiguous affirmation, his mouth full of partially chewed pancakes.

"I looked at your screens," Service admitted. "Looks like there's more than one location."

She said, "I've got a camp over the west edge of the Mosquito."

He knew the exact land parcel. There was no cabin there, at least in his memory.

"An actual camp?"

"Just land," she said. "A nice forty on the two-track, and another twenty out back."

"Traffic?"

"Some hikers and berry-pickers in summer, hunters in fall. Fishermen steer clear because the bugs are real flesh-eaters and always so bad. Or maybe because the name scares them off, not sure which. The nasty bugs in summer are real enough."

"Couple of spring-fed feeder creeks dump into the Mosquito," he said. "Both must cut right through your land. Loaded with brook trout, especially in late summer."

"Not many people left who're willing to bust brush to get to good spec water," she said.

"Ever seen a 2008 silver Ford 350 near your property? Has DRAZEL SISTERS L.L.C. SATELLITE SERVICES & EARTH SURVEYS in red letters on the sides."

Marthesdottir laughed. "Their *services* do get dispatched by satellite, all right, but that's all the truth in that label."

Service didn't understand. She had drawn out the word "services," making it almost pregnant. "I think I'm missing the joke."

Allerdyce nodded. "Sonnyboy dere sometimes ain't sharp as he t'inks."

The woman said, "Drazel's a very old word for a woman of easy virtue."

God. "Really? You know this how?"

"Cameras showed them over by my camp property to the west, and I've seen them on the north side of the Mosquito, too."

"Doing what?"

"Looked to me like they were taking photographs."

"They're actually sisters?"

"Saw but one female twice, and not the same one each time," she added with a shrug.

"How long ago?"

"Past month, not before."

Winter was starting to seriously lose its hold, but lots of snow was still massed in the wilderness area, and some roads were still snowed in and mostly impassable. Most seasonal roads in the area remained unplowed, as they were all winter. A few roads had lost snow and were now moving toward the spring mud phase, which could be worse than snow. Sometimes the mud got deeper than the snow and was a lot more difficult to escape once it got hold of you. "They always with that silver truck?" he asked.

"No, once it was a snowmobile over to the west. A Yamaha, I think, sleek and yellow but no advertising sign I could see."

He and Limpy had seen the silver truck and the woman along the north approach to the wilderness. Service asked incredulously, leery of the answer that might result, "Drazel—what the hell kind of business are they running?"

"Funny business," the woman said. "I did some searching. The company was formed late last year and some of the paperwork isn't filed yet."

Ergo the new truck. "The women own the company?"

"No, I found it impossible to nail down the business owner's name, but I did some Googling and called some friends and there is scuttlebutt around Lansing about a high-dollar lawyer and land and business developer name of Kalleskevich. Drazel is his survey company. He lives down in an East Lansing in a Hummervillage."

Service said, "Never heard of it."

"Because that's a description, not a name. Area of fat-cat McMansions between East Lansing and Okemos. The legal community name is Six Gates, which is how many checkpoints there are to get through."

"This Kalleskevich develops high-end digs?"

"Can't say for sure. I just scraped some surface stuff. But he seems to have his hands in all kinds of things—mines, gravel pits, wilderness travel, trucking."

"He owns mines in Michigan?"

"I don't think so. Far as I can tell, he's a limestone guy, not hard rock or ore."

Service felt his gut flutter. "This Drazel outfit got an address, phone, website, any of that good stuff?"

"They have a U.P. office down to Ford River, just south of Escanaba. It was a party store in a former life."

Southwest of Escanaba in Ford River? There was a retired trooper who owned a little stop-and-rob until his wife passed away. He moved to Oklahoma to be closer to his daughters and grandkids. Could this be the same place? Has to be.

"Any idea what the women were taking photos of?" he asked.

She shook her head. "I could dig a bit, but I'm expensive."

"Do what it takes," he told her.

"Be advised that I don't work for civil servant rates," she said, staring at him. "I'm talking *serious* money."

Service didn't blink. "Like I said, whatever it takes."

She smiled. "You want me to have a contract drawn up?"

He held out his hand. "Nope. This is good enough for me. Go deep and bill whatever works for you. Either of us isn't happy, we'll say so, settle the bill up to that point, and walk. Okay?"

"You're a dinosaur," she said, grinning, and added, "I've seen one other person around."

"Who?"

"Young fella, drives an old rusted-out green Subaru, an oh-three I think. I got plates, cameras filed them. Don't have a name yet, but the boy's a dead ringer for Justin Timberlake."

"When was this?" Who the hell was Justin Tinklelulu?

"After the Drazel girl was out by my camp property."

"Same place?"

"Same day. Didn't look like coincidence, but then I have a suspicious streak."

"Can you get more on him too?"

"Got more coffee?" Allerdyce asked the woman. He was still pounding down pancakes.

"You'll be peeing all day."

"Already do," Allerdyce said. "Da bot' uvus, right Sonnyboy?"

"Thanks," Service told the woman, and handed her his private and personal business cards, left over from his most recent detective gig with the department.

"Nothing on this one about the DNR," Marthesdottir observed.

"The DNR business card's on a leave of absence," he told her. "Just between us."

"How long a leave?"

Service shrugged. To be determined by forces beyond his control. His suspension had already been extended all the way to July 1, an unprecedented seven months by then, and his gut said they might stretch it even longer. Actually the timing of the delay didn't bother him so much. He loathed winter patrols and there was a lot at stake in this situation, too much to think about right now. "Focus on the Drazel women and that

Subaru," he told the woman, "and anybody else shows up on your cameras in the same areas."

"I can deploy more cameras," she said. "No charge. Been meaning to extend my coverage. Eventually I intend to test a full security net and, if it works, maybe market the architecture to land-rich rural barons."

Marthesdottir sounded ambitious. He nodded and led Allerdyce out, the old man pocketing folded pancakes. "You hear any of that?" he asked the old violet, which was his term for a violator.

"After what we done in 'er back bedroom, hard time t'ink much else, hey."

"Kalleskevich, that name ring any bells with you?"

Allerdyce inhaled a last pancake, wiped his hands on his sleeve and shook his head. "Nawf."

"She said he's a limestone guy."

"So?"

"Mosquito."

"Ain't no limestone out dere."

"I thought you were my old man's partner."

"Was," an irritated Allerdyce said. "Same as like wit' youse."

Service climbed into his truck and started the motor. Allerdyce was looking out the windshield, said quietly, "Da Woof Cave."

So he does know. "Now you get it?"

Wolf Cave was the most unlikely natural formation in the unique wilderness area, which was mostly hard rock all around one concentration of limestone. Coincidence, he told himself, but the old stomach keeps rolling with a different take and concern.

"Ain't been out dat way long long time, I t'ink. Still be da deep white dirt out der, hey."

"Snow is a game warden's pal. We'll be able to tell if anybody's been trekking out that way."

They were headed for his Slippery Creek Camp, and Allerdyce was uncharacteristically quiet. "Dat sleep skull bone I given youse, dat come from outten Woofie Cave."

Service stopped the truck and looked over at the man. "When?"

"Like I told youse, long time back, but ain't onny one down dere. Seen, like . . . bunches . . . Wah."

Service had explored the cave as a boy and as an adult. "It's a small cave and I've seen all of it, and there were no bones or remains."

"Dere's heap more youse ain't seen, Sonny. Youse's old man seen to dat. Down deep dere's some wall-pitchers, real old, mebbe old Indi'n bury-bone ground youse's old man t'ought."

In Wolf Cave? Pictures? Does he mean petroglyphs, pictographs, what? Geez. "Are you saying he hid it to protect it?"

Allerdyce nodded. "More like he din't want have to mess wit' it. If word go out dere's old cave, you got all kinds yayhoos and cave-snakes and pot-lickers and pot hunters from all over place, hey. Better for Skeeto dis stuff stay dark and lost."

If this was true, the cave paintings were not the only things hidden out there. He wondered if Allerdyce knew that a rocky outcrop along the river contained diamonds. "My old man's idea to hide it?"

He got a one-nod response.

"But you saw it all."

"Yah sure, youse betcha. Da part youse seen Sonny, is onny da f'ont top room. Goes back, den way down to underground crick, can 'ear crick down dere somewhere under. We follow 'er mebbe quart' mile an' stop. Keeps going, hey. *Big*!"

"Are you talking about The Seam from Wolf Cave?"

"Don't know 'at word, but yah, t'ink."

The Seam was an icy feeder creek that disappeared underground and popped up after a mile or so before emptying into the Mosquito River. He had always wondered where the thing went when it dove into the earth. "Pretty fair distance from Wolf Cave to where it pops back up."

"Wah. Down dere in dark we hear her dance 'round like she Missusstitty River. Sound scary big in couple places, but we only hear, never seen. Youse's old man say, dere was prob'ly shitload more stuff down dere, but dat was nuff for us."

"Pictures?"

"Two, t'ree places, mebbe more. An' some old black crap from old camp-fires or somepin."

Shit, he thought. Underground pictographs meant aboriginal relics and maybe remains, too. How long until the state suits and pointy heads with government research grants would swoop in, and after them, hordes of amateurs trying to beat the academics to the take?

His cell phone rang, and he heard a woman's voice. "Fellow here. The plate on that Subaru comes back to an NMU student, one Tyrus R. Dotz. He's a senior and current environmental features editor for the school paper, as well as a blogger and a columnist."

She continued, "That's just the first turn of the shovel, but the name Dotz is not unknown in Lansing. His old man and his grandfather were state senators. His old man got term-limited out of office. My sources tell me the boy's father was having difficulties adjusting to a life-without-Lansing portfolio. He died two weeks ago."

Service felt his ears prickling. "Accident? Suicide?"

"Not known," she said. "Yet. Possible but not ruled so."

"From where?"

"T.C. area, south, a town called Grawn. The town's chamber of commerce worshipped his ass, and the local greens burned him in effigy."

"What was he doing when he was off the government tit?"

"Billed himself as a land consultant."

"Tyrus R. Dotz. Thanks for the lead. We'll look forward to more," Service said, and hung up.

"Youse said *we*," Allerdyce said in his gleeful chirp. "I like sounda dat, hey."

"Wah," Grady Service said without enthusiasm. "I must be crazy."

"Dat one dose wretchicktorieal t'ings, or youse want me say somepin 'ere?"

"Rhetorical," Grady Service corrected the man, thinking, How sad is it that I can sometimes actually understand this crazy old bastard's slaughtered syntax.

Limpy said, "Dat kid Dotz he might could hep us sniff Lansing, hey." He held up his middle finger and waggled it animatedly. "Now listen me, Sonny. Youse got too much respect for dose clowns down below. Dey lie all time, dis white when it black, black when it white, whatever work best he'p dem. Dose fools care onny seffs, got no bloody idea nottin' down dere real. Dey all white-shoe, flag-waver clean fingernail slick-talk selfish pieces shit and never wore no uniform for country nor put asses on da real line, where win-lose counts bodies and parts, not bloody votes."

He went on, "You invite jamokes like dis to demolition derby, dey come wit' steam-roader, don't want just win, want bloody crush anybody not wit' dem and under dere middle finger. Wah." He waved the specified finger for punctuation.

It was the longest largely coherent speech he had ever heard from Limpy Allerdyce. He complimented the old man, "Outstanding soliloquy. You been reading Shakespeare?"

"What bloody hull is squirrelickwee?" Allerdyce asked.

CHAPTER 5

Marquette

MARQUETTE COUNTY

Since it seemed they were going to bunk out at his camp, Service needed new reading material, and the bookstore owner was the most knowledgeable person he knew on the subjects of books, entertainment, and social crap. Her store had a lot of student customers. Spring was preening outside, but inside Snowbound Books on North Third Street it was perpetual summer. Because he wasn't working, Service figured he might as well read, the one good habit picked up from his old man, maybe the only good thing from him ever. And not detective stories or true crime baloney. Get enough of all that crap at work. Travel books, road stories, biographies, good writing, thoughtful stuff, but nothing too weighty. Reading books about Teddy Roosevelt, a leader who didn't sit on his ass all day and wring his hands over opinion polls. Speak softly, carry a honking big stick. Fuck 'em if they don't like the job I'm doing. Elected to *do* things, and not to sit with pedicured feet on the desk. Yes, Teddy Roosevelt for sure. Talk about tough and determined.

But picking books was never easy. Part of it was that he had already read so many books that he had to look carefully and think about each one he picked up. But even in the thrall of books in the confines of the store, he quickly realized that he had seen a bookstore customer with the same face he'd now seen three times in three different locations. Here it had just sashayed past him, but he had seen the face in his peripheral vision. It had been watching him and trying to disguise interest by turning a shoulder and hip. What had Marthesdottir said, a Justin Timberlake look-alike? He stepped back to the cash register to talk to owner Dynamo Dana. "Do you have a customer who looks like Justin Timberlake?"

She always had a smile. "Yah, several; one's in here now. What about him?"

"You got any photos of this Timberlake guy?"

She smiled. "No, why?"

"Just wondering."

Dynamo said with mocking eyes, "Grady, you don't know what Justin Timberlake looks like, do you? Are you *serious*?"

He shrugged and went back to browsing and calculating. He'd seen the guy by Tuesday's place, and had gotten another quick glimpse near Slippery Creek. This was the third time. Three meant not a coincidence. Confront the guy now or wait for a better time? He decided quickly: wait.

He went back to Dynamo. "Got anything good on ballet?"

"For Tuesday or your granddaughter?"

"For me. Exercises. Ballerinas have great legs. Mine look and feel like crap."

Dana guffawed loudly, quickly covered her mouth, and said through tight lips. "I'm *so* sorry. You know, men do ballet too."

"Just Russian creepoids," he said. "*Tantsovshchik*," he said, his Russian vocabulary worse than rusty and pitted by time and lack of use. "Twinkletoeskies."

He could see her fighting a smirk and ignored her.

"Sorry, nothing I can think of, Grady."

Allerdyce was in the truck up in the Peter White Library parking lot, watching a rust-pocked Jeep with a plow knock back some petrified snow piles. He was eating an ice cream, noxious green in color, like pea soup, the sight of which made Service gag.

"Mint?"

"Pissdashheeho."

Allerdyce and language. God. "Good?"

"Better'n a poke in the eyeball wit' sharp stick."

It was an illogical view of life that steered Limpy, and yet, it somehow made sense, at least to him.

"Where we go' now?" the ice cream eater asked.

"Tuesday's."

"Don't t'ink she like me so much, dat girlie."

"That's okay, the kid, the dog, and the cat do. Three of four is good."

Allerdyce stopped licking and looked over at him. "Dere's vive wit' youse in count."

"I'm still in the undecided column with Tuesday."

Recent verbal scuffles with Friday flashed through his mind in their full fury. Allerdyce said, "Sucks to be youse." This suspension had severely screwed up his routine, such as it was. As a detective herself, Tuesday Friday understood his job, but she did not like the suspension, or how he was coping with it. He knew she would carp and complain, but when it counted, she *always* had his back. Was that love? Who knows. More to the point, he wondered, What did I do to deserve her?

The reformed poacher sighed loudly. "Womens. What I got do make 'er like me?"

"You're still along. Take heart in what you have, not what you don't."

"You buckin for priest?"

Might as well be, he thought, sex and intimacy recently seeming like ancient history.

"Easier work wit' youse's old man," Allerdyce offered.

"That right?"

"He allas Mr. Happy when he tie one on. Youse don't never."

"My father drank enough for the two of us. I like a clear head. The kid Fellow told us about, I think he was in the bookstore just now."

"What youse t'ink he up to?"

"No idea. Time comes, we'll find out." Last night Marthesdottir had sent a two-page email entitled "BG—TRD et al." It was almost astonishing in depth but didn't really answer what the Dotz kid was after. A P.S. on the email read, "Tell your partner it's time again to stop by."

CHAPTER 6

Mosquito Wilderness Tract

Some days later, and strictly by chance, Service caught a glimpse of the rusted green Subaru. He told Allerdyce to jump in back and stay down. The old man slid between the seats into the back. Service got behind the Subaru and followed it at a distance, eventually accelerating, passing him, running hard until he was out of sight and far ahead.He pulled over, jumped out, and jogged into the woods. His last words to Allerdyce were, "Stay here, and follow him at a distance until I make contact." Service got into the woods and left himself just enough of a view to watch the boy park. Service loped through the snow so that the kid could see him and follow his trail, making sure to leave plenty of obvious tracks.

The slow-motion stalk went on for a full two hours—until Service had stretched the boy's woodcraft to its limits. The boy stood in a small clearing, frantically searching the paths. Service knew the boy had totally lost the trail. Marthesdottir had called last night and given him more information about the college kid.

"Tyrus Redpath Dotz Jr.," Grady Service snarled at the startled boy, who lurched, stumbled, took an awkward step back, and caught himself before he fell on his ass. Service was impressed that he managed to get his feet under him, remain standing, steady himself, and look up at the large man in civilian clothes as if they had just met somewhere in town instead of miles from the nearest road. The boy's pencil neck was ringed in tattoos, his hair long on top and spiked up and out like a blond mop of wild greens growing out of a young carrot.

Service challenged him directly, "Why the hell are you trying to follow me?"

Dotz said, "I'm not following you—or anybody. I'm just out hiking."

"Don't bullshit me, kid. You took photos of my truck in Marquette, I've seen you snooping around my house and trespassing on my land. You were in the bookstore with me, and you took the photos three weeks ago. And I've seen you trying to tail me in your piece-of-shit Subaru. You've also been seen out here in the woods a dozen times. I have my own photos of you, and all with electronic time markings." He was exaggerating, with intent.

"You're, like paranoid, dude," the boy said with surprising calm.

"Don't dude me. I hate the word *dude*. Your old man is State Senator Harry Redpath Dotz, once the number three man in seniority in the state and one of Sam Bozian's dearest old pals." Samuel Adams Bozian was the former state governor who had more or less destroyed the state economically and shouldered most of the state electorate outside Detroit far to the political right. After twelve years in office, he moved on to greener pastures as a lobbyist in the nation's capital. He and Sam Bozian had been open, full-on enemies, Service having once been the governor's son's field training officer when the boy buckled in a situation with a biker crowd in a campground. The boy had quickly confessed on the spot that he didn't have what it took to be a peace officer and CO, and that it was his father's idea, not his. The boy had dropped out of training, and the governor had gone after Service every chance he got. Service usually called him "Clearcut."

The nickname grew from the governor's penchant for supporting development over any environmental concerns, to side always with the developer and never with conservationists. Some said Bozian would cover the state in concrete if he got his way.

Dotz Junior's mouth fell open. "How do you know *that*?"

"Day of connections, *dude*. I checked you out, ran your plate, and it was a piece of cake from there."

"You're suspended by the state, not on duty, you can't do stuff like that . . . can you, like legally?"

Junior knows I'm suspended? Confirm nothing, keep pushing him. "You're an environmental communications major at Northern, and you work as a reporter-columnist for the *North Wind*."

"You're creeping me out, Bro."

"You are *not* my Bro, Dotz. Feel a little weird, does it, somebody dropping *This is Your Life* on you out in the woods? Now *you* know how it feels to be creeped, Junior."

The boy nodded, but did not stare at the ground or look away. Dotz was standing his ground, and Service liked that. So many boys this age were spineless yappers squalling for Helicopter Mommy. Service added, "You need to leave me the fuck alone, kid. Trust me, I'm a terrible playmate."

"You're news."

Service flinched. What? "Bullshit."

"You're on suspension for using a convicted felon as a partner during deer season. They're probably going to fire you if they can build their case."

They? "You don't have enough real professor-student crap to deal with on campus?"

"This isn't for the *North Wind*—it's for the *Detroit News*."

The Detroit papers are using students to bird-dog their stories? "Since when?" Service asked. Detroit had two papers, both swirling in the financial crapper, the *News*, which leaned right, and the *Free Press*, which leaned left.

"Since I started working for them after high school. They're paying for my college up here."

"The *News*? I'm not buying that line, Junior. Both Detroit papers are on the fun slide to the financial graveyard. Their unions would kill them if they knew the bosses were throwing money at a kid."

"Doesn't matter if you don't buy it," Dotz said. "You aren't giving me my assignments, or paying me."

"Does the *North Wind* know you're working for a competitor?"

This seemed to bring the boy up short. Service added, "It comes to light, you might have an ethical issue to sort out."

"Is *that* your problem?" the boy came back, changing the focus and shifting back to offense. "A little ethical problem?"

Impressive. The kid's not folding his tent and backpedaling. "My only problem, Dotz, is you shadowing me. If I see you again, I'm gonna get a court order against you."

"How do you think that will look?"

Grady Service grinned. "Junior, if you had done your homework, right now you'd know I don't much give a shit how things *look*."

"Yah, I heard that first thing," the young man said. "That attitude's probably what's got your ass in a sling in the first place."

Service couldn't help laughing out loud. He dug a pack of cigarettes out of his pocket and held it out to the boy. "Word is you smoke dope. How about a real smoke?"

"You don't know anything about me."

The kid's father was dead, possibly a suicide. Marthesdottir had not gotten back to him on this point yet, but his gut said high probability of suicide.

He'd not even seen any coverage of the former politician's death, although this was not all that surprising. The U.P. media sources were often deaf and blind when it came to covering Below-the-Bridge news and goings-on. The U.P. was all about the U.P., even had sports champions they crowned as Upper Peninsula State Champions.And there was a U.P. state fair. A lot of the inhabitants were as blinkered as racehorses, their views restricted to what seemed to be right in front of their eyes.

"I know your old man's dead, and maybe he thought you were a flying fuckup. Maybe he hated your notions about journalism because he saw reporters as lower in the social order than state employees and cesspool divers, which means lower than having a sister as the top earner in a Detroit whorehouse. I know you were a shitty high school student, but your college work is surprisingly good. I know that others your age have their heads up their asses, but yours seems to be on almost straight. I know you like to hunt, fish, and hike, and I know you've got pretty damn good woodcraft skills because I've watched you, even though I did catch you."

"*When* did you catch me?"

Service couldn't help laughing. "Dotz, you clueless knucklehead, do you think I was just out for a walk? I led you around, and I made sure you lost me. And now here I am, like magic."

Service had never seen the boy in the field until today, but the boy clearly had some skills, and now he wanted to see how he handled being off-balance. His answer was a shrug.

"Can't be *too* great; you just nailed me and I'm nothing."

"Dotz, your ass has been nailed for a long time. Game wardens don't show themselves until *they* decide it's time. I set the trail for you, and broke it off. That's why you were looking around, trying to figure out where I went and what you should do next."

"Some woodcraft," the boy said disconsolately, reaching for a cigarette.

"You did okay, Dotz, not great, but okay. I'm a professional, and you're not, it's as simple as that. You ever think about law enforcement, conservation officer work?"

"Is that like a bribe to get me off your story?"

Service lit the kid's smoke and laughed. "One, I don't bribe people and two, I'm not a story. What makes you think I am?"

The kid inhaled and exhaled naturally. "I have my sources."

"Ah yes, the old unnamed confidential sources. That's all so much bull-shit, Dotz, and you know it. You've got bubkes."

"You saying the story isn't true, that you're not on suspension?"

"I'm saying anything happening with me isn't news. That's what I'm say-ing. My business is mine alone, and I don't like being followed—ever—by anyone."

"But that old man, Allerdyce, he's living out to your camp with you, and you're not living with your woman in Harvey. So I guess she broke things off because of the suspension and you're hanging out with a known felon. That can't be too good for a female state police detective's career."

The kid seems to have done some serious snooping and speculating. In fact, Service had moved back to the Slippery Creek Camp partly because Tuesday Friday's supervisors had made it clear that it was one thing to live in sin, and another thing to live in sin with a potentially dirty cop. The kid's knowing this no doubt meant someone in the Negaunee State Police office was talking off-piste. This wasn't good. Cop shops were notoriously ripe and fertile grounds for rumor-mongering and loose-lipped gossip.

"You'll hear a lot of bullshit and wishful thinking as a reporter. You'll need to learn how to weigh your sources—the same way cops have to evalu-ate complaints and witnesses."

"There a method for that?" Dotz asked.

Service tapped his belly. "Time, experience, and this."

The young man studied him for a long time. "You really *don't* care if they fire you?"

"They're not going to fire me," Service said.

"That's not what I'm hearing."

What? If this kid actually believes this, Grady thought, maybe there is something to what he's following. He'd heard nothing from Lansing since Chief Waco had extended his suspension. Put the kid off-balance now, see how he reacts. "Listen Dotz, you ever get interested in a CO career, let me know. I can vouch for your skills in the woods, and if your old man wasn't happy with your journalistic career choice, that's another point in your favor, because I'm pretty much for anything people like your old man were against."

Dotz grinned. "You know what they call you in the legislative halls of Lansing? *Le Grand Boom Boom.* They fear you and they're afraid of you down there."

This was news. "Le Grand Boom Boom?"

"You're like a walking bomb. Everything you touch ends up exploding. My family knows people who are scared shitless of you."

Interesting, even surprising, information. "Your father one of them?"

"Not my old man," Dotz said, "Not anymore. He's beyond being scared now."

"Not a problem when he was alive?"

"We rarely talked when he was alive."

What a bizarre comment. If the kid's father had this sort of feeling, he'd most likely gotten some of it from Bozian. The question now, was Bozian sticking his bulbous beak back into state business? There was another GOP governor in place. Surely the so-called Wonk-in-Charge wouldn't appreciate that sort of interference. "Want some old woods-cop-think, Junior?"

The boy shrugged.

"Every story or case is a kind of picture. And every picture has an artist. Every picture and every case have certain details in them. Every one of those details is chosen by the artist. But in choosing to show us A, B, and C, the artist may be choosing to not show us M, N, and O. You following me?"

"So a cop asks himself what's not in the picture and why not?"

"There you go, like old Rummy Don used to preach to reporters, there's the known-unknown and the unknown-unknown, and the whole damn thing's a nasty swamp. You need to stay out of my backyard, Dotz. If you think you've got a story, go for it, but step back and think things through before you plunge blindly forward."

Dotz seemed to be thinking. "Most state employees who could lose their pensions wouldn't be so . . . you know, like unconcerned."

"Most state employees work for a paycheck and no longer have actual pensions. I think if you look around, you'll find that COs are a different breed. We like our pay, of course, but we look at what we do as a calling, same as journalists are supposed to look at their work. Or used to."

"You wandered way all over the place today," the boy said. "What's up with that?"

"Let me restate your question. What you're trying to ask is how the hell can you find your Subaru?"

"I have a good mind-compass that will get me out just fine, but I'm wondering if there's not a more direct route than the one we came in on?"

Grady Service smiled. There was something he liked about this kid, and realizing it came as a mild surprise. "Yah, c'mon, we'll walk out together."

"Where's the old guy?"

"You haven't seen him?"

The boy shook his head and looked around nervously.

"He was the best in his business in his day. And he's still got it. Fact is he's probably not a hundred yards from us right now, and he was probably closer than that to you the whole time you stumbled around in the snow."

"What do you mean, in his day?"

"He hasn't been busted in years, because he's turned over a new leaf, the straight path of the righteous."

"Lot's of people say differently."

"I know, but check the courts, Dotz, see what his record says." Service stopped walking and handed the kid a card. "If you have questions, call me. Don't guess and don't take anything as gospel until you have at least two sides and two sources for each."

Service stopped again. "Point to your Subaru. Show me a rough direction."

The boy hesitated before pointing, then tentatively raised his arm. "You're only off by sixty degrees," Service said, pointing. "Not bad, but not great." After a pause, Service conceded, "Actually it was overall a pretty lame performance. If you're gonna be in the woods, you need a lot of work, Dotz. Otherwise, follow your GPS around the cities and towns and stay out of the woods." The kid nodded and laughed. Service liked that too.

CHAPTER 7

Lansing

INGHAM COUNTY

The bar was tucked into a seedy industrial area that was called Mextown in the fifties and sixties. Now it was just called the north side. In his day it was Mextown and the bar he wanted to find was called the North Lansing Country Club. By the looks of it, not much had changed since his last visit.

Service checked his watch. Nearly half-past ten, the magic hour when night rats crawled out of their cracks and crevices. He made his way to the bar past vases packed with the same plastic flowers he'd seen so many years ago. The female barkeep was young, chemically blond, genetically perky. "Pour the gentleman a drink?" she greeted him.

"Beer."

"We have flavors these days," she said with a smile.

"Wet and from a tap, not from a can or a bottle—you pick for me."

"That's a lot of responsibility for a girl. Half-pint or pint?"

"Full pint and two double Jacks back."

"You expecting a date?" she asked.

"I expect your boss will be having a drink with me."

"I'm the boss at night," the girl said.

"Nicely played, now go tell her Grady Service is here."

A familiar voice behind him said hoarsely, "Saw youse come in and thought, 'My god, what is *he* doing here?'" Honeypat Allerdyce waved the barkeep away. "It's okay, Loris, he's an old and dear friend."

The girl brought back the drinks. Service pushed a double shot to Honeypat. She raised her glass, said, "You look damn good," and threw it down in one go.

"Back atchu," he said, draining his double. Honeypat had once been married to Limpy's late, crazy, and no-good son Jerry. Rumor had it she had also been Limpy's sometime scromp-mate, which he suspected might have been true. All he knew for sure was that she had tried to take Allerdyce's business away from him and failed, which necessitated she run for her life. Service had stumbled across her years ago here in Lansing, firmly in place as the boss-lady of a high-dollar companion service, a description that fooled no one. Honeypat was fifty or so now, and looked remarkably younger. She was never what one might think of as classically and technically beautiful, but she was one of those women whose parts did not add up to the whole that you met, and the effect was immediate, overwhelming, and real. Whatever it was that attracted men, she had it—maybe even defined it. And, like others, he knew he was not immune to it, but over the years he had been able to resist. So far.

"Loris, bring us another," Honeypat told the barkeep. She turned back to Service and put her hand on his arm. He could feel her heat. "You had dinner?"

"I'm good."

"I need pupus," Honeypat said.

Service was lost.

"Hawaiian for hors d'oeuvres," she explained. "Spent much time in Hawaii?"

"Only on the way to Vietnam," he told her. "Not much local color on a troop transport."

"Loris, give us one order of sweet potato *frits*, mayo on the side." To Service, "Heard they put youse on the shelf—and why." She arched an eyebrow.

"Did you?"

"Limpy as your partner, oh . . . my . . . god! Are you out of your bloody mind?"

"By some accounts," he said, sipping his draft beer.

She laughed. "You've always been out of your mind, Service. It's just one part of your charm. Why the pleasure of your company tonight?"

"Who told you I was shelved?"

"Lots of the white-shoe, white-belt, white-skinned, hit-white-golf-balls-at-the-white-country-club politician set. Odds are being offered on whether you're out of the game permanently."

"What kind of odds?"

The heat from her nearby skin was intense. "Fifty to one you're gone, but you know how odds shift with the winds and events."

"You got any of the action?"

She snickered. "Darlin', Honeypat doesn't ever gamble."

She's changed, dropped most of her Yooper accent. "What if you did?"

"I'd never bet against you, Service. Never."

"Why's everyone so sure I'm gone?"

"The governor plays the naïve Boy Scout, but he's got his big bug eyes on the White House next. Hates anything that might make him look bad or unethical."

"Me?"

"Limpy has a rep," she said. "Casts a long shadow."

"He was just a fish and game violator, not a serial killer."

"He's a legend, a poster boy for bad. And there he was partnering with the poster boy for Good and Righteous White Hats. What's up with that? Did you *really* partner with him?"

The bar had a tacky Tex-Mex décor, including cowboy hat sconces and piñatas over the bar wrapped with tiny red and green Christmas lights. Once tacky, always tacky. "Guilty," he said, as Loris delivered the fries and new shots.

"What *were* you thinking?" Honeypat asked.

"Deer season, who knows more about deer poaching than Limpy?"

She nodded. "A given, but as a *partner*?"

"In my truck for the whole season."

"Wah!"

"Best deer season ever," he added. "For anyone."

She dipped a fry in mayo, played with it, held it to his lip. He turned his head.

"You sure caught you a lot of attention."

He took his own fry, followed it with the double Jack.

"Why are you here tonight?" she asked again.

"You know people, things, stuff."

"Holey moley, are you saying that now you want to partner with *me*? Sweet! Be still my beating heart!"

"That's not what I said, or meant."

"Sometimes takes tits to get tats," Honeypat said. "It's the Lansing way. Mine too."

"I just want some information."

"How much you pay?"

"Name a price."

She rubbed her face on his upper arm, put a long-fingered hand on his thigh.

"Too much," he said.

She pulled back. "Heard you hooked up with a good-looking Dickless Tracy. She must be good."

She keeps track of me? Service wondered. Why? "That's none of your business."

"Everything's my business, Service. Information is power down here."

"Couple of things, then. Kalleskevich, a developer and lawyer. And an outfit called Drazel Sisters L.L.C Satellite Services & Earth Surveys."

"Kalleskevich plays the long game and the short game."

"What's the difference?"

"How much cash he pockets, and how soon. And how many people he crushes to get there."

"You know him?"

"Define *know*."

"The kind of stuff he's into, his business, investments, you know, a detailed profile."

"Guys like him are secretive, got legions of lawyers to create walls to keep it that way."

Service sighed. This felt like a dead end. "Sorry to have bothered you."

She leaned close. "Hell, I've been doing everything I can for years to get you to *bother* me. Mebbe I might have a little something on Kalleskevich."

"Yeah?"

"A date."

"What date?"

"You heard me, there's this wild-child, hey. Sometimes this woman she works some big gigs for me, likes to get down and dirty. You'd like her. Forty, hard body, no limits on anything, if one has the cash."

"Don't bullshit me."

"I ever?" she asked, looking him in the eye.

"All the time when Jerry and your father-in-law were ducking me."

"Hey, that was part of that game, a woman's role in those days," Honeypat said. "It's an entirely different game down this way. Now isn't the good old days."

"What's this 'date's' name?"

"Her performance name is Oheneff. *Omni Noctifugus*; it means all-night-lightning. She has a PhD in classics, whatever that is. She teaches out to the college."

The college to most Lansingites was short for Michigan State University. "You're making this up."

"Cross my heart. Would I lie to you?"

"Would you?" he threw back at her.

He studied her grin and she said, "Top or bottom, both are good for me."

"You're relentless."

"And shameless," she added. "But I always get what I want. Otherwise, why bother, eh?"

"You haven't always gotten what you wanted," he corrected her.

"Net wins and losses," she said with a little smile. "Wins and losses, nobody goes undefeated. Not nobody, not ever."

A Hispanic man came over to Honeypat and whispered in her ear.

She turned back to him, glaring. "You leave something out in your truck?"

"Allerdyce."

Her face drained of all color. "He's here—in *my* parking lot?"

"No worries, he's not coming in."

"Does he know I'm in here?"

"Did *you* tell him?" he challenged.

She looked at him scornfully. "I ain't into suicide."

"You don't know how he is now."

"*Now*? Rattlesnakes bite darlin', end of story." Honeypat looked frantic. "What the hell is wrong with you?"

"It's been years since he's even mentioned your name."

"Snakes don't plan to bite," she said. "They strike from instinct."

"I'm telling you he's not the same man you knew."

"Wah, that one'll never change. He can't. You want to hook up with Oheneff, yes or no? I don't have all night to happy-jaw with you."

"Hook up, yes, but not for the usual business reason."

"Price will be the same," Honeypat said. "Two bills, and for the record she considers it a healthy sport, not a business."

He peeled two one-hundred dollar bills from his wallet.

"Close enough, to start, depending on what you want. Feel free to nego-tiate with the lady."

"How's it work?" he asked.

"My business is the original paperless office, darlin'. It's all off the books." She reached into a pocket and gave him a white cell phone the size of a cig-arette pack. "She'll call you on this. When you finish your business, you give the phone to her and she'll take care of it. She'll need two or three days to arrange it."

Honeypat pushed the two bills back to him "Drinks and frits are on me," she said. "And seriously, Service, you'd like them *on me*. Truth is this is just for you, and if you feel motivated to give me a gratuity, you know what it is, and hint-hint, it ain't hiding in your wallet."

"Not saying I'm not tempted," he admitted to her quite candidly. In fact, he was *really* tempted, as he always was. But this was never going to happen.

She winked. "Not saying you are, either."

He shrugged. "There is that. Ambiguity fuels desire."

"Mine don't need no feeding," she said.

"Hold that thought," Grady Service told her, kissed her and went dizzy, and nearly slid off his stool. She laughed, grabbed his arm to steady him and sent him bouncing off tables and clients as he made his way toward the door. He thought, Don't ever do *that* again, you dope. Holy shit!

Allerdyce was asleep in the truck. "Get what youse wanted?"

"We'll see," Service said.

"How much longer we got stay down 'ere, dis shithole town?"

"Probably a few days."

"Ever't'ing below britch feel nasty," the old man complained. "We don't b'long 'ere, us."

CHAPTER 8

East Lansing

INGHAM COUNTY

They checked into the Jolly Wagner House, a cheap faux-stone façade, a no-tell motel near Frandor, and inhaled an Italian dinner in a restaurant across from the MSU campus on Grand River. Waitstaff and diners alike kept staring at Allerdyce, who had the effect of making everyone in any dining room feel like they were dining with a wolf. Which was not far off the mark, Service thought.

"You up for a little field work?" Service asked his partner over a glass of beer.

"Ya sure, what we do?"

"Dark-walk a property."

"Easy dat, ain't no snow on ground down 'ere."

True. You could feel spring making a real push here. But it was at least another six or seven weeks away for the frozen U.P. It was the weather of two different planets down here and Above the Bridge (ATB).

Back in the truck he called one of the area conservation officers, Torsten Magwire. She'd been in uniform almost twenty years and had a bedrock reputation.

"Magwire," she answered her personal phone.

"Service."

"Holy shit," she said laconically. "This is like a call from God—or the dead—which is it?"

He laughed. "That's so wrong on so many levels. You know someone named Kalleskevich?"

"*Of* him. He's one of our local King Kongs. One of the governor's pals."

"Which governor?"

"All of them is how the story runs. That's what money will do for you—and some jerks think money won't buy happiness. It'll buy everything else."

"Can you find Kalleskevich's address for me?"

"Heck, I'm on duty, Grady. I can show you. You know Schuler Books at the Meridian Mall?"

"Now a good time for you?"

"Yep."

"In ten minutes at the bookstore, see ya."

Allerdyce sat quietly and asked, "Who dat youse callin' up?"

"CO Magwire."

"She not retired yet?"

Service looked at his passenger. "You know her?"

"Made it point know all your tribe, wah."

Tribe of conservation officers. He liked that.

"Don't go pushing any of her buttons," Service warned his partner.

"How I do dat when I don't got no ideas what buttons she got, hey?"

Unfortunately, he had a talent for finding people's buttons.

"Just keep your yap shut."

Allerdyce grunted.

The bookstore had spring displays in its windows. The parking lot was packed full, a steady stream of customers going in and out of the store. Service drove far out into the back rows, looked around, saw Magwire's black patrol truck, gold badge gleaming. Like most Lansing-area COs, officers kept their trucks spic-and-span. Away from the state capital, not so much. They parked nose by nose pointed opposite directions, driver's window beside driver's window. How much of my life has taken place in arrangements like this? Service wondered.

"This seems a far piece from your normal playground," the veteran officer greeted him with a smile.

"I'm sort of without a playground at the moment."

"Yeah, we all go the word," Magwire said, staring past him. "Jesus, is that *Allerdyce* with you?"

Limpy raised his right hand, cackled, and gave her a double-fingertip salute.

"You guys had a great season," she said. "The greatest deer season ever. So many big cases!"

She squinted at him. "He looks kind of old. You sure he's healthy enough to hang with you?"

Magwire had short brown hair and a squarish face with freckles and dimples. She looked like a new middle schooler until you saw her linebacker shoulders. She had been teaching other COs how to fight fast and dirty for many years, and even the strongest game wardens weren't eager to jump on a mat with her to help her demonstrate some new technique.

"He keeps up," Service said. "You heard about the suspension?"

"We all heard."

"Did it say the suspension was extended to July 1?"

"No way," she said with a sharp yelp. "What the hell?"

"The story get shaded?"

"Not especially. Main reaction seems to be we'd all like to have a partner like that for deer season. How many people did you guys nail?"

"We never counted, but we've got lots of court dates ahead. Only a few cases have been adjudicated so far."

"Never mind Lansing, Grady. Great job." She stared at Limpy. "Are you certain *that's* Allerdyce. I thought he'd be a helluva lot more imposing."

The poacher said, "I'm sittin' right here and I can hear ever't'ing youse two's sayin' 'bout me. I play bigger'n I sit, tell 'er, Sonny."

Magwire chuckled. "I expect you do, sir. No offense intended. It's game warden humor."

"Ha ha," Allerdyce said diffidently.

Service asked. "A source told me there's a pool on if I go or if I stay, odds at fifty to one for out."

"You should write a country song with those lyrics," she said. "I heard that crap too, but not from uniforms or anyone in law enforcement."

This he found oddly comforting. Tribe indeed.

Magwire said, "Take us fifteen minutes to get to King Kong's."

"Security?"

"Gated community, private rent-a-cops. They know me and they'll wave us through, so you guys need to jump in with me."

"Limpy can stay here."

She said, "No, it's all right. He can come too."

"You're not afraid of being accused of having a felon in your truck?"

"Hell, Grady, I had six years as a Troop when I transferred to the DNR. I could put in my papers tomorrow."

"They could go after your pension."

"They don't have the balls for that. C'mon Mr. Allerdyce."

Service held open the rear door for Limpy, who hopped up and in, and he got up front in the passenger seat.

Magwire explained, "Most of this outfit's security is for show, especially the uniforms. The development's owner is Kalleskevich, and he doesn't like to spend money except on himself. He's a legendary tight ass business-wise. He contracts his security with the cheapest bidder. The proportions of the houses and properties inside are all different, from five acres to one up to a hundred. Each owner handles his own property security."

"Kalleskevich's setup?"

"He's the only one with a hundred acres. I've heard he's fully wired with cameras and motion detectors, but that's rumor, not fact."

"Fenced in?"

"Out behind the house, eleven or twelve feet high, to keep out the deer. People here see deer as enemies, not cute little Bambies."

Service knew from his decades in law enforcement that economic status and high position were not determinants of lawful behavior, especially out in the bush.

"You okay back there, sir?" Magwire asked Allerdyce, looking back between the seats.

"Keep your hands off the long guns back there," Service said.

"Hey, don't letcher me, I know dis drill, Sonny."

The weapons were in unzipped cases, ready for instant deployment.

Allerdyce was fidgeting around in back, and Magwire stopped the truck. "Hop out sir, I'm going to rearrange my stuff, make you more comfortable back there." Allerdyce got out and the officer began rooting around, moving things. Most COs had cluttered trucks—ammo, extra clothes, first-aid kits, PBT kits, cartons of DNR literature, the list was endless. There were almost always loose pistol, rifle, and shotgun rounds in cup holders and door storage pockets. She soon had a clear area for her second passenger, and he climbed back in and said, "Thank you. How's come youse don't make no space for me, Sonny?"

"Shut up," Service said. "Partners take care of themselves. You comfy now?"

"Peachy," Limpy said.

They drove away.

"You going to advise Twenty of your ridealongs?" Twenty was code for the RAP room full of dispatchers in downtown Lansing. There were personnel on duty there 24/7. Their main job was to relay in-process complaints from citizens to officers in the field. Most citizens were not good about promptly advising when something came up, and as a result, most officers got put behind the eight ball at the start of almost every complaint investigation. Officers called the operation "Twenty," or the RAP Room, after the twenty-four-hour, toll-free call-in program called Report All Poaching.

"Nah," Magwire said. "What they don't know can't hurt or ruffle their feathers."

The guards at the gate looked barely sixteen and acted officious and green as limes when waving them through. With Magwire, all they looked at was the gold shield on her door and waved her on, without even a glance at her passengers.

"Dat was sweet," Allerdyce said.

"They bounced me for having Limpy with me," Service cautioned. "They could bounce you too, Torsten."

"Fuck 'em all," Magwire said. "My husband's a professor at the MSU vet school. This job is strictly play money and for kicks. I believe in our resources and would do this as a volunteer."

"Girlie dere yust say fuck 'em?" Allerdyce chortled from the back. "She look too nice for words like dose."

Magwire snorted. "I've got a lot more where those came from."

"Youse ever fool around on your dog-doc old man?" Allerdyce asked bluntly from his hidey hole.

"Only with people I intend to shoot and bury after I'm done with them."

"I didn't mean nothin' bad," Allerdyce said in a low and quivering voice.

"I was hoping you didn't," Magwire said, looking over her shoulder at him, "because that sort of hit on me would truly piss me off."

Allerdyce held up both hands in a gesture of surrender, and turned to look out his side window.

The house was massive, three floors with a circular drive and extensive landscaping. "Just another palace," Service said.

"They got subway t'ing 'tween rooms?" Allerdyce asked from the back.

Magwire laughed. "Beats me."

Service saw what looked to be a long, low ridge all along the back. "What's beyond that ridge?"

"I-69 North," she said.

"Is there a way back there on foot?"

"Park at the Vandam Exit Park-and-Ride, walk cross-country. It's all state property till that ridge line, and it remains state down to the fence line. Half mile from the exit, give or take."

"Show us the exit?"

Service was watching the circular driveway as she turned around. There was a red Escalade with a black hummer behind it.

"They can't afford a garage?"

"That's *behind* the house," Magwire explained. "Underground," I hear. "Two levels."

Service watched a woman walk out to the Escalade, and when they turned around to come back down the street on their way to security, he got a good look at her as she sat waiting for them to clear the street so she could get going.

Magwire drove through the security gate, and the Cadillac followed closed behind. "Seventy grand for that toy junk," Magwire said. "Can you believe that?"

They got out at the exit along the highway and took a brief walk. The ridge was dense with oaks and sugar maples.

Back at the truck she said, "If they push you out, there could be a rebellion in the ranks."

"That wouldn't be smart. Shit happens. It's my problem, not yours or anybody else's."

"Right and smart aren't synonyms," she said with a snort. "Nice meeting you, sir," she told Allerdyce. "You're not nearly the sleaze I thought you'd be."

"Da girlie call me sir," Allerdyce said when they were back in their own truck. "I like sound dat."

"Don't let it go to your head. She's polite to everyone, even scumbags."

"Da Caddy Hummer joint da one we gone dark-walk?"

"Yup."

"Piece of cake," Allerdyce said. "When we go?"

"Tomorrow maybe, I'm not sure yet."

"Sooner we get done down 'ere, sooner we get back crosst da britch, hey."

"You don't like it down here Below the Bridge?"

The old man vigorously shook his head.

CHAPTER 9

Swamp Lake, South of Laingsburg

SHIAWASSEE COUNTY

The white phone rang early the next morning. Service was alone, and Allerdyce was out in the mall somewhere, snooping around. "Yes?" he answered his phone.

"Oheneff here. Got word you are in the market for company."

"Depends on the company—and the price."

"This is no hobby for cheapskates," the voice said coolly.

"Two yards at the starting line, negotiations from there. Life is à la carte, right?"

"Right. It cost me two yards to get this phone."

She made a sniffling sound. "I heard it was gratis. You must be special."

"Eye of the beholder," he said.

"Say we meet, then decide price," she offered.

"Works for me, when and where? I hate to step on your regular business."

"This is purely a hobby for me," she said. "We'll meet, start with that. Our mutual friend suggested you have something rather special in mind?"

"She exaggerates."

"Not about certain things. How about tomorrow, straight noon?"

"I should bring some protection?"

She laughed easily. "Proactive, I like that. Got something handy to write with?"

Her directions were to a property on Welly Road, south of Laingsburg.

"Swamp Lake." She added, "Locals call it the 'W.' You got a name we can use?"

"Alpha Omega works for me."

"Very funny," she said. "Mr. A.O. it shall be. Noon then."

"Give me a visual."

"42 DD and firm. That enough?"

"Yes ma'am, that should do it, but I meant the house where we'll meet."

He could hear her laugh. "There's a TV security monitor at the back gate. I'll buzz you in. Leave your vehicle out there. There's a place to back it in. Quarter-mile walk to the house, only place on the lake. It's usually a hunting club, and I guess that will hold tomorrow as well. It's entirely private. We won't be interrupted. The owner likes to collect things, not use them."

"I'm not the afternoon-delight sort," he told her.

She laughed. "We'll try to take that into account. Noon, Mr. A.O."

"See you there, Oheneff."

"It's so nice to be on a first-name basis already," she said, and broke off the connection.

Weird.

Allerdyce came in long enough to hear the last couple of exchanges. "What all dat was?"

"Meeting, noon tomorrow."

"Dabotuvus?"

"I go in, you stand security."

"Mebbe I get save youse's butt again."

"Highly unlikely. You'll just give me a bump if anyone shows."

*****

At noon, Service parked on the road before the gate, backed the truck in as directed, making sure to tuck the truck beyond the security camera's reach, and gave Limpy the keys. Allerdyce got out and stretched. "Hear better outside," the old man explained. He was right, of course. Game wardens and poachers alike preferred to be outside where pure sound had a chance to travel with less interference.

He saw the gate camera right away. The driveway on the other side of the gate was wet, one set of fresh tire prints led in. He pushed a button, and a red light illuminated on the side of the camera. A female voice said, "Mr. A.O, it's so nice to see you."

"It's me," he said. The gate slid open, and when he stepped through, it closed behind him. Allerdyce cackled as Service headed down the grassy driveway. He walked steadily, looking around, scanning ahead, behind, both sides, above and down. Only the one set of vehicle tracks. No obvious security devices along the road. Someone felt comfortable and secure here with only the gate camera.

At the end of the road was a tall buck pole by an old house. Swamp Lake stretched out dead ahead. A garage to the extreme left. The vehicle tracks led to the garage. There was a glass panel in the door. He looked inside and saw a red Escalade. Felt his heart skip. No, he told himself, too damn much of a coincidence to be real. But it was real.

The house was two stories, desperately needed paint. The back door was open. Mudroom off the kitchen. He turned the knob and walked in.

Not a mite of dust anywhere, which meant it was not your run-of-the-mill hunting camp. Well cared for, cleaned, probably this morning. The outside made it seem as if it were used only a week or two a year. Inside gave a different impression.

He walked through the kitchen into a living room with a wide picture window overlooking the lake. He looked right. A woman in a scant yoga getup sat on a couch. There was a stainless steel revolver on the coffee table in front of her. A .38 or .357, he guessed, difficult to guess from where he stood. "What a nice gun you have," he said.

She laughed. "That should be *my* line!"

He pulled apart his vest and showed her the pistol tucked in his own belt.

"Yours looks bigger'n mine," she said.

"It's the natural order," he told her.

"That's what you meant by protection?" she asked.

He countered. "What else could it be?"

She picked up a clear bowl from the floor, set it on the table by her Colt. It was filled with condoms in a rainbow of colors. Foil packs.

"What caliber are those?" he asked.

She smirked. "We'll see," she said. "You look even bigger than our friend in common said you are."

"Friend in common?"

"Soon as you lay out the down payment. We don't employ real names in this business."

"Two bills," he said.

"Right," she said. "I know who you are," she added.

"Really?"

"The beginning and the end."

What's she playing at? "That's why I told you that," he said. "The Alpha and the Omega."

"You didn't tell me that you're a game warden."

Amazing. "Am I?"

"I've heard the governor is after your scalp."

This was an interesting development. "Sorry, no idea what you're talking about."

"I think you do. King Kong says the governor thinks you're a world-class shit-disturber, a potential messer-upper of juicy financial deals."

"This King Kong knows the governor?"

"Only superficially socially. This governor walks his own path. They are not what you call asshole buddies, just assholes, each in his own right and way. What is it you want from me, Game Warden?"

"What're you offering?" he asked, sitting down on the arm of a chair across from her.

"That's an array of possibles too extensive to catalog, like a menu in a hash house. Start with why you're here," she said.

"I could ask you the same."

This brought a bitter laugh. "Save the fallen angel? Spare me, please."

"I came to talk," he said.

"That's not one of my better skill sets."

He shrugged, took a guess, based on what she'd said and the red Caddy. "You're King Kong's wife."

She nodded. "That was you riding shotgun with the game warden yesterday by the house. You stared at me."

"Guilty. You seem to have all the toys a girl could want, so why this?"

"The pistol?"

"No, this, your thing, the white phone, all that."

"Ah," she said. "Juice, the edge, the risk of it all—hell, you're a cop, you should know without asking."

He wasn't sure how to play this. "There're all kinds of edges."

"True, but so far I've never met an edge I didn't like."

"That what your old man is—an edge?"

She made eye contact and stared hard.

He continued, "Those who like the edge are always drawn to the antic-ipation and the adrenaline-dump when the moment's passed. It's addictive. I get that."

"So I've learned, the no-drug drug, which eliminates you-know-who. Truth is, King Kong is more like George of the Jungle, totally risk averse, 'Watch out for that tree!' See what I'm sayin'?"

He nodded. "You know much about his businesses?"

"I'm the trophy wife, and that by definition means I know only what I'm allowed and expected to know. What's your interest?"

"Limestone, maybe?"

"Ah," she said. "Now I think I see."

"Good, then you can enlighten me."

The woman stretched like a cat, winding up for a pounce. "Your being here tells me you're enlightened enough," Oheneff said.

What does she mean? He put two one-hundred-dollar bills on the table by the revolver. "That might be chump change for you."

She rolled her eyes. "Perhaps, in the larger scheme of things. *What* about limestone?"

"Same question, back at you."

"Could be King Kong's got his eye on some kind of sweet spot. That's his term, not one geologists would know, a sweet spot heretofore unknown. He lives for such shit—loot, treasure, the magic score!"

Service felt his gut tightening. "Where might such a sweet spot be?"

"One would think, with all the game warden certainly already knows, he would surely know the answer to that question."

"I don't know as much as you think. Give me a name, a hint, a place . . . a something."

"Drinkless nights for me, doesn't do to have the trophy sloppy drunk, some nights the drinkies flow like flash floods down the mountain and names get bandied about. You definitely have enemies, I'll say that for you. They refer to it only as the 'Project,' but I've learned to hear between the lines."

"You called him George of the Jungle? He wants me out too?"

"I gather that your being out of the picture is a key to The Project. As for you, George only hears what he hears and remembers what he wants, usually only those things that directly benefit him. He knows what he hears, and what he hears is that you are a wart on the cheeks of the smooth ass of progress. Think of George as a gubernatorial go-between, the little bird with connections."

"Hears what from whom?" Service asked.

The woman gritted her teeth, puffed her cheeks, and locked her eyes on him. "Look like anyone you know?"

His turn to laugh. "Our way-back governor," he said. "Bozian, *he's* the source?"

"Allegedly," she said. "George's source, not mine. I can't stand that greasy priss. I moved here when Lori was in office."

Lori was former governor Lorelei Timms, his friend, eight years governor and a sometime pain in his ass. She was now out east in a new career as a TV pundit and a pretty talking head. "She was a lousy governor," he said, meaning it. Great intentions, poor executions.

"I agree, but a lovely lady nevertheless, and my friend—and yours too."

"She know about this side of your life?"

"Straitlaced Lori? Not a chance! But she'd kind of understand. The edge calls to different people in different ways. Her way is politics I think, same drug, different name."

He agreed with her assessment and almost laughed. Here they sat before a picture window looking out on a small lake with a bowl of condoms on the table next to a handgun. There was not a ripple on the water. Surreal.

"So," she said.

"Our mutual friend says you're a magnet and she's right. You've got people after your scalp and you seem entirely unconcerned."

"Talk is cheap," he told her. "Thanks for seeing me. Sorry there wasn't more in this for you."

"You didn't get much for your money. You want a sampler for the road?"

"No thanks, this was way more than I expected." More than he could even hope for. If Bozian was back in the picture, that alone potentially clarified a lot. His suspension wasn't about Allerdyce, it was about his being an impediment. The question was to what, and his gut said it had to do with the Mosquito Wilderness.

"One last question?" he asked.

"Let it fly," she said.

"Drazel Sisters L.L.C. Satellite Services & Earth Surveys."

"What about it?"

"It's his business?"

"Don't recall ever hearing that name. Why?"

"Never?"

She sighed. "I've got no clue, sorry. He's got so many contexts and pots boiling. Like I said, I'm just the arm candy trophy wifey, not his business partner."

"Sounds like he's not much on partnering."

She grimaced. "He's got no idea of how to share, and our marriage was over before it even began."

"Sorry to hear that," Service said.

"Don't be. I live the good life. His demands on me are small and my freedom is nearly absolute. What more can a married woman ask for?"

Service put his white phone on the coffee table. "This how we do this?"

"Usually," she said, "but put it back in your pocket, please. You never know when it might come in handy."

He was tempted, but a cell phone, even shut off, could be pinged by the carrier with astonishing accuracy. He didn't need that kind of security risk hanging over his head. "Appreciate the thought," he told her. "I really do. But I have to pass," he said as he stood up. "You always bring that pistol to your appointments?"

"Always," she said. "It jacks up everybody's juices."

"That puffy face you mentioned. He around much?"

She hawed loudly. "Weekly sometimes. I don't see him that much, but George does. Me and puffy cheeks don't much like each other. They meet out at the farm."

"George of the Jungle has a farm?"

"No, the other one's farm."

"Where?"

"Somewhere north of St. Johns."

Strange information from this contact. "Is he living at the farm?"

"I doubt it. He and his wife still live out east somewhere, I forget exactly where. He's not one of my favorite people. But he's been coming back a lot over the past couple of months."

Huh, Service thought. And his suspension got extended in that same time frame. Another coincidence? No way.

"You look like you just swallowed a timberdoodle," Allerdyce said when he got to the truck and lit a cigarette."

"Something like that. You ready to head back above the bridge?"

"Wah, I was ready when we hit Mack City on way down."

CHAPTER 10

Maple River Flooding

GRATIOT COUNTY

CO "Sleep" Bubenko was waiting for them at the Maple River Flooding. Bubenko was one of Service's contemporaries, an old-timer who had been around in the heyday of night poaching and had earned his soubriquet by never falling asleep during long and boring surveillance sessions. He possessed an astonishing ability to function without sleep for many consecutive days and never seem the least bit confused or mentally addled by the lack of rest. Sleep Bubenko, like Service, was one of the last Vietnam vets in a CO uniform.

The man had the posture and girth of a string bean, white hair, and skin mottled with purple and white blotches. "Thanks for meeting us," Service greeted him.

"Is that Allerdyce with you?" Bubenko asked. "I talked to Magwire. She said you and the old asshole were out and about and lurking down this way."

"Sleep, meet Limpy Allerdyce."

The two men eyed each other rather than shaking hands. "Heard a lot about you," the old game warden told the old poacher. "You and Service had a dandy deer season."

"I was just tag along," Allerdyce said. "Sonnyboy dere do all da heavy liftering."

Bubenko turned to Service. "Something special I can do you fellows for?"

"I've heard Clearcut has a farm north of St. Johns."

Bubenko furrowed his brow and frowned, stared out into the flooding. "That's new information to me. How long's he supposed to have had this place?"

"No clue, might be recent, might be old history. Might not even be under his name, but I've been told he's up in the area, maybe as much as monthly, maybe more frequently than that."

"You and Bozian gonna lock horns again?"

"Never can tell," Service said.

"You want me to verify he's up this way, if he is?"

"If you can."

"Any more word on your suspension, when you're coming back?"

He told him what he told Magwire.

"That'll be what, six months? I never heard such shit before. Feels like funny business to me, Grady. Quacks like a duck, eh?"

"Feels like something, not sure funny's the right word for it."

"You'll be back, man. Remember, it don't mean nothing. I'll give you a bump when I learn something. There's a good chance my partner down in Clinton County will know something."

"Who's there?"

"Dover, here a year, keeps to himself, but he's got a hound's nose and the focus of a cobra."

The men shook hands. Bubenko said, "We're all with you, Grady. And we are *all* watching what goes down, and how it goes down."

"Take care," Service said. First Magwire, now Bubenko making masked noises of solidarity. Good for me, he thought, not so good for the state. You need to think on this shit. Your fate is not a reason to destroy the force.

"You guys want to grab lunch?" Bubenko asked.

Allerdyce spoke before Service could. "Just want be over damn britch. We stop outside Iggy, at Wildwoods or da Lehtos' place, get good pasty, yum-yum eatem up."

"St. Ignace is a long haul from here."

"We stop eat down here, I get daspitupitations. He made a rubbing motion in front of his belly."

"We sure wouldn't want that," Bubenko said, glancing at Service, who was rolling his eyes.

"I'm airsick ta down here, Sonny."

"Allergic?"

"I said airsick. I breet dis shitty air, it make me sick, air . . . sick. You got listen better."

It was an odd way to put it, but Allerdyce had a point, and he felt pretty much the same way about almost anything Below the Bridge and the Straits of Mackinac.

CHAPTER 11

Soaring Eagle Casino

MOUNT PLEASANT, ISABELLA COUNTY

Grady Service drove into the casino parking lot, which was, as always, full to the gunwhales. "We need luck," he told Allerdyce.

"I got plenty luck," Limpy said, "go play one-arms, hey."

"They'll drain your wallet."

"Not mine," the old man said. The two men went inside and tried to move through the maze of old folks who had been elder-toured in buses to the casino to chip away at their fixed incomes. They were everywhere, many ambulatory, some on canes and crutches, many with oxygen bottles hung around their necks like necklaces. Many were carrying drinks, and judging by the volume of voices, they were not all drinking fruit juices. The smoke was heavy and hung over the floor at eye level, like smoke over a battlefield.

Allerdyce grumbled, "T'ought dis was no-smoke inside state."

"We're not in Michigan. This is a separate country, a sovereign nation, totally separate, with their own rules and ways of doing things, all in the name of money."

Allercyce frowned, said, "Indi'ns," and added, "Like dat Wally Dicksney jamoke. He got two country of 'is own jest like dis, hey?"

Service said, "Something like that." The old poacher's view of the world was unique, but the points he made weren't all that far off. He was thinking about lighting a cigarette to join the crowd when his cell phone buzzed in his pocket. He answered.

"Grady Service, will you please explain what in blazes is going on?"

It was his friend, the former governor, Lorelei Timms. He said, "Can you narrow that down a bit. The earth continues to orbit the sun, if that's what you're asking."

He had met Timms at a wreck years before. She was on her way to the Huron Mountain Club early one very rainy and nasty morning. She was small, beautiful, smart, and intense, wired tight enough to break wine glasses just with her presence. She had also become a good friend and was someone who believed it her holy right to meddle in friends' lives. It was an annoying combination.

"I'm serious," she said.

"Me too."

"Do I have to go lawyer on you?"

"Aren't you already?"

"You're on suspension?"

"Yes."

"Until September?"

Until September? This is new, he thought, but no doubt lots of rumors were flying. "Until July 1." Originally it was supposed to be until spring. Now September?

"What heinous thing brought this down on your head?"

"Allerdyce was my partner during deer season."

A long silence ensued. "*Limpy* Allerdyce? *That* Allerdyce?"

"Yes, he's the only Limpy I know."

"What *were* you thinking?"

He sighed, hated how she liked to interfere in his life. "I was *thinking*," he explained, "that nobody knows more about dirtbags and poaching than him. And I was right . . . by the way." Not that it matters now.

"For which you are now suspended. You think it was worth it?"

"Yep."

"What's the official charge?"

"I'm not exactly clear on that point. Having a felon in the truck, poor professional judgment, unprofessional behavior—their reasoning is kinda murky, looks bad."

"Originally off till spring, now pushed to September?"

What had she said? "September? This fall thing's entirely new to me. The last I heard it was extended to July 1."

"And what was the reason given for the extension?"

"I don't know. Lansing isn't exactly forthcoming. Something about needing more time to gather more input, you know, the usual Lansing bullshit."

"This is unfair," she said. "Have you talked to Chief Waco?"

"When he took my badge and again when he told me the suspension was being extended. Where did you hear the September thing?"

She said, "Maybe you should talk to your chief."

"What would be the point of that?"

"Are your math skills *that* bad?"

"Two and two is one," he said laconically.

"Stop with the cute. You ever hear of a suspension of this length?"

He had not. "No."

"Then there must be a reason. I mean it's way outside any norm I know of for state workers."

"I put it down to Lansing." The old-time game wardens, the horse blankets of his father's generation, always called the capital the Center of Administrative Incest.

"Don't play cute word games. Your career and pension are on the line."

"Now who's playing word games? None of this is your concern, Lori."

"Friends are always concerned for friends."

"You're meddling, as you love to do."

Silence. "Okay, I can see how it may be interpreted that way by you, but really, I'm seeing an iceberg here."

He had to think about that. "I'm like what, the small visible tip?"

"Could be a certain former governor has his prodigious appetite back in the state trough. There's a rumor circulating that the current director of the DNR will retire and be replaced by Bozian's son."

The governor had only one son, Samuel A. "Trip" Bozian III. "You mean Trip?"

"Trip Bozian is wildlife chief in New Mexico, and very highly regarded," Timms explained. "You realize if he's the director here, that law enforcement will report to him, be *under* him."

"Trip's not like his father," Service said. He hoped this was true, but deep down he knew he couldn't know with certainty. It had been a long time. Maybe he'd heard something about the kid getting a degree in wildlife management, but he wasn't sure.

"Might be that Sam will use his son to try to sweep you out."

"No, not Trip, Lori. He's a good kid, and I can't see him doing that. Now Clearcut, that's a different deal. He'd drown himself to drown an enemy. What the hell are you circling around, Lori?"

"Follow the money," she said.

"Thank you, I'm sure. Are you my Deep Throat?" He cringed as soon as the words were loose.

"Stop making jokes," she said. "Think gigantic commercial fish farms."

Fish farms? This might apply to the Great Lakes, he thought, but the Mosquito? No way for the Mosquito to be involved in any way in any sort of aquaculture.

"I can't buy that, Governor."

"Nevertheless, start with fish farms," Timms directed. "See where that takes you."

"You know there's more?"

"I think there's more, but I can't prove a darn thing with what I know, but you're a detective, so good grief, get out there and *detect*. And talk to Chief Waco, please."

"I doubt the chief will think that's such a great idea."

She laughed sardonically. "I think what you think about what the chief may think is baloney." With that, she hung up.

Geez, he thought. She's such a pain in the ass. But well informed. You have to give her that.

Service turned to Allerdyce, who had come back from the slots. "Fish farms."

The old man grimaced. "Where?"

"Could be the U.P."

"Dis ain't youse's Missistinky or Loositania. Dose pipples down dere like eat all dat soff-meat stinky fish. Not no Yoopers, no."

"Have you ever heard rumors about fish farming in Michigan?"

"None. Youse put one dose t'ings up 'ere wit' salmons, trouts, Yoopers steal dem blind, cut dere nets, all dat shit. Youse know, hey."

"I thought farmed fish was stinky, and Yoopers won't eat the meat."

"Day ain't gone raise no catsfish 'ere. Or eat dat shit. Got be salmons or trouts, hey. Water too bloody cold for whiskerfishies. Could sell down Stink-cago, dose FIBTABs, dey don't know shit."

FIBTAB was Yooper talk for Fucking Illinois Bastard Towing A Boat. It made no sense, linking the Mosquito to fish farms—unless this involved the big lake water at the mouth of the Mosquito River. Even so, this seemed way outside the realm of possible or practicable. But Lori said start there, and she was connected in ways you couldn't even suspect.

"We need to get back to Lansing," Service told his partner.

"Us, we?"

"We're partners, right?"

The old man's leer made his belly roll.

Allerdyce grabbed his arm. "C'mon, we got do firs' somepin."

"What?"

"Eat, collect moula."

"You won at the slots?"

Allerdyce winked.

"Nobody but the house wins at slots. The odds are stacked miles-high against the players."

"I allas win, Sonnyboy."

"No way."

"Youse just got know way to talk da stupid t'ings."

"Talk, as in what?"

"You don't spit out no money, I kill youse's ass."

"It's a machine. It's not alive."

"Shhh," Allerdyce said, "machines dey don't know dat."

God. "How much did you win?"

"One pay one, one pay five, one pay twinnyfive."

"Dollars?"

"T'ousand." Limpy said quietly and stumbled away toward the cashier's cage, leaving Service standing in the smoky air.

CHAPTER 12

Chief Waco's House

INGHAM/EATON COUNTIES

He'd called the chief from Mount Pleasant. "Meet me at my house," Waco had instructed, and hung up. It had been awhile since he'd seen his friend. The chief's place straddled two counties, Ingham and Eaton. Service had no idea which county was the county of record and didn't much care.

"Guess I'm not surprised to see you below the bridge," Waco greeted him at the door, then looked beyond the officer at his personal truck. "Is that Allerdyce out there?"

"Yessir."

"Might as well fetch him into my office. All this concerns both of you fellers," Waco said. "The governor is talking about having him arrested for parole violations."

Grady's voice rose, "Has a warrant been issued?"

"No, but it's being bandied about right now at the governor's staff level. Colonel Sudifant from the MSP called, and I told her all about the deal with you. She's topnotch, knows political crap when she sees it. The Troops will play sea anchor for us as long as she dares, but make no mistake, the governor is out to make some sort of example out of Allerdyce just to get you out."

"I've never had a problem with this governor," Grady Service said.

They both waved Allerdyce in, and he came like a rascal summoned to the principal's office. Waco greeted him with a handshake. "Good to finally meet you. You had a deer season for the record books—if we had such things."

"Sonnyboy's work. I jest dere for da laffs."

"Let's drop all the horse-pucky," the chief said. "The governor is trying to crush Grady and force him to retire. And he's going to try to use *you* for leverage," the chief told the old man. "He wants you back inside for parole violations, but if Service will put in his papers, you'll remain free."

Allerdyce looked bored. "Sonnyboy ain't done nuffins wrong. Me never . . . uh . . . mostly . . . I ain't no saint, okay?"

"This is all sleaze politics," Chief Waco said, "but that doesn't make it less real. Grady's got friends and allies, but most of us can do only so much when the opposing force is the governor's will and office."

Allerdyce crossed his arms and frowned. "I got go back inside, so she goes. None dis is Sonnyboy's fault. He got fault, it's that he cares too bloody much dis bloody state."

Waco said, "You'll get no argument from me, and sentiment and emotion are good things, as is loyalty, but we're dealing with realities of law, politics, and power, which means you guys need a plan. Correction: *We* need a plan."

Chief Waco, unlike previous DNR law chiefs, wore a sparse full-face beard. He had intense, wild gray eyes. The two men had worked a case involving a serial killer who was murdering game wardens and, during a search for a possible victim, had been trapped in a flash flood in Missouri's Irish Wilderness. Both of them had nearly died. They had bonded then and remained so. Later Waco had been brought to Michigan to head up the law division, purportedly to inject new blood into the department, which it had. It was not clear that DNR senior management was pleased with the result. Waco was his highly principled. He had been the same kind of dedicated, hard-charging game warden as Service.

"You having us here," Service said, "puts you deep into potential conspiracy country, Eddie."

Service tried to turn and head for the door, but the chief grabbed his arm. "Hold your horses, Grady. This whole thing is one big political shit sandwich I refuse to eat. The governor wants your suspension pushed back to Labor Day. He's hoping you'll take the hint and retire, but if not, his next move is to go after Limpy, to put him back in the can as additional pressure on you."

"Can he do that, legally?"

"Hard to say, but for the moment he has the AG and his legal team's backing, and that's all that matters to him. Have you heard about his aspirations to higher office? They're true."

"Then he can't let this thing with Limpy and me become public. If it does, it'll look like . . . hell, I don't know exactly what, but my gut says this guy is banking on always looking like Mr. Clean. If this thing breaks publicly, people may wonder if he's captaining the ship of the state or the ship of fools. Going public hurts *him*, not me."

"Exactly. That's why he's using suspend-and-delay tactics, but if those don't work, he might feel he's forced to strike at Allerdyce."

"All this shit is about the governor's concern for his reputation? Jesus."

"That's what I'm hearing, why?"

Grady asked if he could smoke and made a fast decision. "Sit down, Eddie, there's more of this you need to hear." He laid out the Mosquito, Drazel Sisters, fish farms, Kalleskevich, and Bozian. Eddie Waco sank back in his chair. "You mind if I smoke one of your nails, Grady?"

After two or three puffs, the chief said, "We're gonna fight these bastards, whatever it takes and whatever cost. The sitting governor is a tool, and worse, a pompous fool. What the hell do Kalleskevich and Bozian want with the Mosquito? Last I knew there was no commercial market for blackflies, skeets, and ticks."

Now Service had a really tough disclosure decision to make, and after a moment, he said, "The apparent interest is limestone."

"Apparent interest . . . *in limestone*?"

"There's limestone there, but not a hell of a lot of it, and there's sure as hell not enough to commercialize."

"Is there natural gas and oil up there?"

"No," Grady Service said, drawing out the word. "There are diamonds."

Waco blew a ragged blue smoke cloud and coughed. "There are diamonds in Iron County, probably Menominee and Marquette Counties too."

"Not like what's in the Mosquito," Service said. "These are gem quality, *very high* gem quality."

The chief exhaled and coughed again. "Good Lord, that changes the whole game. Do you think they know about the diamonds?"

"There's no other explanation for their interest."

"Who owns the mineral rights?"

Grady Service reminded his chief, "That's irrelevant, doesn't matter, it's a wilderness area, legally and officially. You can't mine a federal wilderness. It's sacrosanct."

Chief Waco said, "You need a remedial wildland law refresher course. The *surface* is wilderness, the mineral substrate isn't. The only way you can stop mining is if the surface rights owner is the same as the underground resource owner, in this case, the state. Otherwise, mineral rights trump all private ownership, even if the land in question has your home on top of it. How many people know about these diamonds?"

This was new ground, and scary. "Limpy and me, and now you. The three of us know the whole thing. Two other people knew I had stones, but not where from." He didn't mention Maridly Nantz, who had found them, because she was dead now, and he hated to think about that.

"I'll ask again," Chief Waco said. "Who owns the mineral rights?"

"Guess we'd better figure that out posthaste."

"Should be right at the top of your agenda," the chief said. "If I were to make even discreet inquiries inside the department, it could raise suspicions. But any distant and indirect help I can give you, I will. And if this thing becomes real, I will resign and bathe the governor in manure on my way out. Gimme another nail."

"Eddie, we can't tell anyone about the real treasure in the tract, not until we're damn sure of our legal grounds, and even then it will be a disaster."

"Won't be a word from me; we'll keep this close until we can't anymore."

"We can't *ever* let this become public," Service argued. "If word gets out, the tract will be trashed by treasure hunters and all the shit that goes with that."

"I hear you, but circumstances will tell, and all battles always boil down to terrain and circumstances. I'm with you as far as a goal, unless we are forced to change the goal, agreed?"

"I've never been much for compromise."

"I know. Me neither. Agreed?"

Service nodded. Allerdyce said not a word during the exchange, just sat quietly looking around, like he was in another dimension.

"There's one more thing," Service said. "Trip Bozian."

"Who the blazes is that?"

Either Eddie hasn't heard or he's a good actor. "Clearcut's son."

Waco shrugged. "This would concern us how?"

"He's going to replace the DNR director."

"The director is in place."

"He's going to resign."

Waco looked flummoxed. "We talk every day. He hasn't said a word."

"It's not his idea. Bozian will use the governor to push him out and wedge his son in his place."

Eddie Waco's chin sank. "This is becoming a madhouse."

"The son, Trip, was once one of my cubs, but screwed up big time and resigned before he was officially fired. He was glad to be out. The whole thing was a burden, and he knew law enforcement wasn't the right road for him, but the old man has been after me ever since."

Eddie Waco said thoughtfully, "None of this makes me happy, but let's keep our eyes on the real ball for the moment. That's the Mosquito. I'd like to tell the governor that you and I have had a heart-to-heart, and that you are going to talk to your lawyer regarding retirement—for the benefit of the force. I'll suggest to the governor that we let your suspension run to July 1, and that we not extend to Labor Day because that might get your back up again. This buys us time. You okay with this?"

Service said, "July 1, right?"

Eddie Waco said, "Yes. The governor won't bring charges against you or Allerdyce if it will risk your not going along with the game. His best move is to swallow his tongue and sit back for a while. I'll advise him that anything else will be regarded as a provocation."

"Okay," Grady Service said. "First agenda item, find out who the heck owns the mineral rights under the Mosquito."

"Which you will find out without inquiry to anyone in the DNR or DNRE. You need to get yourselves into wound-licking mode, and stay unseen and unheard."

"You're making us play with an arm tied behind us."

"You've always been an accomplished head-butter, and nut-kicker, so it doesn't seem like all that big a restriction. You're clever, and I'm confident you'll find a work-around."

"I hate games," Service said.

"Welcome to the secret world of government and greed."

"How do you tolerate it?" Service asked his friend.

"The wife asks me that very thing several times a week, but I swore an oath here and I intend to uphold it by doing what's right, not necessarily what's legal or politically expedient. And, just for the record here, you and Allerdyce? I thought it was a brilliant partnership, same as Cake and me down in Missouri."

The chief's dedication made him ashamed. He was taking this whole thing personally. "Maybe I *should* retire."

"Go ahead, if you want to open the treasure house door. The only thing that has Bozian and the rest of them stymied and slow-walking this deal is your presence and reputation as the Mosquito's junkyard dog defender. Find out who owns the mineral rights. That's enough for you to focus on right now."

"What if the state doesn't own underground rights?"

"Let's cross that bridge if we have to. Our first go-to will be wilderness lawyers, somebody over in the Sierra Club or experts of that ilk. They may know some ways to block exploitation, but if the state owns the rights, this deal will be dead and done, stillborn, no matter what cards Kalleskevich and Bozian have up their sleeves."

Service felt lightheaded. This was so much to take on all at once, but now he knew. Bozian was after him again. He looked at the chief and nodded as he and Allerdyce departed. His pension was meaningless compared to the wealth he had inherited from his late girlfriend Maridly Nantz. Bozian wants war? Let's see how he handles it when it turns hot.

"Did you follow all that?" Service asked Allerdyce when they were back in the truck.

"Yah sure. We got find out state or udder jamokes own unnergroun'd shit."

Something like that. "I'm thinking Fellow Marthesdottir might be a good place to start."

"I had some t'oughts down dat line too, Sonnyboy. She pert smart cookie, dat girlie."

"You might have to take one for the team."

"Wah," Allerdyce said. "I take one, it be for me, hell wit' youses. If dat okay for team, den okay, but not why I taken one for seff."

Grady Service laughed and thought, Polaris and Allerdyce, both invariably in the exact orbit where nature put them.

"Youse t'ink dis all turn out okay?" Allerdyce asked.

"So far so good. It's up to us to make the rest turn out okay."

"We go Yoop now?" his partner asked in a hopeful voice.

"One more stop before we point our nose north."

"Knew dat," Limpy grumbled.

CHAPTER 13

Lake Lansing

INGHAM COUNTY

K Pop seemed ageless in his flashing eyes, but the wrinkles on his face were stacked like flapjacks with liver spots. "Service, you grand and glorious asshole," the retired CO greeted him and grabbed him in a bear hug. "Hey man, I still got all my original teeth. Heard you can't say the same."

Grady Service had lost all of his teeth with the assistance of culvert, a boulder, and an orthodontist after nearly drowning in a river early one Easter Sunday morning. "Bullshit," he told the old officer. "You're on your second or third set of falsies. Word is they fell out just so the Tooth Fairy's dentist cousin could make a living and build a small palace on the Au Sable River."

The old man chuckled and looked down at Allerdyce. "Damn, Limpy, I'da thought them young gang-banger bucks in Jackson woulda butt-fucked you to death."

The old man cackled. "Weren't dere fav'rite flavor when dey see I carry shank."

The CO turned his attention back to Service. "Must be the end of the world, an on-duty CO coming to see the likes of me. The half-life of my usefulness having passed down the crapper about twenty-five years back."

K Pop's intel might not be current, so Service decided to let him think he was still on duty. Decades back the old CO had been wrongfully accused of selling state property and had been fired. The subsequent trial found him not guilty, but the department didn't want him back and chastised him for questionable judgment and unprofessional behavior. The game warden's lawyer eventually got him fully reinstated, with full back pay, including his pension. He then promptly retired.

His name came from his habit of keeping cartons of K-rations in the back of his duty vehicle. He had been a resourceful, aggressive, successful game warden who made cases against people that made all of Lansing pay attention. He especially liked to hammer politicians—and found plenty to concentrate on.

Service saw no shred of irritation or nervousness between the former CO and the famous former poacher. Very unusual for both men. Limpy swore he was allergic to game wardens, all but Service and his father before him. "Dey make me break out in the hides," he would explain.

"You two are a long way from home," K Pop said, suggesting to Service that the old man who swore no interest in anything DNR-related still kept track of who was stationed where. K Pop had left the DNR in Service's third year. Service had bumped into him in a bar up near the Soo one day, and K Pop had urged him to check in if he could ever help him with any of the many mysteries of state government and its foolish ways. Words spoken so long ago, yet Grady Service could still remember the intensity and sincerity of the man that day.

"Knew I'd see you, sooner or later," the man said. "Have to add I was beginning to think it would never happen."

"You know how it goes," Service told him.

The retired officer nodded enthusiastically and grinned sardonically. "Yah, nobody wants to play grab-ass with Typhoid Mary."

"You still running your traplines?" Service asked. K Pop had been one of the biggest, most assiduous trappers among COs, and had taught new officers the sport and how to enforce it.

"Quit that shit years back, and turned to trapping humans as a private dick. Make more money and it's a lot more fun. I specialize in politicians of the egg-sucking persuasion, of which this particular water wonderland has too damn many. What the hell do you want? How can I help? You don't get down to it quick-like, I may keel over dead of old age."

"I seem to remember you had a run-in with Bozian." Service's actual memory was not clear on the details; it was more of a lingering impression somewhere on the edge of his consciousness.

K Pop nodded. "Over-limit of pheasants, twice. This was before his political bulk floated him to the top of the state cesspool. Wasn't much to it. He was up on his farm, and I caught him walking home on a state road, hauled him to a JP. He pleaded guilty and paid his fine. No fuss, no posturing, by-the-bloody-book, politically correct, paid his fines, and went on his way."

"That doesn't sound like the Bozian I know."

"I'm pretty sure he had a lot more shit back on his property, but it was good to stroke him and let him know he was on my watch list."

"No harsh words or aftermath?"

"I heard a few times how the Gov had his own hit list of get-evens and that my name was up high, but nothing ever came from it. Bozian's an equal opportunity believer in payback in spades, no matter how small or large the transgression. But so was I, and I made sure he knew it."

"A list? What was your source on that?" Service asked.

K Pop grinned mischievously. "Where's your favorite morel picking spot?"

Grady understood. Morel mushrooms, trout behind beaver dams, and sources, these were things you kept to yourself and shared with nobody, including your spouse.

The retired officer added, "Okay, it was Bozian himself. He said, 'Listen pal, you'd best step carefully from here on. I've got you on my list.'"

"I said, same here, Governor." K Pop suddenly looked at Service. "Why the hell are you *still* working?"

"I'm not, I'm suspended."

K Pop grinned. "I guess I mighta heard a rumor down that line. And not your first one. What did they nail you for this time?"

"A bit like the deal they ran on you. They suspend guys as a message they should retire—to save legal proceedings and potential embarrassment. They play that game with you?"

"Hell no, they fired me outright, without a hearing and without cause, all based on some stupid rumor. The director told me, 'Own up to it and we'll let you retire.' I told him to go blow his pink Chihuahua; he had the backbone of broke-down hippers. I told him I'd make the state pay for his incompetence, and pay they did, a full million on top of back pay for punitive damages and soiling my good reputation. The guy who sabotaged me had been in our unit but couldn't hack undercover work. We sent him back to a uniform and he vowed to get even, not with our boss, who actually nixed him, but with me. I publicly called him out as a chicken shit and he didn't like that. Ask me, I think he was secretly relieved to be out of the soup . . . he was chicken shit, pure and stinky as they come."

"Titty Bar Tyler," Service said. "Remember the name but not the man."

"That was him. Nothing worth remembering, and I don't know how many times the boss had to tell him that most of our clients weren't of the titty bar persuasion, but he had his own ideas. And he could hide his fear with drinks while ogling tits." K Pop grinned. "What's your interest in Bozian?"

"My nose, gut, an itch, who knows."

"Yah, I know how that works. Look, Service, I just ain't one to give up platinum sources, but if you're looking for night dirt on Bozian, there's only one true expert, M."

"Em, like Emily?"

"No, the letter M."

"That's all? Like the single-letter boss in James Bond's outfit?"

K Pop giggled. "Hell son, M's all you'll need."

"How do I find him?"

"M will find you."

"Hasn't so far."

"Mebbe ain't nobody told M you're fishing the Lansing pond, but I'll take care of that. When time comes to present your bona fides, just say 'K Pop sent me,' and that will open the door and clear the way. But once you're inside, you have to live by M's rules."

"Which are?"

"Different for each of us. You'll be told, don't you worry none about that." K Pop stared at a wall. "Yeah, you'll be told about that."

It wasn't until they were back in the truck that Allerdyce spoke up. "Dat guy back dere give me da big willies. Somepin ain't right in 'is noggin."

Service started the engine. "That's exactly what people say about you."

Allerdyce seemed pleased. "See, takes one, know one, hey," adding, "Dat Titty Bar guy youses say, he da one left 'im and shot offen 'is pajogler?" The old man's eyes were on full twinkle.

"I guess I never heard anything about that."

"Me I keep dis Bobbitt list, you know broad cutted off her old man's whanger? Anybody gets nabbed on dat, I write name on list, don't want date no knife-happy nut job. Dere's a Tyler on list, hey."

A Bobbitt list? "I guess it's good to have standards."

Allerdyce nodded. "Man's got to have 'is tankards." He added, "Bozian ain't onny one keep payback list, Sonnyboy."

"What're you trying to say?"

"I ain't saying nuffing ain't already got saided."

Service studied his partner, whose face was the archetypal violator's mask of neutrality, a real drooler of the plainest sort.

"Where we go now?" Allerdyce asked.

"Fishing."

"We ain't got no gear."

"We're the fish."

Allerdyce seemed to ponder this, tucked in his chin, and announced, "I ain't no easy catch."

Truth in those words, Service could attest.

CHAPTER 14

East Lansing

INGHAM COUNTY

An early morning text message instructed him to drive to an address on Northlawn in East Lansing at a certain time. He could bring his partner. The message was signed "M." Service decided that K Pop had told M about Allerdyce—how else would he know he had a partner? The neighborhood was nice, not modern chic or McMansionish, but the places of people with a pad of whatever to fall back on when times turned hard, as they recently had. Colonials and colonial offshoots mainly, with one outlier, a French-looking thing that was entirely out of step in suburbia. The uniformity of mowed and manicured lawns and ornately trimmed hedges gave Service the willies. He knew people who prized their lawns so much he swore they named every blade of grass and considered each a pet. The snow down here was gone, and it looked like the lawns had already seen at least one pass of the mowing service. Every house, not just one extremist. Monkey-see, monkey-do, keep up with the pack, Jack.

No knocker on the door, but there was a small black camera staring down. "You him?" a voice from the camera asked.

"That depends who him is, doesn't it?" Service answered.

"You'd be him," the camera voice declared. "Word traveled ahead of you that you are a smart-ass and your partner's a thief."

"Thank you," Service said brightly. "It's nice to be thought of."

Allerdyce stared up at the camera and wiggled his middle finger. "I ain't no t'ief, and dat voice piss me off," he whispered.

"Probably a mutual feeling," Service replied. The old violator had a knack for upsetting and angering people. Service was never sure if it was purposeful, or some sort of prickly force field Allerdyce projected.

The camera said, "Excuse me, but do you honestly believe that poaching is not a form of theft?"

Allerdyce looked around and eventually said, "Who me?"

"Yes, you . . . you old reprobate."

"I ain't no reporter, an' I don't use no bait, wah."

"You're a poacher, a violator, a thief of the state's publicly owned natural resources."

"Oh," Allerdyce said. "Dat stuff's old. I retired."

"Without making amends, no doubt."

"Retire means make end, don't it?"

The camera pivoted to Service. "Is this true, he's retired?"

"Apparently," Service said.

The camera: "But has he *reformed*?"

"That's still up in the air," Service said. "It's certainly what he claims, and so far I see no evidence to the contrary."

"Youses is talkin about me," Allerdyce said. "I right 'ere, can hear dat shit, wah!" Then, to his partner: "We got stand out 'ere, take dis shit f'um stupid Pokeroid?"

"If you are trying so ineptly to say I am a Polaroid, at least say it correctly. I am not a Pokeroid. The word is Polaroid," the camera declared. "You are an ignorant man."

"Wah," Limpy said with a growl. "Can you see me while we talk, like right now?"

"Obviously," the camera said.

"Den youse is Pokeroid. Got instant pitcher and you like fat black wart on my ass." To Service: "Why we stand 'ere take dis junk?"

The door buzzed and popped open without further comment from the camera. Service said to his partner, "You know you were talking to a person, not that camera, right?"

"I know it jest machine, Sonny, but hey I t'rw shit back and it shut up. I tell one arms do what I want and dey do. See, dese damn t'ings ain't dumb as you t'ink. All machines is some kind a poodoo."

Another voice inside the foyer directed them. "Please take the left corridor to the living room and be seated."

The hallway had thick-pile wall-to-wall carpet on the floor and a six- by four-foot oil portrait of a man in a World War I uniform, a small gleaming star on each epaulet.

"Old school," Allerdyce whispered with a nod at the portrait. "Ramrod back, spitshinered boots to da knees, real brass all shined up and da Charlie Brown belt."

"Sam Browne," Service corrected him.

"How youse know dis guy's name Sam Brown? Youse been here b'fore?"

"Not his name. His belt is a Sam Browne belt."

"My grandfather," a new voice said from a speaker in the ceiling. "Won the medal of honor twice, first time in Mexico and again in France during the Great War. He lived to 108, still driving his car and commanding the attention of every room he walked into. Five four in his stocking feet, and always confident that he was the morally and ethically tallest man in any assembly. Never had to say a word when he arrived. Such was his command presence that everyone in the room would immediately stand up and go silent. He ran Michigan's selective service the first two years of its life, and he studied military history the way some people cling to their Bibles."

The voice stopped momentarily. "He loathed Robert E. Lee, said if the South had just about *any* other general, even a mediocre one, they would have prevailed and this country would be two instead of one. The general insisted that one does not destroy an enemy in a frontal battle; rather, first the two forces collide, then you make him run, and that done, you destroy him from the rear with relentless pursuit. Lee simply couldn't understand the principle and put all his faith in God deciding battle outcomes. He spent a lot of time praying and waiting for God to kiss his ear with magic intel. Obviously that never happened. Too damn many dead because of Lee and now he gets treated like a saint. The man tried to destroy this country. What's saintly in high treason? He should have been hung alongside Jeff Davis."

"Who *are* you?" Service asked, breaking the ramble.

"Who do you *suppose* I am?" the voice came back.

"Is M here? We came to talk to him."

"Why does M have to be male?"

Service had no answer for this. "Are *you* M?"

"I am, and allegedly you are here to acquire certain information, the gathering of which is my forte. My grandpa taught me when I was a kid that intel wins most battles. He who knows most is likely to fare best. That make sense to you?"

Was K Pop serious about this . . . person? Impossible to guess age from her voice, but definitely female. And then she made her grand entry. Five feet tall tops, short black, shiny hair, pebbled skin, all wrinkles, the tiny hands of a doll.

"So?" she said after she sat down in a pale blue chair across from them. "The two of you are here in my presence, but I am the engineer and conductor, brakeman, and all else on this train, and it shall not depart this station until I see tickets in your hand."

"K Pop sent us," Grady Service said.

The woman sighed contentedly. "Perfect. How old might you guess me to be?"

He pondered this before declaring, "I'll take the Fifth. That's a no-win question."

"What's the ultimate?" she asked.

"I don't have opinions on things like that," Service told her.

"Do I look good?"

Jesus, her questions were no more than potshots. "Depends on who is doing the judging."

"You, for example," she said. "Do you think I look good?"

"I never judge stuff like that."

She smiled and nodded demurely. "I am nine-zero years old."

Is she bonkers? No way she's ninety, not even close. Seventy max, he guessed. He looked at Allerdyce, who, as usual, seemed interested in something else, in this case something on the mantel over the fireplace. He seemed to be looking around and not paying attention to the main business at hand.

"I've been MICHIKOSS since 19 and 75," the woman announced proudly.

"What KOSS?"

"Michigan's Keeper of State Secrets."

"That's an actual state office?"

"In a manner of speaking, but not one bandied about outside the so-called inner corridors. My specialty is cracking secrets that need cracking, or protecting those that best serve our state by being kept secret. I traffic in information, all details and trivia welcome. Everything comes to something from something eventually. A noted historian once wrote that all events form a mosaic. Everything affects and is affected by everything else. How is never clear in the present. It's always a nexterday deal. Time sorts out events, time alone, and only then do patterns appear. We and it and these things we call events or moments are connected in a cosmic sense."

Service was still mired in the KOSS thing, which he had never heard of. "There's a state office called KOSS?"

"No," she said curtly. "Such an office doesn't exist, and I don't exist, which makes it and me damn hard to find."

He was confused. "You don't look invisible."

"I'm not right now, but try to find me tomorrow and see how that works out."

"I don't understand," Service told her. "Are you M or aren't you?"

"M to some, Mph to others, Mageret to my friends, of which I have multitudes."

"M stands for Margeret?'"

She grinned, showing a mouthful of gray teeth. "Of course not, it stands for nothing except mystery. I hope that doesn't disappoint, but mystery is more than adequate, don't you think? And what's in a name? Absolutely nothing. It's what's inside the name that matters, the life force that propels the name. Nietzsche told us this, a name is only a name and no person is found there. I'm paraphrasing."

Weird. "What about Mph?"

"Some call me Miss Potato Head, because for those people who I don't want to know my true appearance, I make it a point to never look the same."

Service sucked in a deep breath. K Pop was reliable, but this . . . person? All the marbles didn't seem to be all together in her ninety-year-old head, if that's how old she really was.

"Are you different people on different days?" he asked.

She granted him a smile. "Aren't we all?"

"And who are you today?"

"The real me, you silly man. You know that old saw about the enemy of my enemy?"

"Is my friend," he completed the ragged syllogism.

"Right, and let me state here most emphatically that I loathe Sam Bozian, and I am told that you loathe Bozian. I want his scalp dripping his cold blood on my warm hands. Would you seek that too?"

Is she legit? Service thought. "I don't loathe or hate him. I don't like or love him either. For me, he's nothing more than a pain in the ass, a kangaroo obstacle that keeps jumping into my path."

"You just don't *know* you hate him yet. He tried all the time he was in office to close my operation and put me out on the street, to pension me off like a post-prime racehorse, but he's a mere politician, and I am a librarian and a career bureaucrat. You can't out-game me. He's gone and I'm still here. And yet, I have not had his blood."

"He's been gone a long time," Service reminded her. "And still you want to get him?"

"Memories have no expiration date," she said. "And hell yes, I still want to get him, don't you?"

"I want to know what he's up to, nothing more."

"He's an octopus, got hands and hands of hands, all grabbing and grasping, everything for money or payback, often combined."

"You work from your house?"

"For your purposes, and today only, yes. Don't you work from yours?"

He laughed. "More from my truck than my house."

"We're similar creatures, you and me," she said. "We both hate playing rigged games, and we also hate losing at anything."

"Bozian's in a rigged game?"

She said in a professorial tone, "Sam's a politician, which is all he knows. His electorate, those fools who voted for him and licked his ass and his much-trumpeted governing principles, have no clue that his words aren't who he is. All he knows is everything is rigged. It's his definition of public servant."

"You know why I'm here?" Service asked the woman.

"Not until K Pop gave me a heads-up RFA—that's Request for Audience. Snooped around a bit since then. They're alleging unprofessional judgment in taking a felon on as a partner in your patrol truck. They don't have anything hard to nail you to the cross with, only this soft judgment-related thing, which amounts to so much pudding at room temperature. It's their legal tool, a delaying tactic to sweep the offender off the field, dump him or her in limbo, and, during that void, push ahead the desired agenda. This is classic bureaupoliticracy, and if you can't move your business fast enough, you keep pushing back your opponent's suspension end date until you achieve your goal."

"Then?"

She shrugged. "By then it's moot. Doesn't matter if the opponent's there or not, done is done, *fait accompli*, we've gotten what we wanted, done deal. By the way, you clearly have way more than enough time in to retire. Why haven't you?"

"Why haven't *you*?" Service countered.

"Touché," she said. "Do I look like a candidate for the drool pool?"

"No ma'am." She had an intensity that, even at ninety, still hurled heat across a room. What had she been like at thirty?

"You know what they say about me?" she asked.

"I didn't know there *was* a you until today, and I have no clue who *they* are. Until I saw K Pop yesterday I'd never heard of anyone known by a single letter, except for the odd superstar entertainer."

She drew in a deep breath. "Familiar with the Hannex?"

"Dutch to me."

"It's my fortress, my hideaway, it's on the campus, attached to Ivy Free Hall, tunnel connecting to the main library. Even cops don't know we're there."

"I'm a cop."

"Moot. Any idea why Bozian wants you out?"

"No doubt I rub him the wrong way."

"Granted, so do I. But for you there's more. With Bozian, there's always more. The truth is, I don't yet know the scope of his animus for you. You see, I'm like the late J. Edgar High Heels. I've been in place so long that it's assumed that I know, if not everything, then way too much. Which is probably true. But I do all of my fighting off stage, behind the scenes, and solely with information, which can be far more lethal than bullets."

She reminded him of his detective job, where information was ammo. Sometimes all you had to trade was information to get better information. "You're an information broker," he said.

"Trade it, sell it to the highest or lowest bidder, depending on circumstances, give it away free, bank it for future use to let it accumulate interest, spread it around in smaller compartments to make the whole invisible to the untrained eye, compile it, contemplate it, manipulate it. Information is currency in this place. Tell me what you think Lansing is."

"The state's capital."

"Spoken like a sixth-grade civics student. Lansing is just a word, short-hand for a meeting ground for the rich and powerful and well-connected, a playground for queen bees and drones alike, a nest and hive for lawyers, analysts, organizationalists, social engineers, religious enthusiasts, rights-fighters for this and that, here of your own volition, or your master's, or your god's. It's a place where tribal reps meet to smoke peace pipes or do war dances, to cavort and fuck and find ways to hurt enemies and enrich those few friends in their own little selected circle. The Capitol is minutes from drugs of all kinds, hookers, dog and cock fighting, S & M houses, opium dens, child trafficking, black marketing, the feeble, the insane, the hopeless homeless—you name any extreme in society and it is here within daily sniffing distance of politicians. Not one of these creatures ever smells it because they're not here to fix problems for people, they're here to line their own pockets and the pockets of their supporters. Have you ever *really* been in love, Service?"

The question caught him unprepared. "Rhetorical?"

"Answer the question."

"I have."

"I mean really, completely whole-hog, out-of-your-ever-lovin'-mind, over-the-top, no-holds-barred love?"

"Yes, like that." And then some, but he had no interest in sharing details with this woman or anyone else. What he'd had with Maridly Nantz was theirs and theirs alone.

"Then you should recognize that when you are in that intense mine-field of love, you can't see reality because you are measurably physically and emotionally blind. This causes you to see your beloved object in the precise way that object wants you to see it. Your instincts, your experience, your peripheral and night vision might ordinarily be second to none, but now, in the aura of this love thing, you are crippled, all your strengths are switched off, because in looking at the other you're really only looking at you. That's how love works. It insists on a way to make everything about you and only what you want. And in the end, sadly and gloriously, the fucking you get is not worth the fucking you get."

Limpy, who had been silent, mumbled quietly, "Girlie right, sonny."

She was a load, this strange little woman. Whether she was effective or not remained to be seen, and his gut was strangely silent on the question.

"Here's the deal," M said. "I'll help you if you'll help me."

"What kind of help?"

"Let's leave that open-ended for the moment and think of it as a player to be named later. You a Cubs fan?"

"No."

"Good, I loathe Cubs fans and all the peace-love-and-peacenutters who follow them like a cult, expecting to be disappointed and to lose, *wanting* to lose." She reddened as she ranted.

"I don't like open-ended deals," Service said.

"No? Then you can't be much of a game warden or a cop, yeah? Ones I've known—the good ones—when they catch someone red-handed, on a triviality or even certain big issues, they let them walk, or reduce the charges. They tell the perp he now owes and if he doesn't come through, the cop will go back and reactivate and elevate all charges and push it like a virgin's defense of her treasured sweet hymen. You've never done that?"

She was quick-witted, opinionated, and forceful and seemed to be knowledgeable. But was she more than talk? "Sure I have."

"Well, this deal is sort of like that. I talked to Fellow up in your neighborhood, and she told me about what you've got her doing for you."

"Did she come to you?"

"Everybody comes to me, sooner or later. This man Kalleskevich out in East Lansing, he's a serious player here in LaLansingland. Shaker and mover, power broker, got lots of muscle and heap-heap throw-weight, and all the charm of broken glass on your bathroom floor." She added, "This outfit, Drazel Sisters L.L.C. Satellite Services & Earth Surveys, was incorporated a week after your initial suspension."

"That's significant?"

"Don't play Colombo with me, sir. You're a detective and you know timing is almost always significant. It takes three to four weeks to process a new corporation, which means the process was no doubt initiated before your keester got drop-kicked."

"Correlation isn't cause, and timing isn't cause and effect."

"Isn't it? Didn't your sappy old pal have the woman you talked to express surprise at your presence because you were supposed to be on suspension and not in your area? From what I've been able to determine, this information was not at all publicly known."

"That's a stretch," he said, though he had entertained similar thoughts.

"A business immediately goes into effect after you get suspended. The business seems to be focused in the very wilderness area formerly under your professional protection. And somehow the people there know you're not supposed to be there, and in encountering you, someone calls one of the women off. You think this is an idle pile of harmless coincidences?"

Before he could respond, she went on. "I let Hollywood, conservatives, and dunderheads drown in their own cockamamie conspiracy theories. I deal in evidence, which sometimes, early on in a case, is purely circumstantial. Shall I continue?"

Service took in a deep breath; he couldn't sort out the woman's extravagant claims to power in such a bland setting. Pale blue walls, pale blue carpet, it was as if all the heat had been sucked out of the room. "Please do."

"I get your reluctance, I really do. Fellow thinks you're pretty much of the Royal Boy Scout School, only in your uniform, a black-and-white warrior while in uniform."

She raised her hand and waved it at him. "In your personal life? Mezza mezza. Not so much. Interesting dichotomy, and believe me, I rather admire that, but no, I was not referring to continuing to talk. Do you want me to take this case or not?"

"It's not a case."

"To me it is, and as old Dubya used to say, I'm the decider here."

"How much?"

"Do you care?"

He thought for a moment, and shrugged. "Not really."

She grinned. "That's because you're loaded and money has little meaning or motivation for you. It took me less than fifteen minutes to get your full financial picture. Very, very impressive. So Grady Service is not about money. He's about honor and other prehistoric intangibles. My reward will be when we thwart Bozian, if God keeps my heart beating until then. I'd love to destroy that son of a bitch, but I'll take thwarting and costing him money in lieu of cash from you. Think teamwork and cooperation toward a shared goal, my friend, you're not the only believer in such things."

"You'll be working with Fellow Marthesdottir?"

"Not exactly. She's taking care of your surveillance needs up in the wilderness. My work will cut a wider swath, and understand this, I'm not going to propose solutions, no tactics, no plans, nothing theoretical or real-world practical. My job is strictly intel, the cleanest and most complete I can compile. Whatever you do based on that specific intel is entirely your decision and business."

The woman, for all her brashness and braggadocio, was cautious and did not want to get nailed for aiding action against Sam Bozian. Interesting. Boiled down, she was like the rest of the Lansing thugs she had described. Could she produce results? His gut said yes.

"Okay, deal."

"Do you even know at this moment what *you* should do?"

"No."

"Good, we'll both figure out what the hell we should be doing, and I'll look out for me and at some point show you mine if you'll show me yours." Her eyes were twinkling.

"You're a pill," he told her.

"Indeed I am," she said.

Minutes later Service backed his truck out of the driveway, which needed re-surfacing, and headed to Frandor. Back in his Michigan State Police days, he had known of a great hotdog joint in the shopping center. He hoped it was still in business. He'd not noticed it the other night. Allerdyce was quiet, almost brooding. Service said, "You didn't have much to say back there."

"I ain't all that gabby in the presence of da bloody devil."

"You think she's the devil?"

"Youse don't? Can we go back up over da britch now? Please?"

"We'll see."

Allerdyce scowled. "Dat's what my ma use to say."

"What did she mean?"

"She mean I keep asking she beat my ass red as sugar beet."

"There you go," Grady Service said. "We'll see." He wondered why he felt the need to make Allerdyce squirm. He's trying to help you. Service couldn't find an answer.

CHAPTER 15

Ivy Free Hall, MSU Campus

EAST LANSING
INGHAM COUNTY

Another text message launched their new day: Meet Lobby, IFH, 1000. Allerdyce looked at the message. "IFH?"

"Ivy Free Hall. Weren't you listening yesterday?"

"Sometimes better look den listen, Sonny."

"Really. What did *you* see?"

"I seen dat ain't 'er place," Allerdyce said.

"Conclusion reached based on . . .?"

The retired poacher made a sour face. "Youse jump track, an' youse start hump it, an' after while youse begin smell dis ain't right. Don't know why ain't buyin, but ain't, hey?"

The old man was right. Sometimes your best evidence came from something in your gut that had no real name. "Let's go see," Service told his partner. "We've got time."

A realtor's FOR SALE sign greeted them as they pulled into the driveway at the Northlawn address where they parked yesterday.

Allerdyce went to the sign and with one hand lifted it from the holes. "Saw da holes yesterday, knew it weren't no fall skunks grubbing dere."

And no more camera at the door. All the windows were blocked with closed blinds. Strange. What had she said? Try to find me tomorrow and see how that works? We're depending on this old nutcase to help us? What am I *thinking*?

"What we do now?" a fidgety Allerdyce asked.

"You interested in real estate?"

"Not b'low britch and on'y if got tree, swamp, crick, critters. Wah! Town shit, no way."

There was a realtor name on the sign, and the closest office was on Grand River Avenue, east almost to Okemos.

They entered a newer-looking building, very spiffy with a lot of chrome and glass, and undoubtedly leased, Service thought. Over the years he was amazed by how realtors aggressively sold structures, but rarely personally invested in real estate, or how financial managers who sold stocks with great enthusiasm and steep fees to customers kept few in their personal portfolios.

They looked through clean floor-to-ceiling glass walls and saw the interior was an eye-blinding antiseptic white. They were greeted by a woman, thirtyish, also in white, head to toe. "House of saints," Service whispered to the old man, who chuckled softly.

Allerdyce's rat nose was twitching wildly. "Wah, don't smell no saints dis place."

"You can smell saints?"

"More important smell devils," Allerdyce said.

"May I help you gentlemen?" the woman in white asked. She came right up to Service and thrust herself into his personal space, but he held his ground, even when she lightly brushed her breasts against him. Instead of retreating, he leaned into the contact, forcing her to pull away, and at that moment he saw momentary panic in her eyes. "We're interested in a property on Northlawn Avenue." He gave her the street number.

She tilted her head and said, "Yes," drawing the word out into at least two syllables.

The woman did not go to her computer terminal or check a sales pamphlet. Interesting, he thought. "It is for sale, right?"

Her left eyebrow danced. No words came out.

Service stepped into the pause. "We're wondering the asking price."

"Currently?" she asked, finally speaking.

As opposed to what, he wondered. "Right."

"Seven fifty," she said, still without consulting anything. Does she carry prices around in her head?

"Seven hundred and fifty thousand dollars?"

"Yes, of course. This *is* East Lansing, you know."

"Excuse me, but that sounds excessive," Service said.

The woman smiled. "You're too kind. Personally, I would characterize it as bloody-way-over-the-top exorbitant or, if you prefer, outright mad."

"How long has this place been on the market?"

"Eight years, nine? A long time."

So she remembers the price but not how long it's been on the market. "You'd think a seller would be motivated to haggle after that long, drop the price, do something to move it. Why pay taxes on an empty shell?"

"The perfect unanswerable question," she said. "But it's *not* empty. It's furnished, and all the furnishings are included in the price. The thing about this kind of work is that you learn quickly how people do things for their own reasons, and often what you think of as commonsense and straightforward logic are not part of anything but your own notions."

"Local owner?"

"The owner is deceased and the property controlled by the deceased's estate."

Even more reason to deal to move it, he thought. "Is there a name?"

"I'm sorry," the woman said. "Just the estate knows the name. All else is private. Are you interested? Really?"

"Just wondering," he said. The real estate was of no interest, but this woman at another time and place might have been. He sensed smarts, attitude, and backbone in equal parts.

"Is there a way to make a direct offer to the estate lawyer?"

"I'm sorry," she said. "All offers must come through us."

"Your rule, or the client's?"

"I couldn't say," she said.

Service mulled this over. Because she doesn't know, or knows and doesn't want to say? "If you ask me, your client doesn't seem overly motivated to sell."

"I would certainly agree with that assessment," she said, inching her way back into control. She was pushing six feet in white flats and had the body type his friend Treebone called "Boney-Maroney, white hippy gal with heap-big honks."

She moved forward and this time he backed up. "Is a showing possible?"

"Theoretically possible, but neither probable nor imminent. It can take two weeks to get a turn-down, which is *always* the answer. But the client inevitably tells us to be sure to ask again, because nothing is forever. And of course we do and still they say no. It seems ridiculous, this whole damn thing. Why list if you have no intention of selling?"

He turned the question back on her. "Why *would* you list something you know you won't sell?"

She shrugged and grinned sheepishly, showing deep dimples. "Because you don't really want to sell it?"

"Only conclusion I can reach," Service said. "Damn foolish, wastes everybody's time."

"I would love to show you something else. There's a lot to see if one has the time and the interest," she said.

Service smiled. "I have no doubt, and while the interest is plenty, our time isn't. We have another appointment at ten."

Perfect professional response. "Not today then. May I suggest an evening showing? No rush that way. We could take it nice and slow. I can get us in and out of anywhere, even places listed by others."

"Except the place on Northlawn," he said.

She stomped her heel in mock frustration and bowed her head in apology. "Except there."

"I'll keep your offer in mind," he told her.

"And I you," she came back. "Shall we exchange cards?"

He gave her one of his private stock, and she read it and looked up at him. "What in the world is Slippery Creek?" she asked, making eye contact. "For real?"

"Very real," he said. Her card said her name was Punner Bonaventure. "Your name is Punner and *that's* for real?"

She smiled. "Every bit as real as 'Slippery.'" She took the card and scribbled on the back. "My personal cell phone," she explained. "I have a condo south on the river, you know, on water that's wet and sometimes slippery."

Full-on hustle now under way. Why? "I'll call if I get the chance."

"Call and I can guarantee you a chance," she said, deadpan.

Driving through the Michigan State Campus, Allerdyce said, "Heat come offen' at one's back dere like crown-out pinefire. Dat girlie got da bad case of da boreds."

"Just bored?"

The old man shrugged. "Wah. Dat bored girlie leave lots trails so she can be founded, rescued, hey."

Service nodded as they passed Ivy Free Hall, which was two storys, its redbrick walls choked in thick green ivy. Service found a visitor parking place with a meter a block away and put the truck there. The two men walked back along manicured lawns and past flowers trying to pop up from black soil beds.

There was no receptionist inside the building and no obvious security cameras inside or out, just eight molded pink plastic chairs that looked vintage 1950s or older. There was only one inner door, unmarked, facing roughly toward Beaumont Tower.

The men looked at each other. Service checked his watch. They were three minutes early. They sat sat on the chairs, feeling every bit as uncomfortable as they looked. Allerdyce said, "Nice chair."

"If you say so."

"Youse don't like?"

God, Service thought, I'm here with Allerdyce, here *because* of Allerdyce. Maybe *this* is hell? What is wrong with me?

Ten straight up, the door opened and a woman stepped out. Familiar face. It was the same woman from the realtor's office, "Punner." She'd been in all white at the office, and now she was decked out in all black.

"Good morning," she said, firmly but politely. Not Punner's voice. Entirely different. She gave no sign of recognition or familiarity. "May I see photo identification please, two pieces?"

"Or what?" Service asked.

"Or you won't be coming in," the woman said officiously.

"You sure have a different tone than earlier," he told her.

She stiffened. "Excuse me. Earlier?"

"At the realty office . . . Northlawn, Slippery Creek, the condo on the wet river, night showings, taking it slow, remember?"

She sighed. "IDs please. We're expected inside and wasting time here."

Service said, "You are Punner, yes?"

She said nothing, took their IDs, examined them, and handed them back. "You were in a white outfit earlier, Punner Bonaventure? I have your card."

The woman took a deep breath. "Have you been using drugs?"

"No, of course not."

"Sir, my name, sir, is Liis."

"Not Punner Bonaventure?"

"I am Liisette Gyttylla."

What the hell? The two women were mirror images. "Okay, sorry, Ms. Gyttylla, I guess my memory isn't what it once was."

"Follow me," she said and held open the door until they were past her. She closed the door and locked it after they were in, and began leading them down curving steel steps. Service eventually counted, seven long flights, not straight down vertically, but at a steep enough angle to feel it on the back of his calves. It was dark, with only small LEDs lighting the way, and after a while he found it difficult to estimate how deep under the campus they had descended. To make it worse, he kept bumping into a hesitating Allerdyce whom he kept gently pushing and urging ahead of him. The last flight ended at a Spartan-green door with a keypad, onto which Liisette Gyttylla tapped something, which popped the door with a hiss. An airlock?

"Like bloody damn summerine dis place," Allerdyce muttered.

"You've been in a sub?"

"Onct over Gorear."

Allerdyce. He had fought in heavy going in Korea, been wounded and decorated there, but a submarine? Is there sweat on his forehead? It's not warm down here and we haven't exactly overexerted ourselves. What's up with that? The little bastard's always been fearless.

The woman held out a hand, invited them through the airlock door, which hissed closed and thumped solidly behind them.

"Where dis is?" Allerdyce asked

This tunnel was darker than the stairs, all the LEDs in strips along the floor. "No talking," their guide said. "It damages the sensors."

Service noted that the floor was heavily insulated, heavy foam. It was like walking on sphagnum moss, a surface he hated, especially when he was fishing.

The woman seemed to tilt backwards as she walked. The new tunnel was narrower than the stairwells. The three walked almost twenty minutes and came to another door with another keypad.

The woman took a tray off a wall mounting. "Weapons, please. This is for your own safety. If you enter and weapons are detected, an alarm will sound and you will be shot on sight by security personnel."

Service said, "I'm clean."

"Me too," Allerdyce said, but under the woman's steely gaze produced a seven-inch skinning knife in a leather holder and, after more staring, a pocket flip-knife.

"Your property will be returned to you when you exit," the woman said.

Allerdyce asked, "We get reseep?"

The woman looked down her nose at him and said, "My word is your receipt."

"Nottin' pers'nal, girlie, but I don't know youse. How 'bout I keep my stuff, stay outten 'ere, wait on youse guys?"

"You may not remain here unescorted," the woman said.

"Don't need no eggskirt," Allerdyce said.

Service squeezed the old man's shoulder. "C'mon, inside . . . now. We're wasting time."

"Don't got pimple-squeeze me, Sonny," the poacher said, and his shoulders slumped in resignation.

"Zip it," Service whispered, pushing the man ahead of him. Another corridor lay ahead, same foam padding on the floor, same low-level LEDs at foot level. "Labyrinth," he told the woman. "Some kind of Halloween scary maze?"

"One supposes that depends on one's view of life," their guide said.

The next stage of the journey took another brisk ten minutes, and again they stopped at a green door.

"T'ink all Old Money Hall like dis?" Allerdyce mumbled.

"I beg your pardon," the Gyttylla woman said, halting and turning to stare at the retired violator. "This is anything but a joke, sir. We are serious people doing serious things."

Allerdyce held up his hands and gave her his bobblehead look, which made him look both ignorant and clueless. He was neither.

The trek ended in a closed bay through another security entrance, with M seated in a soft leather chair behind a small, cluttered, see-through desk. "Welcome," she said. "Right on time. I like that. No, it's not a matter of like, I *require timeliness* as a basic human courtesy." She looked at Allerdyce with scorn. "Two knives, sir. *Really*? Do you fear being assaulted?"

"Don't fear nuffin," Allerdyce said.

"Then why carry weapons," she asked.

"Why ain't afraid," he said. "Slice youse up quickern spicks wit dose."

"Your language is atrocious, sir, and your attitude reprehensible," M scolded.

"I ain't much buy your bullshit neither," Allerdyce said.

M cracked what Service took to be a benevolent smile, maybe a touch amused. "I do like a man who is not easily kowed."

"Don't like being horsed neither," Allerdyce added.

M said, "I'm certain you don't. Who does? May I ask whose idea it was to revisit Northlawn?" she asked.

"Both of us," Service said.

"Did I not tell you I would be invisible?"

"And yet here you are in plain view."

"Only because I choose to be. Your visit to the realtor, did you find it fruitful?"

"Could definitely bear fruit," Service said, realizing it was all part of some cockamamie test. The woman Gyttylla remained impassive in her stone-face mask. *Am I going crazy? That is the same woman and how does she know I visited the realtor? Sexy Miss Punner Bonaventure is one of her people.* "The thing about jigsaw puzzles," he said, "is that you have to have patience. Find one small piece at a time." He could feel M staring at him, sizing him up.

"Like solving puzzles, do you?"

"Some kinds, sometimes," he told her. "Not just any puzzle."

"Selectivity is good," she said.

"Why are we here?" he asked. He had patience but not for everything, and all this beating around the bush was starting to irritate him.

"To solve the puzzle," M said. "Did you really think a visit to the realtor would lead to me?"

"Maybe," he said, thinking on the fly. "The way it plays for me, you own the place through a legal trust and use it as a safe house and meeting place at your discretion."

"That's a bit of twisted logic, but sounds like something you have some familiarity with."

"I've done undercover work," he told her.

"I know. Ionia County, the great tainted salmon caviar case," she explained. "Yes, I do know about that, and I know you had people in your own department after you during that time—your own DNR. That must've felt rather disconcerting."

It had felt worse than that. "It pissed me off, but I'm still here."

"Your record shows you clearly know how to survive," she said. "So far. Who owns the mineral rights to the Mosquito Wilderness Tract?"

"That is the question," he answered. "I don't know. Do you?"

"I do not . . . yet. But let me ask you this: What happens if nobody owns the rights?"

"Somebody *has* to own them."

"Nonsense," she said. "We assume that there was ownership at one point in time. But now is now and proof requires evidence, so I'll ask you again. What if nobody owns the rights?"

"I assume the state would own them," he said, guessing. This was not the kind of thing game wardens were trained to handle or have knowledge of.

"Are you familiar with the fire at the Lansing Conservation Department Office in the early fifties?"

Service knew about it, and was appalled at how one event could have so damn many negative downstream consequences. It was mind-boggling. "It was started by a knucklehead hoping to duck military service in Korea," he said.

"And poof, up went virtually all of the mineral rights ownership records dated before that time."

"Meaning?"

"It means that all we can do is flag various state records and archives and hope to get lucky with a paper find on a duplicate," she said. "The odds are rather long, and definitely against us."

He asked, "There are no statutes that give the rights to the state by default?"

"That, in fact, is exactly how it works, unless someone comes forward with records with which they purport to show ownership."

"What's the burden of proof?" he asked.

"That remains to be seen. I'm advised that this seems to ride on how convincing the claimant and their evidence is."

"They have to convince a judge, right?"

"Circuit court," she said, "with the state supreme court the next step. All mineral rights are addressed in state courts."

"The main thing is it's not a gimme, right?"

"Probably not," she said tentatively, "but you have to realize that this is an area with scant legal precedent and few lawyers deeply schooled in this dark corner of the law."

She keeps staring at me, like she's waiting for me to do or say something. "Could someone push through a bogus claim?"

"Would that surprise you?"

"Not in the least." Where and when financial gain was at stake, nothing surprised him anymore. People could show real genius and no scruples in the free-for-all for money that was the heart of capitalism. "But they would have to convince a court in order to get their claim validated, right?"

She said, "It would appear from here that the provenance of the evidence would be the critical factor."

"Odds?" he asked.

"Given the skinny water that constitutes extant legal precedent, I'd guess fifty-fifty, depending on the strength of the claim, the skill of the lawyers, and who the judge is."

Like rolling dice, win or lose in one roll. "Depending on the minerals at issue, it could be well worth a gamble." But limestone? No way.

"If there are minerals in the claim. What if it's something else that they really want access to, but can get to it only via mineral rights to a particular landmass? They're not going to argue in court about particular minerals, only the legitimacy of their claim to any and all minerals in the parcel in question. Is it possible that Bozian has proof of ownership, proof we know nothing about?"

"I don't know, and it doesn't really matter. I don't know anything, and it doesn't matter what I think. I'm just getting started on this deal."

"Bear in mind," she cautioned, "that Sam's not one to play a game where he's not already calculated the probable outcome. Any time he thinks he might lose, he pulls out."

"Is there such a guarantee?"

"A deed for mineral rights signed by the state would do it."

"Current owner?"

"Assume so, but if there isn't a clear current owner and the claimant can sway the judge . . ." She didn't finish the thought. "You're on the case officially?" she asked.

"I'm on something," he said, and left it at that.

He had watched Gyttylla throughout the meeting and finally realized what it was that was holding his attention. He said to M, "Gyttylla, eh? All black. Her visual twin, Ms. Bonaventure, is the lady in white, but they are the same person."

M sucked in a sharp breath. "How did you figure this out?"

"I'm guessing all the clothes are the same size, and the shoes, but more importantly, both women wear the same heel and both are worn to indicate pronation. I could measure, but I'm pretty sure the wear is identical or nearly so."

M said quietly, "Pronation?"

"She walks on her heels, weight back."

"And you know this how?"

"We're trained to track man and beast."

M smiled. "You're everything they say you are."

He smiled back. "The question for me is, are you?"

On the long trek back to the surface, Service whispered to their severe escort in black, "I like you better as Punner."

She touched his arm lightly. "Me too, and you have my number." She added, "Now we can find out how much of your game is talk."

Not the kind of challenge he liked to have thrown at him. Temptation was a difficult opponent, and Punner was a definite head-turner with an agenda he couldn't figure out, and didn't want to.

When they started to work their way off the campus, Allerdyce chirped, "Youse want go Woof Cave, youse on own dat one. Not go down ground no more. Dis was nuff."

"It was heated and lighted and comfortable," Service said.

"Youse's opinion."

The old man seemed resolute. "You're a claustrophobe, *you*?"

"And I don't like Sanny Claws neither, dumb clown comin' down bloody chimleys. What wrong dat fat man do shit like dat?"

CHAPTER 16

St. Ignace

MACKINAC COUNTY

Dirty clouds were stacked like limestone layers over the cobalt-gray waters of the straits, a color so vile it forced Service to shiver. Beside him Allerdyce, toothless and open-mouthed, buzzed like a cheap saw, his sleep mask not unlike a lot of the dead bodies Service had come across over the course of his career.

The men had talked only perfunctorily since East Lansing, and Service had spent most of the time mulling the situation as he pressed the truck northward.

Ironically, all the lanes on the bridge were clear, and the entire way across the 5-mile-long bridge there was none of the usual construction blocking, slowing, or diverting traffic. Unlike his life.

Allerdyce startled awake within a hundred yards of the toll booths on the north side. "Wah, what dat stink is, Sonny?"

"Wake up, you're dreaming."

"Don't dream," Allerdyce insisted. "Leave dat stuff to shrinkheads, god-pilots, them." Allerdyce pointed. "Somepin goin' on up dere, hey."

Service saw a Michigan state policeman ahead, outside his patrol vehicle, standing beside a toll booth line and motioning for him to pull up to that lane, which he did. Not just any trooper, it was Lt. John "Jump Start" Skelton, the post commander in St. Ignace. He'd earned the name when he saved three heart attack victims in one week.

"John," Service said.

"Sorry, Grady," the L.T. said, looking across at Allerdyce and shaking his head. "We need for you to pull over to the post for a minute." Skelton added, "It's not my idea."

"What up?" Service asked.

"Just pull over to the post for a few, okay?"

"Sure." Now what?

Skelton said mysteriously, "Let me get there ahead of you so I can witness the whole scene," and rushed to his car and headed for the post that looked out over the straits.

Grady Service gave eight dollar bills to the toll-taker. "It's only four for you," she said.

"Four for me and four for the vehicle behind me. Tell him welcome to the U.P."

"Cool," the bridge attendant said and lifted the bar for him.

Service followed Skelton to the post and spotted him waiting at the front door, which he held open. Service also saw a black helicopter in the parking lot. "Got a pen," he asked Allerdyce. "Write down the tail number on the chopper."

The old man did as requested, but said with a sniffing sound, "Stink gettin' worse."

Service sensed something more than smelled it. Two Troops stood inside the front door; one of them pointed down the hallway and said, "Conference room."

Lt. Skelton hurried ahead and held the door open for Service. He stepped inside, saw an immense creature alone at the fake maplewood conference table. Gray layers of lumpy flesh, bushy eyebrows the size of small butterflies, dead eyes. "Sam?"

"It's Governor," Bozian said.

"You termed out, so unless you pushed our current governor aside, it's plain old Sam to me."

"You never mellow," Bozian said.

"And you look more like Jabba the Hut every time I see you."

"Who?" the former governor asked.

"A fat-ass alien. Don't you take your kids to the movies?"

Bozian did not rise to the bait. "What were you doing below the bridge?"

"I need a passport to travel around the state?"

"You're on suspension." Interesting that Bozian knows, and Eddie Waco was right.

"What the hell does that have to do with me crossing the bridge? Am I missing something here?"

"You're always missing something."

Bozian had informants. "What is it you want, Sam. I hate wasting time with jerks."

The governor asked, "How's your blood pressure?"

Service laughed, "A boatload better'n yours, if appearances count for anything. They bring you into the post on a dolly?"

Bozian's eyebrows fluttered nervously. "Why is it you have to do everything the hard way?"

"First, it's more fun, but more importantly, it's because assholes like you make it necessary."

Bozian shook his head slowly. "You have enough troubles without exacerbating your situation by impersonating a police officer. You have been suspended and are not empowered to legally discharge the duties of a state conservation officer. My legal advisors are of the opinion that such egregious behavior would meet the definition of a felony."

"Where do your boys get their information, from a Cracker Jack box?"

"You deny you're suspended?"

Service shrugged, "Is there a point to this, Sam? I've got things to do."

"We'll be seeking a warrant," the former governor said.

"We?"

"The state."

"You're *not* the state, Sam. Haven't been for years. You live out east. I doubt you're not even a Michigan resident anymore."

"I retain interests here," the governor said.

"Such as property?"

"Yes, such as."

Here goes a gamble and a guess. "I sure hope you aren't claiming your farm property here as your primary residence for tax purposes. I'd have to get the law after you. Concerned citizen, you know."

"Make your jokes," Bozian said. "A warrant will be forthcoming."

Grady Service walked over to the governor, pulled out his wallet, flipped it open, and showed the man a laminated card. "My commission as a federal special deputy marshal."

Bozian fished in his pocket for his eyeglasses, and Service said, "It's real, Sam. Federal Special Deputy Marshal. And I'm not the only one. Many COs in the state are federally sworn."

"But you're not a conservation officer. You're suspended."

"Give it a rest, Sam. I'm not suspended as a marshal. I still have that commission. That hasn't been suspended." It was all a bluff. Maybe the card remained in force, probably not, but Bozian obviously had no idea, so for the moment this was a sweet little trick. Even when they took his state badge and sidearms, Chief Waco had told him to keep the federal card. Which didn't amount to much. As a CO he could assist federal officers and do things for them, but he couldn't initiate anything unless directed to do so. What the commission did was give him the freedom to work across state lines.

"I don't think that's legal," Bozian said, but with no force of conviction.

"Get a new box of Cracker Jacks, Sam. The answer might be in it, and if this is all you've got, I'm out of here."

"This isn't o-o-ver," Bozian stammered.

"Count on that, Sambo. Arrows can fly two directions. Next time you come to a word fight, bring more than pidgin shit."

Allerdyce was still in the truck and asked. "Youse find dat stink?"

"A former governor we all love so much."

Allerdyce chuckled. "Sam 'ere? T'ought know dat stink. Like sulphur brimstone dat, the Devil for sure."

PART II: METES AND BOUNDS

CHAPTER 17

Slippery Creek Camp

Back at camp, his home away from home, or as it stood currently, his home in lieu of home. Tuesday and Shigun were in Marquette, and he was here. The old poacher was off on his own somewhere, talking to god knows who or doing god knows what. All that mattered was he knew that if the old man stumbled across something he'd bring it back quickly. Limpy had been gone two days since their return.

After the surprise meeting with the former governor, Service kept thinking all the way from St. Ignace how Hollywood got things wrong. The life of a cop was 99 percent boredom, sometimes more, but nobody wanted to see or read about that. Entertainment showed cop lives skipping from crime wave to wave, creating a picture that bore very little resemblance to reality. It might seem real to readers and moviegoers, but not to cops who were familiar with the 1 percent action and 99 percent tedium.

The real life? Boredom: hours, days, weeks, months, sometimes years. In the interims—the crests—you checked, watched, listened, observed, baited, trailed, and patroled, made your rounds, kept your boots in the dirt and snow, and worked your beat. Every cop anywhere had a beat, even if it never extended more than fifty yards from the patrol vehicle. As a cop, you got to know your beat the way you knew your own body. You paid attention to all changes, however small and seemingly insignificant, seasonal and natural, man-made or unexplained. Anything and everything had potential significance, or would if you could fit what you were seeing into something larger.

Allerdyce had continued with his vehicular sleeping sickness as they made the trip westward from the bridge, which gave Service time to think. The limit for a cop was his brain. Cops were human and all humans had deficiencies. The key was to figure out your own and navigate around them, or find ways to compensate. Sometimes it was a matter of increasing your computing power, in other words, to create and activate a network of people who could act like remote computers. Fellow Marthesdottir, M, the Dotz kid, Honeypat, Oheneff, Friday, his friend Luticious Treebone, these were elements in his network this time around. Every case tended to birth new network contacts or strengthen old ones. The cop who tried to work without extending himself through others was doomed to fail. Policing is a collective effort, not a solo deal. The key was to have eyes and ears that could see and hear and know things you couldn't know on your own. People in your network were like delicate plants, and some needed more water and fertilizer than others. Some needed nothing. They blossomed and bloomed on their own. It was damn near impossible to predict how things would turn out. What you knew, without a doubt, was that a cop who didn't rely on his contacts was soon going to be shit out of luck. You could think of them as plants in your professional garden. Without attention there would be no harvest.

Service interrupted his thoughts to survey the camp. For years it had been only a shell, a rough carapace, in which he slept on a bed made of two army footlockers pushed together end to end. He had nearly finished the interior at one point, but this was as far as he got, and now it looked much like it had before he'd tried to take it to the next level. It was basic shelter, which suited him, filled with fishing and hunting gear.

To Tuesday Friday, it had the "air of a fading gentleman's club—without gentlemen."

Allerdyce, ironically, understood all of this instinctively. He got the logic and had used it in the days when they opposed each other and he was running wild across the U.P. The old man scared a lot of folks and for good reason. But he had been a pro in his day, arguably the best ever, and for that alone he was entitled to respect. In recent days it had become clear that they were a lot alike, and only certain walls of laws and ethics divided them. The governor was out to punish both of us, the dumb bastard, but it was no matter. What they'd done might be outside the box, but it had paid off for the state, and that, bottom line, was the job, wasn't it?

The drive across the U.P. had been downright pleasant. Spring was settling on Lansing and now it was beginning to hint itself up here—not that early spring would be a picnic as mud replaced snow and made travel equally difficult in vehicles and on foot. The weather might be pleasant for the moment, but in forty-eight hours it could rain, dump snow into streams, and start creating snow runoff. Four nights ago while they were still below the bridge, the southern U.P. had gotten ten inches of wet snow, which was already receding.

He hadn't seen Tuesday for a while and, although they talked frequently, phone calls were poor equivalents for proximity. He knew and felt they had been too long without touch, both of them getting the grumples. During their last conversation, Tuesday barked at him, "You asshole, you're treating me like one of your snitches."

"I don't use snitches. They are civic-minded informants."

"You're such a jerk."

The meeting with Bozian was a mild surprise, and he wanted to know the scuttlebutt in state police circles about his minor collision with the former governor. Tuesday had a temper, which made him smile, but he knew he had taken a step too far and amends would have to be made. She was right, of course, but she played him the same way when she needed information. It's a quid pro quo. In his mind, anyway.

At first, when the old man shuffled into the cabin, Service was lost in his own thoughts and paid no attention, but when the old poacher started pouring coffee Service looked up and saw he had two burgeoning black eyes, a scabbing cut lip, and some ragged thread stitches wagging from a jagged head wound that reached down to his right eyebrow. "What hit you, a cuckolded husband?"

"Weren't no bloody cuckoo, Sonny. Was young buck from over da Soo and dumb-cluck Polack from down below somewhere, hey. Dey got me when I don't got da guard up, beat shit outten me, say, 'Tell youse's pal him and his girlie-squeeze, dere brat, youse, udder kittles, nobody gone end good if youse's friend don't retire, take long awaycation, keep 'is nose outten udder pipple's business.'"

Allerdyce kept spouting, "Dey drop da log over road trick, come out on me quick fast, fore could figger t'ings out, den they haul out blades. Got in some good licks but dey big suckers, got hold me, put fist boogers all over my 'ead. And den, one dem let loose a bit and I scoot off."

Translation: Two big young men had attacked him by dropping a tree across the road, and when he got out to move the obstacle, they had jumped him to deliver a message. Not to Allerdyce, but through him *to me*. Assholes. Service felt his temper flare, but forced himself to remain calm.

"How is it you know these guys are from the Soo and downstate?"

"Da buck, he been aroun' hey. Udder one I never seen before."

"You know their names?"

"Indi'n goes by Paint an' he call udder one yo, Polack Prince."

"See a vehicle, get a plate number?"

"Yah sure, I got inna bush 'n dey da chase quit, I loop back on dose guys, write down way your old man taughted me." Allerdyce handed him a note with scribbling.

"These are plate numbers, not descriptions," Service said.

"Youse run dose plates, get description, den I tell youse what I seen, and we see, okay?"

"Great." The old man's logic tended toward the arcane, often too ambiguous to parse; he sometimes complicated things for reasons he didn't bother to explain, but there was always a point to what he did, no matter how bizarre it might seem at the moment.

"Which hospital sewed you up?"

"Hoppytall?" The old man sputtered. "Sew myself, dis not no big deal. Eight stitch, I shoulda been mebbe sawbones, make big bucks, screw nursies all day and night, hey."

"Where *do* you get your information, old man?" His fantasies seemed endless.

Allerdyce looked puzzled. "I t'ink on somepin, den make it up, same way all pipples do."

No comeback for this logic. "When the hell did this happen?"

"Day before taday."

"That would be yesterday?"

"I said dat."

"How long has it been since you last saw this pair of assholes?"

"Never seen da prince guy before, but Paint, been mebbe year back."

"Are they cons?"

"Missingdemanners I t'ink, no falconies. Dey never done no hard-jaw time, hey. Dey pert good, jump fast, do deed, skedaddle quick-like."

"Any idea where they skedaddled to?"

The old man squinted, sipped his coffee, pursed his lips. "Might, jest might."

It will come out eventually. Or not. "Where did this happen?"

"Wah, not far."

Service had to chuckle. "Not far" or "just down the road," these were Yooperisms for anything from sixty feet to six hundred miles. The thing with

Yoopers was that they were hard-wired by history to be helpful to people in need, and if you asked for directions, you would get them, even if they were guessing. Motive could not be questioned, only execution.

"Youse 'ave youse's girlie rund dose plates, hey?"

"No, I don't want her in our shit-stream, and I'm suspended. I'll have to think about who and how."

"Youse got oodles pals," Allerdyce said.

"I guess we'll find out."

CHAPTER 18

Slippery Creek Camp

Service stood on the deck of his camp, smoking. Face your own truth, asshole. A couple of punks kick the old man's ass, threaten Friday and Shigun and maybe Karrylanne and Little Maridly and you keep going ahead? Selfish bastard. Why not just retire and be done with this shit? Everything you get involved in is complex, and maybe you cause things to be that way. Ever considered that possibility, Mr. Motivation? You cannot beat a whole system driven largely by money. Doesn't happen.

He sat on a step.

The system's created to make sure that the flow goes on, no matter what you or anybody else does. Even if you fight the damn system to a draw, where's that put everyone? Nowhere. But sometimes a draw against a superior foe is as good as a win. Oh bullshit, you don't believe that. That's Chicago Cub propaganda, magic crystal thinking, not what you think or believe. What you believe is the Herbie Brooks formula. Take your opponent's skills and style as your own, then beat their asses at their own game. You always have to have luck in your pocket, and if Herbie's boys played nine more games against the Soviets, they would have been toasted, but they played only once and for all the marbles. Like you and Bozian. He's not even living here anymore and he's still trying to get you. Why? Time for you to stop thinking and get on with your work, doofus. Put on your big boy pants and get outside where you belong. No system is invulnerable, and sometimes one win is all it takes.

"The Indian, Paint? Soo Tribe?" he had asked Allerdyce.

"Yah sure, born raised Soo Tribe, t'ink."

"And the other guy's from downstate?"

"Da Polack Prince? Yah, mebbe De Twat, Flintucky, Saginasty, one dose places down dat way, hey."

Flint, Service thought. There's an idea. Flint conjured the name Nosebone in his head. Last time he'd seen the gang leader, he'd been with Trip Bozian and the governor's son had panicked, pulled his sidearm on the gang, and fired a wild shot. Nosebone, the gang's leader, had stayed cool and let me talk the boy down and disarm him. Nosebone had been leader of the Flint Blood Moon Barbarians. Was he still with the gang, in jail, or dead? If the Polish Prince was a Flint guy, Nosebone would know him for sure. *If* he was still alive. *If* he was still around and not in prison. When Service knew him, the man had been a punk with a long antisocial rap sheet, nothing heinous or major, but the lifestyle of a lifetime fuckup. He had to have been in his early thirties then. Now? Fifties? Not sure. Jack Dylan was the longtime CO in Grand Blanc, a town south of Flint, and J.D. had been around that area forever. Good CO, not flashy, but did his job. J.D. answered immediately. "Dylan, Service here."

"This would be the on-hiatus Service?" the CO replied.

"One and the same."

"What can I do you for? You ain't one to call to chew social fat."

Service grinned. "The gang that called themselves the Barbarians, they still around?"

"Lots of new blood in the saddles, but still around and still being run by some of the old heads."

"Nosebone?"

"You're talking about the head motherfucker in charge, Mr. Constantin "Connie" Pendeau."

"That's his name? I only knew him as Nosebone."

"Probably Nose don't even know his real name anymore. Nobody calls him that and I doubt if he ever looks at his driver's license. Bone's done so many drugs over decades that the black holes in his brain have smaller black holes within them, like a piece of modern art."

"You have dealings with him?"

"Happily, no. But Skip has had the pleasure of lots of time."

"Trouble?"

"Nah, some save-face jaw-jaw is all. Nosebone's mellowing, like the rest of us—except you!"

Skip was CO Tom Town, aka Skip Town, though the reason for the nickname was lost to history.

Dylan said, "Give Skip a bump. I think he's on real good terms with a lot of the gangbangers, Bone especially." He added, "Hey, do they let a suspended guy use state phones and credit cards?"

"Only in emergencies. This phone is my own."

"Good thinking. Keep things private, don't give those Lansing bastards any more ammo, not that they need it. They get after somebody's ass, they'll just make up what they need. By the way, if I had somebody with Allerdyce's experience down here, I'd have him in my truck too. So would Skip, so would most of us. Man, you guys had a kick-ass deer season."

"Thanks." Of course, the main ass getting kicked was his own, Service knew.

Skip Town listened for thirty seconds and gave Service Pendeau's personal cell phone number and the gang's clubhouse landline number.

Service punched in the landline number and it was answered after a couple of rings, heavy-metal music blasting in the background. "Grady Service for Nosebone," he told the man.

"He, like, ain't in."

"He'll be in for me. Just tell him."

"You're not the boss of me," the voice responded

"You guys recruiting ten-year-olds to the gang these days? Go tell Nose it's Grady and I want to talk to his hairy ass."

The line lay open for a couple of minutes, exposing Service to music that assaulted his ears, some sort of acid-steel, burn-your-own-balls-off nasty rock that tended to all sound the same and be played at jet engine decibel levels that could be used to make attacking drones crash. It was amazing gang members could hear anything.

He heard the phone being picked up and the background music fading. "Yo, Grady Service, you shittin' me? What happened to that trigger-happy junior fish cop partner with you that night?"

"He decided to pursue other career options."

"Heard he was the governor's son, that right?"

"Your source is solid."

"You make the little prick walk the plank?"

"Didn't have to. Jumped off all on his own."

"Would you have made him walk the plank, man?"

"Yup."

"So what up, dude? Been, like a long, long time."

"I'm looking for a thug who calls himself the Prince. Supposed to run with a Soo Tribe Nish calls himself Paint." Nish was short for Anishnaabe.

Nosebone grunted softly. "The Prince and Paint. I know those dudes, Service. Low-run head-knockers, mostly freelance. What they done this time?"

"I just need to talk to them."

"Why call me?"

"Heard that the Prince might be a Flint guy, or was, and I figured if anybody would know, it might be you."

"You calling me a thug, man?"

"No, an expert."

Nosebone laughed. "He's a Doo-rand boy, the Prince, you know, south of Flint. Big sonuvabitch. He was a crotch-sniffer in high school, football, all that pussy shit, got him scholarships to Eastern to wrestle, but he burned out first month there. He dropped out and we heard his old man liked to have killed 'im."

"You know the father?"

"Was outside captain of Saginaw Po-po, sayin. We call 'im GZ, but his last name is some fuckin' consonant horseshit, like all kinds of z's and y's and like dat?"

Service had to think for a minute. "Zyzwyzcky?"

"'At's 'im."

"He's a former state trooper."

"Dat's the man, man. Papa to da Prince of Stoopid."

Mind wandering, flashing back to the State Police Academy, hand-to-hand combat class, a huge candidate named Zyzwyzcky, six-five or six-six, all muscle and square-jawed, hissing and huffing and ready to do battle with hands the size of prize French hams. Knocked me out within ninety seconds, left my head spinning somewhere between Pluto and Uranus, and everybody laughing at me on my ass. Tree, naturally, jumped up and also lasted only ninety seconds, and then the two of us sat with our backs against a cinderblock wall, trying to clear the cobwebs, and Treebone mumbled, "Man, he kicked your ass like nothing."

"Less than nothing on yours."

"Man, somebody had to defend your honor."

"I've got no honor."

"Make sure you remind me next time," his friend had said. Then, in a confessional tone, "No honor in it, man. I thought I'd kick that Polack's big white ass and show my man how fights supposed to be made. I was gone hold 'at over yo head for like, forever."

"How's that working out?" he'd asked his friend, and both of them broke down laughing.

Zyzwyzcky had gone from the academy to the Saginaw post and from there, some years later, to the Saginaw city cop house, where he had risen to outside captain, a title for a job that worked outside all of HQ's paper-storms and concentrated on supporting officers where it counted—in the field. Z had never been much of a swimmer in the bureaucratic paper sea, but he was brave, a natural leader, which made the outside captain job a perfect fit.

Back to Nosebone. "The Prince is Zyzwyzcky's kid?"

"Maybe his only kid, too, and a by-the-number freaky fuckup Numbah One, sayin'."

"The son lives in Durand?"

"No, man, not no more. I hear he live wit' 'is old man, got place up to da Big Lake west of Cheboygan."

"Thanks Bone, I owe you one."

The gang leader giggled. "Too old to need one now, Service, but thanks. Keep your wheels on the see-ment, sayin'?"

Zyzwyzcky, Five Z, they also called him, and Big Z, Grezgorz Zyzwyzcky. Small damn world, which was always the case in the cop community. Everybody knew everybody and gossip moved like honey in a hive, for better or for worse. Big damn Zyzwyzcky.

Service called Treebone's cell phone. "You snowed in over there?"

"Depends on who is doin' the askin' and for what."

"Want to go visit Big Z?"

Long pause. "Long as we don't have to fight that gorilla again."

"No, we're gonna emotionally kick his son's ass. They jumped Allerdyce. Thought you being along would give us more weight."

"You mean gravitas, my friend, this being the word you are so hopelessly groping for, you cretin. I wouldn't miss this gig."

"Good, we'll text you when we pull off US 2 to pick you up tomorrow, say, oh seven hundred?" He knew his friend was at his camp in the swamps north of Rexton.

Service found Allerdyce at the side of the house smoking one of his cigarettes.

"We're gonna go visit your pal the Prince."

"He know we comin'?"

"He'll know when we meet him."

"He run, dat kind, allas run if dey get sniff."

"Not that far, he won't. Turns out that his old man's a pal of Tree's and mine. We went to the academy together."

"Treebone?"

"We're picking him up at his camp. You okay with that?"

"Why I wunt be?"

"Because Treebone scares the shit out of you."

"Not no more, him and me now what you call BFF."

"What the hell's a BFF?"

"Best Friends Forever, don't you fish dicks keep up wit' da social neck-works, Sonny?"

CHAPTER 19

Point Nipigon

CHEBOYGAN COUNTY

Service easily located the address for Grezgorz Zyzwyzcky on a smartphone app. The listing was for Cheboygan, but his map app showed the location at Point Nipigon, south of town. When they got there, they found a split-level house with a spectacular view of Bois Blanc Island, about four miles north into Lake Huron.

The house was modest and well cared for. No surprise there. Big Z, Mr. Spic and Span, had always been the most conscientious of all of them in terms of personal appearance. There was a large pole barn to the side and in front of the house, and a black Ford 150 sat in front of the driveway into the pole barn. The truck was uncapped, with a crew cab, and not a spot of rust. The thing had to be ten years old, but it looked like it just came off a dealer's showroom. Big Z had always had a thing for appearances, and this truck made him look like a poster child for motor-heads everywhere. If the son was not there, Big Z would help them find him because Z was a fanatic on right and wrong and law and order, almost an apostle for all related subjects.

Service nosed up behind the Ford and parked. The big door to the green pole barn was open and out strode Big Z with a huge smile on his face as he grappled first with Treebone and then with Service. "You assholes!" Zyzwyzcky bellowed happily. Allerdyce hung back from the collision of the three giants.

"Vodka for you guys?" Big Z asked. "It's the best and right from the old country."

Service said, "Big Z, it's not even nine."

"Hey, we're retired coppers and it can be any time we want it to be, am I right?"

"Not for me," Service said. Treebone held up his hands. Allerdyce said, "Vodka sound keen."

Zyzwyzcky said, "Leave it to the dwarf to be the real cop."

Limpy bristled. "Name's Allerdyce. I ain't no cop, and I ain't no dwarf, asshole!"

Big Z looked at Service, then turned back to Allerdyce and said, "I'm sorry, old-timer, I was just kidding."

"Bite me," Allerdyce said. "Polack."

Tree's eyes bobbed nervously, and Service stepped between the two men. Big Z said to Allerdyce, "Looks like you already shot off your mouth one time too many, old-timer."

Service took the retired Flint captain's arm. "How about some coffee, Big Z? You used to drink it by the bucket."

After a moment Service asked, "Your son's Thad?"

Zyzwyzcky cocked his head like a bird taken with curiosity. "Thaddeus, yah. You know him?"

"He lives with you?"

The former trooper straightened up and turned serious. "What's this about, Service?"

It felt like Big Z's famous hair-trigger temper was ready to go off, but his edge quickly turned reasonable. "What's that dumbass done this time?"

Service said, "We'd prefer to talk to Thaddeus."

"You'll talk to me," Big Z said.

"Your son's eighteen, Big Z. You know the law."

"His age is higher'n his IQ," the man said bitingly.

"Is he here?"

"You want his butt out here?"

"We can talk inside if he wants," Service said, but the boy's father was already talking away and huffing with emotion. "That would be good," Service said to his old friend's disappearing back. He could imagine little worse for a cop than to have another cop come calling about your kid. It was bad juju for all involved. "Get on the other side of the truck," Service told Allerdyce. "We'll give the kid a surprise."

Limpy chuckled and scuttled back to the truck.

Ten minutes went by. No Thad, no dad. Service looked at Treebone. "The house doesn't look all that big from out here."

"He'll be out," Tree said, just as the front door exploded open and out stumbled a blond bearded giant clad only in red boxer shorts. Barefoot, head askew, bloody lip, shouting, "What the fuck is wrong with you, old man, what the fuck!"

The young giant's pitch went up an octave as Big Z burst out the door with his fists clenched and the boy turned to run, saw Treebone and Service looming in his path, stopped and curled down into a protective shell, like he was expecting an attack from the front or the back. After a second, the boy squawked, "What is this shit?"

Service said, "Thaddeus Zyzwyzcky, also known as the Prince?"

Big Z stood directly behind his son. "What of it?" the boy snarled at Service.

"You run with a partner they call Paint?"

"I got lots of partners, man, and that name don't seem like one of them."

Treebone whistled and Allerdyce strode out from behind the truck and marched over to the boy. "That is him, sir," the old poacher said. "Name is Prince. His Indi'n partner's called Paint." Allerdyce pointed to his stitches. "They done this, the botuvum."

Young Zyzwyzcky didn't react but asked, "Who let you out of your nursing home, old man?"

"How big's this Paint?" Treebone asked.

"Size of my boy," Big Z said.

Tree said, "Took two of you short-dunk lunkheads whoop this itty bitty old man . . . this *dwarf*? What kind pussies are you two?"

"He ran," the boy complained. "He's sneaky quick."

"I ain't no dwarf!" Allerdyce shouted.

"You admit to beating this man," Service said to young Zyzwyzcky. It was not a question.

"I swear to god I ain't never seen this dwarf dude before," Big Z's son said.

His old man said, "Thaddeus," and thumped him in the back of the head with the knuckles on the back side of his right hand. The boy stumbled and stammered, said, "F-f-fuck. If I'm lyin', I'm dyin.'"

Allerdyce surged forward and viciously and accurately kicked the boy between the legs, dropping him to all fours, holding his crotch and gagging.

Service spun Allerdyce over to Tree, who said, "We might could get you tryout as a kicker for the Lions. They ain't had shit since Hanson hung up his jock."

Allerdyce grinned, pointed at the boy, leaned down, and said, "T'ink I busted 'em."

The boy moaned. Treebone said, "Good chance."

"What the hell is going on?" the elder Zyzwyzcky demanded.

"Your boy and his friend Paint beat up Allerdyce to send a message to me."

Big Z grabbed his son by his long hair and jerked him to his feet. Service guessed the muscled kid would go three hundred pounds easily, and his old man had snatched him up like a bag of popcorn.

"We didn't want to hurt him!" the kid yelled. "Was just meant to be a message, swear to god."

"Don't swear at God!" Allerdyce hissed at the boy, who dropped back to the ground, groping himself.

"*What* message?" Big Zyzwyzcky asked his son.

Service answered. "That I should retire from my suspension and stay away from a certain place in the U.P."

"What suspension?"

"Mine," Service said.

"Now?"

"Until July 1."

"For what?"

Service pointed at Allerdyce. "Having him in my truck for deer season."

"The dwarf, you got suspended for hauling a dwarf in your patrol truck?" Big Z asked with a huge grin.

Allerdyce was too quick for either Service or Treebone to stop him, and once again he aimed a perfect snap kick, this time squarely between Big Z's legs, and like his son, the retired cop dropped to his knees, went to his side, and began gagging.

"I *ain't* no dwarf!" Allerdyce said with an angry hiss.

"Déjà vu," Treebone said.

Allerdyce glared at Treebone. "What youse call me?"

Treebone put his hands in front of his crotch. "Hey old man, we're on *your* side."

"Howzcum youse let dem call me dwarf?"

Service said, "If they hadn't called you that word, you wouldn't have gotten in your kicks. We did you a favor."

Allerdyce went bobblehead. "Wah, felt *really* good, dose kicks."

The elder Zyzwyzcky rolled on his side. "I believe that old fellow may have killed me, Grady."

Treebone said, "You're just wishin' you dead, Big Z. It'll pass."

"We need to know who paid Thaddeus and his partner and what their exact instructions were," Service told their old associate.

The father kicked his son. "Stop gagging and tell these officers what they want to know, and do it now."

Thad rolled on his back and exhaled. "Was a woman, paid us two hundred each, easy money. Just kick his scrawny ass and tell him to tell his friend to quit the damn game before somebody gets seriously hurt."

Service evaluated what he had heard. "This woman met you guys where and when?"

"We were in Marquette. Joint called Scallywags, out on the road to Big Bay."

"How'd she know to find you there?"

"Kinda like our hangout over that way. Over this way it's Beaudoin's up to the Soo."

"You talk to her inside or outside?"

"I want a lawyer," the son keened.

His father kicked him halfheartedly again and the kid said, "Outside, in the parking lot."

"She paid you guys two bills each and what else, drugs?"

"Nothing," the boy insisted. "Just cash. We're professionals."

Another kick from the old man, but hard, and it rolled the boy over and the old man yelled, "Professional *what*? Fuckups?"

"Convincers," the boy said. "We got more work than we can handle."

Treebone blocked yet another kick from the young man's father. "Steady Zyzwyzcky. There's nothing personal here, okay?"

Zyzwyzcky nodded, "I'm cool, Tree. You got kids?"

Treebone nodded. "I hear you, brother."

Service looked at the boy. "Two bills and no drugs. She blow you guys in your vehicle or in her truck?"

The kid's eyes went wide. "How do you know she had a truck?" the Prince asked.

His old man popped him lightly on the back of the head.

"We aren't coming in here blind, Thad. We've already talked to your partner. He says the whole thing was your idea."

"Bullshit," the boy said. "He all for it. Who you think got her to give us blow jobs?"

"In her truck?"

"Yah."

"Tell me about the truck."

"Silver, man, new shit painted on the doors."

"What was painted on the doors?"

"Picture of a doohickey," the younger Zyzwyzckyi said, and pointed up at the sun in the sky. He waved his hand in a circular motion.

Doohickey. "You mean a satellite?"

The kid nodded. Service said, "Still not buying. What exactly did the words say on the truck?"

"I don't read good," the boy said. He was blushing.

"You read satellite pretty good."

"No, was the pitcher over the writing, that doohickey."

"What color was the writing?"

"Red, man, bright red."

"On a silver truck?"

"Silver, dude, like that Long Ranger's horse."

Can the kid be that thick? "The *Lone* Ranger's horse was white," Service said. "Are you sure the truck wasn't black or white or blue or something?"

"I tolt you, dude. Silver truck, red words, like blood."

"What's Paint's actual name?" Service asked.

"Angevin."

"How do you spell that?"

"P-a-i-n-t," the boy said. "Paint, like you puts on a brush."

"A-n-g-e-v-i-n," the senior Zyzwyzcky said. "Thaddeus cannot read well and can't spell a lick. He was always too cool for school. His jock creds carried him."

"But Eastern Michigan took him," Service said.

"Only for a lousy month. Being a jock there didn't trump ignorant."

"Where's Angevin live?" Service asked the son.

"He moves around."

"How do you guys get together if he moves around?"

"Cell phone."

"We want his number."

"He don't got one, got borrow phone. He always call me. I don't never call him."

"Got his own wheels?"

"No wheels, no number."

"And no home," Service said, "and he calls you."

Big Zyzwyzcky was back on his feet, albeit a tad unsteadily. "You see where this strong-arm stuff leads you—or worse?"

"Just some fun, Dad, no biggie."

Big Z looked at Service. "Does he need a lawyer?"

"No, we just want information. Mr. Allerdyce does not wish to file charges, do you, Mr. Allerdyce?"

The old man was glaring at the kid, and Service said, "Limpy?"

Limpy shook his head and grinned.

The older Zyzwyzcky began to chuckle, which turned into a laugh and then into a howl and uncontrolled laughter as he shook his finger at the old poacher. When he recovered his breath, he managed, "Limpy Allerdyce, *that* Allerdyce?

"One and only," Service said.

"Damn, boy," Zyzwyzcky said to his son, "Did this woman tell you this man's name?"

The boy shook his head, said, "She just say he a worthless old bum."

The father said, "You and Angevin are damn lucky you're not dead and carved up for wolf-bait."

The boy struggled to his feet, looked at Limpy. "From that . . ."

Allercyce took a step forward, said, "Go 'head boy, say it."

Zyzwyzcky covered his groin and moaned.

His father said, "We're sorry, Mr. Allerdyce."

Limpy said, "Had me dumbass kid, too, you. Not our fault."

The son said, "Paint lives with his auntie in the Sault, and he's in Beaudoin's almost every night."

"Druggie?"

"No drugs, he don't even smoke."

Service backed the truck out to the highway, trying to think.

What had happened back at the house left his stomach sour. Silver truck with red writing. This *has* to be the Drazel Sisters again, but where do Bozian and Kalleskevich fit? If at all? We've got some direction now, faint, but at least something to trace. The Zyzwyzcky kid had gone bad and left his father mired in frustration. He put himself in Big Z's shoes. He had known his own son only briefly before he'd been murdered along with Maridly Nantz. The Zyzwyzcky boy had gone to Eastern to wrestle, play college football, and get an education. Everything must have been looking rosy and a month later he was unceremoniously out on his ass, his future shifted from bright to none, all the sunshine gone from the sky. Luck, Karma, predestination, whatever it was that guided such things, it shit on humans with little regard for anything but its own unspoken, unknown ends, whatever the fuck *those* were. Big Z and Thad: He felt bad for them, but there wasn't a damn thing he could do for them. If the kid couldn't read very well, he was as good as dead.

Allerdyce complained from the back seat, "I never got me no vodka."

CHAPTER 20

Brevort

MACKINAC COUNTY

Fellow Marthesdottir telephoned as they were approaching Brevort, a village high above the north shore of Lake Michigan. Service told her he'd call her back and wheeled into Gustafson's to park.

Limpy opened the back door and said, "I go get us smoke-fishy."

Treebone also got out and said, "I'd better go with you and make sure you don't bring back no nasty waterskunk."

Allerdyce retorted, "Lake trout good, not no skunk fish, what wrong wit' youse De Twat boys?"

Treebone and the old poacher went off together like the oldest and dearest of friends. It had not always been so. Back when Allerdyce had been released from prison, Treebone had gone with Service and some Marquette County deputies to make sure the newly minted con knew he'd better be on good behavior. Service felt pretty sure the incorrigible poacher was too old to change his ways and fully expected to find parole violations on Limpy's first night out of the can.

Allerdyce's feral clan lived in a remote compound in extreme southwest Marquette County, and the law crowd had found the conditions they had expected—guns everywhere, booze, drugs, and stoked naked savages dancing in front of bonfires, shrieking like banshees.

They found Limpy in his rocking chair, looking mildly amused by the goings-on, and when Treebone hove into view the old man growled at Service, "Youse brung a nigger here to my home?"

Treebone had stepped forward and said, "This nigger's glad to make your acquaintance."

Later, after the old man was cuffed, he had looked up at Service and asked him, "Take you a nigger and a bloody army to get an old fart like me?"

Now look at the two of them: asshole buddies, a reminder that time had a way of scrambling what once seemed absolute.

Marthesdottir said, "There's been a lot of activity out in the Mosquito."

"It's a big area," he said. "Where exactly?"

"Stafinski's fox farm."

He laughed. "That's a myth." Old-timers insisted that a former copper prospector or logger, the stories all varied, had grown weary of life in the Copper Country and relocated to what was now the Mosquito Wilderness, where he bought hundreds of acres, built a cabin, and established a fox farm to meet big city pelt needs. Fox furs at the time were a big fashion among certain city women from Chicago to New York. At some point in time—and nobody knew when or how—the so-called Stafinski land had passed into the hands of the state, which had either bought it, or taken it for back taxes. When the wilderness was declared officially in 1987, the alleged fox farmland became part of the much larger wildland. The thing was, nobody could ever find any public record of anyone named Stafinski ever owning anything either in or near what was now the wilderness. The fox farm was considered to be a specious story.

"There's evidence," Marthesdottir said, and she gave him the relevant section numbers. He ran them through his mind, in which he had long ago memorized the topography of the entire wilderness. "That's all black spruce and swamp down that way," he told her. "No place to build a cabin, not a piece of solid ground anywhere near there. I don't know what your source is, but I think it's worthless."

She said, "I have a 1925 plat book and it says W. Stafinski on it."

"How much land?"

"Four eighties at the corners of four sections."

He could think of only one place where such a picture might apply, and there was some high ground for sure, and the Mosquito itself, and some caves, not to mention the diamonds he'd found and hidden years back. The diamonds were just off one edge of the so-called Stafinski land. So maybe it wasn't a myth after all? He shook his head. How can you live all your life in certainty that you know all there is to know about your little corner of the world and then you find out you're wrong? And now it makes you wonder if there's more you don't know. "How'd you end up with a 1925 plat book?" he asked her.

"To go deep and narrow in any research project you usually have to go as wide as you can to begin. A net cast wide catches the most fish. I was trying to get a better picture of the full dimensions of the wilderness, the dimensions, topography, hydrology, all that good stuff. Besides, what girl doesn't love paper maps?"

He loved maps too. "Is there any way for you to run down more information on this W. Stafinski character?" Might as well dispel or verify the myth, uncover the real history.

"Possibly," she said. "There are a lot of sources to comb through. Fact is that this has me interested too. And by the way, I had a chat with M. She thinks Allerdyce is a dish."

"A dish of what, moose doots? Good god, Fellow, that woman's ninety years old."

"You bloody ageist! Even when we get too old to play any longer, we can still remember. At your age, it might do you well to remember that. Besides, I told her to keep her mitts off my man."

He found no words for this. Allerdyce is Marthesdottir's man. Wonder if he knows that? "Good god, Fellow."

She laughed. "Affairs of the heart, Grady, affairs of the heart."

"I follow, Fellow." God, women. Sometimes Tuesday's logic made his head ache, and Maridly Nantz had positively made his head spin with some of her thinking about . . . everything.

"How do you think cougars came to be?" the woman asked.

This bizarre aside pushed W. Stafinski aside for the moment. "What is it about Allerdyce that attracts women?"

"You really *don't* know?"

"If I knew I wouldn't have asked."

"BBQ," she said.

"Barbecue?"

"No, Bad Boy Quotient, B-B-Q, which *surely* you know about. You've never heard a lady ask why it feels so good to be bad?"

"Not in so many words," he said. Maybe sometimes, he thought.

"Exact words don't matter, it's the sentiment. Sometimes a lady needs to be less than a lady, which then makes her more of an independent woman. Most people live their whole lives between the lines either because they can't see outside the lines, or most likely, they're afraid to go too far out because they might not make it back, or get caught. Or worse, might like it so much they don't want to go back, ever."

Enough. "I don't want to talk about this anymore."

She laughed in his ear. "I do sense a desperate need for control over there in Brevort. You need to loosen up, Detective."

He'd been hearing this control thing his whole life, and he had rejected it as fatalist thinking on the part of some people, over-control on the part of others, or some stupid, petty motive he'd never been able to pinpoint, much less understand. Almost every damn fool alive knows you can't control everything. But he'd read some Chinese guy who'd said, "Misfortune comes from the little crap, from cumulative error, and it was the little shit you *could* control."

An old CO in Luce County called Tombo Smyks had gotten in his face at a district meeting not long after he transferred from the state police. "You think all the time you spend on the job will actually change—anything? Look how it turned out for your old man." Smyks had been a contemporary of his father, one the old man never much cared for.

"Wouldn't be in uniform if I didn't. What would be the point?"

"All you young bucks with your hair on fire. Listen, Service, all that does is get your head burned. No one person ever makes a difference, a least not the likes of us."

"Jesus made a difference," he'd retorted, said it just to be a smart-ass.

"Ain't none of us Jesus," the old CO had come back, "and thank god for that small favor."

He'd ended up laughing that day. The old COs were damn good at their jobs, and a lot of them far more dedicated than some of the newer breed. Never mind that they were underequipped, poorly trained, sadly underpaid, little appreciated by the public, and worked over pretty badly by prosecutors, juries, and judges. None of this mattered. The good ones were all committed, keen observers, hard-nosed, in-your-face curmudgeons and eccentrics.

Concentrate, he told himself. Get refocused.

He said to Marthesdottir, "I'd like to know when and if Stafinksi bought those eighties and how and when the state got hold of them. There's a myth up here that Stafinski once owned almost all of the wilderness property. Is that true?"

"I doubt that but I'll do what I can," she said. "But you aren't asking where exactly the activity is that I called about."

"Because there is no Stafinski fox farm," he said. Humor her, "Okay, *where*?"

She gave him the section and plat book numbers again. "No Fellow, there's nothing down there, and what the hell are you doing monitoring a place that's six miles from the nearest road?"

"Steady, Grady. The section numbers changed after the 1920s. The numbers I'm giving you are current in the newest plat book."

This shut him up. "I've always understood that the original survey lines were done before the Civil War, and not changed afterwards." As he said this, he was recalibrating the coordinates and realized now that she was talking about the shortest route into the Wolf Cave area. *Shit.*

Fellow said, "As with most things in life, there's no 'always.' Stuff we've learned sometimes turns out to not jibe with what actually happened. Michigan's survey history is . . . interesting, to say the least. You want details?"

"Only to the extent that it relates to the Mosquito."

"Well, I don't yet know how this exactly relates to the Mosquito Wilderness Tract, or even *if* it does, but most surveyors were contracted and their work results varied a lot, despite specific contractual requirements. A lot of the work was apparently pretty damn shoddily done, and later large tracts had to be resurveyed and maps and charts readjusted. Most of the U.P. was laid out in the period 1845–1849, but some parts weren't done until 1850–1853. Every surveyor was required to draw a precise map in triplicate to reflect what he had done. One copy went to the US Surveyor General and another to the state land office. The USGS got the original, and what's on record now may vary some because of poor administration, fires and floods, and other disasters that hit record storage," she said. "Still with me?"

"Like a tick," he said.

"This is interesting. The only place in the United States that has a complete set of the originals and copies is Bentley Historical Library in Ann Arbor. Only place in the whole country and nobody knows why or how they landed there. Purely a fluke maybe, but get this, we're also the only state of fifty with two principal base lines. This is the point where the baseline intersects the Meridian. The baseline runs east to west along the north borders of Wayne, Washtenaw, Jackson, Calhoun, Kalamazoo, and Van Buren Counties," she said. "And the principal meridian runs north–south with the two lines coming together on the Ingham-Jackson County lines."

Okay, this was too much. "Shoddy work had to be redone?"

"That's the short of it, but here in the U.P. you have to remember that county boundaries shifted as regularly as teenage girlfriends, and over decades new counties were made from portions of old ones. I'm sure you know what kind of strife that must have caused."

He knew about the historical scrap between Crystal Falls and Iron River over which city would be the county seat, with the former winning out after a nefarious card game and midnight raid that moved records to Crystal Falls from their original place in Iron River. There were still hard feelings among some old-timers over in Iron County, the same way that residue from the Civil War still hung like a pall and irritating reminder over southern states. That bloody war was supposed to remake the country and give everyone a new start. The laws changed, but sympathies and emotions didn't, and some conflict still remained. "There could be errors involved up here?"

"We shall see," she said.

"How soon?"

"The unanswerable question. Shouldn't you be more concerned over the traffic I've been seeing?"

Service thought, Why does my mind keep wandering? "You're right." He closed his eyes to again explore his mental map, this time with the new information. Now he could picture it in his mind. "How much activity?"

"Sometimes daily, sometimes every other day."

"Any sign of law enforcement?"

"No sir, none."

What the hell is the name of the new CO who's supposed to be partnering with me? Can't remember. Some female. She's being paid, so why the hell isn't she patroling the Mosquito, learning her territory?

"The Drazel trucks again?"

"Yes, and some ORVs as well."

Wheeled vehicles of any kind, even bicycles, were outlawed throughout the Mosquito Wilderness, and ORVs were major no-nos. Where the hell is my partner?

"That boy's been there again too," Marthesdottir reported.

"Tyrus Redpath Dotz?" he said. "On an ORV?"

"No, he's on foot and he gets there well after the women have headed into the area."

"Women, plural?"

"Yes, the two of them in a side by side. Looks brand new, a Ranger RZR 800."

"Let me guess, painted silver?"

"Red logo and blue earth ball too."

Are they clueless about the law, or don't they care? No motor vehicles are allowed in the wilderness. Has someone told them they're not exempted for whatever reason? "Are they in there today?"

"No, and they didn't come out to their truck until late last night. The boy didn't get back until just before sunup. If history holds, Drazel will be back tomorrow, get there about seven o'clock and push off."

"Oh seven hundred. Okay, we'll take a look. Thanks. Let me know about that Stafinski thing, all right?"

"It's your dime," she reminded him.

"Take a look at what?" Treebone asked.

"That fish you've got smells like a locker room."

Tree grimaced. "Well, that answers that puzzle. Look at what?"

"*We* doesn't include you."

"Does now, right old man?"

Allerdyce shuffled along chuckling. "Three muleteers, dat's us. Wah, team!"

Service sighed.

"Seriously," Treebone said again. "Look at what?"

"Drazel Sisters. They're running ORVs in the Mosquito."

"That's neither legal nor copacetic. Who's your department got covering the Mosquito with you out of the picture?"

"Why?"

"Uh, you're suspended. Ask your partner to deal with the problem."

"I am a CO and that's my turf"

Treebone shook his head. "Really, is your head *that* hard?"

Son of a bitch. Tree was a strict constructionist in some ways. When did this happen? Back in Vietnam he'd been the definition of loose and going with the flow.

"We'll just do a little recce for her," Service said smugly.

"Her whom?"

"W something."

"You haven't *met* your partner?"

"Don't use that tone of voice with me, you big asshole. I had no reason, I'm suspended, remember?"

"You're a jerk is what you are."

The name suddenly came to him. "Wildingfelz."

"Her mama give her a first name, this Wildingfelz?"

"Harmony," Service said sheepishly.

Treebone laughed so hard he had to grab his old friend by the shoulder to steady himself. "Lansing give the great Grady Service a partner named Harmony? I *love* this."

"I wasn't asked."

"Imagine that," Treebone said with his eyes bulging.

"We gone jaw all night?" Allerdyce complained. "She nice girlie, dat new one," Allerdyce said as he bit off a chunk of stinky fish.

The two men turned and stared at him. "*You* know her?" Service asked.

"Somebody got greet new girlie. I don't hang out wit' youse all time."

Service looked at Treebone, who was suppressing a laughing fit.

"Get in the truck you two," Service ordered. "There's work to do."

Treebone said, "You may have a honey-do list with Tuesday, but your DNR list is empty."

"Get in the damn truck and stop your damn preaching."

CHAPTER 21

Marquette

MARQUETTE COUNTY

Dotz was on camera going in and out of the wilderness area, ostensibly following the Drazel Sisters. Service wanted to hear firsthand from the boy why he was interested in them, if at all, and what, if anything, he had seen or done. After that he'd call Wildingfelz and put together a plan for tomorrow morning, if today's meeting pointed to the Drazels in any way at all.

The address took them to an apartment building just south of the Northern Michigan University campus. The place was on a tree-lined street with hundred-year-old houses, most of them freshly painted in pastel colors and in some stage of gentrification. When he paused to look, it struck him how prosperous beat-up old Marquette was becoming. He wasn't sure if such prosperity and the reams of out-of-town traffic were positive things. He'd once read that if it took you more than a morning to walk out of a town, it was too damn big. How much longer will the city qualify? This place felt like deep-seated liberal-land, with every lawn showing various political signs or flags declaring anti-gun, pro-recycling, anti-capitalism, and LGBT rights, the whole array of the liberal philosophy. If such a place reflected conservative values, the liberals would flip out and tear down the signs. Can't stand extremists, left or right, religious or secular. Whatever happened to live and let live? Nowadays, politics was about taking your opponents' souls and bathing them in your beliefs.

Treebone looked up at the stairs that led steeply up to Dotz's apartment. They stretched up the side of the house, nearly *straight* up. "Like the damn Matterhorn and not one damn landing," his friend complained. There was one small landing up top at the door, and it reminded him of a time when they were in training with the Marines. A serial rapist had gone up a similar set of steps and had been shot by a young wife from Brooklyn, both she and her husband the children of made-men. She had grown up with guns and had put three 9mm slugs into the intruder, lit a cigarette, and calmly called the police. The officer climbed the steps, looked at the body, which was half inside the door and half on the landing, and asked her if she had any coffee. She did. The officer took a cup and, according to base scuttlebutt, told her, "I'm gonna go back downstairs and drink my coffee and have a smoke. When I come back up, I want to take another look at the body, inside the house, right?"

While he was downstairs, she pulled the dead body inside.

The cop had come back and looked at the body and said, "Yes ma'am, righteous shoot, him being inside your house and not outside." Odd thing to recall, Service thought.

Treebone was still grumbling about the steep climb. "This place has the reek of landlord liability."

"You're just too damn lazy to walk all the way up," Service told his friend.

"There is that. I'm not lazy. I economize my energy. You remember our Juicy Fruit run? That was 'posed to be straight up too."

Service remembered. An Air Force F-4 had crashed in the karst of Laos and the two crewmen had punched out. They made contact with Search and Rescue Forces, reporting they had parachuted into the middle of a huge swarm of bad guys in what amounted to impossibly difficult terrain.

Service and Treebone were recon guys, not ordinarily involved in Air Force Search and Rescue efforts, but this time someone reached out and they were selected to go to the location to "assist the extraction."

The plan was to drench the area with Juicy Fruit, code name for a central nervous system gas that put people out cold for fifteen minutes to a half hour. The gas was new and experience with it in combat meager. Their CO, a mustang captain named LaFarge, had choppered out with them and given them the rules of engagement. "These ain't mine, copy?"

"Copy, sir," they had answered in unison.

"We are to use Juicy Fruit *solely* to extract our fliers. Call Jolly 5 when you have them, and pop red smoke, copy?"

Again in unison, "Yessir."

The captain was not quite finished. "The bad guys may be recovering by the time you're ready to get pulled out of the shit. If they are afoot and armed and threatening you, you have the green light to engage, copy?"

"Sir, yes, sir."

"But," the crusty old combat veteran continued, "so long as said bad guys are incapacitated by the gas, they are to be left alone. Your mission is to save two of ours, not to ice bad guys."

"What fool drew up this monkey fuck?" Treebone had asked.

Their captain grinned and rolled his eyes. "I share your frustration, Marine, but rules are rules. We are not the goddamned barbarians. They are."

"Dinks don't got rules," Treebone insisted. "Why do we?"

"Because we're not them," the captain said.

"Too motherfuckin' bad for us," Tree had muttered.

"Inerts are off-limits, men, red-lined all the way, copy?"

Eight hours later they rode the sling back up to a chopper from the crash site. The fliers were extracted first and had been taken back to their base in Thailand. Wiggling into the belly of the chopper, the two Marines braced their backs against a bulkhead. Treebone unsheathed his K-Bar and wiped dark blood on his fatigues. Service did the same.

Jolly 5's crew chief said, "Skipper says great job, thanks for your help. This was our first Juicy Fruit dance. Any problems?"

"None," Treebone said.

"How quick were they waking up?" the crew chief asked.

"They weren't," Service said, and didn't elaborate.

"Guess that shit lasts longer than the test-tubers expected," the chief said.

Treebone had said at the time, "Ain't that the truth." He did not look at his partner.

Allerdyce went up the apartment stairs like a mountain goat.

Treebone asked, "*How* old is he?"

"Older than us."

"That man is scary, like supernatural," Treebone muttered.

Dotz did not answer the door. Instead, an entirely naked redhead with both arms covered with tattoos opened the door and yawned. "Like, what time is it, man?"

Service showed her his watch and she grimaced. "I need me a real clock, old guy, not one of them sundial-dealeys."

He understood. She had grown up in the digital age and could not read a clock with hands—a sad comment of social directions. "It's seven p.m.," Service said.

"Shit," the girl said. "I got to be at work in half an hour. Don't know why you people here, but thanks."

She padded to a bedroom and prodded her bedmate. "Ty, Ty, *Dotz*, wake up dude, you got like three old fuckers want jaw-jaw."

Dotz popped up, rubbing his eyes, and asked with a slurred voice, "S'up?"

Treebone popped the bottom of one of the boy's feet. "Delicious thing like that running around and you grabbing z's in the rack?" Treebone said. "Shame on you, son."

"I had a difficult night," Dotz said.

"We saw," Service said, sitting in a purple and orange chair across from the trashed bed. "We'd like to hear all about what you've been up to since last we met."

The girl flounced back into the bedroom in tights, Ugg boots, and a fisherman's knit sweater. "You gone again today?" she asked Dotz.

"No, I've got stories to write today. I'll be out tomorrow."

"Good," she said, kissed him hard enough to break his neck, said, "back at four, dude, see you then," and bounded away.

"Mr. Dotz," Service said.

"Can I get a drink of water and take a piss?" the boy asked.

"Have at it. Who's your girlfriend?"

"Just a friend," Dotz said.

Treebone said, "Friends don't sleep with each other, man."

"Her name is Ballou, and she's my bunkie."

"Bunkie?" Treebone asked.

"Right, bunkies. Like we sleep together but it doesn't mean anything."

"You've been down in the wilderness," Service said, trying to redirect the group's attention. "More than once."

"How do you guys know the shit you guys know?" the boy asked.

"It's our job to see and not be seen until we choose to be seen."

"It's like, jiggy, you know? No offense."

"None taken. Not creepy to us. What about the Drazel Sisters?"

"You already know everything, why ask me?"

"To confirm facts, bonehead," Treebone said. "We use multiple sources and standard evidentiary practice."

"What?"

"It's normal to check data," Service said. "Drazels?"

"They've got ORVs, but you already know that."

"We do, silver with the same logos as on their trucks. You've been following them on foot."

"First time was a nightmare, but now that I know they head for the same area, I can relax and take my own route to it."

"Where have they been going?"

"It's a damn wilderness, man. Nothing's labeled, right? Even the map app shows it blank."

"Use English."

"There's some higher ground down on the edge of some swamp country. Lots of melt-off in pools, but they have a route they follow to the same place every time they go in. Must have it on their GPS units, and they're getting through without any trouble. Spring's sort of coming."

"What are they doing on the high ground?"

"Surveying, taking photos."

"Can you see them all the time?"

Dotz nodded. "Even when they take leaks."

"That's sick, you watch those ladies," Treebone said. "Got laws against that stuff."

"You asked," Dotz said defensively.

Service pushed his friend to tell him to stay out of it. "Same place every time?"

Dotz said, "The piss or the work?"

Treebone coughed.

Dotz said, "They've been working their way all around the high ground."

"And never out of your sight?" Service asked.

"Nope, like I said."

"Will they be out there today?" Service asked.

"No, I'm thinking maybe tomorrow, but I don't know. Last time they came out really, really late and I had a hard hike out in the dark. They aren't staying as long each time, so maybe they're finishing whatever it is they're doing. Do you guys know how far it is from where we park to the high ground?" Dotz asked.

"Five-point-six miles," Service said, "give or take. Forecast says snow tomorrow."

"Snow doesn't seem to bother them. They went in that ten-inch dump we got. Got to give it to them, they get out there and get to work."

"They haul gear each time?"

"No, they have a cache."

"You know where it is?"

Dotz said, "Yes."

"We want you to show us."

"Now?" Dotz asked.

"No, tomorrow. What time do the women go in?"

"Usually it's seven a.m."

"We'll meet at eight, at the place where you hide your truck," Service said. "Give them time to get on their way."

"You know where I hide my truck?"

"He knows the all, kid," Treebone said. "A game warden's definition of a hide is not in any dictionary."

The three men made their way back down the steep stairs outside. This time Allerdyce stayed with them and asked, "Youse keep ask kid if womens ever outten sight, like mebbe dey found Woof Cave?"

"That was part of my thinking," Service said.

"Cave safe," Allerdyce replied. "Got know is dere to find and den got have some of da good lucks to get down in 'er."

Service didn't want to hear any more details. They would emerge soon enough. The good news seemed to be that they weren't surveying along the river, which is where the diamond-bearing kimberlite pipe was located. So maybe this isn't about diamonds? And if not, what? What the hell are the Drazels up to?

He called Friday at her office in Negaunee. She answered, "Huck Finn, I presume. How's Jim and what role is Allerdyce playing, the evil Pap?"

"I miss you too," he said.

"Prove it," she came back.

"How's our kid?"

"Don't change subjects. When are you coming home?"

"Soon."

He heard her sigh. "I feel like the wife of Columbus, always alone."

"You're exaggerating."

"Which is what one is forced to do when one is left alone all the damn time. Or fantasize, but that can lead to trouble. Seriously, where have you guys been?"

"Downstate."

"I find no reassurance in either the itinerary, or the statement."

"I had an unscheduled visit with Clearcut."

"Where?"

"Troop post in Iggy. Haven't you heard?'

"I heard, just wanted to back-check your truthfulness."

"You think I lie?"

"No, but this time the rumor is true. The Troop drums were going wild."

"Dumb," Service said.

"One tends to hear about every step the legend takes," Friday said.

"I hate that word."

"Face it. The label is permanent, at least while you live, which I hope is a very long time."

"We have to roll," he said.

She came back, "Trying rolling through our bedroom sometime."

Grady said, "Wilco."

"I thought you Marines say aye aye, sir."

"You're not a sir."

"How would you know?"

"Are we arguing?"

"No, dummy, I'm whining and you're giving me no satisfaction whatsoever."

"Got to get," he said. "Conversations are, for the record, usually two-sided."

"Not in our relationship," she said.

"This is okay by you?"

"Not by a long shot, Bucko, and goodbye. I have mayhem to investigate, murderers to collar. You boys try to stay clear of trouble."

"We always do."

She laughed and hung up. It was not a happy laugh.

CHAPTER 22

Skandia

MARQUETTE COUNTY

It became Treebone's mantra, *call your partner, call your partner, call your partner.*

And instead, out of the blue, she called Service, catching him entirely off guard.

"Service, Wildingfelz. What the hell do you think you're doing mucking around in *my* territory?"

"Wildingfelz?"

"What, you have to be told things twice to get them into that thick brain of yours, or is it just age? Read your phone, asshat. Hello! I'm your *partner*, you know, partner: one who shares when and if the coequal partner may assist the other partner to untangle his goddamn legal bonds and get him off the damn suspension list where said partner was consigned for making dumb-ass decisions, back into the woods, where said partner belongs. Taking a lifelong poacher for a partner? During deer season? Totally dumbass and lame."

"I was just about to call you," he said.

"I had an asshat boyfriend used to say that. He is long gone and unmissed. I was just about to call you," she said in a whiny voice. "You are so lame!"

"But it's the truth," he argued.

"Bullshit, don't be sliming me. Mr. Bigshot's got aholt of his precious gonads and he's squirming like a run-over snake on a hot-tar road. You're off fucking around on *my* turf, and not a damn word to me? No head's up, no nothing? You don't even have the common courtesy to give me a bump or, god forbid, ask for my help."

Her voice was high-pitched and nearing scream level, and he held the phone away from his ear and listened as Tree and Allerdyce leaned closer.

"Whoa," he ventured.

"Whoa? What am I, one of your fillies. Don't you dare whoa me, you oversexed, sexist misanthrope, or should I say, more to the point, museum piece?"

Treebone mouthed, "Start—with—I—am—sorry."

"Sorry," Grady Service said, and the word was out before he could run it through any of his filters.

"No, you're not," Wildingfelz threw back sharply. "Once a prima donna asshole loner, always one."

Temper tipping, he could feel it squirming in the search for air and light. Keep it back, stay cool. "You want to talk or rant like you've got the mother of all PMS cases?"

She shrieked, "As advertised, bigshot sexist asshole. No wonder women refuse to partner with you."

"What the hell are you jawing about. I've had lots of female partners. Ask around."

"Define had," she said.

Another piece of straw was added to the camel's back. She kept digging into him. "I didn't have to ask around. They came to me at the academy and told me to stand clear of you and your Neanderthal games."

"My *games*?"

"Order everyone around, poach cases from others, cheat across territory lines, play every thing for yourself, always for yourself."

"What lines? Listen Wilkinghell, look at your goddamn patch. It says *Michigan* conservation officer, not county, not area, not district, but Michigan, state of. We need to meet and I need to square away your thinking. If you represent the shit being dumped out of the academy, those assholes need to take another look at what it is they're supposed to be doing."

She paused and said, "Good, that's why I called."

Where the hell did all the venom and aggression go?

She said, "I live just off US 41 in Skandia. Got a moose roast in my slow cooker. You and your homeys eat yet?"

My homeys? "No." How does she know it's not just me?

"Good, bring your appetites and straighten out your attitude for mixed company. You remember mixed company, right, boys and girls talking as equals? How soon can I expect you to grace me with your exalted presence?"

"By the way," she concluded. "The bit with the old poacher in deer season was brilliant."

After she hung up, Service looked to Tree and Limpy. "Weird, huh?"

"What part wired?" Allerdye asked.

"Weird, not wired. She asked if we had eaten yet. How could she know I wasn't alone? I never told her."

"Phone got picture-taker gizzy?" Allerdyce asked.

"Shut up, Mr. High Tech." Service turned toward Treebone, who was looking off in the distance. He knew his old friend, all his little tells. "Want to tell me what the hell is going on?"

"Got me," Tree said. "I'm not part of your sorry outfit."

"You called her, didn't you?"

"No sir, I did not talk to that woman."

"Define *talk*."

"Don't make me no Bubba-Bill Clinton, man. I never had me no kind of intercourse with that woman whatsoever."

"Your words say no-no, but your tone says otherwise."

"Tone is not evidence admissible in a court of law. You've got nothing, man."

"Tone counts with juries," Service said. "The truth will come out."

"Take your case to the prosecutor, see if he'll go for warrants . . . oh wait, you can't. You're suspended and you can't do diddly squat. But your partner can, so you talk sweet and make nice with the girl."

"Asshole," Service said.

"BOYS," Allerdyce said, raising his hands. "We got fight bad guys, not each udders."

Tree said, "Are we going to sit here and jaw or go eat the lady's moose? I'm starved."

"You could afford to miss some meals," Service chided, then asked, "What's your weight at?"

"Classified, need to know only."

Service plugged Wildingfelz's address into his map app, and a syrupy female voice navigated them to a small hilled driveway. The house sat under the trees to the left of a garage. A black CO truck was parked with its nose pointed down the hill, a small detail, but one that suggested Wildingfelz was always ready to roll.

His new partner was on the porch of the house, a walk-out ranch. "Thank god for modern electronics," she said. "Half hour, on the button. There's wine and beer inside, boys." To Service she said, "You stay right here with me. We need to talk."

Treebone and Allerdyce went inside and his partner said, "First item, it's Wildingfelz, not Wilkinghell. You did that on purpose," she said.

"Might have."

"Second point, my friends, family, and my partners call me Harmony."

"You're new. You don't have partners."

"There you go," she said calmly. "Ready, fire, aim. What *is* your deal, man? Listen up. I was a Troop out of the Jackson post for five years, so stick your superiority complex where the sun doesn't shine. FYI, I never listen to gossip. I start all relationships at a zero sum, blank pages, copy that?"

"Copy that," he said sheepishly.

"I know the whole story of you and Allerdyce, verse and chapter. I asked for a transfer from Van Buren County, where I had my first partner. Chief Waco visited me the day I got my assignment and told me he'd hand-picked me for this area because you and I are one of a kind. I wanted Grand Traverse County."

"He never told me."

"He's chief. He doesn't have to."

She went on. "I understand the politics of your suspension. It sucks, but we have to deal with it. I also know you've been fucking around the Mosquito, and I know on your present course you are headed for serious trouble. How about we shake, start as a team. I do the legwork. You can't until you're reinstated . . . *if* you're reinstated."

"Why're you in my face like this?"

"Because you'd do the same for me?"

"You don't know that."

Wildingfelz grinned. "Everybody knows you, Service. You never leave anyone behind. You don't know how."

"There's always a first time," he told her, the only comeback he could manage. She had him on his heels and he did *not* like the feeling.

The young CO dished chunks of moose, carrots, and potatoes out of the slow cooker and they all sat at her dining room table. "I shot this animal in Newfoundland," she said with a mouthful. "Saved this roast for a special occasion."

"Moose is moose," Allerdyce pointed out.

"Wrong, sir. This is a special cut for my new partner . . . moose-ass roast."

Grady Service could only laugh and as the meal continued, Wildingfelz looked over at Treebone and said, "Your wife says you should call home."

Service sat back in his chair to listen.

Treebone turned to him. "Get that damn notary public. I did *not* talk to this officer."

"No, but somebody near and dear to you seems to have."

Harmony Wildingfelz said, "Actually I talked to Kalina and to Tuesday. They had a whole ration of suggestions for ways to get your attention."

Treebone said, "This is conspiracy."

The CO said, "Call it what you want."

"What suggestions?" Service asked.

"You'll be the first to know when the winds and time are right."

"I t'ink I like dis girlie," Allerdyce said.

"And I like you too, Mr. Allerdyce, and I'll always treat you with the utmost respect, but if you ever again call me girlie, I will break off your thumb and make you eat it, and if I catch you breaking the law I will respectfully bust your ass and take you to jail."

The old poacher let out a cackle. "I don't do dat stuffs no more. I'm wit' youse guys."

Wildingfelz said, "Words are cheap, Mr. A. We shall see." She looked at her partner. "Right?"

"Uh, yeah, right," he said, and nervously scratched his chin.

CHAPTER 23

Hancock

HOUGHTON COUNTY

Service learned early in his career that all plans were written on tissue paper. Intent meant nothing. This was to be the day that the motley team would hump the Mosquito, but late last night former governor Lorelei Timms telephoned.

"Big trouble, Grady. The lawyer of Bozian's friend Kalleskevich is claiming in certain circles that they have proof that one of Kalleskevich's companies owns the mineral rights beneath certain portions of the Mosquito."

"Real evidence?" An old cop reaction: "proof" is a mere word. Evidence was something you could hold in your hand, and until you could do so, it wasn't real. She was a lawyer and knew this. Must be something to it or she would not have called.

"That's not clear, is it?" she said. "The lawyers can claim what they want, but until the court sanctifies said claim on paper, it's just a claim. I've managed to have my source transfer the details of said proof up to Frosty in Houghton."

"Frosty who or what?" She spoke so fast sometimes he couldn't understand her, and she threw names around like everyone on earth knew them, not because she was playing the big shot, but because she knew so damn many people and assumed others did too.

"Attorney Fallon 'Frosty' O'Halloran. You need to get up there and talk to her. More importantly, *listen* to her," Timms said.

Why does the former governor keep nosing into my business? We need to be in the woods trying to figure out what the Drazels are up to, not sitting in an office listening to some lawyerly blather. "I don't have time," he argued.

She chuckled mirthlessly. "*Make* time, Grady. Besides, it'll give you an excuse to see little Maridly. You do remember she's in the same town, yes?"

"You don't do sarcasm worth a damn," he told her, but her snark changed the equation. Little Maridly was the daughter of his late son, who had been murdered along with his girlfriend Maridly Nantz, who was the child's namesake. He had no legal link to the little girl, but considered her his granddaughter, as if his son were still alive. The girl's mother, Karrylanne Pengally, had been a student at Michigan Tech, as had his son, and she was now in a post-doctoral program. The couple had never married, but he considered Karrylanne to be a daughter, if not almost-daughter-in-law, neither of which was the reality.

Legally he had no real link to the little girl or her mother, but his heart was stolen by her, and every time he saw the little girl he wondered how much of his son was in her burgeoning personality. He had known his only son for only a short time, the boy a product of his only marriage. When he was being entirely honest with himself, he knew the real question was how much of himself had gone through his son to little Maridly. Only rarely did he allow himself to dwell on what sort of children he and Maridly Nantz might have had. They had never married, never had a kid; she was dead, and they would never have a kid, and in his life of priorities the past was worthy of only the briefest of glances. Why dwell on what you can't change? But Lori was right, this would be a good opportunity to visit Karrylanne and Maridly. He wrote down the lawyer's phone number and office address.

"Is this Frosty person expecting a call from me?" he asked the former governor.

"No, but you could surprise her."

Surprise her? Why would that be? Is Lori telling stories about me? Damn meddler.

He called the woman moments later, expecting to get an answering machine. He was surprised when she picked up on the first sound. "Law Offices of White, Kobera, Moody, Moody, and O'Halloran, this is Frosty."

"Sorry to call so late. This is Grady Service. Lori Timms spoke with you."

"She did. We're old friends. You and I need to meet. My office is in Houghton, but how about breakfast at the Kaleva in Hancock? It's on Quincy Street."

"I know the place, what time?"

"Not intrusively early. I have a quite heavy real work load right now. Shall we say 0700?"

This wasn't too early? He and the crew would have to be on the road by 0400. "It's midnight now," he said, hoping she'd take the hint.

"You're right. Let's make it 0715," she said, "and before we disconnect, tell me how much you know about someone named Stafinski, first initial W. He may have owned land in what now is the Mosquito."

"Don't know diddly," he told her, "but this is the second time in a short while that name has come up."

"The W is for Walenky," she said.

"You win the Trivia game, good for you."

He heard an odd snorty sound. "You think this is a . . . game?" she asked, and hung up.

Good start, he told himself. You're smooth as broken nails on a wall top. Did the sudden hang-up mean meeting, or no meeting? Do I call her back or not? No, you go and act like the meeting is on and if she doesn't show, you'll understand and you'll also know she's a kook. Either way, you win . . . not counting the 0400 departure time.

*****

His crew finished off a two-quart thermos of coffee as he drilled across the U.P. on dirt roads before swinging up to US 41/28 and making his way through Houghton across the lift bridge to Hancock. The two towns faced each other across the Portage Shipping Canal, but were invariably described as a single place: Houghton-Hancock. Every time he crossed the bridge onto the base of the Keweenaw Peninsula, he was reminded of the story of a ship's captain who had been drunk and bounced his ship off one of the bridge pilings. There was a day in this country, where such behavior would hardly warrant a second look, and it made him wonder what being a game warden had been like a hundred years ago.

The other two men, having inhaled all the coffee, went to sleep and spent the trip trying to outdo each other's snoring, both of them so loud he considered getting his ear protectors out of the JoBox in the truck bed.

He hadn't been in the Kaleva Café in years and thought he'd heard it had gotten new owners a few years back. If so, they'd made no external changes.

He could see the three-story building from a block east, "Kaleva Café" in huge white letters on an old brick wall, "Café" in a gaudy script. A new sign over the front door advertised "Fresh Hot Pasties." Inside were rows of tables and booths, red chairs with metal frames, salmon and odd yellow walls. There were red condiment boxes on the tables with words in white,

"Start Your Day at the Kaleva Café." Not a new slogan, or a catchy one, unless this was 1954.

They were met inside by a waitress with a name tag that said Lilach. "Officer Service," she greeted them. "Em Ess O'Halloran awaits your party in the meeting room."

"Em Ess?"

The waitress rolled her eyes. "You know, it's like the mizzzzzz thing? She fries butts if we don't get it right. Says it's a matter of common courtesy. Ask me, it's a matter of her being uppity. This *is* the U.P., not DeeeTroit."

"She finds Em Ess acceptable?" he asked.

Lilach grinned. "Not so much, hey, but it's technically correct and everybody knows us Yoopers don't talk so good, eh. This stops her from going all high-horse with the new owners."

Service smiled. The people who now owned the restaurant would still be referred to as the new owners until they sold the place twenty-five years from now, at which time the purchasers would inherit the "new owner" label. Same way if one moved to the U.P. from somewhere else, you remained new, no matter how long you lived up here. Not born here? Then you're not *from* here.

"Patty, she works here too," Lilach went on. "Patty says it's a passion-aggression thing, ya know, like wet spaghetti? Youse can't even push it, hey. Is everyone nuts these days?"

The meeting room wasn't a separate room. Rather it was a corner of the main dining room, and there a woman sat like a professional gambler with her back to the wall. Scarecrow-thin, dishwater blond, thirtyish, jutting jaw, little makeup, no jewelry. She wore a Finlandia University sweatshirt over a yellow shirt and black jeans. The shirt was emblazoned with the letters F U, which made him wonder if the lawyer had a quirky sense of humor.

"Service?" she said, glancing up.

"Yes ma'am."

"Sit," she ordered, and then to the waitress, "My guests will have breakfast, Lilach."

"Yes, Em Ess, would the gentlemen have coffee to start?"

Treebone and Allerdyce winced, and Tree asked where the men's room was. Service told her he'd have a cup.

"Full stuff or half ethel?" the waitress asked.

"Both," the lawyer asserted. "Bring urns. We don't want any interruptions."

"Me," Allerdyce said, "Wunt mind da tea, hey."

"Half and half in the urns, or an urn of full and an urn of half, and a separate pot of tea?" the waitress asked, and Service guessed she was showing her own "passion aggression."

"Whatever," O'Halloran said.

The waitress said, "Yes, Em Ess, whatever," and with that she was gone.

He knew he had just watched one small battle in one very small war, the stuff of daily life in small towns.

O'Halloran looked at the old poacher and said, "Sit down, old man, before you end up back in jail."

"Youse got no cause talk me dat way, girlie."

The lawyer said icily, "Don't you dare call me girlie, you pitiful, duplicitous, pompous, frivolous, homicidal savage. You are the poorest excuse for a human being in the entire Upper Peninsula, which offers a lot of candidates. Sit your scrawny corpus down and do not speak unless spoken to. I'll need two showers after just sitting at the same table with you."

"Okay den," Allerdyce said, sat down, and added, "girlie."

The woman gave Treebone such an evil eye that he immediately fled to find the men's room.

The lawyer said nothing more until the waitress came with her tray and Treebone returned. They all placed breakfast orders, and when the waitress was gone, the attorney said, "The three of you together, two old-timey head-knocking dicks and an ex-con deer-stealer—not exactly the holy trinity."

She looked at Treebone, "How many times have you been suspended by Metro?"

"I never counted, is it important?"

O'Halloran turned her attention to Service, who shrugged and said, "What?"

She looked back to Treebone. "I am shocked that the city of Detroit allowed you to retire. With a record like yours, an indictment might have been more to the point."

Service saw his friend's eyes light up, but it was Allerdyce who spoke. "What got youse all righty-tighty, girlie?" It was his high-pitched voice, the one that came as a prelude to physical action.

"I told *you* to zip it," the lawyer said, glaring at him.

"Youse can piss up da ropes," Allerdyce snapped at her. "Dese guys 'n' me we don't take no shit offen no fools. You mind dat mout' or I take you in da bat'room, wash dat nasty mout' out wit' da Mule Team."

"You wouldn't dare," O'Halloran said.

Service saw she was clearly horrified, and that she had turned pale and shaky, but he couldn't figure out why the edge and such in-their-faces nastiness. Any lawyer, like any cop, needed to have very thick oil in their feathers. You heard crap from people all the time, including threats, and you learned to let them wash over you, or found another career. He didn't know why, but he reached over and touched her arm. "All right, enough, you wanted this meeting and we left at oh dark hundred to get here on time."

"Correction," she said. "Our mutual friend wanted this meeting, not me. And, if you must know, I objected most strenuously, but relented solely because that's what one does with friends of a certain political magnitude. If you must know, I do not like people and I do not like to work with them. I never go to court. My job is thinking, which is the only job I want."

He wanted to ask if her favors were granted based on some sort of friend rating system, but kept his mouth shut. She was clearly agitated, and making it worse would only waste more of their time. "All right," Service said as self-appointed peacemaker. "We're here, so let's get on with this. We're all busy."

She wasn't ready to get to the point yet. The woman sniggered. "*You're* . . . busy. Good god, sir? You are suspended without pay by the state." She looked at Treebone. "That one is retired and spends all his time hiding in his camp in Chippewa County, while that old and reprehensible creature is marking time until they put him back in prison." The woman got up, turned her back to them for a few seconds and sat down, her hand shaking violently. Service saw she was sweating. Her upper lip looked pasted against her teeth. She fumbled with her purse, tore paper off a tube of hard red candy, put several pieces in her mouth, bit hard and chewed vigorously and loudly, kept crunching and added two more. After a while she said weakly, "Sorry, I'm diabetic, my sugar's down. Too much work, not eating right, all my fault. I'm so sorry about this. I know better."

With that declaration Service knew she was someone they could like, and he now understood why she was Lori's friend. "You eat here a lot?" he asked her.

"Every morning," she admitted.

"And sometimes you're in dire need of food?"

She nodded. "Worse, I'm *not* a morning person."

"Do you need insulin?" Service asked.

"No," she said, "I thought I had glucose tabs in my purse, but all I could find are hard candies. They work, not as well as glucose, but they work. Thanks."

Waitress Lilach brought their meals and coffee and tea and stared at the lawyer. "You okay, Em Ess O'Halloran?"

The attorney said wearily, "Yes, fine. Thanks."

To the men, she commanded, "Eat," and Service realized she had not ordered anything for herself. He stood up, whistled, and waved Lilach back. "Does Em Ess have a regular breakfast she orders?"

"Youse betcha," Lilach said."

"Bring that," he told her. "Please."

O'Halloran said, "I forgot to order? God, I hate it when I get like this. And I know you're wondering about the Em Ess thing. It's like a word knife. It's so typical up here. If you insist on civility and common courtesy, some people get entirely bent out of shape. I grew up here, hated the place, couldn't wait to get out, and said so. They all remember that, and up here, once something is said, it never goes away." She patted a folder with her hand.

"Let me tell you the reason for this meeting. Researching Stafinski, certain rumors suggest that at one time he owned a series of properties that would become part of the heart of the Mosquito Wilderness Tract. This is, like most rumors, not entirely true. But it's also not entirely off base. He apparently did own several eighties but never more than that, never anything like that entire area."

"Source?" Service asked.

"Plat book, but not backed up by any known official state records. Those, unfortunately, were among the Conservation Department records that burned in 1950. For some reason, the state register of deeds was then storing all its archival material in that doomed facility, and this has been the source of nothing but problems since then regarding mineral rights claims, some of which are very contentious, let me tell you. Now we have Mr. Kalleskevich's lawyer claiming his client owns a company that holds the deed to the mineral rights."

"An actual deed?" Service asked.

"We don't know."

"What's the date on this alleged evidence?" Treebone asked

"Also unknown, but I started further back and asked myself if W. Stafinski is real or not. Assuming the plat book is real, the answer is that he is real and not a fictional character created by the claimants."

"And?" Service said.

"Again, it's not crystal clear. The plat book certainly says W. Stafinski, which means there was *a* real landowner by that name, but no other record corroborates that. I've looked at the state office of deeds, at births and deaths, marriages, everything. The man's a blivet. Familiar with that word?"

Service thought he knew but didn't want to guess. Limpy stared at his tea. Treebone scowled.

"A blivet is a nothing that looks like something—a kind of optical illusion some call 'an impossible fork.' The painter M.C. Escher used such visual tricks in his bizarre creations, which is to say, they look real until you really see what's there. On closer examination, you learn you're not seeing what you think you're seeing."

Service was having trouble tracking her, thinking perhaps her flux in blood sugar was maybe causing some screwy thinking. He'd run across this now and then, but not often, and his first impulse was always to think it was bullshit, but it was real enough. He'd had one case where a man claimed that too much sugar made him kill deer illegally. The jury laughed through the trial. The gambit had not worked. Too much sugar could make certain people wacky. Too little could have similar effect. Finally he gathered his thoughts and asked, "If Stafinski is a so-called *blivet*, what the hell does that *mean*?"

The attorney tilted her head. "Incisive question."

"Is there an equally incisive answer?"

"I'm not altogether certain," she said. "The governor found a source who pointed her to a grave in Lakeview Cemetery in Calumet."

Service let her talk and tried to listen to her reasoning and decided eventually that what he was hearing was real, not sugar-talk. He knew her type. She was driven with an intensity few mortals could understand, most couldn't tolerate, and even fewer could match or accept.

"Here's what we know from the graves registration and what additional information they retain, most of which is now at the university. The family immigrated to the United States, to the Copper Country, attracted, it seems, by mass advertising in newspapers in Europe, in this case the paper in Poznan, in Poland. The family name was Stafocyzyki. They arrived in Red Jacket in 1890. Red Jacket is now called Calumet. Son Walenky was born in 1892, and the boy's father was killed underground in a mine fire in 1898."

Frosty O'Halloran stopped, took a sip of water, and resumed her recitation, all from memory. "His mother died of consumption in 1911. Both father and mother are buried in Lakeview Cemetery outside Calumet. When the big strike began in 1913, young Stafocyzyki lit out for Detroit where Henry Ford was offering five bucks a day to his auto workers, a lot more than unskilled labor miners could make on their best day. And people weren't being shot by those opposed to auto plants."

She paused again. "We have records that show he got a job with Ford, but by then he had changed his name to Stafinski. He apparently found the regimentation and routine in the auto plant even worse than mining and moved back to the U.P. to live with a distant relative named Philomon Staffoneski, in Michigamme. Staffoneski was originally Stafocyzki. Walenky started by working in the woods, and later became a builder of houses and other structures. Walenky disappeared from Michigamme in the winter of 1972, age eighty, senile and prone to wandering. His remains were found in the McCormack Wilderness the next summer. He was identified by his rifle and dental records."

Allerdyce suddenly became animated. "Hey dere, dat sound like old man Wally Staff we call't 'im. Change name short get rid all da Polack gunk. Was real good guy, loopy at da end. Had no real fambly."

Service stared at the old poacher, whose knowledge was forever surprising him. "You know this how?"

"Yah sure, I go school Michigamme when I go school. Wally Staff he dere in town den. I din't like school."

He continued, "My ma she got us cabin Witbeck Rapid and dem days I start work on own, go school sometime, build cabin, help Wally Staff, yah. Michigamme onny seven mile or so crowfly from ma's cabin."

"Did you know the uncle? What was his name?" Service looked at O'Halloran.

She said, "Wilby Staffoneski."

"Don't really know 'im dat name. He allas go by name Wally Staff. We know dat not 'is real name, but peoples can be funny wit' da names, hey."

"Did your Wally Staff ever go by Stafinski?"

"Mightamebbe, but not when I knowed 'im."

"How well did you know him?"

"Know pert good. He he'p teach me build stuff. We drink hootch he make, hey."

O'Halloran said, "Mr. Allerdyce, this is important. How well did you know Mr. Staff?"

Allerdyce rolled his eyes, hemmed, hawed, looked away. "Mebbe we done some business."

"Would you care to elucidate?"

Allerdyce, obviously befuddled, looked at Service. "Loosed date, hey?"

"She means explain," Service told him.

Allerdyce grinned. "Could say mebbe I was in supply business."

"Supplying *what*?" the attorney asked.

"Dis, dat, youse know."

She has penetrating eyes, Service thought. He heard her say coldly, "Actually I do not know and would appreciate you enlightening me."

"Umm," Allerdyce said and looked to Service for intervention. Service wasn't quite sure and then it dawned on him. "Mr. Allerdyce was a violator, full-service, market hunter, dirty guide, out of season. You needed it, whatever *it* was, he'd bag it for a price or set you up to do it at an even higher price."

Allerdyce added, "I kep da prices down real good, lower den udder guys."

"You had competition?" O'Halloran asked.

Allerdyce looked at Service again. "She claim she grow up 'ancock and she dunno?"

Service said, "Not everyone who grows up here knows about all of that stuff."

"Wah, all kinds competition back in old days," Allerldyce said.

Service suddenly thought of a question, given that Allerdyce and his father had allegedly spent so much time together. "Did my old man know Wally Staff?"

"I t'ink did, sure, you betcha."

"You think he did or you know he did? If you were the old man's partner, you'd know."

"Me an' youse's old man come later, Sonny. I t'ink youse's old man he make da pinch Wally, two, t'ree time. Wally he never make no stink, no fight, not run, just go JP, plead guilty, pay fine, no hard feeling, hey. Cost of doing business, pay da fine, shake youse's old man's hand, man to man, each man doing his job. Dey liked each udder, dose two. Respect I t'ink."

"Ten seconds ago you couldn't be sure if they even knew each other," Service pointed out.

"I 'member now is all. Day okay wit' each udder, youse's old man, Wally Staff."

Service pondered all this. My father knew Wally Staff and they "liked" each other? How much stuff do I not know about my own father? How much more does Limpy know that he's never mentioned? Is he intentionally holding back from me?

"Did Mr. Staff own property?" the lawyer asked.

Allerdyce thought for a few seconds. "Wah, he own land all over U.P. hey. Buy, sell, trade, he din't even care what kind land, just want land, say God he don't make no more, so year from now, ten years, hunnert years, land she be wort' a lot more. One time him and me drinkin' an he tell me his peoples back in Polackland don't got no land, dat all dat over dere belong uppity mucks and he not let that happen him in 'merica, whole reason his daddy come here."

Service studied the old man's face. "Did Wally Staff own land in the Mosquito?"

"Weren't call't dat when he own it," Allerdyce said. "Jus' mile 'n mile green nasty-nasty, swampety swamps."

"The plat books use the name W. Stafinski," lawyer O'Halloran reminded them.

"Dat Wally Staff. We call name Staff, but he like squirrel an' hide nuts all over, Wally use all kinds names business."

"Logging?" O'Halloran asked.

Allerdyce nodded. "Dat, build, buy, trade land, do anyt'ing can make bucks dose days. Same like today, hey."

"And he employed aliases?" she asked.

Allerdyce cackled. "No, Wally don't hire no helper pipples. He work alone most of time."

"And you're saying he poached and violated too?" she continued.

"Like said, dat don't make man special up 'ere. Ever'body violate little bit. Game is good cheap food. Wally Staff, he honest man. He tell me one time, 'Beef is for making money and venison is free.'"

"Who happened to be a violator," O'Halloran said.

"Just tole youse dis don't make a man unhonest he violate a little. Dat *not* 'is job," Allerdyce said forcefully. "*Build* stuff was Wally's job."

"My old man pinched Wally Staff?" Service asked, to break the verbal contest.

"Two, t'ree, mebbe could be four time?"

"Over here?"

"No, Wally he allas get him wit' swells from Shitcagotown. Come up, want shoot big bucks, couldn't shoot selfs in foots, want catch big trouts, all dat man-stuff dey call it, pay Wally good money an' he show dem where and how."

The attorney said, "So, not just a little violating. This is not the business of an honest man."

"Was all legal, guide dose city pipples," Allerdyce insisted.

"Legal doesn't get one arrested," O'Halloran pointed out.

"Guide is legal, but sometimes da swells say dey got big bucks for big bucks, so he take 'em where big bucks was at."

"Mosquito River country," Service said, remembering how it had been when he was a kid. There were still some big bucks in there, but not as many, and you had to hunt even harder and smarter to even get a chance at them.

"Sometimes," Allerdyce said.

"Were you assisting Mr. Staff's . . . endeavors?" O'Halloran asked.

Allerdyce looked at Service, "How tall dose statues of reservations?"

"You're clean," Service told him, fighting a smirk.

"Okay, den, mebbe I he'p Wally Staff sometimes, but never dose times he got busted."

Service had another thought, said, "Seems like the old man was pretty lucky nabbing Staff all those times, and him presumably being so good in the woods."

Allerdyce didn't blink. "Was damn good game warden, youse's old man. Good ones got have luck too, jus' like good hunter."

"Sometimes game wardens get a little extra help, which helps them to be lucky," he told the old man.

Allerdyce shrugged.

Service turned direct. "Did you drop a dime on Wally Staff?"

"Not me, cross my harp, hey. But somebody mighta, coulda."

Service knew from the old man's tone that he had indeed informed on Staff—and he understood. All rules short of mayhem were permissible when the situation concerned a competitor, and it didn't matter the activity. His old man had all kinds of informers working for him and all for the cost of a shot or two.

"Wally Staff ever get pissed at you?" Service asked.

"No reason be, I never done nothin' to 'im."

"Staff held no grudge against the old man?"

"Not I ever seen or heard."

"What else?" O'Halloran asked.

"What else youse want?" Allerdyce answered, question for a question, a standard U.P. conversational technique that usually appeared anytime there was a faint hint of trouble.

"You're sure about all this, would swear to it in a court of law?"

"Remember where we live, hey."

Tree sat up from a slump and declared, "Damn lot of words said here. Where the hell are we? Staff sold land and owned it all over the place and some of what he owned, according to Limpy, now comprises part of the Mosquito Wilderness." He turned to Allerdyce. "Do you know who Staff sold the land to?"

O'Halloran intervened but focused on Allerdyce. "I almost bought your tale until you told me Staff had no family when we know there was the uncle and there is also evidence of a wife and son, Elder, and a daughter Etta. How could you not know that?"

O'Halloran turned to Service. "Governor Timms and I have been talking a lot. Bozian wants your scalp. Could be something to do with his son, or something entirely different, we don't know, we may never know, and it doesn't matter."

Service and Treebone glanced at each other, but the message was clear. His longtime friend was telling him to stow it and withdraw. He'd seen the look a million times in many different situations.

Service said, "Okay, thanks for all this. You have my number and I have yours. Let's stay in touch."

"I'm not finished," she said. "Bozian is also talking openly of proof of mineral rights, and both men are making noises about the land having been purchased from W. Staffoneski."

"Bullshit what all dat is," Allerdyce said. "Da uncle never own shit for land, and Wally Staff don't sell nothing to nobody he don't know and like."

"This was a long time ago, and land frequently changes ownership over time," O'Halloran pointed out.

"No," Limpy said emphatically. "Wally Staff don't *do* stuff like dat. Dis guy what make claim is lie t'rough ass, wah."

The lawyer said, "Did you not just tell us he did business under several names?"

Allerdyce looked at Service, frustration on his face and in his eyes. "Thanks," Service told the attorney.

The three men went out to the truck. Tree said, "Bozian's after you because of your old man, not you. I don't know how, but the link smells like it's way back there and not up here."

"Explain?"

"I can't. It's just a feeling."

Neither could Service, but he had similar feelings, the kind of hunches that formed out of the ether for detectives and investigators in the middle of some important moment.

Tree said, "There's got to be something else bearing on this business. The evidence, whatever it is, has had to be in their hands for a while and only last fall did it dawn on him that you could be a big-ass fly in his poached egg."

"Evidence?" Service asked, his head beginning to throb. "There's no way I can do anything to Bozian. He's way bigger than me."

"Keep your eye on the ball, friend. He *thinks* you can, which means we need to figure out why and what and how. Sometimes they're not even in shouting distance. In this case it seems *you* look like the insurmountable obstacle."

"That's all speculative, Tree. Worse, it's fantasy."

"Listen to me. I was a long damn time in vice. I've seen this behavior from three-card monte up to mayoral politics and big-time Black-Bottom Ponzi. There's a scam alarm sounding in my gut."

"We need more than your gut to make a case."

"In vice work, first you need to *feel* something working. Then you find out what and how, and then you kick their asses."

CHAPTER 24

Houghton

HOUGHTON COUNTY

When you got right down to it, Karrylanne Pengally told him no more about her job than general bureaucratic boilerplate, and the air of secrecy in and of itself suggested she was on contract with a Department of Defense project, or more likely Defense's super-secret research and development arm, the Defense Advanced Research Projects Agency, known as DARPA. If this was how it was, it would be many years, if ever, before any information from the work ever saw public light. Not that he cared about government black ops. What mattered most was that Karrylanne and Maridly were still only a couple of hours away. The alternatives were too awful to consider.

Service crossed the bridge to the Houghton side, made his way south to Green Acres Road, and pulled into a long, paved driveway that ended in a one-car garage. It once had been a small barn. Karrylanne had tried to buy the property on her own, but lacked the resources, and her former to-be father-in-law had bought it with her, leaving it to her to figure out how to wrestle with all the updating the place needed.

A silver pickup was tucked in by the side of the house, and for a moment he thought it was a Drazel truck. When he realized it wasn't, he parked at an angle at the garage and saw his five-year-old granddaughter standing on the side stoop of the house with a huge smile. "Bampy!" she squealed as she charged him. He held his arms wide and she leaped like a cat and wrapped him up, and when he passed her to her "uncles," she drowned them in messy kisses and giggles. When she was back in her grandfather's arms, she waved her arm like a wand and shouted gleefully, "*We live on top the whole world!*"

The eighty-acre parcel sat on the edge of a steep hill into the Pilgrim River Valley; on a clear fall day you could see thirty miles south. He loved her enthusiasm. "Where's your mum?" he asked her.

"Upstairs, having one off," the girl said happily.

The three men made eye contact but said nothing until Service asked, "Do you think we should go in?"

"Sure!" she said, opened the door, and yelled up the stairs "Bampy's here in our new house!"

Karrylanne yelled down the stairs, "I'll be right down, honey. Show them the coffee."

This was only Service's second time here and the place still felt somewhat strange to him. The girl pounded a cabinet and growled, "Cups!" Service got out three.

"*I* drink coffee," Maridly announced.

"Not with me you don't," Service told her.

Limpy said, "I give her sippa mine."

Service glared at him and Allerdyce just grinned.

"Karrylanne lets me," Maridly said.

"You mean your *mother*," Service said.

"Mum is Karrylanne, Bampy," the girl said seriously. "She says if I'm to be a big girl I ought to talk big girl talk."

He strongly disagreed with this approach, but said only, "Okay."

"*You* call her Karrylanne," the girl pointed out.

"Got you there," Treebone said.

Service bowed his head. "You're right, kiddo. But you're not me."

"You're *part* of me," she said.

He exhaled and said, "Absolutely."

Karrylanne came downstairs tucking a blouse into her shorts. Her hair was disheveled. "You guys headed somewhere?"

"Had an early meeting across the canal," Service told her.

"I've got the day free," Karrylanne said, "to work on the house."

A man clomped down the stairs behind her. He had a pencil stuck behind his ear. He had a head filled with thick white hair, and his skin was shiny pink with sweat.

"Dante," Karrylanne said. "Our contractor. Dante, meet Grady Service, Luticious Treebone, and Limpy Allerdyce."

"Allerdyce?" Dante asked, staring at the old poacher with bulging eyes.

Limpy said, "Dis guy and me, went over Gorear same time to zap Gooks."

Service gave his partner the evil eye and Allerdyce modified the statement to, "Go Nort' Gorear, kill Nort' Gorean Gook guys."

"He's right," Dante said. "Damn lucky we got out. A whole lot of city boys were not so fortunate."

"Dose guys dey needed dere mamas wit' dem," Allerdyce added sarcastically, nodding his bobblehead.

"Bampy and Uncle Tree went Feet Nam," Maridly said. "And they didn't got killed. I'm glad they came home!"

Service looked at Karrylanne. "Your daughter told us you were upstairs having one off," he whispered, and the woman immediately turned red and her jaw dropped and eventually she snorted with real delight. "I told her we were going to pull off the old cabinets in the bedroom." She looked down at her daughter. "Scamp!"

The girl rolled her eyes, causing Service to wonder if she knew exactly what she had done. It wouldn't surprise him, and this possibility disturbed him even more.

The girl's mother asked, "Are you back on duty, then?"

"Not yet, this trip is personal business."

"Have you given serious consideration to retiring?" she asked.

"Why is everyone trying to run my life? I think about everything, keep it all on the table."

"You don't understand," she said, keeping her voice low. "I think you should fight these assholes, no matter what. They're screwing you over. If you retire, they win."

No wonder his son, Walter, had loved her. She was feisty and smart. "I'll take that under advisement."

No doubt she's been talking to Tuesday.

She poked his ribs. "You want to see what Dante thinks we should do to this place?"

"Long as it's not on my dime," he said.

She laughed. "All mine."

Dante and Karrylanne led the way up the stairs.

Service got to the top of the stairs, then asked his late son's girlfriend, "How's your job going?"

"Too soon to tell," she said. "But they aren't stingy with time off."

Feds, Service thought. Law enforcement, despite 9/11, remained a Balkanized creature, each out for his own. The narrow views pissed him off, but there was nothing he could do other than personally do it differently. His own outfit had its own issues, and organizations tended to reflect the weaknesses and prejudices of their sponsors and mentors.

He paid scant attention to Dante's house plans, interior decoration ranking just behind lawn care and decorative gardening in his priorities. Any lawn that looked slightly green was good to go. But he tried to act like he was listening and from time to time tossed out some active-listening cop talk, "Really." "No way." "Amazing." "Sounds good." "OK."

Karrylanne gave him a long hard hug as they got ready to leave. "Tell Tuesday hi," she whispered.

He would when he saw her again. When he saw her, if he saw her, which based on recent events left the outcome somewhere between questionable and a long shot.

"What did Dante do in Korea?" Service asked Allerdyce when they were back in the truck."

"Ya sure, same business youse two in Nam. Army seen how good he shoot, move in woods, pull him out to work alone. Said, good Dante, good, go get endemies."

"What's Dante's last name?"

"Boner-gotti, like dat wop marble-chopper."

"You mean Michelangelo?"

Allerdyce made a face. "Why dose wops got so many names, hey? Don't dey know cops keep akas in dere jackets?"

"A fine question," Tree said.

Service thought, another prime reminder of the old violator's deep knowledge of police procedure. Record jackets indeed included lists of known akas for criminals.

Service kept quiet. He knew the old poacher's ways. If encouraged, the man would shamelessly entertain as the clown and later not remember a word or thing he'd said. What if this had been going on at the lawyer meeting? Allerdyce swore he was reformed and perhaps he was, but how much could a man change himself? It was a disturbing thought.

CHAPTER 25

Wolf Cave

MOSQUITO WILDERNESS TRACT

The day after the Houghton-Hancock trip, young Dotz hardly complained when Grady Service called and told him to meet him at the Slippery Creek Cabin at 0600. Hard to suss what the kid was thinking or if he had talked to his grandfather or one of Bozian's legions of minions. All he knew for sure was that Dotz had not asked for directions to the cabin, which confirmed earlier suspicions that the kid had been snooping around his camp.

After Dotz, he called Harmony Wildingfelz and asked her to join the "group grope." She laughed, "Goat rodeo, hey?" she said. "Start at your cabin? What time?" First Dotz, now his new partner, and neither had asked for directions. Damn place is being overrun by snoops.

"Oh seven hundred here," he told her.

Allerdyce was first out of the sack and carping like a hoarse old tomcat. "Why we got beat feets oot bush so early, wah? What youse's tink out dere won't still be dere two hours later in day, hey?"

"I don't know what's out there; ergo, we'll go have a look-see and Dotz can retrace his trail."

"Dis alla waste of time," Allerdyce complained.

"Then stay here," Service told him.

"Partners don't split up," the old violator said with a pained grunt.

"He got you on that one," Treebone said. "Semper Fi."

"You can stay, too. There's no need for the whole damn herd out there."

Tree said, "No stops, Woods Cop, all the way together, like the old days."

*****

Dotz appeared on time and came reluctantly into the cabin. "Nice place," he said softly.

Treebone said, "My friend's got him a style we call footlocker-barn. It gets the job done—just. This particular domicile was once on its way to imminent habitability, but he fell off the previous quo, which put us pretty much back to the starting status quo."

"It is big," Dotz said.

"And empty," Treebone amended.

"You got enough stuff?" Service asked the boy. "Plenty of water, some sammies?"

"It's just out and back, right?"

Service said, "Always plan past your intentions—in case."

"I'm good for overnight," the college boy said. "Maybe two if I conserve."

"You're good then. What's new on the Drazel front?"

"Nothing new. I've sort of been busy with school, and I had to work at the paper so I sent Ballou out to watch for them, but the silver trucks never showed."

"Surprise you?"

"I'm not writing a damn dissertation on them, man. I write news."

Service thought about the no-show. If Bozian's people were already pushing their ownership claim public, would this be the reason for the Drazels not to show, that whatever they needed they now had?

"How many times did they go into the bush?"

Dotz said, "That I saw and followed? Four . . . no, five times."

Another question without adequate answer, he thought, and in any event, does it even matter? The Drazels are up to something, which may be perfectly legitimate, but we need to know what. And I need to get down into the cave and take a long look, see the alleged petroglyphs and pictographs, and the human remains Allerdyce said are down there.

"Could you see what the women were doing?"

"I think surveying, ya know. They had one of those transit-things used to run property lines? Beyond that, I'm not sure. They set up a big pop-up ice fishing tent in a clearing and operated out of that."

Surveying seemed a reasonable superficial observation, but not necessarily accurate. "Throw your gear in my truck. We'll all ride together."

"Make a great movie title," Treebone said. "*Four Rode Together*, the update of *Two Rode Together*. Are Dick Widmark and Jimmy Stewart still on the planet?"

"In it," Service said. "Not on it."

"Damn shame, I liked both of those guys," Treebone said.

*****

More wet snow last night, unpredicted by the TV weather whizzes who rated no better than seers and carny fortune tellers in the accuracy of their predictions. What a damn mess, crusty snow in some places, slush-mush in others, standing water on the year's last skiff of ice, and the noise they were making—unacceptable and unavoidable. "Did the Chinese army blow bugles when they attacked?" he asked Allerdyce.

"Wah, make spine turn Jell-O, hey. Bugles blow and in they come yelpin' like damn barred owls and spooks."

Treebone said, "Say what?"

Allerdyce grinned and held up a hand. "I meant to say ghosties."

"Good man," Treebone said, trekking on with giant strides.

Even Allerdyce was moving loudly, which was rare. Why? Usually he moved with the weight of a warbler.

Their luck turned when they hit the hard rock area. The snow here was mostly gone and with it most of the ice. If we come back after dark tonight, he warned himself, some pools here and there in the glacial pans will still be iced. Have to get real cold to make it sliding ice. Mostly it will be more of a hindrance to moving quietly.

Friday called as they caught sight of the high land, said, "US Attorney called. Needs you in Marquette day after tomorrow, something about a ceremony? 1100. You okay?"

"Sure, and you?" he asked.

"Fine," Friday said. "Your voice is weak."

"From missing you."

She said, "Bullshitter," and laughed at him.

"Weak cell service here," he lied. "We're out in the Skeet. I may lose you."

"Not a chance," she said, and the contact evaporated.

Cell phones. He shook his head. So things were moving fast on the US Attorney front. Leave it to Eddie Waco to jump on priorities with both boots. Last time he had been seconded to the US Attorney, some DNR Fish people had been after his scalp for investigating questionable (in his mind and by the evidence, illegal) practices. A few had been on the take because of a coziness with commercial outfits they were supposed to be regulating. Such coziness led to some questionable decisions in favor of the outside firms.

Unfortunately, his whole internal investigation got squashed, but the department let him run hard against the commercial entities, and his team had built a case that crushed a couple of fish companies and put people in jail for long stretches. The halting of the internal investigation still galled him, but all those people were now retired and the whole thing moot. One aspect was certain, he had liked working for the US Attorney out of Grand Rapids, had felt tremendous support from her, and he was thankful his chief at the time had had the wisdom to realize the transfer was even feasible. He would never have thought of such a thing, but it had opened up his seeing other possibilities should future opportunities arise, which they now had, although it was hard to think of this mess as an opportunity.

When they climbed up onto the hard rock knob, they found Wildingfelz sitting cross-legged on a boulder with a cup of coffee and a metal thermos.

"You were supposed to meet us at my place." he scolded.

"Why waste taxpayer gas. I knew where you were going."

"Been back this way before, have you?"

"Brought my snowmobile out here several times in winter, but no tracks and I had other cases going so I never even unloaded it. I gather you know the area pretty well," she said, tongue in cheek.

"It would pay for you to spend some time just looking around," he said. "That's how we learn our areas!"

"Is that a gotcha?"

He shook his head. "Friendly advice. I pretty much grew up out here, but you never can know everything about something as complex as a big mess of landscape. Like us, it tends to change, slowly, but it's changing for sure. You don't know that yet."

He added, "Next time we make a plan for a time and a place, let's all stick to it."

She touched the bill of her hat and nodded.

Allerdyce limped over to a flat rock and sat, patting his knee.

"Are you all right?" Service asked the old man.

"Leg's gone bum."

"Stay topside with Dotz. Tree, Wildingfelz, and I will go down into the cave."

"Youse don't even know where get down."

"Show us."

The old man grumbled, got up, and shuffled slowly across the gray rocks. "See t'ree hemlocks over dere on etch that little clift? Dere's big rock got some red stripe. Below dere is letch. Sit on letch and down youse go maybe four foot and you turn on lights and can see from dere. Be tight but can get t'rough. Youse's old man allas bitched but he made it okay. Why you want down dere, Sonny? See all dat shit I tell youse is down dere?"

"That's the idea."

"Why?"

"It's the job."

"Youse's old man din't t'ink so."

"Times have changed, the job too. He drank while on duty. I don't."

Allerdyce said, "Listen Sonny, don't be so hard on dat man. Dese was bad jobs back den, took hard men do dis crap for lousy pay and worser gear. Some dose men, dey pick up bottle to keep strong. Others, dey pick up God. Dose with drink and God dey're the hard charge fellas, all da rest in betwixt and most of them not so anxious take no risks. Was how it was."

"Thank you for the history lesson."

"No problem. Now listen good, can get real confucius down dere and dere's at least two places where can break youse's neck real quick." The old violator described the two places, but Service could not really decipher the details. Allerdyce had his own language, which Service was still trying to figure out.

"Confucius?"

"Yah, all giggedy-jumbly, hey."

"I just can't go down dere dis time," Allerdyce said suddenly. Service thought he saw dark rings under the man's eyes.

"No problem, your knee is bum. You gave me a word-map, right?"

"Tried. Youse know where youse go now, right?"

"You want to come with us partway and make sure start off in the right direction."

"Bum knee," Allerdyce said again, wincing. "An' don't believe dat chink crap 'bout trip of t'ousand miles start wit' first step and all dat shit."

Service said, "Ledge beneath the big boulder under the three hemlocks. Sit on our butts and slide down into Alice's rabbit hole."

"Ain't no Alice out 'ere, and ain't no rabbits in dat shit," Allerdyce mumbled. "Hey," he added, "dat upper part, can't get down lower dat way. Dere's nothur cave hole below where go high room to small low room."

"How far down and in?"

"Don't 'member. While."

"This where the skull came from?"

Allerdyce nodded. "T'ing work?"

"Probably not. It's in my pack. I'll put it back where it belongs."

"Won't be alone down dere," Allerdyce said. "Youse sure want go down dere? Hard-ass climb down, back up, all of 'er."

"Got to go look," he told the old man, thinking that if this had all the archaeological features Allerdyce claimed, he was going to be faced with some nasty decisions that could potentially affect the future of the Mosquito, maybe with more impact and political entanglements than mining. In fact, could this be what the hell Bozian and Kalleskevich were after, the cave with artifacts?

"You ever hear of anyone else being down here?"

"Never and never seen no sign up here nor down deep below, hey."

That, at least, was probably good news. "You come out here often?"

"Usta."

Huh. "How far down to the pictographs and cave paintings?"

"Halfway, mebbe."

"Halfway to what?"

"Youse'll see," Allerdyce said.

Wildingfelz came over to them. "This cave wet or dry, a walker or a crawler?"

"No water can see. Can walk pert easy, last time down dere. Mebbe next time I climb dere wit' youse, show use 'round, like fudgie guide."

The spelunkers found the ledge, and after Wildingfelz got down on the ledge and crawled around, she located the entrance with her flashlight and dropped in. She called back up, "Four feet, four and a half, an easy in."

"There room for Tree and me down there?"

"At the start, yeah. It's tight but you guys can squeeze through."

Service and Treebone got out their headlamps and set the beams on low lumens. Service followed Wildingfelz into the earth.

Tree had his legs hanging down, his upper body still outside. "We are not made for this shit anymore."

Service called up. "Then stay, man. We can handle it. All we want is a fast look and some photos and out. Meanwhile, you can help the cause by thinking about ways to block and hide the entry. I don't like how it is now."

"Roger that," Tree said. "I'll stay topside."

Service picked up his pack and slid into the straps. "You've got the lead," he told his partner.

"Copy, I have the lead," she said with a matter-of-fact voice, entirely professional, all business. "Looks like lots of room up ahead," she added. "There's an old trail. I've already been down about fifteen feet and come back up. I think we're good to go. We can always drag our bags if we have to."

"Seepage?"

"None yet. I felt the walls pretty good with my bare hands. You comfortable caving?"

"We'll find out," he said. "You?"

"I'm okay. Let's get this show moving."

Tree yelled down to them, "How long before we send cavalry?"

"Twenty-four hours, then come running on the double. I doubt we'll be that long, but you know how this tunnel-cave complex crap can go." They had been in countless sucky places in Vietnam and Laos, some of them huge, stunningly beautiful, or ugly, man-made, and tight confines, and all of them potentially deadly. They inflicted high casualty rates in the caves, but the enemy had taken a toll too, and both sides inflated results and fudged losses so that the war was reduced to me, myself, and I. Guys who worked tunnels exclusively were referred to as Section 8 Squads. He took a deep breath and slid down into the dark behind his partner's voice, turning his headlamp off so he didn't blind her. They would need to conserve light all the way.

CHAPTER 26

Wolf Cave

MOSQUITO WILDERNESS TRACT

So far, so good. There was a kind of raw path leading downward at a reasonable angle, although he could tell the climb out might be on the strenuous side and would no doubt play havoc with his leg muscles. Wildingfelz moved soundlessly, and did not appear to have an idle need to talk, or to be reassured the way young officers often did. A good sign. She seemed very secure in herself and her own skills, and focused on the business at hand.

After thirty minutes Wildingfelz stopped, and sat and looked back at him. "Rest stop."

"Why here?"

"There's a steep drop right next to me," she said. "The trail runs down the right side of the thing, and the next tunnel isn't as clear as this one. I'm guessing whoever used this place before us didn't come much deeper than where we are now."

"You can see the next tunnel?" he asked.

"The first part, sort of," she said.

"How far to the bottom?"

"My sonar's broken," she joked. "No clue." Her light beam angled to the right. "The trail from here is visible, but it's not as clear as it has been. We'll have to go down from rock to rock, but there seem to be plenty of good handholds going up and down."

He wondered how many humans had been down here and why his old man had never told him about this cave. He'd been in the upper cave many times, but apparently that was unconnected to this maze. How many other secrets had the old man taken to the grave with him? Dumb bastard, drunk on the job in the dark. "Let's hang here for a while," he told his partner.

"Cool by me. Why here?"

"I think Limpy was trying to tell me there are cave paintings around this location. Look over to your left."

She stood up and he could see her flashlight blade carving the darkness, and then it froze on one place. "Jesus, Mary, and Joseph," she said, her voice thick with awe. "This cannot be real."

"What?"

"You've got to see this, let me scrunch down the trail to the right. When you get to the edge, be damn careful, but lean out and look to your left with your light. I'll throw mine that way to add to the effect."

"Is there room for me?"

"I think," she said. "I'm on a nice lip here, but there is a zigzag of ledges to the left, and believe it or not, they look man-made." Her light started moving again and stopped before arcing back behind and above her. "Jesus, partner, somebody carved little ledges down here, like rock scaffolding—maybe so they could work? C'mon," she said.

Service moved cautiously, got to the opening, could feel moving air, felt the wall to his right, stood straight up. Wildingfelz's light illuminated his boots. He blinked to get his eyes adjusted, and when he saw the side of the cave he gasped. Deer, buffalo, elk, and stick-figure people with horns, some of the figures prone, and some with small single straight lines sticking up from the bodies. Arrows? One of the lines was much longer than the others. Spear? Arrows and spears. "What the hell is this?" he asked.

"Major cave art," his partner said. Her light beam lit the dream-like glyphs on the wall, showing bright reds, whites, yellows, and even blues. The colors were intense and looked like they had just been painted. How much humidity was in here? No light to degrade them, he thought. His mind ticked through technical observations, but his eyes were riveted on the paintings. Damn creepy, yet somehow comforting, men thousands of years ago, drawing pictures, trying to figure things out, just like us who walked on the moon and left evidence.

Wildingfelz said, "Look at the zoomorphs over there, and anthropomorphs over here, separated. Jesus! I think they're two different things, like separate canvases?"

"There's a picture of Jesus?" he said.

She laughed. "No, you cretin, that's a cry of astonishment."

"Glyphs, zoomorphs, anthropomorphs, how do you know about all this stuff?"

"I got a teensy bit in college, when I took some summer classes in France and Spain. I love caves, always have. I didn't know the Mosquito had caves!"

"Nobody is supposed to know," he said.

She was silent for a long moment. "Uh, partner, isn't it our job to protect natural resources, not hide them from the public?"

"It's complicated," he said, knowing that his instinct was always to hide things until he could figure out the right thing to do. *If* he could.

"You knew there were caves here?"

"I only knew about the upper one until Limpy told me about this place. I probably should have known because when you've got limestone, you often have caves and sinkholes. It's not automatic, but there's a correlation. There're limestone caves over in Mackinac County, and more I think near Millersburg, near Alpena, and maybe one more in southwest Michigan." He was truly impressed by what was on the wall, and even more impressed when he began to imagine what it had taken to paint the images in such an unlikely place. Had artists died?

"Let's get photos," he said.

"Switch your headlamp to full beam to help me. I don't want my flash to go off."

He did as he was asked. She moved next to him and brushed so closely he could smell her skin. She whispered, "Partner, this is potentially a huge deal for science and art and history." He heard her camera whispering and then, "Good god, there are at least five rectiforms here."

"English, Harmony, English."

"Comb-shaped glyphs," she answered.

"Meaning?"

"Nobody knows, but people are studying this stuff other places and aggressively protecting it. This find alone is priceless. Academics think they are the key to understanding who put this stuff in these caves."

"Like aliens?"

She guffawed. "No, people, but when and what do these rectiforms mean? They're not everywhere, but they're fairly widespread."

The smell in the cave was dry, yet dank. "There has to be a reason people crawled all the way down here to make these things."

"And build ledges," she said. "That's maybe as amazing as the art. Man, you'd have to be one of the Fratellini Brothers to make these pictures?"

"Who?" Service asked. She seemed overflowing with information he knew nothing about.

"Italian clowns. They were the first trapeze artists."

My partner's brain is very different than mine, Service thought. But her enthusiasm reminds me of me.

She said, "These pictures may suggest hunting and some kind of war."

"They teach you to read caveman in college?"

"Why does it have to be cavemen who made these? Why not women?"

'"I got nothing," he said. "It was just a word."

She touched his arm. "No problem. Archaeologists, paleontologists, most of them assume men controlled almost everything in such societies. Until forty thousand years back, Neanderthals were the ruling hominids on earth, but we *Homo sapiens* nudged them aside in pretty short order, and there's evidence in Europe and Turkey that cave art took a huge leap forward at that time."

"As in how much was being created?"

"Probably that too, but more in the sophistication of the art itself. Academics say they can see more creative and experienced brains at work, and greater abilities to manipulate pigment."

"The Neanderthals, them and us, did we . . ."

"Did they dot-dot-dot?" she said. "Yah, for sure. You are *such* a guy. Academics think they dot-dot-dotted a whole lot, so much that there are people walking around today with Neanderthal genes. Hell, maybe *you're* carrying them. It might explain a lot."

Her closeness and voice made him feel uncomfortable, something about the honeyed softness in the sounds she made. "Let's move, we're on the clock here."

"Since when, B'wana? The way I hear it, there's no time clock for you when it concerns the Mosquito."

******

Forty more minutes brought them to what he assumed was the lowest level of the cave. It was still dry, without seeps, but he could hear water moving somewhere beneath them. "You hearing the water?" he asked her.

"Roger, I think it's below us yet."

"Does this whole system terminate here?"

"I got nothing," she said.

Both turned on their lights and flashed them around. They were at the bottom of a crude and steep cylinder. The walls had to reach up fifty feet at least. Six feet in front of him was a stone pedestal, a sort of stalagmite that was sheared off. All around it were bones and skulls.

"Human," Wildingfelz said, squatting to look. "Definitely."

He took off his pack, dug out the skull from Limpy and carefully placed it on the pedestal.

"Thought you didn't know about this place," she said.

"Limpy gave this thing to me to help me get rid of headaches."

"*No shit*. Did it work?"

"Hell no," he said sharply. "That's when I learned about this place. You think these are Ojibwa remains? They usually put their dead in spirit houses, with a hole in one end so the spirit can escape to make the walk to wherever they travel."

"I'm guessing these are much older," she said. "*A lot* older. You realize that stalagmite where you put the skull means it was wet in here at some point?"

"Only one, and only here?"

"So far," she said. "Geologists will have to deal with that issue, but could it be this being the only one made this a special place?"

Good thinking on her part. Ergo the bones, a natural ossuary. "Could be. Can we count skulls, estimate the number of remains here?"

Her light danced again. "Seven, eight, nine, some smaller than others. Kids maybe."

Shit. "Any sign that there are cultural artifacts?"

"Like burial stuff?"

"Right."

She looked around for a few minutes. "Don't see anything that jumps out at me, but everything could be in tiny shards if they dropped bodies from above, hey?"

He looked up at the place where they had come down from the level above. "This is way outside my competence. Listen, did you guys learn about NAGPRA in the academy?"

"It was mentioned, but we didn't get anything of depth."

"Did they tell you that COs are responsible for sites like this as well as historical sites?"

"Mentioned only in passing. Are we?"

"Yes, under the light of NAGPRA, the Native American Graves Protection and Reparation Act. Any site that gives evidence of cultural burial has to be reported to the Feds."

"You have some actual experience with that?"

"Some, not much."

"I'll follow your lead, partner."

Wildingfelz gasped and pointed with her light. "Jesus, Grady, look up there!"

He looked up. There were many more cave paintings, not as fancy as those on the level above, but the same curious mix of human, abstract, and animal.

"What do you make of it?" he asked her. "This is over my head."

"Me?" she said, and laughed. "Not a damn thing. This stuff needs the attention of experts."

Alarm bells. "Whoa."

"We can't keep this secret, Grady."

"It's been secret a long time." Even from me, he thought. "It can't harm anything keeping it that way a bit longer." Damn the old man. *Why* had he not shown me this?

Wildingfelz's light was moving again. "Check out the far wall," she said. "Looks like bank swallow holes."

This deep? Not very likely. He checked his watch. "Let's get out of here," he told her. "They're waiting topside."

"Partner, there's a lot of interest in how and when this continent got peopled. All this stuff combined, painting, carving, symbols, I don't know if this variety of stuff has ever been seen before anywhere in the United States. This is better than, or equal to, the stuff in Spain and France. We can't sit on this, Grady. It would be unethical."

"We need to climb out, Harmony. I hear you. We'll talk it through later."

"But," she said.

"Academics can't keep secrets," he told her.

"You don't know that."

"Like hell I don't. You wave something like this at them and they'll claw each other to get at it, and some will steal the site blind and lie about it later."

"But we are also under land that belongs to every citizen of the state," she said. "This is a treasure, Grady. It's priceless."

He felt his sphincter tighten. Is *this* what Bozian and Kalleskevich are after? How the hell could they know this is down here? I thought it was the diamonds they're after, but my partner says *this* stuff is priceless.

"Harmony, this place does not belong to everyone except theoretically. This place truly belongs to my old man and me. We've protected it since long before wilderness designation and there's a lot about this place you don't yet know."

"Things you *do* know?"

"And damn few others."

"Does the chief know these things?"

"Some, not all." He told her about the diamonds and the ex-governor and Kalleskevich, and let it all sink in.

"No way," she said after a long while.

"Get my concern now?"

"God yes. You think they're after the diamonds?"

"I did until I saw this. Now I wonder. We need to evaluate all of this calmly when we're well rested."

"And fed," she said. "Fed is always important. What if it is all this and not diamonds? They wouldn't try to claim mineral rights to get hold of all this. Do mineral rights even address this sort of thing?"

"I don't know and I don't know, but they're willing to gamble fake ownership documentation to get control, and if they win, we can't rule out that they could completely clean out this place and *still* have reasonable access to the diamonds."

"You have a twisted mind," she said.

"You will too," he assured her. "Let's climb out."

Just short of two and a half hours later, they crawled onto the entry shelf and breathed in the air and sighed. "Do you carry a flask?" she asked him.

"Sorry," he said.

"And here I was led to believe you were a hairy-legged knuckle-dragging male."

"You can't trust testaments."

"Warnings, not testaments," she said. "Grady, I think there's *another* chamber below where we were. I almost took a flier off a drop-off. My light wouldn't even hit the far wall."

"This just gets worse," he said.

"More remains are on a small ledge in there too," she said. "Weird placement, separated from the others."

Treebone said from behind them. "You two got a serious case of the heebies. I've got a flask if you're interested."

Wildingfelz said, "Ah, one real man in the crowd."

Service said, "Did you find a way to block this?"

"For now." Tree explained, "Trail cam, infrared, small, and damn near invisible."

"You put devices in place?"

"Hell no, those things go for a thou a pop. You'll have to req them through channels."

"Earth to Tree, we have no channels. I'm suspended. Over. We need to do this fast, get cameras in place. Soon as."

"What about your partner? She's official."

"She's mostly a rookie and rookies get what's given to them, mostly leftovers and hand-me-downs. They don't rate high-end specialized gear."

"Aye, aye. Too bad."

"A grand a pop is peanuts compared to what's underground here," Service said. "We think there's a major cave system starting here. We have no idea how far or deep it goes."

"Shit," Treebone said.

"Get Dotz aside somewhere. Don't tell him anything, I need to talk to Limpy. Where is he?"

"With the kid."

Treebone led Dotz away and Service sat beside Allerdyce. "You saw everything down there?" he asked the violator.

"T'ink so, mebbe. Bones, pots, wall pitchers, junk all over place."

"Pots?"

"Pieces, ugly."

"What's below the level where all the skulls are?"

"Din't know dere's anyth'ing below dat."

"Who showed you this place?"

"Youse's daddy."

"Who showed him?"

"He never said."

"You tell others?"

"He swore me keep zip. I did. Dis a big deal?"

"Maybe."

"How did the old man find that second cave?"

"Yore old man he never get nuffa dis place, hey, down here an' pokin' around all time."

"But he showed you."

"Partners."

"I'm his son and he didn't show me. Did he leave instructions of who to tell if he died?"

"Said hold it for youse 'til youse old enough. Said wait 'til youse game warden."

"I didn't even know I wanted to be a game warden."

"Gibby knew. Raise youse to it, hey."

"And if I didn't become a game warden?"

"He tell me blow it shut."

"That's all?"

"Dere's dynamite down below and blast caps too. We blast it now?"

"Not yet."

CHAPTER 27

North of the Mosquito Wilderness Tract

Treebone had gone to Ford River on a mission, leaving Service and Aller-dyce for the day. Service's cell phone buzzed, and he saw it was Tuesday and flipped it open. "Molly Cloud's gone missing," she said in her cop voice. "Disappeared yesterday, last seen in the afternoon. There's a BOL with all agencies. No official Missing Persons Report yet, but Linsenmann was just here asking if you could jump in on this—unofficially. It's not been twenty-four hours yet. Grady, Ms. Cloud's been diagnosed with Alzheimers."

Marquette Sheriff's Department Sergeant Weasel Linsenmann was an old friend and longtime colleague. He'd dragged Linsensmann into all kinds of weird situations, knowing the man would always have his back. Now his friend needed his professional help. No hestitation: "Of course," he told Friday. "He knows my number."

"Wake up, Grady, there can't be a paper trail. Unofficial means invisible. He says you've had special training and a lot of experience, more than almost anyone else he can pull forward."

He had indeed been through all sorts of training and had many, many practical experiences finding people. "Why is Miss Molly out there alone if she's been diagnosed with Alzheimers?"

"There's no time for questions, Grady. Find her, then you can ask your questions."

"Anybody else on this?"

"Just you for now. Linsenmann wanted to leave the path and site clear for you."

Tuesday Friday was calm, as she always was, making her way through a mental checklist that would ensure everything she needed to do would get done. "Okay," he said. "Bump you later."

"One can only hope," she said, ending the call.

Allerdyce was staring at him. "Miss Molly Cloud's missing."

"She been tooken?"

"Alzheimers. She's a walk-away."

"Holy moley, geez oh Pete," the reformed violator said. "Dat gunk's nasty."

Service focused on the problem as they raced to the woman's camp, which was five miles north of the northern Mosquito Wilderness border. He felt a burning in his gut. Molly had been in this camp for several years. She had taught high school English downstate. As soon as she retired, she moved across the bridge to the semi-remote camp, which had a handle-pump well, an outhouse, and a generator for emergencies. Mostly the woman used propane lights and generally went to bed and got up with the sun. It was a helluva way for a retiree to live after spending most of her life in more civilized circumstances, and he admired her grit. In recent years she had begun spending winters downstate with a son, but he couldn't remember his name, or where. He'd met her when she first moved in, liked her immensely, and made it a personal matter to check on her as regularly as his schedule permitted, but it had been what, weeks? No, damn, it's been *longer* than that. It had been before last deer season, just before she headed south for the winter. Usually she didn't come back until late April, so if she was here now, she was a little early.

They drove to the narrow trail that led to the woman's house, and parked, leaving the engine running.

Curious. He had gotten a first impression of her that she was playing a few marbles short. Over time he had changed his opinion, deciding he'd been wrong, that her directness was just quirkiness. Now he wasn't sure. "Limpy, jump in back and look around for a blue softcover book. Title's *Lost Person Behavior*."

Allerdyce held it up. "Here youse go."

Service reached back for it, opened the index, found what he wanted, and flipped to the section on dementia. The book was from a course given to search and rescue people all around the country. It grew out of a thesis that there were various kinds of lost people, and it had gathered huge case numbers. The ongoing study concluded that people of certain ages in certain circumstances tended to react in similar ways. It seemed so damn obvious that he couldn't understand why this hadn't been done years ago. Even better, the lost-person database and behaviors were now being updated regularly.

Knowing the high population of elderly in the U.P., he had been most intrigued by the dementia section and had made multiple notes in the page margins. Dementia victims tended to develop a kind of tunnel vision, which meant they tended to go straight until they got stuck, or hurt. There was no real attempt to understand the mental processes that made this happen, only to know the behaviors it caused. People with mild dementia tended to have some goal or destination in mind, and the distances they traveled could be remarkably far. Worse, one in four would be dead if not found in the first twenty-four hours, meaning there was no time to dick around with this. Cold rain and extreme heat jacked up twenty-four-hour mortality rates. It was cold up here and damp, which meant hypothermia was a real risk and often fatal.

Got to move, he told himself. He raced the vehicle up the rough trail that had once been a wagon road, and skidded to a halt. The front door was standing open. "Stay here until I check the place," he told his partner.

Allerdyce stepped out to check the front. Service went inside, called, "Molly, it's Grady Service." No answer. Ample heat inside, even with the door open. Out front Allerdeyce had found two sets of footprints that seemed to lead from fresh vehicle tracks by her mailbox. The size of the tire imprint and the width of the axles said it was a pickup. In and out. Two people had gone to the house, two had come back, and the truck was gone. Who discovered Molly missing? These people?

Service went back into the house and came out the side door. Another set of tracks, small, shoeless, might be her, heading due south into the woods. He followed for a few yards. "I think I've got her," he called to Allerdyce, who bounded over to him. Service's mind was racing through calculations. Seventy-five percent of dementia walk-aways on flat terrain would be found within 2.4 kilometers, approximately a mile and a half, far short of the Mosquito border where the black spruce swamps began. He pointed at the track, and Allerdyce said, "Okay. See good, move slow, how come she barefeeted, hey?"

No time to think about extraneous details. "I'll take left of track, you take right," he told his partner. "Maintain visual contact. Statistics say she'll be about a mile and a half out."

Allerdyce commented, "Stride look strong, but barefeet slow down most pipples."

It was just this kind of situation when he felt total comfort with Limpy Allerdyce, who transitioned into all-action in an instant. He was right. "Let's go," Service said. The old man was the best tracker he knew, probably would ever know, and if the two of them couldn't find her, nobody could or would.

"Quick pace," Service told his partner and stepped it up, constantly pointing to the tiny tracks running between them. Straight as an arrow south. Amazing and lucky this was an old tote road. Most of the Mosquito had never been logged of its white pine and still held some massive first growth, but these pines north of the wilderness had been logged, and the area was a maze of old tote roads, on which loggers had dragged out their take.

Allerdyce saw her first, tapped his head, put forked fingers to his eyes to say, I see her, then held up one finger, I see one person. The old poacher's left hand made an arc over, up, and over. Service understood. The land was beginning to get a little hilly. He waved Limpy on and followed him. They found the woman sitting on a rotting log.

"Miss Molly," Service said.

She was tiny, with a thick mop of silver hair and dangling gold earrings that gleamed under their flashlight beams.

She rolled her eyes momentarily. "Yes?"

"You went for a little walk."

"Yes."

"Are you cold?"

"Yes." Limpy draped his jacket over her shoulders.

"Can we take you home, Miss Molly?"

"Yes."

"Do you want us to help you?"

"Yes."

Each man took an arm and gently helped her up, but Service then picked her up and carried her and she settled her head against his chest. She had the specific gravity of a shadow, no weight, no bulk, hardly a physical presence.

"Thirsty?" he asked her.

"Yes."

He stopped and Limpy helped her drink from a water bottle.

So far, no matter what he said or asked was answered the same way. "You stopped to sit on that log, Miss Molly."

"Yes."

"Were you tired?"

"Yes."

"And sleepy?"

"Yes."

"Were you going to keep walking after you rested up?"

No answer. "Miss Molly?"

"Yes."

Slight change, she was responding to the inquiry, not answering. "Were you going to keep going after you rested, Miss Molly?"

"Grady?" she said, and his name startled him and he felt for an instant like he was going to drop her.

"Right, Miss Molly. It's Grady. You're okay. We'll take care of you."

"Grady," she said, pawing lightly at his chin. "I'm not . . . you know . . ."

"I know," he told her.

"Yes," she said and smiled. "I'm not."

"Want me take her?" Allerdyce asked.

"No thanks, I'm good."

Try to remember what you learned. Some dementia victims had trouble finding the right words. Some couldn't walk or move easily, or smoothly. Some couldn't recognize common things, like familiar faces. Some lost the ability to organize, plan, think in the abstract. But Molly had been walking with a nice gait, as Limpy pointed out. She recognized me, not right away, but eventually. And she was stuck mostly with one word.

"I'm not crazy," Molly said into his ear.

"Of course you're not," he said.

Allerdyce said, "Look, girlie, smile for Limpy." He stopped walking and got right in her face, and she shrieked so loudly that nearby ravens fled squawking. Service pulled her closer, felt her trembling. He looked at Limpy, who had removed his teeth and looked like a gargoyle. "What the hell are you *doing*?" he snapped at the old man. "Maniac!"

"Stroker test," Allerdyce explained. "Pipples get strokered can't make no smile, hey."

"If she'd had a stroke, she couldn't have walked this far," he told the old man.

"Could be quick stroker, ones leave pipples dizzy and drunk like cuckoo."

"Put your damn teeth back in and don't do anything else until you check with me."

"Just try help," Allerdyce muttered hoarsely.

Service wondered if Allerdyce was the one with dementia. Or certifiably bat-shit crazy.

"We're sorry, Miss Molly," Service told her and resumed walking.

"Yes," she said brightly, and grinned. "Good golly!"

Geez, this is completely surreal. He said to her, "From the song, right, 'Good Golly Miss Molly'?"

"Yes," she said. "My song."

"Let's get you back to your house."

"Yes," she said, then, "*Your* house?"

"Not my house, your house, Miss Molly's house."

When the house came into sight, the woman hugged him tight, and he could feel her stiffen up.

"What is it, Miss Molly? Something there?"

"Yes," she said. "No, was."

"Something, or someone?"

"Yes," she said.

"Spoon," she said. "Fork."

What the hell was she trying to say? She pointed at the house and he took her inside. Allerdyce came in behind them and closed the door. He put her down and kept contact in case she wasn't steady, but she seemed fine and shuffled to a kitchen cabinet drawer and pulled it out. "Fork," she said, touching one; "spoon," and she touched a spoon. She pointed at a tea kettle on the stove and nodded. "All."

All? What's she mean by all? "Miss Molly, you saw something like the spoon, the fork, and the kettle?"

"Yes," she said resolutely. "Truck saw."

Truck saw . . . saw truck? "You saw a truck?"

"Yes."

The connection then popped into place. "A silver truck?"

"Yes," she said, smiling, and added meekly, "And red, yes."

"The silver truck had red on the doors or the people had red hair?"

"Yes."

"Doors?"

She nodded enthusiastically. "Yes."

She was shivering. "Limpy, find her some shoes and socks."

While Allerdyce searched for shoes, Service hit the speed dial on his smartphone. Reception was good, he noted, three good bars. Friday answered. "We've got her," he told her. "She's fine, but cold. Call Linsenmann, tell him to dispatch EMS. We'll stay with her until they decide what they want to do."

"On it," Friday said and hung up.

He called Fellow Marthesdottir. "Recent Drazel activity?"

"Yesterday, four p.m. or so."

"Where they've been the other times?"

"Yes, what's wrong?"

"Not sure," he said and hung up. Had the Drazels spooked her? And if so, why? This could happen with dementia patients as well. Had they spooked her into running yesterday? If so, she'd been out all night with bare feet. Damn.

Allerdyce had helped her into socks and shoes and she was closing the Velcro straps while Service was boiling water on the stovetop and getting out fixings for tea and some bread for toast.

The woman sat at her small table and traced the top of her cup with a finger and at one point tapped the cup with one finger and looked up at Allerdyce and said, "Yes."

Allerdyce beamed.

Service wanted to press her while he had her partial attention. "You were in the woods all night."

She smiled.

"You went into the woods after the silver truck was here?"

"Yeah."

"Why, Miss Molly, why did you go into the woods?"

"Warn," she said.

"Warn who?"

She stared at Allerdyce. "*You*," she said. "Warn Grady, yeah."

"Warn me about what?"

"Want yours, yes."

He felt uncomfortable pushing her like this, and maybe it was all bullshit, but it had to be done. "Try to concentrate, please. A silver truck, Miss Molly. With red letters on the doors?" She smiled and didn't respond. Losing her, back off. "Are you warm enough?" More smiling. He tried to read her eyes, was she here or not here? "Miss Molly?" Yes, he thought, her eyes are still here. I hope. For how long?

"Miss Molly, Have you seen this silver truck before?"

"Yeah," she said, glowering. A shadow seemed to cross her face.

"Did you talk to the driver, Miss Molly?"

"Yes."

"A man?"

"Not a lady, no. The woman drives, a woman talks yeah, drive-talk."

"A man and a woman?"

Molly shook her head.

"Two women? Miss Molly?"

"Yeah," she said with a cautious, tentative voice.

He almost laughed. She had made the point—crudely—that one of the women was not lady-like. Don't leave us yet, Molly, we're almost home. "What did they want, Miss Molly. Can you tell me?"

She lifted an arm and pointed at a small vertical desk. Service nodded at Allerdyce. "Something in there, Miss Molly?"

"Yeah."

Allerdyce opened the thin middle drawer, took out an envelope, looked at it, and passed it to his partner.

Her name was typed on the front of the envelope, which was open. He read quickly. It was an offer to purchase her place for $250,000, but the original figure had been lined out and $400,000 scribbled above it. Service looked at the woman. "They want to buy your property, Miss Molly?"

"Yeah. Yours."

Why the hell does she keep dragging me into this? "This is a lot of money; why wouldn't you sell?"

"No," she said.

"They said something yesterday that sent you into the woods," he said.

"Yeah."

"Can you tell me what they said that upset you, Miss Molly?"

"Three word. Sell. Or. Else."

"They threatened you?"

"Sell. Or. Else," she repeated.

"This is what made you run into the woods, a threat?"

"No," she said firmly.

"You didn't run away?"

"No, go find Grady."

"Find me where?"

"Mosquito," she said.

"You thought I'd be in the Mosquito, Miss Molly?"

She beamed a smile. "Yeah. Always."

"I'm glad you found me, Miss Molly."

"Yes," she said, proudly. "Find Grady."

Someone, possibly Drazel, wanted to buy her property. But there was no limestone anywhere near here. What the hell was going on?

An EMS truck and Linsenmann showed up at the same moment. EMS decided to take her to Marquette, just to be safe. Linsenmann confirmed that she had a son downstate and he'd gotten in touch with him. "Told the son it's not safe for Molly up here alone, but the son said she's always been batty and, in any event, she has her own full-time caretaker. He didn't want to hear what a cop thought."

"Some people spooked her out of here," Service told the Marquette County Sheriff's Department sergeant.

"Know who?"

"Just might."

"Want to share?"

"Not yet."

With Linsenmann, the EMS, and Miss Molly gone, Service and Allerdyce closed up the camp and locked the doors. Service wondered if Molly really had a full-time caretaker. If so, where the hell had he or she been since last night?

Allerdyce said, "Miss Molly ain't all dere in noggin, but she more dere den some I know, hey. Dey gone put her inna rubber room?"

"I don't know who *they* are or what will happen next. I think we need to make a run to Ford River tomorrow."

"Old days," Allerdyce remembered, "old-timers get treated real good, get respeck. Respeck elders, kids learn. Now treat old pipples like dog shit on boot bottom."

A sad reality, Service thought.

"We he'p Miss Molly?" Allerdyce asked.

"I'm not sure we can, legally or otherwise."

"Dey can't put rubber room dey can't find 'er."

Ever the outlaw, thinking outside the box. Steal Molly and hide her? "Stay out of it," he told the reformed violator. "This is not the time for bush justice."

Allerdyce harrumphed.

Why in hell would Drazels pay $400,000 for Molly's land and camp? No damn way to know at this point. When he got to the Drazels tomorrow, he would make sure cages got rattled.

Halfway to Slippery Creek it dawned on him that he had to meet the US Attorney in Marquette tomorrow. At first he was irritated, but then he realized that a fresh and legal badge would open a lot more doors than huffing and puffing like the big bad wolf.

CHAPTER 28

Marquette

MARQUETTE COUNTY

His meeting was on the third floor of the Federal Building on West Washington Street, the city's main east-west drag. Business types loved to brag it up and call Marquette the next Traverse City. The thought sickened him. He hated Traverse City. Too much traffic, too damn many mindless liberal tree huggers who grazed on broccoli spears for breakfast, neighborhood healthy-lifestyle vigilantes who spent their time policing dogs crapping on neighborhood lawns and saving injured chipmunks and fawns. Michigan's own fruit-and-nut coast. One thing was for sure, the city's fast-talking, mon-eyed, harbor-front developers were having their way with the city, and it almost made him grab for a Zantac everytime he had to go downtown past froufrou storefronts filled with yuppie-blood merchandise and eight-dollar cupcakes.

He'd telephoned this morning and confirmed a meeting with Tator Brezek, the US Attorney currently running the regional office for the Western District.

Brezek was trim, of average height, pink-skinned and with the long fingers of a born pickpocket. "Where's your partner?" the man greeted him after they shook hands.

"We don't have actual partners." Service felt he should explain. "It's just the way we talk about having a second officer nearby."

"I meant Allerdyce," Brezek said.

"He's not a CO."

"But he acted as your partner. Care to explain your thinking?"

"He knows more about poaching and violating than maybe anyone up here, living or dead. I took him as an asset. It was a temporary thing."

"Yah, I heard. Let me say up-front if you want him along with you now, that's no problem for me or the government, as long as he doesn't violate his parole. This work gives us some pretty damn strange matchups, and you'll get no guff from me." Brezek took a badge out of a desk drawer and said, "Raise your right hand, and repeat after me."

The difference between this federal oath and the one he had already taken was one word. Instead of Special Deputy Marshal, he was now appointed fully as a deputy marshal reporting to the US District Court of the Western District of Michigan. Every time he swore any oath, it put a lump in his throat and jacked up his adrenaline. The new badge was a single circle surrounding a cutout star in the center. Fifteen seconds later he had the sidearm and badge of a special investigator for the US Attorney.

"Limitations on this commission?" he asked Brezek. "With COs we're limited in the things we can do on behalf of the Feds, like half-breeds or something."

"Nope, no limits here. You have the full powers of your commission, which will remain in place until your situation with your own department gets resolved. Welcome aboard, Deputy Marshal Service."

He got two badges, one to pin on his clothes, and another in a leather folder for his pocket. His new weapon was a Glock in the S&W.40 caliber, pretty much the same as the Sig Sauer he had carried as a CO. Brezek said, "Pam's my assistant. We call her the armorer. She caches ammo and holsters and stuff. Feel free to grab what you need; just make sure to sign for it."

Pam led him into another room. He selected a holster to wear in his pant waist and passed on ammo. He had too much at home to even count it. The DNR believed in keeping officers well supplied so they could practice and keep their skills up for that one moment when they might find themselves needing a firearm.

A thermos of coffee was waiting for him when he returned to Brezek's office. "Have to tell you we're all looking forward to watching you rattle some fat-cat cages. Kalleskevich and Bozian: You do set your bar high."

"I don't set the bar," Service said. "Others do."

"I hear you. Those boys like to play all their games with the finesse of gorillas. You want to take me through what you're dealing with here?"

It took awhile, as he made his way slowly, leaving out almost nothing, including Miss Molly's strange story, the astonishing cave system, and a brief mention of pictographs. He withheld his knowledge of the other cultural artifacts and the human remains. He knew he was skirting the legal and ethical edge, but felt he needed to protect the Mosquito for as long as he could. The only thing he kept entirely to himself was the diamond-bearing kimberlite pipe in the vicinity. He tried to calmly assemble everything into a coherent story, which was not easy. Brezek made only an occasional note and, like most government attorneys, listened more than he talked or reacted until the telling was at an end.

Brezek smiled. "You have a helluva record for making some very bizarre and complex cases. I read all about your work against the Piscova outfit with the tainted salmon egg caviar. You chased that fella Fagan all the way to Costa Rica."

"He fled when he was supposed to report to serve his sentence."

"It was a great case and a great job. Anniejo Couch asked me to convey her regards."

"You know her?"

"She's my mother-in-law."

"Small world," Service said. Anniejo Couch had been his protector in the US Attorney's office when he went after a case involving Michigan and New York companies dealing tainted salmon eggs to the Russian mafia on the East Coast.

"And getting smaller every day," Brezek said. "The way I see it right now, you've got several things on your plate, beginning with finding the owner of mineral rights for the land in question. If Kalleskevich can prove out his claim, you realize he's pretty much going to be home free? Your department will have to give him permits to explore and all that."

"Understood." Not liked, but understood.

Brezek said, "Let's talk about those cave paintings. Did you see anything to suggest formal burials, cultural practices? You know where I'm going with this."

"I didn't see anything particularly significant, and neither did Officer Wildingfelz, but this stuff is not in our normal work experience. If you are asking if we found enough to activate NAGPRA, then no, I don't think so. But that doesn't mean we won't find something later. As for the paintings, I have no idea how they fit the NAGPRA notification requirements. The paintings are cultural but they're not burials, and pretty much what we concern ourselves with are human remains and all that. We didn't see the entire . . . cave." He almost slipped and said cave system. "Could there be burial remains down there? No answer to that. The other thing is that the cave entrance is damn marginal and unstable. It could seal up any time. Dangerous down there." He hoped he had given himself wiggle room. Was throwing a dead body into a cave the same as a ceremonial burial?

"I hate all this NAGPRA junk," Brezek admitted.

"Me too," Service said, wishing the man would get off this subject. "Why are you interested in this?"

"I guess it's more for you," the government lawyer said. "You realize that if this is a site that meets NAGPRA notification, that would probably trigger a delay in any development—on cultural grounds. If so, that will allow us and you to explore other legal strategies."

"Are there others?"

"I don't know. I'm just trying to think ahead."

Service said, "But if the state owns mineral rights, all that becomes moot, right?"

"Not exactly. Now that you've told me about the cave and painting, that pretty much cinches that we involve certain agencies and people."

"Meaning what?"

"First and most importantly, we need archaeologists to get in there and evaluate."

This was not what he wanted to hear, and it sickened him momentarily. "What if all the painting predates the Ojibwa and the Sioux, if it was made by people here long before our Indians? How can NAGPRA apply to pre-tribal people? Hell, we don't even know what to call them." Shut up, you're rambling, he told himself.

"Those are interesting questions, and I guess the archaeologists will have to make such a determination, or paleontologists or whomever. If it's prehistoric, scholars may be able to link it forward to existing tribal populations."

Service added, "But if there are remains and they predate all the local tribes, what then?"

Brezek sighed, "I take your point, Grady, and again, I don't know, but I'm sure we can find an archaeologist who will jump at such a rare find."

"That's what I'm afraid of," Grady Service said. "Does the find *have* to be made public?"

"Yes and no," Brezek said, "but I'll have to have a chat with my colleagues and the judges on this. If it is announced, there is a system in place for masking and hiding where the place is from citizens. The system's been on the state's books for decades. Only approved scholars and scientists will know exactly where the place is."

"And their secretaries and their research assistants and their spouses, blah, blah, blah. That's *not* a secure system, sir. And you can't hide anything like this from locals."

"The whole process for this could take years, maybe ten, maybe longer. Hell, you and I will be retired and dead by the time it's resolved."

Service understood this, but it was the period between the public learning about the site and the whole issue getting settled legally that concerned him. Now he was sorry he'd told the US Attorney anything about the cave. "The process will take years even if Kalleskevich has mineral rights?"

"If the man has damn deep pockets, and determination, he might get to do whatever he thinks he is applying to do—quarry limestone, right?"

Decision time. "That's his public reason."

Brezek looked across the table at him. "There's something else?"

Service took a deep breath. "Diamonds," he said quietly.

The attorney said, "Are you shitting me," and sucked in a loud, deep breath. "Really?"

"Seriously and definitely."

"Industrial size and quality?" Brezek asked.

"Gem quality. *High* gem quality."

"Ouch," the attorney said. "Really?"

"I had samples appraised some years back."

Brezek got up, locked his hands behind his back, and started pacing the conference room, and after awhile a huge smile crept onto his face and he stopped. "I think this is going to be some major damn fun, Service."

"Only if we win."

Brezek agreed.

Service understood that the irony here was that the federal Wilderness Act was written in such a way that all legal matters fell to circuit courts and the Feds had no legal redress, meaning this was going to be a state show, start to finish, unless NAGPRA got dealt in, which could lead to separate complications and problems.

"Here's something," Brezek said, "and remember, I'm no expert, but if Kalleskevich gets permitted for limestone, he can't extract diamonds unless he amends his filings and gets permits for diamonds as well. If he's permitted for limestone only and evidence shows diamonds coming out of the operations, his ass will be in a huge legal sling."

"Even if he owns the mineral rights?"

"It's one thing to own them and another to ask permission to take something specific from a site. You can't just dive in willy-nilly and do what you want, without letting the state, as the steward, know and oversee."

"But if he's caught saying he's doing one thing and actually doing another, how does that break down legally? Bait and switch is bait and switch."

"That's all outside my technical ballpark, but it's at least conspiracy to defraud the people of the state. Where are the diamonds relative to the cave?"

"Roughly adjacent. I know about where the kimberlite pipe is, but nothing about depth there, or anything else." Here he decided to keep his mouth shut about the likelihood of the cave being a major system that could, at least theoretically, have a kimberlite pipe running through it and damn diamonds laying all over the place like King Solomon's mine.

"May want to involve geologists on this too, USGS, bring all the guns to the fight."

"But if we bring in all the guns, we're sure to have a leak. Then we'll have to deal with every asshole diamond hunter in the eastern United States. There will be fights and killings and every social problem known to man, and with that we can kiss the wilderness goodbye."

"No choice, Special Investigator Service," Brezek told him.

"I don't like it," he said. "It's too risky for the Mosquito. The wilderness is priceless."

"I hear you loud and clear, Grady, but we are compelled to set in motion certain processes created by law. The good news for you is that you have a badge now and you're sworn. If you need anything else, give me a bump. Keep me informed as you develop more information."

"What about setting those processes in motion, when does that happen, like contact with the state archaeologist?" The process always began like this, and Service had been through it once before and had no respect for much of Lansing and some of its people.

"Not until we know enough to make that determination."

"What if this is all we ever know about this deal?"

"It's not enough to push the GO button," Brezek said. "Listen, do me a favor. Sometime when you have a spare, quiet moment, I'd like to meet

Allerdyce. Everyone knows of him. Few have met him, and I've heard he is a very complicated piece of work."

Grady Service smirked. "You heard right." And he'd heard too. If further exploration of the cave was physically impossible, then the hordes of government, academic, and general snoops would be averted. For how long, he couldn't guess, but for now it would prevent violation of the cave system and what was inside. Only one decision now: Close the cave. ASAP and as permanently as possible.

CHAPTER 29

Slippery Creek Camp

While Service was getting sworn in at the US Attorney's office in Marquette, he sent Treebone to recon and probe Drazel Sisters L.L.C. Satellite Services & Earth Surveys at the company offices in Ford River, south of Escanaba.

Treebone had been a huge success as a vice cop, his skills remarkable. He had a rubber face and complete control over every nuance in his voice. He could be a clown or wear a funeral mask. His normal voice and timbre tended to be deep and tense, but when he inhabited an alternate personality he quickly became an entirely different person. This ability to play different roles with all types of people made him an outstanding detective. Service knew his friend could have been a successful actor.

Treebone came back to camp that night wearing a neutral mask, his eyes flat as slate. "They see you?" Service asked.

The retired Detroit detective put a tiny digital tape player on the kitchen table and flipped the on-switch. "Better than just see me."

Service listened to the disk play.

TREEBONE: Good morning, ladies, this the place to come for a land survey?

FEMALE VOICE 1: Do you have an appointment, sir?

TREEBONE: Listen darlin', I just drove me all the way over from Chippewa County. Do I really need an appointment if I'm here and got business to do and money to pay?

FEMALE VOICE 1: I guess not. Did someone recommend us to you? We're quite new.

TREEBONE: I've got friends in Lansing. Big friends, see what I'm sayin'? But see here, I got to ask a few question—like do you got your own satellites, and if you got 'em where they be shot up from? I think satellites and such be way cool.

Service heard his friend pronounce ask, "axe," and knew he was shining the Drazel crew. It made him smile. Treebone could speak the Queen's English as well as an English toff.

How many taped interviews have I listened to over my career, Sevice wondered. Transcripts were fine, even necessary for evidentiary purposes, but woods cops learned early on that no transcript could let you hear a raw voice the way a tape could. Sometimes tone, pauses, emphasis, and other immeasurables told you more than mere words on flat paper.

FEMALE VOICE 1: You're from the east side?

TREEBONE: Got a camp over Chippewa-Mackinac County. Great deer, bear hunting, high land, marshes, a stream, acres and acres of limestone, some ponds, a small sinkhole, sayin? I be just north of the Fiborn Quarry.

FEMALE VOICE 1: Fiborn, the old worked-out limestone quarry?

TREEBONE: Weren't worked out. Got abandoned 'cause they found cheaper limestone sources. Money talks, sayin? Got a whole lot of limestone still over there, sister. On my property and all the property around it.

FEMALE VOICE 1: You want your limestone surveyed?

Service heard a level of caution in the woman's voice.

TREEBONE: No, no, no, I don't got me no interest in no damn limestone, I just want my camp lines set. Got this neighbor, five nasty trespassing signs, say'in? Gone fence my place in, prosecute all the way, stop them keep stealing my game.

Treebone was laying on the heavy black brother shtick.

FEMALE VOICE 1: Has your limestone ever been worked?

TREEBONE: Not I heard of, no ma'am.

FEMALE VOICE 1: Any sinkholes or caves?

TREEBONE: Well trut' is I hear stories sayin', but me I don't know. Never seen none. God, maybe two sinkholes, little ones. Why you ask there be caves?

FEMALE VOICE 1: Call it professional curiosity.

TREEBONE: If there be a cave on my place it ain't no easy find. No cave.

FEMALE VOICE 1: And you're surveying so you can post against trespass?

TREEBONE: That what I tell people.

FEMALE VOICE 1: There another reason?

TREEBONE: I got to say?

FEMALE VOICE 1: A client's goals help us to design the survey plan to help us get you the most for your money.

TREEBONE: I hear you people more expensive than others, but worth the money. You folks don't come cheap and I be okay with that.

A new voice pops in here.

FEMALE VOICE 2: Heard that about us from whom?

TREEBONE: I ain't at liberty to say exactly. Republicans, Lansing? Catch my drift? You go around annoucing all your clients? See what I'm sayin?"

FEMALE VOICE 2: We announce only if potential clients make a formal request and insist on it.

TREEBONE: There you go. You understand I ain't gone spit it out. I tell you ladies my land be almost full section? I think maybe sometimes I divide it, give each parcel some fine feature to sell it. Do this need them maps got them up-down lines, sayin? Can read hills and such.

FEMALE VOICE 1: That's very forward thinking. A topographical survey to begin and a land survey to determine parcels after that. May I ask if you own the surface and subsurface rights for your property?

TREEBONE: I didn't, I be here axing you ladies do work for me?

Silence here until Tree breaks it:

TREEBONE: You ladies use latest 'quipment?

FEMALE VOICE 2: Yes, the latest and the best. Would you care to see?

TREEBONE: Yes, ma'am.

Here Service can hear the women talking and can sense separation from Treebone, and then the first woman is talking again.

FEMALE VOICE 1: This isn't everything, but it will give you a good idea of our capabilities.

TREEBONE: Shit, this look like tool shed for Indiana Jones. Who do actual survey work for you little ladies?

FEMALE VOICE 2: That would be us, the little ladies. (low laugh)

TREEBONE: Where you be learning survey business from?

FEMALE VOICE 1: College.

TREEBONE: You go codge be surveyor?

FEMALE VOICE 2: Western Michigan University in Kalamazoo.

FEMALE VOICE 1: Professor Emerson Jay. His course of study is *very* demanding.

TREEBONE: I can imagine college be demanding. You got be trained by a professor to be a surveyor?

FEMALE VOICE 1: *Doctor* Jay is the gateway to the future.

TREEBONE: You go codge and start business?

FEMALE VOICE 2: Not right out of college. We worked for a Lansing company for a few years and then we decided to go into business for ourselves up here.

TREEBONE: That take some big cajones these days.

FEMALE VOICE 1: No risk, no reward.

TREEBONE: Not for me. I got some maps somewhere. I come back, we talk details.

FEMALE VOICE 1: How large a survey are you contemplating, the entire section?

TREEBONE: Not whole thing. Can't say widdout my map. You got the limits on what you do?

FEMALE VOICE 2: Our only limits are time.

TREEBONE: How's that?

FEMALE VOICE 2: We're on another very large job right now, and it is devouring our time.

TREEBONE: Dee-vouah. You learn that word up codge from that Dr. Jay? How soon other job be done?

Laughter here, and Service guessed Mr. Charming was making goo-goo eyes and entertaining the women.

FEMALE VOICE 2: How soon are you thinking you'd want us to get to your job?

TREEBONE: Sooner be better than later, am I right? Like this spring?

FEMALE VOICE 2: If we win this other contract, it could be fall or later.

TREEBONE: That must be some client all y'all got.

FEMALE VOICE 2: It's a considerable challenge but a real rewarding one. Which of our clients did you talk to?

TREEBONE: Which you think give you the big thumbs up?

FEMALE VOICE 1: All of them, we hope—and expect.

FEMALE VOICE 2: Client satisfaction is among our very top corporate value statements.

TREEBONE: That what I hear, you ladies go extra mile, that give you hint who client be? Any way you can get to my job *before* fall?

FEMALE VOICE 2: We don't even know the dimensions of your job yet, and like we said, fall would be the earliest. To be honest it would be nearly impossible to get a plan in place and start work before next year.

Service heard Treebone whistle, then jack up his shine mode.

TREEBONE: You ladies seem to sure be sittin' pretty.

FEMALE VOICE 1: We hope we earn it.

TREEBONE: Understand won't be this year, okay, any way to rough-spec, help me do my own budget?

FEMALE VOICE 2: I think we could manage that.

TREEBONE: Today?

FEMALE VOICE 2: Day after tomorrow?

TREEBONE: Best you ladies can do?

FEMALE VOICE 2: Sorry.

Another pause here.

TREEBONE: Day after tomorrow, here good? Say noon? I'll bring some real folk soul food. You ladies like pasties?

FEMALE VOICE 1: Noon is fine, but pasties are Cornish—English.

TREEBONE: Bullshit, don't be believing those lying Cousin Jacks. Pasties were invented by *Africans*, how you think soul food come this country? Come over on slave ships.

Service heard a shift in ambient sound and then the recorder went off.

TREEBONE: I'm recording again, out in my truck now. Their equipment looks to me to be state of the art and they seem technically competent and superficially legitimate. I called their Dr. Jay to confirm their story, but he's never heard of them. I also called the state to see if the Drazel women are licensed. Ain't nobody by that name got a license to survey in the state of Michigan. We got some shit here, my friend. What be said and what be—ain't jibing. I'm about twenty miles out now. Talk tonight over food. Wait till you hear how they homed right in on caves, and no prompt from me to move it that way.

Here Treebone turned off the machine and looked at Service, who was thinking, my friend, the great black god of charm.

Treebone said, "I talked to Department of Licensing and Regulatory Affairs. That's the LARA on the recorder. Just over a thousand licensed professional surveyors in the state and there's nobody named Drazel in those ranks. LARA told me all the profesionals have a four-year degree, an internship, and have passed a slew of state tests in order to be certified. It's damn hard to get that. There's one other thing. I also talked to MSPS in Lansing. They've got an office not far from the Capitol, other side of the Grand River."

"Spare me the initial soup."

"Michigan Society of Professional Surveyors."

"We planning a visit?" Service asked.

"Man, you wanted detail, Tree brings home the detail. The folks at MSPS, they never heard of no Drazels, not as members, not as a company. Far as they're concerned, Drazels don't exist. I find that real interesting."

"You intend to keep your meeting with them day after tomorrow?" Service asked Treebone.

"I don't know. It's your case, and your call. One of the ladies gave me a handout as I was leaving. Says I have to bring some paper—deed, title insurance policy—something with a legal description of my property. Thing is, if I do that, they can check back through the Registrar of Deeds, could learn you owned North of Nowhere before I did. This being true, our ship seems to be headed for the beach."

"Maybe not. I think my accountant had that land in another name, so it may not easily link to me. We'll have to call Marschke and talk to him."

"You want me to gather my paperwork? I got it in a box in the bank in St. Ignace."

"Go ahead and get it, just in case, but we'll hold on the next meeting until we see where we are and how this thing is developing."

"Partner," Service said to Allerdyce, "how about you call Dotz and ask if he can meet us and hike back out to where the Drazels were working."

"Already done that," Allerdyce said, grinning, "Sonny."

"I want you to do it again."

He thought the old man might challenge this, but he didn't. I'm still missing something out there, and the only key we have is Dotz.

Allerdyce went bobblehead. "Okay den."

Service to Treebone. "Bottom line impressions?"

Tree said, "They talk a really good game. That equipment room? It blew my mind: GPS, laser scanner, something called robotic something or other—I just got a glance, and no time to memorize everything. I did manage to sneak a couple of phone photos. Want a look?"

Service shook his head. "Later on for the photos. But let's make sure Dotz gets a look at them. Appearances aside, Drazels aren't licensed or registered and their business doesn't show up among other surveying outfits."

"That's true, but I asked the gent at MSPS if somebody has to be licensed to do surveys. He told me they have to be licensed to sign off on legal work, but unlicensed people can and do work for a licensed surveyor; all he's got to do is supervise their daily work. Maybe there a head hen or rooster hiding in that chicken coop?"

More digging to do, Service told himself. The key to successful investigations was to have all relevant questions answered before you asked them for the record.

"You think it's weird how the one lady dove straight to questions about caves?" Treebone asked.

"It's odd, maybe, no way to know yet."

"You want I keep 'axe' around?"

Both men exploded in laughter, and Allerdyce chirped, "What funny, what funny?"

CHAPTER 30

Mosquito Wilderness Tract

Even for a college boy, he looked seriously undernourished. "Dotz, you look like you just came off the Bataan Death March," Service greeted him when the boy walked up onto the cabin porch.

"The what?"

Jesus, what are schools teaching nowadays? "You're so skinny you could sleep between Venetian blinds. That girlfriend of yours, she needs to add carbs to your diet. This is white dirt country, Dotz. The skinny bones die first. To survive up here a man needs extra insulation."

"Ballou is my *roommate*, not my girlfriend."

Allerdyce came outside and intervened. "You wingy-dingy dat girlie's t'ingey?"

Dotz took a step back from the old violator. "Ya, sometimes, I guess?"

Allerdyce poked the college boy in the chest. "Den she youse's girlfriend, chuck-knuck. You college kittles can't speak no normal Hinglitch, wah."

Dotz said to Service. "What is *his* problem?"

"The unanswerable question," Service said. "In fact, I find it to be entirely imponderable."

"Ballou is *not* my girlfriend," the boy insisted.

Service said, "Knock it off and show him the photos."

Treebone showed Dotz some of the photos he'd shot with his phone during yesterday's visit to Ford River. The photos showed the Drazel women and their equipment in the equipment room. Service said, "Those women look familiar?"

Dotz said, "I guess?"

Treebone went right at the answer. "You know or you guess, they aren't the same thing. This is binary, Dotz, yes-no, and like that."

"I think I saw some of that stuff, maybe . . . yeah . . . yes . . . I've seen it."

"Where and when?" Service asked.

"Mosquito," Dotz said, "Out there where we went."

"You saw the women in these photos using the equipment shown in these photos?"

Dotz asked, "Is this important?"

Service nodded and said, "It is."

"I seen, man."

"These women using the equipment in the photos?" Service repeated.

Dotz looked confused. "No, not *these* women. I saw the women I've been seeing using equipment that looks like that."

Service and Treebone exchanged glances.

Dotz said, "The equipment they were using, this stuff coulda been the same, but it's just an impression. Truth is I'm just not sure."

Service asked, "What did you think the women were doing our there?"

Dotz said, "Surveying?" After a pause, "It was surveying, right?"

"We want to go back out to where they were, and go through everything again."

"We *already* did that, man."

"Cops keep doing stuff until they get it set in their heads," Treebone said. "We ain't as quick on pickup as college boys." Treebone leered at the smaller man. "What your ACT score was?"

"My ACT? Uh, 27, I think."

"Mine was 32, hear what I'm saying?"

Dotz looked confused. "Can somebody *please* tell me what's going on?" Dotz asked.

Service said, "We're investigating."

Dotz furrowed his brow. "How can you do that—legally? You're not a cop right now, right?"

Service flashed his deputy marshal badge. "Is that real?" the boy asked.

"You think I bought it at the Dollar Store?" Service said.

Dotz pulled a reporter's notebook from his back pocket and clicked a ballpoint. "Okay if I write that down?"

Treebone said menacingly, "You're a reporter, that's what you do. You think a source won't like you making notes and might shut up, then you find a minute, moment, whatever, step aside, and make notes. You don't ask if it's okay for you to write down something. Learn to *do* your job, Dotz."

"That seems unfair," Dotz said. "Or something. You know, like sneaky?"

"You need to lose those feelings," Service told the boy. "Journalists and cops have the same job up to a certain point: cops to discover the facts and see if the facts tell a story that tells us we need to develop charges. You need to determine if the facts and that story hold together and if your audience ought to know what you know. We take our facts to the court and you take yours to the public."

"But if you're investigating someone, they ought to be aware of that, right?" Dotz said.

"Was it ethical the way you were sneaking around following me?" Service asked.

Dotz hung his head.

"Get your head up, Dotz," Treebone said. "Put some damn oil in your feathers. Anybody wants to run down the real facts on anything needs to maintain a mean streak and keep some ice in the blood. Remember, we're looking at somebody because we think they're dirty or done something bad, and if they've done something bad we don't owe that somebody a damn thing, except to find the facts. You got to lie to a source or suspect to get what you want and need, lie to his ass."

"I should lie to my subjects and sources?"

"Whatever it takes to get the truth."

"*You guys* lie?" Dotz asked.

"To suspects and shitbags," Grady Service said, "damn right we do."

The retired Detroit detective said, "You don't lie and spin a tale, you won't be finding shit."

Dotz said, "That makes me feel dirty."

Treebone shrugged. "You see an asshole indicted and later convicted because of what you done, you'll feel plenty clean, b'lee me."

"The ends justify the means?" Dotz said.

"In investigations of serious wrongdoing," Service said, "absolutely."

"Burnin' daylight," Allerdyce announced, sniffing the damp morning air and spreading dawn.

"You eager to get out in the woods?" Service asked the old man.

Allerdyce shook his head. "Don't want go at all, me."

"Then why bother?"

"Youse said we go, an' partners stick together, no matter what, hey?"

"This isn't critical do or die," Service said. "We're just gonna take a walk, talk, and look around."

"Youse crawl back down dat hole out dere?" Allerdyce asked.

"Don't know yet," Service said. "Why?"

Allerdyce shook his head.

They all got into Service's truck and drove to the jump-off point.

Out at the site, they immediately headed into the woods. Allerdyce trailed alongside Dotz, and Service listened to them.

"Dat girlie youse got," Allerdyce said. "What name is?"

"Ballou," Dotz said.

"Balloons," the old man said in his marble-mouth way. "She sure got her da nice ones, her. How many times youse bone dat girlie every night?"

Dotz said loudly, "Do I have to listen to this shit?"

Tree said loudly "Learn how to go deaf and shut out everything but the stuff you need to hear."

Dotz looked at Allerdyce. "Not your business, old man."

Treebone laughed. "Best learn this fast, Dotz. This skill of selective hearing could be useful with your boss and your old lady."

"You mean spouse?" Dotz said.

Treebone said, "Walk, Dotz, I'm done showering wisdom on your scrawny white ass."

*****

By day's end Service concluded that Dotz was a typical observer, seeing only the most obvious things and missing even some of those. But in one particular area his observations had been excellent and potentially significant.

Once they were out on the high ground, Service walked Dotz through his days with the Drazels, step by step, and Dotz answered quietly and confidently, sometimes closing his eyes and pausing before answering.

He would say things like, "She had the device pointed *that* direction."

"What was the position of her legs?" Service would counter.

"Her legs?"

"Legs, the things our feet are connected to. Right leg, left leg, was one forward and if so, which one. Were they close together or spread out. Make the picture in your mind. It's there. You just got to pull it up out of the server."

In this way he began to educate the boy on how to anticipate what information they were after, and Dotz responded nicely. The boy's patience in being the focus of so many questions was remarkable. Service doubted he would have been as patient, given a reversal in roles.

Up on the higher land Dotz showed them where the one woman had set up "the one with the viewfinder thingey."

"A transit?"

"No idea, man. Could have been a telescope or a camera from where I stood."

"One woman with the device is there, and where's her partner?"

Dotz pointed. "Around that hump."

They were, according to the young man, standing where the woman with the device had been standing. "She wouldn't be able to hear her partner from here," Service said. "What about her legs and body position relative to the device?"

"The one with the big thingey had her left leg forward and right leg back, I think, but then they were looking up again," Dotz said. "And I don't really remember anything except that."

Service squinted and rubbed his eye. "You said she was looking up . . . *again*."

"Right," Dotz said.

"*Again*, that means this was not the first time."

"Right, it wasn't."

"Why is it we haven't heard about a first time before the again?"

"I didn't tell you they were looking up?"

"You didn't. So when was the first time?" Service asked.

"Every time the plane buzzed them."

Service felt almost flustered. "There was a *plane*?"

"It kept like, buzzing over, you know?"

"How many times?" Treebone asked.

Dotz puffed up his cheeks. "Eight, ten, twelve times, I didn't count, you know? I didn't write it down or nothing."

"You didn't think the plane flying over was relevant?" Service asked.

"Is it?" the boy asked.

Treebone said calmly, "Everything you see, including things you didn't expect to see, is relevant until you evaluate it and determine how it fits."

"But it was in the air and we were on the ground," Dotz said, his voice quavering.

Service thought, a typical response for witnesses, who rarely could think beyond a single item, observation as horizon. Go easy on the boy.

Service said, "Take a deep breath, Ty. Are you sure they looked up at the plane?"

Dotz said, "Yes, for sure."

"Each time?" Service asked. "Each time it flew by?"

"Yes," Dotz answered.

Service pressed on. "Where did this plane come from and where did it go?"

"I don't know where it went, because we were down here and it was up there, you know, like in the air?"

"Right, can you show me the directions it came from and went away toward. Pretend your hand is the airplane," Service said.

The boy crooked his hand like a bird's head and looked at Service for approval.

"That's good, now show me the first pass, if you remember it."

"Remember just fine. It scared the shit out of me." The boy reached up and zoomed his hand from one direction to what appeared to be its antipodal point—the exact opposite side of where it first appeared.

"Thanks, good job. How long did these passes take place?"

"Roughly an hour? Yeah, an hour. Seemed like a long time. I kept thinking, what's this guy want?"

"Can you describe the aircraft?"

"White," the boy said decisively. "Two engines, and the engines, they like made a high-pitched whine, you know, like some sort of phase shifter for a guitar that goes too far? Man, the plane, it was *really* fast. And, oh yeah, it was skinny?"

"Are you asking me if it was skinny or describing the plane?" Service said.

"No?" Dotz said. "It was really skinny from the cockpit back?"

Talking to young people was like listening to staggering serial doubt. Every damn sentence ended in a limp-wristed question mark, like they weren't sure of shit.

"All right, one vertical stabilizer or two?"

Dotz tilted his head like a curious dog.

Service amended his question, "One tail or two?"

"One," the boy said.

"Doing good," Service said. "Two engines, whining sound, really fast, and the skinny aircraft is white with a single vertical stabilizer. What were its other markings?"

"I didn't see any?"

"Nothing?"

Dotz shook his head. "Maybe it was moving too fast? You couldn't hear the damn thing coming until it flashed over you."

Treebone said, "So they look up, the two women do, at every pass. They do anything else?"

"Not until the last pass, and then the woman standing here looked up and waved, like this." Dotz showed them. "It was like magic, man. I couldn't hear the thing, but she did."

"What do you think the wave meant?" Service asked. All of this information today had not been mentioned before, or even hinted at. He wondered how much more the kid had buried in his head.

"Goodbye?" Dotz offered weakly. "I mean, I guess she was waving goodbye."

"After how many flyovers?"

"Like I said. Ten or twelve, I'd guess."

Treebone said, "She waved goodbye, why you think she did that?"

"I don't know," Dotz said.

"Tyrus," Treebone said quietly. "What were the ladies wearing for headgear?"

The boy puffed his cheeks and shrugged. "Like hats, you know?"

"What was *your* headgear?" Service asked.

"My blue Tigers ball cap."

"Were the women wearing ball caps?"

"I'm trying to remember."

"You're doing great," Treebone said.

"Well, they had bills like ball caps, but they also looked like mad bomber hats, except the flaps were like, you know, rounded?"

Service used his boot to clear a patch in the dirt and handed a stick to the boy. "Draw one of their hats."

The resulting diagram was crude and shaky and sort of looked like a mad bomber hat, but something was off, and Service had to study it for a while, until he realized what was bothering him. There was a horizontal line across the bottom of the face. "What's that line, Ty?" Service pointed.

"I don't know," Dotz said.

"How close did you get to the woman who was standing here?" Treebone asked.

"Sixty yards, maybe fifty? I was over there." Dotz pointed at a thick grove of straight paper birch trees.

"That's close for recon," Treebone said. "You usin' binos?"

Dotz tapped his backpack. "Yah, but they're not so good?"

Service ignored the comment. "Did you have binos on the women when the plane came over?"

"Not the first time, or the second. Shook me up too much. After that, yah, on some of the passes?"

"Binos on the women when the plane wasn't around?"

"Sometimes?"

"Did anything catch your attention?" Service asked him.

"With which one? Crazy Lady or the other one?"

Service asked, "Crazy Lady?"

"She kept talking to herself?" Dotz said.

She did. "How'd you know?"

"I saw her when I had the binos on her."

Treebone said, "Okay, take five and smoke 'em if you got 'em."

"I don't smoke," Dotz said.

"Figure of speech," Treebone said. "Course you don't. Suck a handful of wheat germ instead . . . and don't be so damn self-righteous."

"I have chocolate chip Clif bars, not wheat germ."

"Good for you, chocolate chips'll make you fat and plug your arteries. On second thought, eat two. You need the calories, and you're too damn young to worry about plugged arteries."

Service looked around and found Allerdyce sitting Indian style on the lip of the entrance to the lower cave with a grave look on his face.

"Planning a spelunking expedition?"

"No way," Allerdyce said, then unfolded and popped to his feet with the agility of a ten-year-old.

"We're saddling up. Walk with Dotz and try not to creep him out. He's been a big help."

"I don't creep out nobody."

Service laughed softly and walked beside Treebone on the way out. Halfway along he had a thought and stopped. "Ty?"

The boy turned back to him and Service pulled out a pad and a pencil. He drew a small x and gave him the pad and pencil. "That little x is you," he said. "Draw lines to show us the angle of each flyover, put an arrow point on each line for directions."

"I don't remember all of them."

"Do your best."

The boy made seven lines. Service said, "You think there were ten or twelve passes?"

"I think so, but the lines there are pretty much the tracks they followed, I think."

No question mark this time. Service took the pad and returned it to his pocket.

"That what you wanted?" Dotz asked.

"Perfect."

"What's it mean?"

"Won't know until I look later. It might mean nothing."

They resumed the hike. Service said to Treebone, "Radios between aircraft and ground, you think?"

"Sounds likely. And with each other."

"My thought too."

Tree said, "Unmarked aircraft is the outlier here. What're the chances of that?"

"Not likely, but we can't rule out that under some circumstances it might be copacetic. We'll have to check it out. But whatever happens, we've got to get an ID on make and model."

"Could take a lot of time." Treebone said.

"Time is all we have—for the moment," Service told his friend, but his mind was on the Drazel women asking Treebone about limestone formations at his camp, and caves. Do they know there are two caves here, or just the upper one? Surely some people know about that one. Just doesn't seem possible they could know about the lower cave system, so this is most likely about diamonds, not artifacts. If true, the questions the women asked Tree about caves and sinkholes on his property were not significant.

Service recalled the last time he had dealt with diamonds in the U.P.; a Huey had been used to haul around a spheroid magnometer to take readings that computers could interpret as various natural resources. But there was no ball hanging under this fast-moving aircraft. Something's different here.

Treebone said, "Good thing your brain's not fried from old age. You smelling some deep shit in all this?"

Service nodded. "Maybe."

Back at the Slippery Creek Camp, Service told Dotz, "Do us all a favor and forget any of this happened. If a story develops, you will get the exclusive, only you."

"No problem," Dotz said, grinning. "And thanks, guys."

What the . . . ? "Okay Ty, thanks. If you think of anything else, no matter how trivial, call me."

Dotz walked ten feet away, stopped and turned, said, "How could I forget, *jousting*!"

"Jousting?" Service repeated the word.

"Yah, knights of old and lances and shit like that?"

"You've lost me Ty."

Dotz looked burdened. "Wait, wait: hummingbirds."

"Hummingbirds and jousting?"

"The airplane, man. The bird, that thingey on its nose. Dotz picked up a stick, walked to the side of the driveway where there was dirt, and drew a crude picture.

"Twin-engine hummingbird," Service said. "Unique."

"Yessir, sorry I forgot that part."

"The aircraft had a long proboscis like your drawing?"

"Like a big hummingbird but with a thingey on the end."

"A thingey on the end?"

"Like a ball or a bulb or something, ya know?"

"Draw it," Service said, and the boy did, but neither he nor Treebone could work out what the boy was trying to tell them. How do you tell a kid that every fact could be critical and you can't ever predict which fact will unlock the rest.

"Can I go now?"

"Sure," Service said. "Thanks, we'll be in touch."

"Wish I could have done more."

"This is a start, and you'll get your chance for more. Investigations take time."

Allerdyce cackled at the boy. "Now don't go wear seff out wit' dat Balloons gal youse got."

"You are a sick and disgusting old man," Dotz said, stomping away.

Allerdyce looked at his companions. "What I say?"

Service shook his head. "I'm hungry."

Allerdyce walked over to the side of the driveway. "Who draw dat pitcher in dirt?"

"Dotz," Treebone said.

"Mine-diggy compys use da plane like dat pitcher with long nose," Allerdyce said.

"Mine-diggy compys?" Service said. "Mining companies?"

"Yah, dose make da mines deep down in da grounds."

"You know this how?"

"I seen fly up, down Menominee."

"The county or the river?"

"River."

"And you determined this thing was from a mine-diggy company?"

"Ast my first cousin So-So. He work down airport Menominee. He say dere guys down dere, looking glow-rocks and got plane dere."

Treebone said, "Glow-rocks, as in uranium?"

Allerdyce laughed and wagged a finger. "Yah, Uranus, glow-rock."

PART III: BEYOND BOUNDARIES

CHAPTER 31

Slippery Creek Camp

Early in the morning, Treebone had run over to St. Ignace to fetch his camp ownership documents, in case they had to meet with the Drazel Sisters. He returned mid-afternoon spitting and frustrated.

Treebone said, "Hey old man, come look at these photos." He showed the old poacher the photos from his phone.

Allerdyce looked, held up his chin, said, "Seen dem girlies down Skeeto when all dis crap start, hey."

Treebone said, "But Dotz says he saw different women, not the ones you guys saw, or the ones I met in Ford River, so what the hell is going on?"

Service said, "We're missing something."

"Sherlock Holmes," Treebone said.

Service said, "The women will be identified as we move on. Right now we need to verify Limpy's claim on the aircraft." He looked at Allerdyce. "Can you talk to your cousin in Menominee, get more information? If there's a mine exploration company over there, what's its name and does it have a plane hangered somewhere near there, or across the river in Wisconsin?"

"Got no wheels," Allerdyce said. At some point the old man's truck had ended up back at his camp compound in southwestern Marquette County and he had been riding with Service since then.

"Use the telephone," Tree said.

"Can't see man's eyes on phone."

"Use Skype," Treebone said.

"Dere ain't no eyes up in sky," Allerdyce said. "What wrong wit' youses?"

"You expecting your kin to lie if you can't look him in the eye?" Treebone asked, continuing to press.

"Eve'body lie sometime, cover ass, whatever."

Treebone flipped his truck keys to the old violator. "Bring it back in the same shape you drive it away."

Allerdyce chuckled and was gone.

Tree watched the truck leave the camp, said, "At least he didn't spin my skins."

"It's a long road to Menominee," Service teased his friend.

"Don't remind me. I ever scratch that truck, Kalina will skin *me*."

"I thought it was *your* truck?"

"On paper, on paper. Kalina assumes moral ownership over all in the domain."

Service poured coffee for them. "Let's call Dotz and tell him we want to see him here."

Service checked his watch. Friday would still be in the office if she was not out on a case or wrapped up in some paper jungle.

She answered right away and greeted him with "Has your cell phone been dead?"

"No, why?"

"Coulda fooled me. Where are the Three Musketeers *now*?"

"Tree and I are at camp and Limpy left a little while ago for Menominee."

"Fun aside, my dear," she said. "There's a lot of scuttlebutt on the float. Bozian, you, Lori, DNR management changes, nothing specific, but the one constant in whatever comes in is you and Lori's increasing involvement."

"How's our kid?"

"Shitstorm hovering in the sky and you want to talk about Shigun?"

"Can't do anything about the weather. But then neither can paid weather forecasters."

She laughed. "Rumor mill suggests that you alone are the human equivalent of political climate change."

"Not me. What climate change?"

"People believe what they want, come down with the conspiracy virus, think they're all Nostradamus, and they tend to follow whoever they think is going along the path they want to be on."

"I lead no one," he said.

She tsk-tsked him. "Word is out you have a shiny new badge," she said.

"Law enforcement is a sieve with secrets," he told her.

"Your secret's safe with me."

"It's not you I worry about," he said, "but the US Attorney's office, I've got to say I have doubts."

"Think how they must feel having badged you. By the way, Shigun misses his big guy."

"He *said* that?"

"No, but I know he's thinking it."

"You can't *know*."

"Sure I can. Mothers know everything about their kids. This mama also knows you need to find some time for a home visit," she said.

"Conjugally speaking?"

"You're such a romantic, Service. We're not married. Remember?"

"I forgot."

Friday laughed. "Liar, liar, yah conjugal, connubial, call it what you want."

"Probably overdue," he said.

"Seriously, how much longer is this dance gonna go on?"

"No clue yet. I wish I knew."

"Me too," she said. "My best to the boys."

"We're hardly that," Service said.

"Do you well to keep that in mind before you guys try to act like eighteen-year-olds, Big Guy. I'll hug Shigun for you."

"Keep your ear to the ground for more drums."

"Clear, Kemo Sabe."

Treebone said, "If cops needed wives, the agencies ought to be the ones issuing them."

"She's not my wife," Service said.

"Why not?"

He had no answer, had asked himself the same question many times.

*****

Dotz rolled in just in time for dinner: sweet citrus-marinated tofu on a bed of lettuce, peas and corn on the side, with pure black wild rice.

"Come in and grab a seat, kid," Treebone greeted the boy. "Them shiny things 'longside the plate are called eating utensils. Do not use yours like shovels. It will detract from your image and damage your chances of winning fair lady."

"You twenty-one yet?" Service asked the boy.

"I could lie."

"Great, you want red wine or tap water."

"Those are the only two choices?"

"No," Tree said. "You can select nothing."

"Red wine," Dotz said. "Why am I here?"

"To share; see, we're breaking bread," Service said. "It's symbolic."

"I don't see bread," the boy said.

"Don't be literal, Dotz," Treebone carped. "Try the wine."

Dotz took a sip.

Service said, "You followed me for quite a while before I tricked you out into the bush."

"What's your point?"

"Why?"

"The rumors about you being suspended and wondering if maybe the DNR was hiding some sort of scandal."

"Rumors heard where?"

"A tip, not exactly a rumor," Dotz admitted.

"Tip from what source?"

"A journalist isn't obligated to reveal sources."

"I'm talking about *you*, not some theoretical scribbler."

"I'm not talking," Dotz said.

Service said, "Then eat, the food's getting cold."

"You've looked at photos of four Drazel women, two that Tree took in their office and others from another source, and you've not seen any of those four, correct?"

"I guess."

Service got up from the table and dialed Fellow Marthesdottir.

She said, "I've seen you guys coming out of the Mosquito. You and Tree and Dotz, and now Allerdyce is gone in Treebone's truck."

This was jarring. "You've got cameras *here*?"

"No, I'm a good guesser."

"Hardly," he said. "You've expanded your surveillance."

"Not really," she said. "Allerdyce called, he's on the way over here."

Service shook his head and cupped the phone, told Treebone. "Limpy took your truck for a bootie call."

Treebone sputtered, "That better not take place *inside* my baby."

Service noticed that Dotz had refilled his wine glass. "What is it with old farts and sex? Ain't no big thing, sayin'?"

Treebone said, "Shut your mouth, Dotz."

Service said to Marthesdottir, "We're in a bit of a quandary. Could Drazel employ more women than the two we first met?"

"Could and do. You haven't called or I would have updated you."

"Tell me now."

"I've indentified six potential employees, all female. Not by name, only by faces."

"All blond?"

"That too. At least on the surface."

"All six in Ford River?"

"They appear to rotate from downstate. I've got bridge pix verifications. Plates are all Drazel trucks, nothing personal. Names I can get, I suppose, but this will take some more time."

"Are any of them licensed surveyors?"

"Unanswerable until I have actual identities," she said, "but that doesn't mean they can't work."

He said, "The way we heard it, if unlicensed personnel do survey work they have to do it under direct supervision of a licensed professional. So far, we've seen only them in the field. Maybe one of them is actually a licensed surveyor. If so, it would be helpful to know which one and her name. Also, does Drazel have an aircraft for exploration and geosurvey work?"

"What kind of a plane?" she asked. "I confess, all cars and planes look pretty much alike to me."

"One source says it looks like a hummingbird."

"Hah," she said. "That's interesting. Want me to dig?"

"With the greatest dispatch. Make, model, registration, owner, tail number, where hangered, crew names, everything you can get, and flight plans and local jobs if any of that information is findable."

"On it," she said.

Service said, "Tell Allerdyce to never mind on Menominee, explain what you're doing and tell him there's no need for him to drive all the way down there."

"You know he'll still do what he thinks he should do."

"I know, but tell him."

"Don't hang up before I finish," Marthesdottir said. "Dotz's father is *not* part of the Kalleskevich-Bozian thing. He was mostly a father in name only. He was on the boy's periphery, but there was some argument or disagreement and a parting of the ways."

Service said, "The father's dead, right? So he was part of it, but isn't now? That's what happens when you're dead."

"It's the boy's grandfather, not his father. Yes, the dad's dead, and I've dug out more information on that. He ate a .357 mag after he term-limited out. Tyrus found him."

Service stared at the boy. Why had they not heard this before now? "Thanks, Fellow."

"Yah, later. I have company. Listen I won't be talking to you until tomorrow because, well, my brain gets kinda addled in the slipstream, if you know what I mean."

After he hung up, Service turned to Dotz and said, "Ty, we're really sorry about your dad, but we have to ask about him."

The boy said, "Don't be sorry. He was only my biological father. Everything except family was important to him."

"You don't have to answer this. You found him?"

"And his note."

"He left a note? Can I ask what it said?"

Dotz looked Service in the eye. "It said, 'Messy, isn't it.'"

The boy drained and refilled his glass. And pulled the wine bottle closer.

"You're bunking here tonight, Dotz," Treebone said.

Dotz took another swig of wine and said, "Grandpa gave me the tip on you being suspended and the state maybe hiding some sort of scandal. I needed a story and this sounded pretty interesting, the kind of thing that could get me noticed. So I start looking around and I ran into the Drazel women. So what's with the Drazel Sisters and their interest in the Mosquito? They're not tourists and they're not on any government contract I can find, and I can't even find their company registered and licensed with the state."

Service said, "We've been down the same roads. We'll tell you what we know, but this is deep background and meant only to help you understand. If this turns into a story, then we'll discuss attribution and all that stuff."

Service paused and then asked, "You pissed at your old man?"

"Very," Dotz said. "He was a loser."

"It will pass," Service said. The longer he lived, the more he found out about his own father, and the more he had to alter his negative opinion of the man.

Dotz didn't reply.

"What about your grandfather?" Service asked.

Dotz said, "You mean, His Royal Majassnasty?"

"Problems with dad *and* grandad?"

"All my grandfather wants is greatness bestowed on his name. He feels ignored. A former governor promised to get a state park renamed for him if he helped him with his legislative agenda, which he did, but that governor's gone and no state park."

This had to be Bozian. "Which governor?"

"Sam," the boy said. "I've known him since I was little. Apparently everything was on track until my dad ate a bullet and Sam told grandad the deal was off, that they could not risk a scandal of the name given the suicide."

"Now my grandfather is despondent and depressed and moping around and mumbling to himself, stuff like, 'After all the shit I did for that son of a bitch and his toadies.'"

Service had no idea of the load the boy was carrying and decided to leave him alone for the moment. One fact gleaned: The key link here is Dotz's grandfather, not his late father, and the boy just revealed that the tip on my suspension came from his granddad, which seems to throw the link toward Bozian.

Fellow Marthesdottir called, and Service stared at his plate and wondered if he was ever going to get to eat. "Yah?"

"My mind's a tad-bit flummoxed. I've been talking to M every day. She said I should tell you that Kalleskevich's lawyers are pushing hard for a court hearing."

"Court, not the Department of Environmental Quality?"

"Title issues need to be cleared in court before he can ask the DEQ for permits."

"Does M think there's a case?"

"She's not sure yet, and she has her lawyers looking into it. I gotta go, there's a pest in my house!"

Service looked at Tree. "Limpy's there."

"I don't want no more details," Tree said.

CHAPTER 32

Slippery Creek Camp

Grady Service had extensive experience in criminal courts. The prospect of court dealings in this situation bothered him because it was in a sea of case law he knew nothing about. Despite that, any courtroom tended to unnerve him. Over the decades he had come to understand that while precedent in fish and game law was long and deep and tended toward cut and dry, laws governing mineral rights were not just different, but based on what the lawyer O'Halloran had told them, essentially unknown. This suggested any court case would be a crap shoot, above and beyond what it normally was. Under normal conditions he had learned that the behavior of defendants, witnesses, experts, cops, lawyers, judges, and juries was largely unpredictable even in cases that theoretically should have been open and shut. And now this case, which appeared to be even more unpredictable.

There had been a time in his career when he pinched a man named Clayband with two illegal deer. He had watched the deer be shot and killed, had watched the suspect gut them, and had arrested the man red-handed. A confession had been forthcoming, with his excuse boiling down to "because everybody else does it."

The t's were crossed that time, the i's dotted, the paperwork in perfect shape. Just before the trial began the ADA had said to him, "No sweat. We'll be out of here in ten minutes." Then came the curveball.

The prosecutor had him on the stand as the arresting officer, and the defense attorney was pecking for grounds for dismissal. Judge Stimac, who had a longtime hard-on for game wardens, sat listening with obvious impatience. When the judge couldn't take it anymore, he said to the defense attorney, "Excuse me for butting in, counselor, but Officer Service, how many illegal deer cases have you made in your career?"

"Sorry, your honor, I don't know and I doubt the department maintains such numbers. A lot is the best I can do for an answer."

"A lot, you say?"

"Yes, Your Honor."

"With each case in that 'a lot,' what was the penalty?"

Why the hell was he asking this? It was a matter of statute passed by the state legislature and in force forever. "Statutorily, Your Honor, it's a mandatory year in jail and a thousand dollars for restitution to the state, court costs at the judge's discretion, and the loss of hunting privileges for the individual for at least one year, but typically two years or more."

Stimac squinted, grinned, then sat back and joined his hands behind his head. "Tell you what, Officer Service, if you can provide the court with a detailed cost accounting of how the state establishes one thousand dollars as the price of restitution for one miserable whitetail deer, of which we have millions of the nuisances chewing their way through the state—you do that, and then I shall direct a verdict of guilty and we'll be done with this folderol over a miserable pest. Your turn, Officer."

How the fuck was he supposed to know something he had no involvement in establishing. It was a calculation made decades before. "Your Honor, if we *could* have a short recess, I'm sure I can provide the information you seek."

"No good, Officer, no good, unh-unh. I want your explanation and I want it now. You are the arresting officer, you accumulated evidence for the case, and surely you must think about the precise effect and implications of all your work on the citizens you collar."

"Your Honor, I also represent the citizens. It is their representatives who make these laws, and perhaps if you directed your question to the legislature on behalf of the citizens, an answer would be forthcoming."

The judge glared at him. "Nice try, Service. Case dismissed." He hammered his gavel down.

"Objection," the assistant prosecuting attorney yelped weakly.

"I imagine you do," Judge Stimac said. "Overruled." The judge then turned to the defendant. "Mr. Claybank, the next time you get the itch to shine a deer, you will do well to understand that this court will focus on the untoward practice of discharging firearms at night and take appropriate action. I don't condone anything you've done, sir, none of it, but I expect game wardens upholding state laws to understand the reasons they are charged with the job they are doing, for all facets of the law, and I expect them to be able to explain such rationales to citizens such as you, or jurists such as me."

The gavel came down again. All stood—including the judge, who sashayed to his chambers.

A week or so later the same APA called him while he was on patrol. "Apparently, Judge Stimac had a brother who was just pinched for shining after shooting seven deer that were snacking on his soybeans."

"Wish we'd have known that coming in."

"Would it have made a difference?"

Service had no answer.

Treebone poured coffee and sat down across the table from his old friend and comrade. They had heard last night that some sort of preliminary hearing was on the docket for today in Lansing, something to do with the case, but there had been no details. Tree said, "We heading south to sit in the peanut gallery or are we gone sit tight?"

Service sighed. "Fish and game law I'm comfortable with. Real estate resource ownership rights, I know less than zero. We'll get a transcript. In any event this is just a hearing to set a date for the actual hearing, so it's no biggie."

"Not afraid you'll be blindsided?"

"They can blindside us if we're there or here. Our presence is irrelevant. The lawyers have to lead on this and we have to follow as best we can."

"There are good lawyers and bad," Treebone said.

"We've seen both extremes," Service said. "The space between those extremes is pretty thin."

"I hate the waiting shit," Treebone said.

*****

Chief Eddie Waco called later that afternoon. "Lis was at the hearing," he told Service. Lis was Captain Lisette McKower, Service's longtime friend and onetime partner.

"And?"

"The claimants tried to present evidence purportedly to demonstrate inarguable rights to said parcels in the Mosquito. But the judge told him to not be in a hurry, that there's a process in place and the judge intends to follow said process step by step until he reaches the endpoint."

"So?"

"Bing-bang, no quick on-the-spot decision, a lucky and fortuitous start for our side. The judge did in fact take a fast recess and review evidence in his chambers, but when he came back to the courtroom he set the date for the actual hearing, told the claimants their evidence seemed interesting."

"When's the actual hearing?"

"Six weeks from today. Claimants wanted two weeks. Judge countered with one month, and when the claimants' attorney tried for three weeks, the judge set the date at six weeks. You get your new badge?"

"I'm all set."

"Good. I don't know what to tell you, Grady, but you've got six weeks to birddog this thing and come up with evidence the case needs. If the judge rules for the claimants, our own attorneys say that will be that, end of game. Without state records to counter the claim, they'll have no options."

"If the claim is bogus and bullshit and the judge buys it, that's all she wrote?"

"About the size of it," Waco said.

"Even if it's bullshit?"

"It won't be bullshit if the judge buys it."

"This is not right. Justice should mean right or wrong."

Eddie Waco said, "You know better, my friend. All justice requires is a decision, nothing more and nothing less. The captain will give you a bump tomorrow, and she'll make sure you get a transcript of todays' proceedings."

"Thanks, Chief."

"Grady," Waco continued, "I never met a man with more sand than you, and now's the time to let loose on the opposition. Most people stumble through life and never even see an opponent of your strength, much less have to go head to head with one. It's time for you to attack, Grady. Over the top and all out."

Sand and grit? Meaningless tripe from his chief and friend, but all said with the best of intentions, which he appreciated. "What I need, Eddie, is something that undoes bad paper—scissors or a damn rock, I can never remember which one."

"Scissors cuts paper," the DNR law enforcement chief said. "You've got six weeks. Use it all."

Treebone looked at his friend. "We been hosed?"

"It don't mean nothing." Service said. This phrase had arisen among combat troops in Vietnam and come home with them, a statement that came from when they were looking at the worst possible consequences and circumstances. He had never understood the logic of the words, but the emotional load in it was clear: Get the job done, no matter what, no matter how. Service said, "Let's get us some beers. Where the hell is Allerdyce?"

"Said he had some stuff to take care of."

"You loan him your truck again?" Service asked with a sneer.

"Me and my truck had our turn, Bro. I loaned him your truck."

Service needed something else to focus on, so he called Chippewa County Undersheriff Hawkins Shoebear. "Hawk, Service."

"Been a long time," the undersheriff said.

"How it is. You know a guy over your way goes by Paint?"

"Sure do, our winnable warrior with no war. Not a bad kid, good family, but his thinking's mud and he hangs with shit birds."

"I need him picked up."

"Charges?"

"Person of interest in an aggravated assault. There's no warrant. He and a pal beat up an old man. We already talked to the other perp and he admits to it, but we need some time with Paint."

"That's our Paint, and no doubt his partner was that dumb-ass Polish Prince. Glad to help. We'll yell at you when we have him. It'll be my boys or, more likely, the Bay Mills crew."

Tribal cops? Hmm. "Okay, Hawk. I owe you one."

CHAPTER 33

Negaunee

MARQUETTE COUNTY

Allerdyce and Treebone dropped him at the state police post and headed to Econofoods in Marquette to shop for groceries. Allerdyce had not come back to camp until late last night and had little to say about where he had been or what he had been up to. Friday's boss, Lieutenant L'Lonnie de Leon, met Service at the entrance to the state police office and stuck out her tiny toy hand.

"What's that for, El Tee?" he said, shaking hands with her. She was five-four, petite, and bright-eyed, with the voice of a finch.

"For fighting the good fight."

"Which fight would that be?" It was unlike the lieutenant to engage in personal chitchat. De Leon was usually about business and only business.

"Your suspension, the gang rush to push you out the door; the US Attorney gambit is a great thing and a tremendous vote of confidence in the kind of officer you are. Don't let the bastards wear you down, Service. We're all behind you, two hundred percent."

Should I thank her, kiss her, hug her, or ignore her and play dumb? She was fairly new, had been sent up from Below the Bridge to take the post commander job and had no real knowledge of the U.P. or its ways yet. How much does she really know? She's stringing together a bunch of things on what, inside knowledge, instinct? Friday as her source? Not a chance there. She'd die in torture before disclosing anything to anyone. "Thanks, El Tee."

"Detective Friday's over to Fletch's," the post commander said.

Fletch was Sergeant Egon Arrington, his nickname from his passion for archery, especially hunting deer with bow and arrow. If Tuesday was with Fletch, they'd be close to coffee, because Fletch was a major caffeine addict who slugged full *cafento* night and day and was always wired because of it. Fletch had once been a great road cop along the Chicago-Detroit corridor, and then as road sergeant, but one day he looked at his workload and odds down there and used his seniority to transfer Above the Bridge, where trooper duty was a piece of cake relative to the risks on downstate interstates.

Ironically, Arrington had grown up in Pickford in the eastern Upper Peninsula and, unlike most native Yoopers, chose to stay Below the Bridge when he left the academy. He had been a great mentor to young troopers.

Service saw Friday smile when she saw him coming. "Look what came in from the cold," she greeted him.

"It's spring, and not so cold," he said, and Fletch laughed.

"You're not exactly in either, are you bud?" she whispered when she leaned close to him.

Arrington handed him a cup of coffee and made for the door. "I'm sure you two have much to talk about. The room is yours. Take no prisoners, Grady." The sergeant gave a sharp fist pump and was gone.

"Your El Tee met me outside. She was positively gushy, even gave me sort of a half-time pep talk, I think. I'm not sure what was in or on her mind. Now Fletch's 'take no prisoners'? What the hell does that *mean*?"

"Word's spreading around Michigan that the state is trying to force you out and that the Feds have intervened in your behalf."

"You know it's not quite like that."

"How was it Mark Twain used to put it? People like stories with stretchers. Perceptions, Grady. The world's social fuel is half-fact and seven-tenths rumor."

"That's more than a hundred percent."

"Ain't that something," she said, smiling.

"Someone downstate has the blabs."

"Bozian pigeonholed me in St. Ignace."

"That's one of the big logs on the rumor fire."

The Michigan State Police community of sworn officers on active duty as well as retired officers was statewide, but small and tight. Active duty or retired, Troops kept track of and supported each other, like Marines. You were on active duty for twenty-five or thirty years, but you were a Troop for life, just like COs in the old days, his old man's day. Nowadays, with COs, he was no longer certain of similar solidarity. He suspected the seeds were there, but emerging from the ground was yet to be seen.

"Surprised to see you," she said. "Consider yourself hugged."

"We could close the conference room door," he joked. "Fletch said the room is ours."

"Fletch says a lot of things," she said, and flicked her eyes left where Service saw a surveillance camera.

"New toys?"

"Directives from East Lansing, for every room here. Some legislator got it in her mind that if cop cars need cams and street cops need body cams, offices should have cams too. She pushed a bill through and the governor signed it and, voila, we now have statewide state police CCTV, just like we're our own big lawless city."

"Politicians," he muttered.

She said, "Are you here to make a big happy announcement that you're coming home so that we can resume our special flavor of family life?"

"I wish."

"That means no," she said.

"We're moving around a lot," Service said. "Do these cameras record everything?"

She said, "I bet my man needs him a smoke."

They walked outside to her car. He went to light a cigarette and she rolled her eyes and said, "What I said was to get us outside so we'd have some privacy, not so you'd have a damn cigarette."

"Good to know," he said and brought her up to date, Fellow Marthesdottir, M, Kalleskevich, Clearcut, the current governor, the MWT, Ty Dotz, the Drazel Sisters, all of it, concluding with the Prince and Paint beating up Allerdyce. Friday, as she always did, listened attentively until he was finished. He included diamonds and the marvelous cave artifacts. He confessed to her that he had not quite leveled with the US Attorney when the questions of NAGPRA notification came up.

Treebone and Allerdyce drove into the lot and parked beside Friday's vehicle.

"Lovebirds," Treebone said when he let down his window. "Should we let you two alone for a few?"

"A thoughtful gesture," Friday said with a smile, "but we are adults in full control of our animal urges."

"Damn shame," Treebone said.

Friday looked in the truck window at Allerdyce. "Looks like they gave it to you pretty good," she said, "but it's statistically impossible to uglify past baseline."

Allerdyce grinned. Treebone smirked.

"Are you guys going to find the thugs who pounded Allerdyce?" she added. "They need some education."

This surprised him. "You don't especially like Allerdyce."

"True, I especially don't like him, but that doesn't mean I want his ass kicked by jerks trying to use him to get to you."

"We'll be attending to that forthwith. I stopped to tell you we're headed to the Soo to find Jerk No. Two when we leave here."

"Damn," she said, "and here I thought you came for a smooch and a hug. Listen to me, Grady, this whole thing has you playing very close to the edge, and it makes me uncomfortable for you and for us, especially this thing with the US Attorney."

"I know, I know, but if what we know becomes public, that's the end of the Mosquito."

"Lying to the US Attorney can be the end of you, too."

"I didn't lie," he said. "Exactly. I can live with my conscience." So far.

"All right," she said with a reedy voice. "I guess you've gotta do what you've gotta do. Whatever happens," she added with a deep sigh, "I'm with you."

What had he done to deserve her? "Thanks," he said, and they embraced, and he closed his eyes and decided maybe retirement and more of this might beat the hell out of all the stuff he was juggling now.

"Our kid and dog send their love."

"Not the cat?"

"That cat is about hate—and food." She took hold of his elbows and held them. "Tell me this thing *will* end."

He nodded.

"Say it," Friday said.

"It will," he said.

"Will what?"

"End."

"Good boy, give us another big smooch."

"You're working."

"Big whoop," she said, pursing her lips.

"The guys are watching."

"Oh no, heavens no, the boys!" She looked at Treebone's truck and said, "Turn your heads, you animals!"She kissed him and whispered, "You're not the only hardhead in this family. Now beat it and go earn your paycheck while you still have one."

"I don't have one," he said. "Do I?"

"Pretend you do; all money's an illusion and theoretical concept—unlike sex, which is real and needed way more than money."

CHAPTER 34

Bay Mills

CHIPPEWA COUNTY

Undersheriff Hawkins Shoebear called as they were climbing up the steep hill south of Munising. "We've got your subject out in Bay Mills."

"He say anything?"

"Tribals picked him up and you know how that game goes, both sides posturing for whatever they posture for. I'm sure he knows better than to mouth off to them, since they are a sovereign country and have their own notions. They've got him on ice, no hurry. Want to grab a bite while you're over here?"

Should they take time for a social lunch? Service wondered. It was often important in cementing relationships between police agencies. "Rain check on chow, we're on a tight timeline."

"Rain check," his colleague agreed. "But let's not forget. Be good to jaw a bit."

Service tried to remember the Bay Mills village layout. "The jail's on West Lakeshore?"

"That's the one. Call if you need anything."

How was it that most local and regional state law enforcement could get along just fine, but the Feds seemed to find it impossible. Eight years after 9/11 and he was still hearing disturbing stories about silos and self-serving bureaucratic behaviors. *Not your problem. Keep your mind on your own problems.*

"Dere still good sin-mans in MacMillan?" Allerdyce asked as they hit the Seney Stretch coming out of Shingleton.

Treebone said, "Closed a long time, family health issues, flu in the family, divorce, some bullshit excuse to save face, who knows why for sure."

"That kind of flu causes all kind of nasty," Service said. "Kind of stuff you don't see till it slaps you up side the head."

Tree said, "Kalina leave me, she reach for nukes on way out. When say till death do us part, she got in her mind maybe she'll be doing the killing on the other end."

"Could use Ind'in frybread," Allerdyce said. "Put da sin-mans on dose too, squooch out some horny, nice." He smacked his lips.

"Horny?" Treebone asked.

"Wah, horny from butts and beets."

"Horny comes from beets?" Good god, talking to the man was like trying to connect with a Martian.

"Horn-y, not horny, you no listen good your problem," Allerdyce complained.

"Button it, you two. Allerdyce, you may have to swear charges to get this guy to talk."

"I can do dat?"

"You bet."

"Dat be new, me, make charge against udders. I work t'other end of dat most my life. I tink I like dis change."

Allerdyce had his mask perfect. Who'd think such a simple fool would be the one-man scourge he had been for so long. "Don't get used to it," Service told him.

The old man frowned. "Youse don't t'ink I changed?"

"Never say never."

"What dat means dat never never?"

Service said, "I believe you've changed. But I'm still trying to figure out your angle and how long all this may last."

"Last forever."

Service shrugged, turned his mind to Gerard "Paint" Angevin. Thaddeus Zyzwyzcky was a dumb ass, much to his old man's obvious chagrin, and who could blame him. Big Z had been a lifelong poster boy for white hats, and Service wondered which of the two boys, Paint or Thad, was hardcore and which was the lesser of the two cement-heads. One had to be a bit smarter than the other, and be the ringleader, otherwise both would be doing hard time. Service was determined to find out.

*****

The Bay Mills Indian Community had its own police force of three officers, its own court, its own jail (for short-term, immediate post-arrest purposes), all the good things casino income could bestow on a tribe, at least for a while. The police department was in the Tribal Justice Building, which also housed the court. The jail was a block away in a stone cube that reminded Service of military architecture: plain and solid, no art, no frills.

The jailer offered them a room, but Service declined. Angevin was alone in a holding cell with no windows, external ambient light, or other distractions. Service decided it would be a good location, with tight space so they could squeeze the man psychologically and physically. The goal here was to capture the man's attention and make sure he understood that what was going down here was not some half-ass deal.

The man was as described, six-four, three hundred pounds, and ripped the same as his partner, the Prince. Where Thad was fair, Angevin was dark-skinned with long, shiny black hair and black eyes. Huge hands, lots of scars on his knuckles, a veteran of a lot of close-in dustups and no doubt accustomed to using his size to set the tone and the pace.

"Mr. Angevin, I'm Deputy US Marshal Service. Mind if I call you Paint? That's an interesting name. You did take it for yourself, right? Because your folks they named you Gerard, and it seems you took a different name the way actors take new names, you know, to be cool and send a message and all that superficial, meaningless crap, right?"

Angevin said nothing, but Service could see he had the man's attention.

Treebone said in an extreme falsetto voice, "Those actors, most of them are gay gay gay, man, high-heel sneakers club, pumping iron. They looking at themselves in mirrors to get off on themselves, eyeball masturbation, ain't a pretty picture, pretty pretend-man."

"I ain't none of them *things*," Angevin said through his teeth.

Got him going, now keep him on his heels. "You mean you're not an actor?" Service asked.

"Not one of them others," he said.

Treebone kept pressing. "What you thinkin' run around with a pretty boy like Polack Prince. He alla them things you ain't, see what I'm sayin'?"

"Polish, not Polack," Angevin asserted.

"That what your gay boyfriend say, Pole-ish? He like that word *pole*, do he, the prince's *pole*."

Angevin looked at Service. "What is *his* problem?"

"You, you're his problem, Paint. So you're not gay. The word around Bay Mills is you like to wear ladies' shoes, so we should pay no attention to that kind of talk, sayin'?"

"Sir, I don't wear no damn high heels."

Sir? Good, Service thought, really got his attention. "I believe you, man. Where would a man with feet like yours *find* shoes that big?" He continued, "Mr. Angevin, you and your love-bro put a nasty whipping on our friend, Mr. Allerdyce."

Service would swear forever that all the color had drained out of the Indian's boy's face like it was loaded on a freight elevator and his face had gone from dark to pink to a color approaching parchment-paper pale.

"Man," Angevin said very carefully and deliberately, "that woman she did not never say the dude's name, I swear."

"She?"

"Call herself Andy. A *gon-gos-ik-we*. She hire us to convince an old guy to give a message to friend of his."

Service said, "A *gon-gos-ik-we*, a Swedish woman, right?"

Angevin's eyes widened. "You speak Nish?" He looked appalled to learn this.

"I'm rusty but sometimes I can dredge up what I need. Here's the deal, Gerard, I'm the friend in question. No charges have been filed . . . yet. But Mr. Allerdyce there behind us is just waiting for us to tell him if that's going to be necessary, right, Mr. Allerdyce?"

"Absolutely correct," Allerdyce said, and Service was startled by the man's normal human voice and diction. He glanced at Tree and saw it had rocked him a bit too.

Service said, "If you cooperate at a level we find satisfactory, no charges will be filed and you and your 'boy-girlfriend' will be free."

Angevin didn't attempt a comeback this time. Instead, he sat quietly, listening.

Limpy said, "We shall all behave like civilized adults here."

Service ignored the old man, who was embellishing his new role. "You've got to level with us, Gerard. We've already talked to your partner. Your story better match his."

"Yes sir, but how will I know what he said?"

"We'll tell you, is how. This Andy, this Swedish woman, how do you know she's Swedish?"

"Blond hair."

"Natural, you mean?"

"I don't know man, just blond. How I know what hair goop she use?"

Oh shit, dumber than a post, the twin of the Prince. "Okay, this allegedly Swedish Andy, how did she find you two? Did you put an ad in the phone book or on Craig's List?"

Cat eyes, light bouncing, no penetration. "We hang out down to Beaudoin's, Soo, yah?"

"She met you there, came in and just walked up to you guys?"

"Pretty much," Angevin said with a nod.

"Bullshit, Paint. How would she know you were for hire and for what?"

"Word gets around about me and Prince, what we can do."

"So you have a reputation as beasty gay boys?" Treebone asked with a smirk.

"No man, we friends, Prince and me—not *that* way. Why this dude keep saying that shit?" Angevin asked Service.

Tree kept after the man. "Not *that* way? What way *are* you two sweet fairy friends? You afraid I keep saying it I gonna turn you that way, or maybe you've already like got thoughts like that?"

Service saw that Angevin was beginning to hyperventilate. He tapped Treebone's boot with his own to let him know to lighten up and lay off this line, but his friend was pumped. "What did this Andy offer?" Service asked, trying to take back the interview and steer it elsewhere.

"Couple bills each, gas money, some beer and, you know, stuff."

"Stuff, what the hell is stuff?" Treebone demanded.

Paint stiffened, "Yah, just stuff, you know?"

Service asked, "The job for the Swedish lady was to be done where, and how soon?"

"Soon as."

"And you guys agreed to it?"

Angevin shrugged and looked perplexed. "*Sha hi-sa!*"

This exclamation meant nothing to Service. "Had you met her before?"

"No, was first time."

"This how you and the Prince do business, some stranger comes up to you cold and offers you money to assault a guy and you say okay, just like that? What if she was plainclothes setting you guys up?"

"Blow jobs," Angevin said. "Cops don't do that stuff."

Quick response there. Maybe he's not entirely thick. "Did she say why she was targeting Allerdyce?"

The boy shook his head. "Just say kick some old man's ass and tell him tell his friend need retire or everybody will have to pay."

"I'm that friend. Do I *look* ready to retire?"

Angevin stared at the floor. Service added, "And the others include my woman and kid. How'd you feel if somebody threatened your woman and your kid?"

"Just words," Angevin said. "We wun't hurt no kid."

"But old people, they're fair game?" Tree said.

Service said, "That what you beat up Mr. Allerdyce with, just words?"

Treebone asked, "Swedish woman give you a name for your target?"

"No man, if I'da heard that name, I'd have said no deal, no way."

"You've heard of Mr. Allerdyce?"

Angevin said, "*Everybody* knows who he is, man."

"What did she tell you?"

"She give us an address."

"Where?"

"Place over McFarland, spooky place look like redneck hillbilly Radio Shack shit, wires, poles, antenna shit, all that. Dr. No shit, sayin'? Creeped us out, dude."

"Did your employer tell you when the target would be there?"

Angevin shook his head, "Said just wait and watch, he'll come. She say, 'get him when he come out. He'll be weak when he come outside.'"

Service looked up at Allerdyce. "This happened in McFarland? You never told us where it happened."

Allerdyce said, "Youse never ask where, and what diff'rence dat make now, hey?"

None now, but who would know that Allerdyce and Fellow Marthes-dottir were seeing each other? Was there a leak, and if so, who and where?

"Your Swedish woman paid cash?"

Angevin said, "Cash, used bills."

Why those distinctions would make a difference to the punk, Service didn't understand. "And she never said where she was from, or who wanted the job done?"

Paint said, "She never say, but while she doing Prince, and I wait'n my turn, I see Escanaba newspaper in back seat."

Ford River and the Drazel's office were just south of Escanaba. The only building he could think of had to be the retired Troop's former business. Having a newspaper was by itself meaningless, but it was a piece of information that might come to have the feel of weight to it.

Treebone put the camera on the cot where the detainee sat and told him to look. Prince looked, shook his head, and passed the camera back. Service handed the boy surveillance photos from Marthesdottir's cameras. More head shakes.

Service looked at Treebone and thought that's four who didn't order the job, which means there are others. Service did not want to break off the interview yet. "What time were you at Beaudoin's?"

"Early, like eight?" Paint said.

"That your usual time to circulate?"

"Circalake?"

"You know, get out and get around, hang out, visit and such?" Thick as a brick.

"Oh yeah, pretty much."

"What kind of weather that night?"

"Cold, clear."

"Roads dry?"

He nodded, "Yah. And her truck clean."

"Her truck?"

"Where we make deal."

"What color?"

"Gray, silver, like that."

"Anything on the doors?"

"Enh-enh, but I don't read good."

"Anything, color of what was there?"

"Was red writin', red and blue ball above it, man."

Silver truck, red writing. Shit. This had to be the Drazels. Dry night, easy drive south to the Escanaba area, three to four hours max, probably no motel stop and too damn many potential routes for fuel stops to try to run gas sales.

Service took his friends outside. "It's them, but no way to pinpoint anything. What I'm wondering is how they would know Limpy's been seeing Marthesdottir. He looked at the old man. You tell anyone?"

"No, just youse guys."

They went back into the cell, and Service said, "No charges this time, but put one more blip on the radar and we will activate all this plus whatever new shit you're tracking in."

Angevin stood up and stuck his hand out toward Allerdyce. He looked down at the outstretched hand. Allerdyce snapped a kick between the man's legs, putting him face down on the floor. "I got ten-year-old grand-girlie-kittles hit harder than youse two assholes. Next time youse come after me, I come back after youses wit' knife, not no boot."

Service opened the cell door, looked back at Angevin and said, "*Megwich*," thank you in Ojibwa, and followed the old man out. "We've got to figure out how the Swedish woman knew about you and Fellow," Service told his partner.

CHAPTER 35

North of Nowhere Camp

CHIPPEWA COUNTY

The camp name was misleading. To reach the place you had to drive almost forty miles south of it, so you could sneak back to the north through a maze of eroded two-tracks. He'd bought the place after Maridly Nantz's murder and gave it to his friend Tree as a retirement gift—a hideaway, a place to provide his wife, Kalina, with more space and an abundance of solitude. Later he and his friend had quietly sprinkled Nantz's ashes into the unnamed little trout stream on the east side of the property, a spring-fed ribbon of water that stayed frigid year-round, and in summer brought schools of fat brook trout up from warmer waters. He'd bought the camp from the retired writer, Bowie Rhodes, whom Tree and he had first met in Vietnam and had been friends with ever since.

Service still owned Nantz's huge house on the Bluff above Gladstone, along with his Slippery Creek Camp. He and Tree had decided to head directly to Ford River from the Soo, and he had momentarily considered holing up at Nantz's house, but Tree wanted to check on his camp where they decided to spend the night. They would push on to Ford River in the morning, hit there early, and have all day to work the situation, whatever that amounted to.

Given the sort of clout attached to Kalleskevich and Bozian, it was difficult to understand how anything in their name could be affixed to such rank amateurs as the Prince and Paint. The fact that someone hired the pair of cretins suggested that their alleged employer was herself a rank amateur and lacking in judgment. The combination of amateur with amateur could be disastrous by all measures and for all people involved.

This woman, this Andy, Service thought, had sent the two punks after Allerdyce in an attempt to get the old man to pressure him to get out of the way. It was interesting that Paint, stupid as he seemed to be, was not totally unaware, because he had nearly fainted when he heard the name of the old man he and his partner had beaten up. Everyone in the U.P., northern Wisconsin, and northern lower Michigan with an IQ above room temperature seemed to know who or what Allerdyce signified, and most people tiptoed around him the way they would tiptoe around a bear with a nasty disposition, or a minefield. Did Andy know this and intentionally withhold the old violator's name, knowing she'd have a difficult time finding anyone who would go after someone with such a reputation? She could have saved herself the trouble by hiring a professional from one of the cities, but they wouldn't come cheap and two hundred dollars seemed like peanuts. So was this Andy person perhaps trying to operate on the cheap? And if so, why? What the hell is this all really about? Especially since his gut was telling him Bozian and Kalleskevich were after diamonds, not artifacts, and if so, why the hell was the woman playing cheap when such big bucks seemed to be at stake? His gut, he knew, wasn't infallible, but it was rarely off, and his first impression rarely changed later.

It was a quarter mile from the North of Nowhere gate to the cabin, which was a two-story thirty-by-thirty-foot log box with only a single small window above—a porthole facing northeast. Even on the brightest summer day the interior of the cabin was as dark as a hangman's heart. He loved the location but had never felt comfortable in the cabin. Tree loved the place and that was all that mattered. His friend had paid for power to the camp. He dug a well and installed a hot water heater. Tree spent much of his time up here fishing and hunting, out of his wife's hair. As gregarious as Tree was, Service found his friend's love of solitude less surprising than satisfying. It reminded him of the old saying about how the more one knows people, the more they like their dog. Most of Tree's career had been spent in and around Detroit, and he was peopled out.

Allerdyce dropped his small duffel bag inside the camp door, stood there, and looked it over the way a burglar might examine a potential target.

"Got all the basic food groups here," Treebone announced.

"Watermelon and Kool-Aid?" Allerdyce asked, tongue in cheek.

"Cram it, you racist insect," Tree said, and laughed. "I refer, of course, to Ball Park dogs, baked beans, beer, and ammo. Not your store-bought canned beans, but my own recipe for shoot-fire-out-your-ass specially spiced by that classy firm, Brothers 'n' Others."

"My taste birds don't fly," Allerdyce said. "And I ain't youse's brother nor whatever."

"We'll excuse your deficiencies," Tree said, "just this once. If you're gonna whine, there's peanut butter in the cabinets and jam and jellies in the fridge, and a loaf of limpa rye, in the freezer, but it has to be unthawed."

Service smiled. Tree was up here so much he was beginning to talk like a Yooper. *Unthawed* indeed.

"Real food," Allerdyce said. "PBJ on limpa. Okay, dat work."

Tree pulled Service aside to confirm his observation. "Is he acting ouchy-owly or is it my imagination?"

"I feel it too," Service said, "whatever *it* is." With Allerdyce, it could be anything, but Tree was perceptive and Service sensed some sort of extreme unease in the old man. As long as he had known the violator, he rarely expressed real feelings.

They turned in early. Service had a last smoke outside before climbing up on the deck above to a cot. As he smoked he studied the bear claw marks on the corner logs of the house and saw that his friend had added bear-proof metal shudders to the windows. Allerdyce stood outside with him, staring up at the tops of the cedars around the cabin. It was a cloudy night, with almost no light getting throught the treetops. "Violet's delight," he told the old man, who grunted and made no other response.

"Was a time," Allerdyce whispered in a scratchy voice.

"I'm packing it in," Service said. "We've got to roll early."

Allerdyce said nothing.

Just before 0400, Service awoke with a start to tomb-like silence and none of the usual camp sounds—no heavy breathing, no snoring, farting, coughing, choking, or rasping, none of the symphony of nasty sounds sleeping old men tended to make. He rolled over and could make out Tree's breathing but couldn't see him. The two of them had spent so much time together in darkness in their various lives that they no longer needed to see each other to know the other was close.

"Problem?" Tree asked in a hoarse whisper.

Service reached over to Allerdyce's cot and found no Allerdyce. "Did you hear Limpy climb up to bed?"

"I ain't heard nothing," Tree said. "I died when my head started down toward the pillow."

Service felt his way to the ladder and climbed down and told Treebone, "This place needs a nightlight."

"I sleep better in dark, and since I'm the only one here most of the time, it will remain that way."

Service found Allerdyce squatting just outside the door, with his back to the log wall. "You okay?" Service asked. No response. Service nudged him slightly with a sock-foot.

"What?" Allerdyce sputtered.

"Everything okay out here?"

"Was till youse woken me up."

"Sorry. You coming up to your cot?"

"Just fine 'ere."

"Okay," Service said just as the inside camp light came on and Treebone came out in his skivvies and sweatsocks and stretched. "What's with you two? I can't sleep with two old men down here whispering like old women. We're not even close to the ass of dawn yet."

Service said, "We're good here," as he pushed Tree back inside and stepped inside with him.

"You want to tell me what's up?" Tree asked.

"I don't know for sure. He's acting more squirrelly than normal. I found him squatting with his back against the wall. Asleep."

"Damn, he'll be lucky if he can unfold his legs in the morning."

"I think something's bugging him."

"How can you tell?" Tree countered. "He doesn't say shit, except for his cutesies."

"I can tell."

"Grady, the man's a wood tick. He doesn't think like normal humans. I'm going back to bed. Call me if the patient takes a turn for the worse."

Service went back to bed too, and lay on his cot watching the doorway below. Eventually Allerdyce came in, but got only to an inner wall where he went into the same squat as outdoors. Service fell asleep wondering what was wrong and awoke to the sound of bacon snapping in a black iron skillet, the smell of coffee brewing, toast popping from an old and very athletic toaster. He checked his watch 0500, still black outside with the main light on below him. Tree might believe he needed the dark to sleep, but the main light had not awakened him.

When Service rolled out to pull on his trousers, Tree grumbled in his deep voice, "What the hell is going on?"

"Allerdyce is making breakfast," Service said.

Treebone yelled down from the loft, "Don't cook my eggs hard, old man. I get hard eggs, I want shoot the cook."

"I hear dat," Allerdyce said from below. "Eats is on. Move it, we burnin' daylight, boys."

"Sun won't be up for at least another hour," Tree yelled back.

"I can see da dawns out dere," Allerdyce came back. "Get butts moving."

Grady Service wiped sleep from the corner of his eyes and yawned. This had the feel of a long day.

Allerdyce put a cup of coffee in his hand. Service asked, "What the hell is going on? You slept all night on the floor?"

The old man said, "I slep worse places, wah."

Had whatever was eating at the old man passed? Need to keep an eye on him.

CHAPTER 36

Ford River

DELTA COUNTY

Grady Service's mood was dark as loon shit. Tree was angry and seeth-ing. Only Allerdyce seemed unaffected, and his thoughts were impossible to know. The Drazel Sisters facility was cleaned out, and they were gone, vamoosed, off to terra incognita. Damn.

The windows had been spray-painted black inside. A nice touch, Service noted, if you were looking to delay any pursuit. Expecting to find something and then finding nothing tended to dump his personal gyroscopes into a dizzy tumble. It was one thing to theorize these people might boogie and yet another to actually find them gone. Psychology affected cops as much as civilians.

Who had tipped them off? Paint? The Prince? How had they known to send the twin goons after Limpy at Marthesdottir's place, in the middle of nowhere, when his schedule and presence were badly erratic at best? This left a bad taste.

Service said, "Smoke 'em if you've got 'em," as he leaned against a chest-high yellow metal post in the parking lot in front of the old Drazel Sisters building. Definitely the old Troop's place of business. "Somebody around here has to know something," Service declared as much to himself as to his companions. He stared at the building. Did the Drazels work and live here, or if they only worked here, where did they live? Fellow said they rotated employees from downstate. And where the hell was Andy the Swedish woman in this mob?

Allerdyce reached out to Service with a hand-gesture Service recog-nized as "gimme smokes." Not just one or two, but the whole pack. How has it come to pass that I'm now financing both of our habits with damn ciggies topping five bucks a pack? "Maybe I should quit smoking and improve the health of the both of us," he said out loud. Allerdyce was nonplussed and kept wiggling his fingers.

Having gotten what he wanted, the poacher lit up and grinned. "I like how youse laugh when t'ings turn shit. I gone take little walk-about now, hey."

Service told him, "We'll probably head for the county building to see what they know about this business, or we'll canvas neighbors. Meet back here in a couple of hours?"

Allerdyce grunted and shambled away looking like he might fall over dead any minute, which was just part of his act. Service wondered if this whole shtick was developed gradually over time, or if it was situational and designed to match his new-leaf persona. Ought to mention this to somebody at the college, see if they want to study Allerdyce. The problem with the old man was that even when he was acting normal, he wasn't, and recently he had been acting odd beyond his normal odd, a difference almost unparsable but to a select few. Whatever the source of this change was recent, and the weird sleep at Tree's cabin was a pretty strange symptom. Usually the old man went to bed and was out immediately. He did not sleep on his heels against cabin walls. Service tried to think back to when he first noticed a change. But nothing came.

Treebone interrupted his thoughts. "Black paint job inside the windows suggests this was neither a sudden decision nor a short-term one."

There was an old gas station across the street, repurposed into the "WHOLESALE PAINT EMPORIUM, ALL BRANDS, ALL WHOLESALE PRICES." Service pointed at the building. "What're the chances the good neighbor knows something?"

Tree said, "Don't ask questions, don't get answers. Let's go talk to the man."

The two walked across M-35. One end of the building had been painted in a primitive camouflage pattern, which was becoming the fashion statement of the day in the U.P. for all sorts of products, from toilet paper and romantic candles to T-shirts. He'd recently seen a bumper sticker on a black Hummer, CAMO IS THE NEW BLACK. Treebone, who had seen the sign at the same time, quipped, "What is wrong with people's heads?"

A sign in the paint store door said, CLOSED, OPEN AT 9 A.M., and it was just past eight, but there was one man moving around the store and Treebone knocked to get his attention. The man was thin, early thirties, with gelled spiky hair and gold posts in each earlobe, yet another sign of the changing times. Was a time when piercings and jewelry were exclusively for pirates, Gypsies, women, or drunk sailors. These days it seemed everywhere.

The man inside came to the door and pointed at the CLOSED sign. Treebone banged his fists aggressively on the glass, yelled, "We don't want to play your game. Open up."

Service stepped over and flashed his badge and the man reluctantly opened the door and said, "What up?" followed by a stupid grin and "What kind of badge is that?"

"The badge you're looking at, is what. I'm a US Deputy Marshal. When did your neighbors across the street move?" Service asked.

The man stuck out his lower lip. "I'll be. Are you like a Fed?"

"Not *like* a Fed, I am a Fed. You never noticed they were gone?"

"Sorry, I was out to my camp," the man said.

Service tried to look him in the eye but the man kept looking elsewhere. His instinct said the man was lying. He seemed edgy. "If you didn't notice the move, how do you know you were at camp when it happened?"

The man chewed his lower lip. "How do I know?" the man repeated. A sure sign a lie was working came when people repeated your questions. "Not sure," the man said.

"Did you work yesterday?"

The man shook his head. "Nope."

"Who did?"

"Nobody. Yesterday was Sunday and we never work on Sundays, you know how that is, I'm sure."

Yesterday was Sunday. Damn, I'm losing track of everything. "Did you know the people over there?"

"No, and now I guess I never will."

Odd way to answer the question. Gut says game-player, but why? What game?

"So you didn't know the people?"

"Define *know*," the man said.

Smart-ass. "Coffee now and then, say hi to Andy, ask how's business today, sell them some paint, you know, like interact with and know them."

"I don't know no woman Andy," the man said.

"I never said Andy was a woman," Service said.

"It's a woman's name," the man came back.

Tree glanced at Service.

Service said, "Andy Devine, Amos and Andy, all men."

Treebone pressed the man physically, using his size to loom over him. "Like my partner just said, nobody said there was a woman named Andy," Tree said, stepping closer to the man and pressing his blackness into the man's personal space. "Why would you say there's a woman named Andy?"

The man looked like he would have preferred to have been anywhere but here. Service was sure he was sorry he'd opened his door.

"I don't remember," the man said.

Tree leaned toward the man. "You don't remember why you said Andy's a woman?"

Service jumped in, "You're telling us that the people across the street pulled out lock, stock, and barrel and you didn't notice."

"I'm not gonna lie. I didn't notice and that's the simple truth."

What fools came up with that phrase? Cops heard it all the time. This was not the time to get hung up on trivia. "When did you see them last?" Service asked.

The man looked at the sky. "Friday, or was it Thursday? I guess I don't really remember. Sometime last week, could have been Monday, I just don't know."

The old runaround. Why? What's this jerk's angle? "Did you ever sell them any of your paint?"

"I don't believe so," the man said. "But my memory's not what it used to be."

"Listen up, we can have a federal subpoena here for your records faster than you can call a lawyer," Service said. "Does that help your memory?"

"I guess there's only one way to find out," the businessman said.

Is he consciously playing for time for the sake of neighbors who are watching? Up here this happened all the time. People didn't mind talking to cops, as long as nobody else knew. He claims not to know about the move, which seems like bull. Or is this guy just a lamebrain? Either is possible.

"How many employees do you have, Mister . . .?"

"Trelawney, Nalor Trelawney," the man said. He made no effort to shake hands.

"Cousin Jack?" Treebone asked.

The man took a step backward. "I'm not your cousin, man. No offense."

Thirty-year-old ignoramus. "You from here originally, Mr. Trelawney?" Service asked.

"I moved up from Milwaukee for this franchise opportunity."

"How's that working out for you?" Treebone said dryly.

"You know, good days and bad days," the man said.

"Listen up," Service said. "The way you're playing our questions, this could end up being one of your worst days ever, Mr. Trelawney. People down in Milwaukee, do they smart-lip the Feds and try to impede official investigations?"

"I've done nothing of the sort."

"You've done nothing but," Treebone said. "Obstruction of a federal investigation ain't no small thing, Cuz."

The man squirmed. "What is it you men want? I don't know when the people across the street moved, I swear to god. If you have to get a subpoena, go right ahead."

"You got something to hide back among your paint cans?" Treebone pressed.

"No, of course not. I can't tell you about something I know nothing about, and to answer your earlier question, I am the sole employee of this business. Just me."

Service grabbed Tree by the arm. "Let's go."

"You Feds can't march onto private property and push around innocent people," Trelawney said to their backs.

Tree said to Service, "I see a dumpster peeking out behind the Drazel building. Couldn't see it till now. Want to go do some diving?"

*****

They spent an hour in the refuse bin. "Our age and doin' this shit, what's wrong with us, man?"

"I'm kind of enjoying it," Service said.

"You always been what Canucks call crook. Allerdyce ever coming back?"

"I told him he had two hours to remove whatever was bothering him from his system."

"You say it exactly?" Tree asked.

"No, I just told him two hours. Where the hell could he have gotten off to?"

"It's Allerdyce."

"Right, sorry."

"The man's got him a questionable record in the reliability column, right?"

"He'll be back."

"This calendar year I hope."

"He doesn't have enough smokes and his wallet's in my truck. He'll be back."

*****

As foretold and promised, Allerdyce shuffled back a minute before the two hours were up with an excited look on his face. A dottering old man with a game leg limped along beside him. The man had no cane, but sort of threw the stiff leg in an arc and then shifted weight onto it to step forward. The two of them combined in a sort of herky-jerky bobblehead dance.

The violator's aged companion was equally grizzled and toothless, mostly bald with smoke-colored patches of thin hair sticking out here and there—like islands of old rushes in a marsh.

"Dis 'ere Weikko Teppopihlamaki," Allerdyce said.

Some Finnish names were unpronounceable to normal humans, which accounted in part for how easily Allerdyce ripped this one off without even taking a practice run.

The man said, "How're you fellows doing?" His English was flawless.

"Dis guy," Allerdyce said, clearly tickled, "he was best Yoiker of all da Finlands pipples."

"Yoiker?"

"Yoiking is throat-singing," the man said. "I learned it from the Sami people."

Service had no idea how to respond and didn't have to. Allerdyce raced on, "Fought dose Red Russky Commies in da White Dirt War, nineteen and da t'irty nine. He just fourteen den, and kill dose Russkies, pop-pop-pop."

"*Talvisota*," the man inserted with a grin. "Icy Hell."

Allerdyce pressed on. "Also means dat word, sniper-helper, hey. So now dis guy he eighty-four. Weikko, dis kid, he crawl out der wit' 'is *pukko*, finish off wounded enemas, take dere ammo and stuff." Allerdyce made a slashing gesture across his own throat, and a sound that Service thought a perfect representation of a knife cutting flesh.

"One day Russky bombs hit close, mess up Weikko's leg bad, and dey send 'im over Helsinki, den down London to sawbones and when he all good again, Finland war she all done, so Brits dey send him to US Army and dey ship Weikko over 'ere to da Yoop, translate kraut and Russian from Nazi POW. He live over Pelkie long time, den move down here get place close to grandkittles."

Service said, "It's a pleasure to meet you, sir." Cutting throats at fourteen? Jesus. Wars made for so much sick shit. "Throat singer?"

"More of a poet," the man said, his English pronunciation far superior to anything Allerdyce could ever organize. "I wrote pieces and the BBC broadcast them during the occupation."

Service knew Finland had been occupied both by the Nazis and the Soviets.

"Dey give him da gold *pukka* after war," Allerdyce said."

"You got a gold knife for writing poetry?" Treebone asked.

The man smiled sheepishly. "No, for my work in Talvisota."

"You've been here since the war?" Service asked.

"I come here in late 1943. I speak some German, Finn, some Swedish, some Russian. I helped with Nazi POWs and I stayed when the war ended. I was in Pelkie then. After that I went down to Ann Arbor, got my degrees, moved up to Northern, and taught there until I turned seventy-five. After retirement, I moved down here to the U.P. Riviera." The man laughed. "I married my wife in the U.P. and we had our family here. This is Finland for me, this place."

"And you know Allerdyce?" Service asked.

"Very much so. We liked to hunt and fish together. We did everything in the woods. For years."

"*Everything?*"

"Things like back in the old country," the retired professor said.

"Tell Sonnyboy," Allerdyce urged the man before Service could think of what to say next.

Teppopihlamaki pointed north up M-35. "House with the widow's walk is mine," he announced.

"Tell him what up dere," Allerdyce urged enthusiastically.

"Lord Nelson's telescope on a tripod, a reproduction of course."

"Far-looker," Allerdyce said. "Dat Nelson guy get killed over Hegick get sent home to da Englands in pickle barrel."

"Horatio Hornblower?" Treebone suggested.

Allerdyce scowled and hissed. "No, *Nelson* guy, not jazz guy, pickle barrel, youse can Goople it." The violator looked at his companion. "Tell 'em Weikko, tell 'em."

"There was a moving van here yesterday. They looked like they were emptying the building."

"What moving company?" Service asked.

"Two Men and a Truck, I think the name was. Very odd name for a business."

"How many people did you see?"

"Two movers in blue overalls, five blond women, and Trelawney."

"Trelawney?"

The professor pointed across the street. "Trelawney."

"The owner?"

Teppopihlamaki nodded solemnly. "He's been over there a lot."

"Really," Service said, pure rhetoric with no need for an answer.

The old Finn suggested, "I believe he might be seeing one of the women. Is that how they put such things these days?"

Treebone said, "It's euphemism for get some leg."

The professor grinned. "Yes, I would think that would be the intent."

"Did you know any of the Drazel women?" Service asked.

"Not personally. They are all blond, but one seems older by a bit and she is the one I saw most frequently with Trelawney. Frankly, I couldn't guess her age. I'm better at gauging the doneness of a steak on the grill than the ages of women, who all look young."

Tree joked, "I hope you haven't been using that telescope to look in bedroom windows."

Service cringed, but the professor laughed. "Certainly not since I was eighty-one, or was it eighty?"

*****

Trelawney was at the door by the time they crossed M-35. Allerdyce remained with the old Finn. He had both hands up, and a crooked grin on his rat-like face. "Okay, okay, I was just jokin' around with you fellows. No harm, no foul, am I right?"

"You helped the people across the street load a moving van. Yesterday, Trelowney."

The man said, "I'm so glad you came back. I just now remembered something and wondered if it, you know, might be relevant to your inquiry."

"That's good on account your neighbors saw you with the Drazels."

"Ah, the neighbors; alas, we are not on a solid footing with them. It's an anti-Wisconsin thing."

"They've also said you have been seeing a certain blond," Service added.

"As I said, I am not a favorite among neighbors and you are likely to hear anything and everything about me." The man sucked in a deep breath. "She was a fellow commercialist and colleague and a neighbor."

Service said, "What's her name?"

"It's like this," Trelawney said, holding up his left hand and tapping a wedding ring.

"Ah yes," Tree said, "it's the old it sucks-to-be-you moment. What's her name, your blond colleague?"

"Then you understand," Trelowney said with a trembling voice.

"Nope, can't understand no man who cheat his wife, unh-uhn," Tree-bone said. "My wife find out I do that, she empty a twenty-round mag in my sorry ass and be screaming for more clips."

"Truly," the man said, "you must understand my dilemma."

"We understand it," Service said, "but we don't give a shit. We want that woman's name, and where she lives."

The man sighed and his shoulders slumped. "Andronica is her full name, but she goes by Andy. She lives somewhere around Traverse City, but alas I have no address or phone number and no way to make contact."

The man had a smug look. "Her last name?" Service asked.

"Alas, she never said, and I never thought to ask."

"Alas my ass," Treebone said. "Our next stop is to talk to your old lady, and we'll see how you sing then."

The man tore a piece of paper from a small notebook and scribbled a phone number.

Service looked at the paper. "That's not a name."

"I don't *know* her name, but that's how I can get in touch with her. Please do not tell her who gave you the number."

"Are you afraid she'll think badly of you?"

"I do have principles."

"So did Hitler," Service said. "We'll say it was a little bird."

"Yeah," Tree said, "stool pigeon. How old's this lady?"

"Forty she claims."

"You doubt her?"

"I would guess closer to fifty, but you know, she's like sensitive!"

Treebone said, "FYI, Ms. Sensitive hired two young bucks to beat the living shit out of an old man. I hope she don't find out you dimed her ass."

Service asked, "What were the Drazels doing here?"

"Loot," Trelawney said. "Treasure."

This caught both of them off guard. "What the hell does that mean?" Service asked.

Trelowney held up his hands. "I assume you know as much as I know, you being law enforcement."

Treebone asked, "Your arrangement with Andronica, a matter of heart or cash?"

"I resent the implications of your question," Trelawney said.

Service said, "Resent what you want. Did you pay for it, or not?"

"Different people see intimate relations differently."

"If you say so," Tree said.

Service asked, "When did the woman leave?"

The man sucked in a deep breath. "You missed her by thirty minutes."

"She stayed *here* last night?" Tree asked.

"Well, I couldn't very well take her home, could I?"

Trelawney had stalled them earlier to give the woman time to get farther away. Now his only concern was his wife. Scumbag. Service said, "Let's have a look at your receipts. I assume you sold them something."

"Paint," the man said. "The records are in back."

It took an hour to get more information to go on. The bill was from a credit card in the name of Drazel Sisters, A Subsidiary of D&D Hop Farms, Leelanau County.

"What about my wife?" the man asked as they walked out the front door.

As they crossed the street, Service gave Treebone a phone number on a different scrap of paper. "His home number, presumably his wife's as well."

"You're a mean sumbitch."

"I learned from you. You gone call his lady?"

"Not sure yet."

CHAPTER 37

Slippery Creek Camp

Various police agencies were looking for the woman Andronica, aka "Andy." Service had little hope anyone would find her. Eventually, maybe. She was typical of a slew of certain modern humans who slithered along beneath the radar of decent folks. It wasn't so much that these people were adept at evading detection as it was that authorities and police agencies were too strapped for bodies to conduct anything close to focused, sustained searches.

They had hoped for a line of inquiry into the origins and ownership of D&D Hop Farms, which should have been a straightforward proposition, but this didn't happen. Even Googling the name turned up nothing remotely useful, and nothing at all in Leelanau County, including its phone book. Wherever they looked it was no dice, and one cop or a few, no matter how well intentioned, could not do everything alone. This conclusion resulted in Service pushing the search effort to M in Ivy Free Hall, and to Fellow Marthesdottir in McFarland.

Thirty minutes after transmitting the requests, M reported back, the first time he'd talked to her since East Lansing. "Just to let you know, this is going to be a slog through the quirks of offshore-holding-company-land. I've tapped Delaware, which is easy enough, and I already have pointers at Ireland, Belgium, and Cyprus. I have no doubt this will lead to many other locations."

She continued, "What happens is a rich fella can build himself what looks like a huge empire, by borrowing and building and continuing to borrow more until even he can't really determine what he owns or what he's worth. Even if it's legal, you have to ask how much tax they pay. The answer is often not even one thin dime and it's all perfectly legit, a legal tax dodge."

She paused, waiting for Service to absorb the info. Her voice crackled to life again, "I have a superior source close to the judge for the minerals case and I'm hearing some early leanings in the MWT. Is it all right to call it that, MWT, which is shorter and more succinct than Mosquito Wilderness Tract?"

"Fine by me."

"Well," she went on, "said judge is apparently not leaning in the direction you desire."

I desire? I thought we were all in this effort together. What *is* M's angle? "The judge is leaning toward finding for Kalleskevich?"

"So it would seem. If you have some magic up your sleeve, now would be an opportune moment to bring it out into the light."

"I thought you were the master miracle worker."

She said nothing. "We can always file an appeal," he said, "to buy us time."

"This is one of those cases," she said, "where an appeal will surely be lost—assuming the original adjudication has used Cadillac academic and forensic sources to evaluate the provenance of claimant evidence. What would be far more helpful would be a competing claim based on equally compelling evidence. You can, of course, appeal, which is the nature of our system, but like the Bible says, 'the end is writ plain.'"

Service had never considered the Bible a plain source for anything, and he could feel his shoulders drooping as the conversation drew to a close. "Are you trying to tell me we're about to have a fork stuck in us?"

"That is certainly not how I would characterize the situation, but that visual certainly has some merit. You are a very blunt man."

After hanging up he walked outside, telling himself he needed air but knowing he was going outside to be alone so he could sulk and bathe in self-pity. Two generations in his family, their lives given to the Mosquito, and why? What has been the damn point of so much sweat and blood. Both the old man and I have shed blood in and for the damn land.

Tree followed him outside. "Bad news?"

"If news is consistently and continuously bad, does new data qualify as bad qualitatively?"

Tree said, "You need to see your woman, if you take my meaning. Your mind fluids are all mixed up."

"That bad?"

"We have known each other a long, long time. Whole lot of folks, maybe most, got no clue how to read you, but me, I don't have that problem. You're feeling something, I know."

"The judge is leaning toward Kalleskevich's claim on the mineral rights."

Treebone stood next to him sniffing the wind, said only, "Man."

"Exactly."

Allerdyce came out on the porch and looked the direction the others were looking. "What out there?"

"Nothing," Treebone said. "Grady just heard the judge may rule for the other side for the property in the Mosquito."

"Wah," Allerdyce said, "how he can do dat?"

"Evidence analysis and evaluation," Service said.

"What means dose words?"

"He believes the other side."

Allerdyce was quiet and frowning and said after a while, "Wah, can't be right, dat. Know it ain't right. When we eat, hey?"

"I'm not hungry, help yourself," Service said.

"Me either," Treebone said.

"Limpy need food," Allerdyce insisted.

"The cupboard and fridge are full. Help yourself," Service said.

"Don't want none dat crap. Take truck?"

"Keys are inside," Service said.

Allerdyce drove Service's truck away.

Treebone said, "You're right, something's wrong with him. I need a drink, you?"

"Why not."

Treebone poured double jiggers of pepper vodka, set one in front of his friend, held one in front of him, and said, "It don't mean nothing," and chugged it down.

Service hesitated just for a moment, then picked up his telephone and called Marthesdottir.

"Fellow, we learned that Limpy got jumped coming out of your place. Did he tell you?"

"Are you sure it was here?" she asked.

"Who knows that you two are seeing each other?"

"Nobody," she said.

"You're certain?"

"Let me think on it, all right?"

Service broke the contact and drained his shot.

"Another?" Treebone asked, bottle in hand.

"Hit me."

After another shot, he made coffee and called Marthesdottir again. "We're coming your way."

"When?"

"Now, tonight. Make coffee."

CHAPTER 38

McFarland Area

MARQUETTE COUNTY

Fellow Marthesdottir looked past the two men towering over her at her door. "Where's the wee one?"

"We're not welcome without him?" Service asked.

"Of course you are, it's just that he's always with you."

She showed them in. "You seemed out of sorts when you called," she said. "I have coffee." She paused, then continued, "I've been thinking on your question of who knows about Allerdyce and me and no answer pops up. You two and nobody else, unless you two or Allerdyce told someone. There's one sort of vague possibility," she added. "I wonder if someone saw me when I was out installing new equipment and servicing disks and batteries. Maybe they recognized me."

Service said, "Or followed you back to your place. But seeing you alone doesn't put a link to Limpy." Service looked over at Treebone, who nodded and said, "I'll go take a look at her surveillance gear. Got to be set only so can see the back door or a vehicle with someone getting out, right?"

Marthesdottir said, "Are you suggesting someone has cameras on *me*?"

"We'll find out," Service said. "Goose, gander, right?"

"That's a disturbing thought. I have all kinds of security with no holes in my perimeter. I even have an app that provides a continuous evaluation."

"May be nothing," Service said, "but Tree will take a look—for peace of mind if nothing else."

Treebone said, "Shouldn't take long," and departed.

The woman poured more coffee for Service. "I take it things aren't going well?" she asked.

"More like not going at all. We're missing something here. How about we go over the W. Stafinski stuff again, chew it like a cud."

"Certainly. I thought you said it was a myth."

"I might have been a tad wrong."

"A tad?"

"Like totally wrong." Every time the Stafinski name had come up in his life, it had been bantered and joked about by his old man and Allerdyce, who had said it was bullshit and not important.

Service said, "Limpy knew W. Stafinski as a man named Wally Staff out of Michigamme."

"I've just begun getting the wind on that story, and I learned that apparently Mr. Staff caught Mr. Allerdyce poaching his land one night and turned him over to your father."

Violator games. This fit the pattern of the old-timers. "I never heard that exact story, but it may fit somewhere in all this."

"Challenging my veracity?"

"No, ma'am, not in the least. I didn't mean it that way, sorry."

"We're both stepping on our tongues tonight," Marthesdottir said.

Service explained, "Limpy confirms he knew Wally Staff, aka W. Stafinksi, who was an extensive landowner and builder *and* one to bend the fish and game laws now and then. Limpy also knew my old man busted Staff for fish and game violations."

"My research shows that Mr. Staff was a rock in the community—sober, disciplined, hard-working, all that—and he had a son who was nothing like his father, a profligate with serious drinking and spending problems," Marthesdottir told him.

"A son?"

She said, "Yes, Elder Staff, originally Elder Stafinski, and it was said in some circles that when Wally died, the boy got everything and quickly squandered it all. Sorry to be so earthy in my word selection."

"I hear a but in that story."

"You do indeed. Wally Staff also had a daughter, who was just like him, and who got an education and moved downstate. She was a teacher and school administrator. Her name is Molly."

Service felt a stab in his gut. "Are you *serious*?"

"Yes, I am, and I have learned from a good source that Wally Staff made sure son Elder did not get any of his estate."

"He gave it all to his daughter?"

"Possibly, probably, but there are no records anywhere of who owned various land parcels, except of course people Wally Staff sold land to over the years. My understanding is that he was very active in land sales and trading. He once sold eighty acres for two draft horses and a wagon."

"What happened to Molly Staff?"

"She married, lived downstate until she retired, and then moved back to the U.P."

"Her name is Molly Cloud now?"

"Yes," Fellow Marthesdottir said, "and she owns property just north of the Mosquito."

Service said, "Five miles north of the Mosquito, to be precise, and she has been diagnosed with early onset Alzheimers."

"You already knew about her?"

"I did not know her maiden name was Staff. She had an episode not long ago and I got called in to find her. Allerdyce was with me. Actually it was him who found her. She was loopy and claimed she was coming to see me because she possibly was being pressured by Drazel Sisters to sell her property. That's not confirmed, but that's where my gut is right now."

"Why you?"

"Because I think in her mind she links the Mosquito to my father and to me, and she must think we are defending the land around there. I suppose in her mind I'm a safe haven. But she also may be too damn confused most of the time to have a clue what she's thinking, much less saying."

"How awful," Fellow Marthesdottir said.

"It looks like the judge may find in favor of Kalleskevich," Service told her.

"I know. M called me, and I reminded her that judges rarely talk about cases under active consideration and this is more likely some sort of disinformation game designed to make a loop back to the judge. Kalleskevich and Bozian both know how to manage such games. The thing is, Grady, Kalleskevich may have evidence that is clear and indisputable, or a bit cloudy, but at some point that evidence has to be shown to the state and then it's *res ipsa loquitur*."

Service shook his head. "I failed Pig Latin so badly I didn't dare take a run at the real stuff," he said.

Treebone came back into the house and held up a game trail camera. "It was in the cedars fifty feet from your back door and aimed right at it. They came through the swamp behind your property and never got into the open so your stuff wouldn't pick them up. And that Latin, my Woods Cop friend, translates to something like 'the cards will speak for themselves.'" He held up the camera. "Top of the line, you want me to put it back?"

Service said, "I'm going to assume it was Drazels and they're gone, so why leave it up?"

Marthesdottir said, "The judge will decide based on opinions from experts he interviews, selects, and hires to advise him on the validity of the provenance of the submitted claims evidence."

"Experts who will be known to the public?" Service asked.

"Not as I understand the process," she said, "unless, of course, His Honor decides to make that information public, which I think would be unlikely unless the case is appealed by the losing side."

"I feel . . . ," Service said.

"Helpless," she said, finishing his sentence for him. "You have no control and that fact is weighing you down."

"No luck either, it seems."

"You're just used to mankind's greatest shared condition," Fellow said. "You always exude control because right or wrong—and it is wrong—you think you have control. When we think we have control, luck is our servant and when we don't it's not."

"Is that supposed to cheer me up?"

"I had no idea that cheering you up was part of our contract," she said.

"It's not. You think the daughter got the land from her father, but you have no proof of that and can't find any evidence, pro or con."

"I got this from a good source, but it's not yet confirmed, and it may be only Molly Cloud who can set the record straight."

"Allerdyce and Grady's dad both knew W. Stafinski?" Treebone asked.

"Yes," Service said. "Allerdyce claims he was tight with W. Stafinski and thought my father pinched the man several times, and he claims there was never any lingering personal animosity. Limpy mentioned a son, but gave us no details, and I don't remember any mention of a daughter. What I *do* remember is that he told the lawyer O'Halloran that Staff had no family."

Service closed his eyes and tried to remember exactly what the old poacher had said. With his eyes still closed, he continued, "He said that Staff had no *real* family." Was this one of the old man's silly, twisted definitions?

"What the hell does that even mean?" Treebone asked.

"Same question," Marthesdottir said. "He had to have known the daughter if he knew there was a son, right?"

"You'd think," Service said. "Why did you ask if he was with us tonight?"

"Because he told me he'd be back after I saw him earlier."

"He was *here* tonight?"

"Three hours ago. Said he had errands."

"Did he say what errands and where?"

"Not exactly."

"But you have a notion?"

"We were relaxing, you understand, and he told me how you rescued an elderly woman, but he did not tell me her name and I was . . . uh, too distracted at the time to ask?"

"It was not a big deal," Service said. "We find people regularly. This time the lost one was fine. Often we find them too late and they're dead or seriously hurt." But it had been Allerdyce who found the woman, not him. Why had he not told Marthesdottir that? The old man's thinking was impossible to follow.

"Well, I personally thought it quite a feat and certainly befitting a knight of the woods."

The phrase made him nauseous. "But he never said the woman's name?"

"No, and that's too bad because I would have told him you fellows saved the last in a historical family line."

"Molly Staff has no heirs?"

"No, she was married without issue."

But Linsenmann told him she had a son downstate and she was living with him in winter. What the hell was going on? Service asked, "And Stafinski, Staff—Allerdyce never mentioned a lawyer we met with and how he told us all about his relationship with Wally Staff?"

"Not a word, and if I may be so bold, *you* didn't bother to inform me either. At any rate, he and I were relaxing, and after we talked about the rescue he jumped up and left and said he'd be back later. The man is just not reliable by any standard human measure."

Service tried to remember. Miss Molly had been borderline batty through the whole episode—convinced that the whole point of her sortie into the woods was to get to me. What had she said at one point? Her reason for walking away was that the woman who was trying to buy the property "want yours." It hadn't registered. Not hers, but yours, meaning mine? Everyone who had ever spent any time at all in or around the Mosquito knew the Service name was almost a synonym. That's what she had to have meant by "want yours." Shit, but "yours" can mean only one thing, that the Mosquito belongs to me? No way. "Fellow, if you don't mind, we'll load a thermos with coffee and run."

"Why?"

"Because I'm hearing something I didn't quite pick up on earlier and maybe I should have."

He felt antsy without clear reason, a gnawing sense of dread with no specific source other than it had vaguely to do with Allerdyce.

"There was one other thing I told Limpy," Fellow said. "I told him that everyone talked about what a beautiful red-haired kid she'd been, and he just about jumped out of his ever-loving skin."

Service had Treebone's truck started before his friend jumped in with the coffee. "Who said *you* could drive?" Tree asked.

"Shut up," Service told him.

"What am I missing here?" his friend asked. "You're amped up like you're in payback mode. Something I ought to know going down here?"

"You'll know when I know," Service said, then backed out and raced away into the night.

CHAPTER 39

North of the Mosquito Wilderness Tract

There was a whale-shaped woman sitting on a kitchen chair in Molly Cloud's cabin, duct tape around her mouth, her eyes free and wild and screaming. The woman's skin was beet-juice red, and she began to kick and make the chair jump around. Tree grabbed the woman by the shoulders and said, "Easy, you're okay."

The woman said "Mmph-mmph-mmph" and kept making the chair buck.

Service left the kitchen and swept the rest of the house quietly and efficiently. He searched for Miss Molly and the old violator. My partner, reformed *my ass*! That miserable son of a bitch. Gagging and hog-tying a woman, for what? Maniac. Good god, they should fire my ass for ever letting him near my truck much less in it. What is wrong with me? My old man was the drunk. I'm not. I'm just a bunch of bad judgment.

Then he saw Miss Molly sitting on the bed in the back bedroom, a peaceful look on her face and a pink pillow in her lap. No sign of Allerdyce. "Are you all right, Miss Molly? It's Grady."

"Yes," she said, her voice devoid of any inflection or emotion.

"Was there a man here?"

"Yes."

"A man you know?"

"Yes."

"Did he hurt you?"

No response. "Are you hurt, Miss Molly?"

"Yes."

"Where are you hurt, can you show me?" He was looking her over trying to see if there was anything obvious. Nothing, no marks. Slow down your heart rate. How do you deal with people in this condition? "Did the man touch you, Molly?"

"Yes."

Go easy with her, he thought. Call Harmony? Call deputies? No, not yet, she's not hurt, do this yourself. Just take it easy here. Go slowly. "Where did he touch you, Miss Molly?"

She made a face and started to say something just as a scream ripped at them from the front of the house and just ahead of the whale woman, who charged into the room snorting like a bull and screaming, with Treebone right in her footsteps.

"She head-butted me," Treebone said, blood dripping from his nose.

"I want a cop, get me a cop!" the whale bellowed.

"I *am* a cop!" Service yelled at her.

"With a badge!" She stomped her massive feet like a child in a tantrum. He showed her his badge.

She shook her head, screamed "In a uniform!" and kept stamping her feet and raising dust. Miss Molly began to shake and cough and cry.

"I was assaulted," whale woman shouted. "Me a decent person, assaulted and fondled by that toothless monster! He soiled me."

"I was assaulted too," Treebone yelled back at her. "By you! Calm the hell down or *we're* going to calm you."

"I *am* calm," she screamed.

Service sucked in a deep breath. Who is this whale, why is she here, and why would Limpy hog-tie her?

The woman pivoted and threw a hard, straight punch at Service, but he saw it coming out of the corner of his eye and easily deflected it in one motion. He put an armlock on her and flipped her onto the bed where Treebone pinned her and said, "Calm the fuck down, superwoman."

"I want . . . that . . . man . . . arrested," the woman said, her breathing in gasps.

"Which man?" Service asked.

"That man, *all* men."

Whale woman kept looking toward Miss Molly. "*She* saw him, ask her, she saw, she saw, she saw, she saw—the whole thing," she keened, nodding toward Miss Molly, who sat calmly with tears sliding down the sides of her face. "Ask her, ask her!"

Service told the woman, "Miss Molly gives the same answer to every question."

"Ask her, ask her, ask her."

"You want me to put the sleeper hold on her?" Tree asked, still holding the woman on the bed and sweating from the strain. The woman was grunting and squealing like a captured sow.

"Not yet, this shit has gone way too far. Lady, please shut your mouth!"

The woman went silent, then started in again. "That old bat's out of her bloody head."

"Lady, the only person out of control is *you*," Service said.

"And just who the blazes are you?" the woman asked him.

"The cop you wanted."

"I hate cops."

"Imagine my surprise." Service told his friend, "Get her out of here. Restrain her if you have to."

"I don't *take* orders," the whale insisted. "I *give* orders. The old bat pays me to take care of her."

This is Miss Molly's caretaker?

"You are about to learn how to take them," Treebone said, then yanked her to her feet and frog-walked her toward the front of the house. Service saw his friend had a pinch-hold on the woman's obese neck, the hold draining all the fight from her in a hurry.

Service returned his attention to Molly Cloud. "We're really sorry about this. Everything's okay now. Can I sit next to you, Miss Molly?"

"Yeah."

"Do you remember me, Miss Molly?"

"Yeah."

"We found you when you took a walk that one night."

"Yeah."

"Think before you answer this next question. Can you do that for me?"

"Yeah."

"You're sure the man who was here tonight touched you?"

The woman paused and finally said, "Yeah."

"Did he hurt you?"

She stared at her right hand.

"Did he hurt your right hand, Molly?"

She sighed. "Yeah."

He looked at the hand, no marks and no sign of violence. As he studied her hand, she patted his shoulder with her other hand.

"Molly, is that how the man touched you, with his hand on your shoulder. Are you saying he patted you?"

"Yes."

"The man was Allerdyce and he's your friend, right?"

"Yes," she said. "Nice man. Long time. Your daddy too."

My father? Good god. "Allerdyce didn't hurt you."

"Yes."

Dammit, think about how you're wording the questions, doofus. "Yes, he did *not* hurt you?"

"Yes."

"Did he talk to you?"

"Yes."

"Can you tell me what he talked about? I know this must be really hard for you."

"Yes," she said. Then, "Yours."

This stopped him. "Mine?"

She smiled and nodded. "Yes." Then, with great deliberation and seriousness, Molly said, "They want yours, Grady. Want yours, yes."

"Want my what?"

"Yours," she said, her eyes burning with obvious frustration.

"Okay, Molly, we're just about done. You need rest. But just so we're certain, Allerdyce did *not* hurt you."

"Yes, no hurt."

"He patted your shoulder, affectionately?"

She smiled. "Yes."

"And you did not feel threatened by Allerdyce in any way."

"Yes, not."

Good, this is connecting. "Okay, let's try this one more time, all right? We need to be absolutely certain about this, okay, Miss Molly? Did he want to talk about me?"

"Yes. Yours."

"Can you remember about what?"

In reply, she opened her mouth and ripped off a wolf howl so real it sent chills down his spine. What the hell? Oh shit. "Wolf? Miss Molly?"

"Yes."

"Wolf Cave?"

She smiled. "Yes, yours."

"Did Allerdyce go to Wolf Cave after he left here?" Did she mean the upper or lower cave and does it matter?

"Yes," she repeatedly emphatically. "Yours."

"Have you known Allerdyce a long time, Molly?"

"Yes."

"Okay, Molly, come with me. We're going to get you out of here and get the docs to check you out. Where are your coat and boots?"

She pointed at a closet.

"Tree will help you get ready, okay? He's my friend."

"Yes."

Service went to the front of the house. Whale-woman was sitting on the couch glaring at Treebone. Service said, "Call Harmony for me and tell her to meet me at the jump-off point we used most recently. Same destination after that. Tell her to bring lots of lights and batts and so forth."

"Got it. Should I tell her why?"

"Tell her I'll explain it when we meet up. I think Molly is okay, but I want you to call Tuesday and take Miss Molly there. Ask Tuesday to get her to a doc for a check." Service pointed at the whale woman. "I don't know who the hell this woman is or why she's here, but the Department of Social Services needs to jump into this clusterfuck PDQ."

"Is Allerdyce all right?" Treebone asked.

"I don't know, but I know I have to go find out."

"He took off for that . . . *location* at night?"

"Remember, for him our night has always been his day." He liked it that Treebone knew not to mention the cave in front of the whale.

"How you going to get there?" Tree asked his friend.

"The old-fashioned way, beat-feet, boots in the dirt."

"Got to be five miles."

"Done it before. It's what I do."

"As soon as Molly is squared away, I'll drive back to your partner's truck and hold there until you need me. Tell her leave to stick a key in the JoBox so I can have radio contact."

"Good, later." But one detail still sticking.

Service went back to Molly. "Miss Molly, some women called Drazel wanted to buy your property for a lot of money. Is that true?"

"Yes."

"Do you know *why* they want to buy it?"

"Yes. To get to yours."

Get to mine? What the hell is she talking about? he wondered. No time for more of this. Got to find Limpy. She's secure, focus on finding Allerdyce.

Whale-woman had her coat on in the front room and was holding out an open hand. "I refuse to work under these conditions. I demand to be paid."

"I don't blame you," Service said.

"I'm not coming back. I want my pay. I earned it."

"Doing what?" Tree asked.

"Caregiving," the woman said.

"How much?" Tree asked.

"One hundred for pain and suffering."

"For causing it, not receiving it," Tree said. "Get the hell out of here, lady, and don't let the door hit you in the booty. You'll be seeing the cops. I don't know what's going on, but I'm guessing if there's an assault here, you weren't the victim."

The woman stomped out, grumbling and cursing.

Miss Molly was suddenly in the living room, pointing at the open door and the woman who had just departed. "*Bitch!*"

Service watched the whale drive away in her PT Cruiser. He stuffed his sweater into his pack and headed into the night in a modified recon shuffle. He hoped to beat his partner to the rendezvous. Otherwise he might have to pop out and scare the shit out of her, and he began to giggle as he felt the night enveloping him. Don't think, son. Go, left-right-left-right, fly baby, fly like the owl: low, fast, silent, and deadly

CHAPTER 40

Mosquito Wilderness Tract

Wildingfelz was already waiting patiently by her truck when he popped up beside her. To his surprise, his sudden appearance seemed to have no effect on her.

She turned right to business. "Treebone didn't say it directly, but this has to do with the cave, right?"

"Yah," he said, sucking for air now that he had stopped moving.

"Cool," she said. "I'll lead."

Before he could object she was gone and invisible, and all he could do was cinch his pack straps and start moving again, following as best he could, focusing his ears on the faint sound of her boots somewhere in front of him. She runs with the weight of a shadow, he marveled. Impressive.

Eventually he got into a rhythm and nearly slammed into her, but she blocked him with her forearms and jarred him to an awkward stutter-step stop. "Where in the hell did you come from?" he whispered harshly. He was pumping sweat and dried his forehead with his sleeve.

"Tired?" she asked. "Legs a little rubbery from all the exercise?"

"No," he lied.

"I was right in front of you, kept watching your snail's pace and then decided I'd better come back to make sure you were all right."

"I just ran five damn miles," he said defensively.

"Want me to take it easy on you?"

"Is that an age joke?"

"No, sir, not at all, sir."

"I'm not a sir."

"I know, but it's a customary address for elders," she said and laughed out loud at him, and he couldn't help but laugh with her.

"You're gonna kill yourself running in the dark at that speed," he told her.

"You sound like the mother in that old-timey Christmas movie: 'You'll shoot your eye out.'"

He started to object to her calling *A Christmas Story* an old-timey movie until it dawned on him that it was out . . . twenty-five years ago? Where in hell did the time go? "You should listen to your mother," he reprimanded.

"I do when she knows what she's talking about. She's blind as a mole. I was born with something doctors call Sunshine Syndrome. The distribution of my cones and rods is different than most people. I'm what they call a quick-dark adapt, or QDA, with scotopic vision. My weird deal lets me see color longer in the dark than others."

"Did I ask for a medical report? You could still poke out your damn eye with a branch."

"Granted," she said, "but statistically it's more likely to happen to you."

"Are you wanting a competition between us?" he asked.

"Absolutely not, but stop patronizing me. I'm your partner, not your baby-girl daughter. I have a father, and believe me, one is more than enough. Are we going to stand here and yack-yack or get to the cave and get on with whatever it is we're here to do?"

"Cave," he said, sucked in a deep breath, let it out slowly, and took off after her again, content now simply to follow, with no need to catch her, even if he could.

He found her waiting for him twenty feet from the lip entry to the cave, holding out a water bottle.

"Thanks." He took a long pull.

"You want to have a smoke and explain what we're doing?" she asked.

"No," he said and then, seconds later, "Yah okay, a smoke is a good idea." Still sweating heavily, his hand was shaking slightly from exertion when he tried to light up. Wildingfelz took the lighter away from him and lit him. He puffed it to life and let the smoke find its way.

"That shit will stunt your growth," she whispered and giggled.

"From this day forward, your name is Stealth," he said.

"I prefer Harmony, which is a girl's name, not Stealth, which is a spook plane. So, why are we out here?"

"Looking for Allerdyce."

"That'd make a snappy book title," she quipped. "I thought he was attached to your hip these days."

"Right tense," he told her. "I think he may be in the cave."

"The cave?"

"Think so."

"Now that's a surprise," she said.

"Why?"

"Didn't you see his eyes when we were out here earlier?"

Service tried to think back.

She continued, "Every time he got near the cave opening, his eyes bulged like Ping-Pong balls and he started to hyperventilate. Every time he even *looked* at the cave opening, it looked like he was staring into a wolf's maw."

He had not noticed any of this. Some hesitancy, even malingering, but what she was saying, no. "You think he's afraid?"

Wildingfelz said, "I think he's scared shitless. I'm guessing he's claustrophobic, which is a four-syllable word. Any time a four-syllable word gets into your system, you've got deep trouble."

"Yah," he said, "Just like Sunshine syndrome."

"Shut up," she said and poked his arm. "Why would he be here?"

"I'm not sure," Service said and pinched the ember off his cigarette.

"Want me to lead?" she said. "Be easier for me to turn around if we get into a tight spot."

"Yah, good idea. How many lights did you bring?"

"Headlamp with red-white alternates, three SureFires, one red-filter penlight, one green-filter penlight, two boxes of new nine volt batts, AA and AAA batts, and two extra SureFire bulbs. You?"

"Same for all, but only one box of batts."

"Light's not going to be our problem," she said. "I'm going to strip off a layer and leave my overcoat outside the entrance. Have you got a full-size space blanket in your gear?"

"In my pack."

"Good, two is good; let's get this deal done."

He could feel her excitement and enthusiasm and, even more, her confidence.

*****

One hour later they halted at the main chamber. There had been boot marks in the dust up top, just inside the entrance where it dropped down to the rock path. Service recognized the pattern and showed his partner. "It's him."

She aimed a red-filtered light onto the track for several seconds. "I've got him."

They spent five minutes at the main chamber for a quick bite of an energy bar, shared from her supply. "Okay," he said. "Let's go.

The down-slope seemed worse than the first time he'd been down here, the angle and tight squeeze more extreme, but this was normal psychology. The second and third reps you always saw more. How does someone with claustrophobia even do this? If I feel it confining, Allerdyce must be near out of his mind. Why in the world is he down here, crazy old coot?

Another forty minutes and Wildingfelz said, "Probable nadir. I hear water. This is where that steep drop is. I almost took a flier here last time down."

"We still have a track?" he asked.

"Yeah, he came down here for sure, on his hands and knees in some places. You want me to keep pushing downward?"

"Yes, I'm pretty sure he's here, it's just a matter of catching up to him." He wanted to add *alive*, but didn't dare say it out loud.

"How long of a lead does he have?" Wildingfelz asked.

"Hours, many hours."

"Are we in a foot pursuit?" she asked.

"No . . . maybe . . . I don't know. Let's find him first and then we'll figure out what to call this."

"Well, the damn cave can go only so far, right?"

"Theoretically."

"Caution at this next descent. Let me find a safe way down for us."

He sat and waited in total darkness, but could hear her shuffling and moving around ahead and below him. After a minute or so she said, "Grady, crawl directly to my voice."

He did as she asked and felt a tap on the top of his head. "That's good. Hold here."

He could feel a light cooler air current, presumably from below. She had her red light turned on; he could see the beam dancing and make out her silhouette in front of him.

"Okay, here we go," Wildingfelz said softly. "Crawl forward and keep your right shoulder against the rock wall. When you get to the end, you can feel it with your hands. There's a ledge, maybe three feet wide, but it's down from where you are maybe five or six inches. Keep your right shoulder along the wall and crawl toward me. I'll be at the next steep spot. Once you're ninety degrees right, use the wall to stand. The chute will be right in front of us, off our left eyes. I'll go first."

Her red light bobbed again, and fifteen seconds later she said, "This is a piece of cake, partner. Just don't crawl straight off because it's a helluva long drop to the bottom. There's heaps of space ahead, okay?"

"Yeah, good."

"Okay, do it."

It was precisely as she had described. When he got to his feet she snapped on her red light. "Keep going," he said, feeling a need to rush cautiously.

They made their way down the steep trail and heard a wobbly voice say, "What took youses so bloody long?"

Allerdyce. Service was so startled he banged his head on a rocky outcrop. He tried to figure out where the voice had come from, but Wildingfelz was already on it.

"So there you are," she said calmly. Her red light lit the old man.

Service saw blood on his hands and face, his right leg twisted in an unnatural direction, his right arm too, nauseating angles. "Fall down on my ass," Allerdyce cackled.

Service turned on his red headlamp. His partner was kneeling beside Allerdyce, quietly assessing injuries, calmly asking him questions and cracking jokes. Her voice was as relaxed as a mother would be with a baby. "Are you feeling lightheaded, Mr. Allerdyce?" she asked him.

"Wah, onny when youse touch me, girlie. Okay youse call me Limpy."

"He's fine," Service said. "Allerdyce, the officer's name is Wildingfelz, not girlie. Show some damn respect. She crawled all the way down here to help your sorry ass." The old snake. Only way to kill him is chop off his ugly little head.

Wildingfelz stood and leaned over him. "Pupils enlarged but not bad, his skin isn't cool to the touch, he's not light-headed. Double bone fracture in the lower right arm, single bone in the right leg, no compound stuff, no poke-throughs, the head stuff is superficial, but it's gonna be a long-ass haul out of here and I want him splinted before we even begin. I think there's some light shock. I'll have to pop back to the top. He's in no immediate danger."

Allerdyce had the pain threshold of a reptile. Service said, "Might as well bring Tree when you go back to your truck. He'll be waiting there for you. We can use his muscle and bulk down here."

"We'll get your friend warm in space blankets and get some liquid into him. You guys can make tea on your jet burner while I'm up top. I've got a tump-line and a pull strap in my JoBox. With Tree above and you and me below, this should be a straightforward deal."

"You believe that?"

"Positive thinking; you should try it."

"Like Custer," he said, and she stuck him with an elbow.

"Wait," Allerdyce said. "Over my head put to wall da light, yah?"

Service shone a beam where the old man directed. "Something shiny?"

"Yah, dat's what I come get, but forget dat stupid right turn up dere."

"What happened to your claustrophobia?" Service asked.

"Fall knock dat shit right outten me. Own damn fault fall. Afeared of dark? Tell self I ain't no kittle no more."

"Any drops between me and the shiny object?" Service asked.

"Clear as new whore's heart," Allerdyce mumbled.

"You have a gift for words," Wildingfelz told him. "You're just like Shake-speare."

"I know dat," Allerdyce said, "but t'anks, Officer Wildingfelz."

Service came back with a dust-encrusted small metal box and rubbed the dust off a metal plate on top of the box riveted under a metal handle. It read: SERVICE, G. Next to it, the old man's badge number, the same badge number he'd worn before being suspended.

"Open 'er up, ain't got no lock," Allerdyce said.

"How do you know?" Service asked.

"Cause I put 'er der, din't I."

Jesus. "When?"

"Be nineteen and fiffy-seben, I'd say. Open 'er up Sonny."

"I'm out of here," Wildingfelz said. "Leaving my extra water. Will do this as fast as I can."

"Not yet," Allerdyce said to her. "Got take look-see, you, be witness."

Service guessed the box was fourteen inches by nine by five, the top shaped sort of like an old Dutch barn. An old iron miner's lunch box? There was an unsealed envelope inside. He pulled it apart and took out two folded documents, folded so long they seemed pressed together. The top one was in his father's chicken-scrawl: "For G. Service, My Son and Heir." It was signed "G. Service." The second document robbed him of words. He handed it to Wildingfelz.

"I think this says you own some land, right?" his young partner said.

"Not some," Allerdyce corrected her. "Dis land 'ere we in. Now Sonny's she is, ever't'ing under da ground 'ere is 'is."

Where the hell to begin? "Harmony, boogey. Go get Tree. The sooner you get back the sooner we can get him out of here."

After she departed and was climbing back toward the surface, Service exploded at the old man. "You son of a bitch, you've got a lot of explaining to do," Service said sharply to Allerdyce. "You assaulted and hog-tied a woman."

"Did not. Look my nose. She head-butt me when she open door. What I gonna do? Den I worry she do bad to Miss Molly so I head-butt 'er back and use da ducks tape to shut 'er big mout' up. I din't do nottin' but defend seff."

"And," Service said, banging the metal lunch pail.

"Nuttin' funny dere. Molly Staff she buy land to keep from Elder. Youse's old man, he say, 'Sell me mineral rights?' Old Wally, he real sick den, ask, 'What youse gonna do with that useless crap?' Your daddy said, 'Let the land sleep, like it ought. No good somebody own top and bottom unless it be da state.' Old Wally Staff he bray like da mule got lucky, said, 'I'd be insane to turn down an offer like that,' stuck out hand, say, 'Youse got deal, Gibby.'"

"What's Molly Staff's connection?"

"She marry jamoke called Cloud. I know her when she little girl. Pretty red hair like strawberry."

"Molly Staff is Molly Stafinski," Service said. He'd already heard this from Marthesdottir.

"No," Allerdyce said. "Her name is Ellie Stafinski, but she like dat name Molly more better."

Service felt his heart jump. E. Stafinski, Ellie Stafinski. Wally Staff's heir. Holy shit.

"What was my old man thinking?"

"Youse know what near 'ere, yah?"

"The old man knew about the diamonds?"

"Back since he was kid, and kep mout' shut."

"But he showed you."

"Yah, partners don't hide nuttin fum each udder."

"So you tell your partner, but hide it from your son?"

"He'd a told youse when old enough. Too young kittle don't know when to keep da mouts shut."

Speechless. "Why's the lunch box down *here*?"

"Youse old man, he tell me take box bank up Gwinn, and I want do dat but had udder stuff do down 'ere and so I put 'ere, tell seff come back later, take to bank."

"Yet here it remains."

"Couldn't make seff climb back down. When youse's old man die, too sad come down 'ere widout him. I t'ink, if it down 'ere, dat good enough as bank an' I tell youse when time get right, hey."

"What if you had kicked the bucket before you told me?"

Allerdyce said, "Youse bring eats? Limpy hungry."

"But what if you'd been hit by lightning, a jealous husband, or a truck?"

Allerdyce said softly, "Weren't none a dat stuff, was I? See if all stuff unnerground is youses and dis down 'ere safe, ain't no way udder jamoke can say 'is deres, hey? Dis place down 'ere good as safety report box."

"Did you think about what would happen if somebody forged fake papers?"

One word response. "Wah."

"You have broken bones, don't they hurt?"

"Not if I get foods. Youse bring lunch?"

Wah, Grady Service thought.

CHAPTER 41

Houghton

HOUGHTON COUNTY

The offices of White, Kobera, Moody, Moody, and O'Halloran were located in the upper warrens of the Douglass House, the longtime hotel reborn in the late eighties as a commercial building on Shelden Street in downtown Houghton.

Allerdyce was in the hospital in Marquette in fair condition, which was just short of a miracle. One of the doctors had remarked, "At his age he should be en route to eternal dust." Instead of dead or dying, he was undergoing tests to assess other damage due to the cave fall. On a closer look, they estimated he fell just more than thirty feet. Service, Wildingfelz, and Treebone all kept the location and details of the fall site to themselves, and when they left the old poacher at the hospital, he was wide awake and making lewd comments to nursing staff.

He'd talked to Frosty O'Halloran as they were racing toward Marquette with their victim. They dared not call EMS for fear of disclosing the deep cave. Wildingfelz had given Allerdyce a thorough on-site assessment once they had him out, and she had been confident they could get him to the hospital without killing him or aggravating his injuries.

O'Halloran had not been happy to be awakened, but she rallied quickly and assured him she would clear a two-hour block for discussion. "Can you be here at ten? Bring all the paperwork you have on this case, including the metal box."

With what remained of the night, he, Tree, and Wildingfelz crashed at Friday's house where he immediately realized that Tuesday and Harmony had met before.

Service packed notes and other material in a cardboard box before he turned in for the night, and had it all done when he noticed the rough diagram that Dotz had drawn of the overflight tracks. He looked at the thing for nearly a minute. His gut searched for an answer in the scribbles. But it didn't or wouldn't come, and he went to bed and crawled in beside Friday, who grumbled, "Don't steal the covers."

"Hey," he said. "You and my new partner, have you been talking?"

"Gawd," she said, and rolled over, giving him her back.

So they had, which explained some of Wildingfelz's aggression. She'd been well coached.

*****

A twenty-something woman with pixied purple, green, red, and white hair and multiple piercings showed them into a conference room. The girl's scrawny arms were replete with ornate tattoos. He wondered if the tattoo needles had struck bone. If she loses her job here, she'll be a shoe-in for a carnival sideshow. He dumped the contents of the investigation out of the briefcase and looked at the clues, which at this point amounted to an unfinished puzzle. Tree carried the metal lunch box and its precious contents. Service stared at all the items on the table, and it seemed something was missing. He groped in his trouser pocket and found Dotz's crumpled drawing. He dropped it on the table just as he heard an aircraft's jet turbines howl overhead. It was rare to hear aircraft this close to the city. He asked the tattooed girl, "What's with the jet?"

"Wind's like different today or something, and they have to like land on like a different runway?" The wind, he'd noted walking from the truck to the Douglass House, was brisk out of the northeast, or close to it. Aircraft land into the wind. They can fly with the wind, or against it, but to land, the pilot has to put the nose into the wind. He found himself remembering Dotz's drawing. Damn thing is telling me something, but I'm too stupid to hear it.

Treebone took the materials out of the foot-long metal box and set them on the conference room table. He took the envelope out of the metal box and set that in front of a place they prepared for their attorney.

Miss Tattoo wheeled a video monitor over to the table and set down a laptop computer. "It's all set up. Do you guys know how to manage a Skype connection?" She looked skeptical.

Treebone said, "I got this. My Kalina and me talk this way all the time." He sat down to make the link.

Connection made, they saw Wildingfelz with Allerdyce in his hospital room. "Can you guys see all right?" the tattooed girl asked. "Volume all right?"

Tree said, "We're good to go, just waiting for the lawyer."

"You guys want me out of the room?" the girl asked.

"Hold tight for now," Service told her.

Frosty O'Halloran strode in, said nothing to anyone, sat down, looked first at the pile of various notes and papers, then to the envelope in front of where she sat. She opened the envelope, took out the two papers and opened them, and read. Her jaw seemed to sink as she read. She put on her glasses. "*Gibson . . . Service?*"

"My father," Service said.

"This is rich," she said with a snort. "Your father bought the mineral rights in question? How ironic, how fortunate, how absolutely downright handy. Do I look like I just fell off a turnip truck?"

Service understood her frustration. He'd already been down this lane. He said only, "It's real."

Frosty O'Halloran rolled her eyes. "And how long have said papers been in your possession?"

Service looked at his watch. "About forty-eight hours."

She harrumphed. "Why didn't you let me know right away? This might have caused a huge reduction in needless legal angst."

"I was kind of busy," he said. "And I knew nothing about them until forty-eight hours ago."

Her voice took on a patronizing tone. "The magic coincidence. Find any beanstalk seeds while you were 'busy'?"

"Dis crap all my fault," Allerdyce said over the Skype connection.

O'Halloran slid her eyeglasses down her nose and squinted at the video screen. "Ah yes," she remarked, "Mr. Malfeasance, Master Minor League Criminal."

"No need use dat voice wit' me, girlie," Allerdyce said. "Listen me. Sonny's father he give me paperswork, say take safety reproduction box at bank Gwinn, but I had some work need get done first so I put in cave for while, and den I sort forgot."

O'Halloran pressed her hand to her forehead. "You put the papers *in a cave*. Now that is *truly* creative. And may I ask when was it that you placed said 'paperswork' in said cave?"

"Dat she would 'ave been nineteen and fiffy-seben."

"Ah, 1957, three decades *before* Congress passed the Michigan Wilderness Act. This gets richer and richer."

Allerdyce said, "Don't know nottin' bout no conkress junk."

"Why did Mr. W. Stafinski, aka Wally Staff, sell the mineral rights to the detective's father?"

"Dat was sorta Gibby's idea. Land above went to Wally's daughter cause Wally didn't want give to idiot son Elder. So Gibby say he buy min'ral junk an' keep it separate, so somebody could own da land, but not mess it up wit' mines and crap."

"And he did this because . . .?"

"Gibby had da big heart," Allerdyce said.

"Last time we talked, you didn't seem to know Staff had children." She picked up the old papers again and looked at Service. "What're these numbers by your father's name?"

"His badge and social security numbers."

"Would those be commonly known?" the lawyer asked.

Service said, "They would not, no."

She went on, "This metal thing is what, a . . . lunch box?"

"For miners," Service told her.

"Made by da Canucks Subidderry, Hontarioak," Allerdyce said over Skype. "Gibby an' me gone over dere for week fish specs, and dis guy dere just start company make dose lunch boxes. Gibby he buy one, hep guy get start, hey."

Last night Service had dug around in old family photographs for almost forty minutes. From the moment he'd seen the box down in the cave, he thought he vaguely remembered it. Service handed the photograph he'd found to the lawyer.

"Who might this be?"

"That might be me," Service said.

Allerdyce squawked on the Skype, "What dat dere is?" Tree put the photo in front of the camera and the old poacher cackled wih obvious delight. "I 'member take dat pitcher! Look wall t'ing behind youse."

Service took the photo from Tree and saw there was a calendar on the wall and the year on top in red was 1957.

O'Halloran said out of the corner of her mouth, "What's this supposed to be, a message to Garcia?"

Allerdyce yelped on the screen. "Who dat she say, who dat?"

"Listen to me," O'Halloran said. "To any sane and sober jurist, all this looks too good to be true, so the question immediately becomes one of verisimilitude and believability of the documents, not to mention the credibility of those claiming to have discovered said documents. Given Mr. Allerdyce's interesting history and *long* reputation, I think we can all see we have a long uphill climb facing us."

"But," Treebone said, "the judge now gets to choose between this or the other and not just between the other and their verbal claim."

"True, to some extent," O'Halloran conceded. "But here's the point. Had these papers been in your hands when all this started, I doubt the other side would have had a prayer. But this stuff was elsewhere and now appears under what can only be called 'magical' conditions."

"Not ain't no magic," Allerdyce insisted. "My screw 'er up."

"We get it," Service said. "A hearing will be a crapshoot."

"Something like that," she said. "If what you're showing me *is* real and verifiable, and I'm not saying it isn't, but if this is real it shows that their evidence appears to be a blatant attempt to defraud the state. In my mind of minds, I wonder what deposit of limestone could possibly justify the inherent risks of criminal charges and jail time, not to mention reputational destruction. One would have to be dangerously deranged to be the ex-governor and risk, based on your evidence, an astonishingly stupid and naked criminal act."

"They're screwed?" Tree asked.

O'Halloran said, "*Au contraire.* Here's the irony: Because it looks on the surface to be too stupid a move and risk to take, your average judge may very well conclude it must be valid because nobody could be so stupidly brazen as to push through such a bald-faced lie. Add to this calculation that the opposition—that would be us—has taken so long to come forward with apparent competing documentation that it would now seem that the second set of data is more likely to be fraudulent than the initial offering. You see the point I'm trying to make? The first big lie can carry the day. For all their positioning to show themselves above human foibles, judges are every bit as human and subject to mistakes and prejudices as the rest of us." She looked at Service. "How long has your father been gone?"

He told her, and she clamped her jaws and shook her head before she looked at the video monitor. "What *were* you thinking, Mr. Allerdyce?"

"Was on accident," the chastised old violator said. "But now we got papers, ain't dat somepin?"

Service was watching the lawyer, who was squirming, and asked her, "Are you trying to tell us that our evidence doesn't matter?"

"I would not state it with that degree of certitude. Ownership claims, even with trunks-full of compelling documentation, are always dicey legal undertakings."

"You a poker player?" Treebone asked.

"On occasion," she said.

"You know what a push is?"

"Of course. Even-steven, nobody wins." O'Halloran's attitude shifted slightly and she leaned forward with a set jaw. "Until this claim by Kalleskevich, the state has been the assumed owner of the mineral rights; thus if neither claim is ruled upon, the status quo will pertain and the state will continue to be assumed the owner of mineral rights."

Service asked, "That happens, the other side can't push ahead with developing whatever it is they want to develop, right?"

She nodded. "Presumably, yes."

Service asked, "And if Kalleskevich withdraws his claim?"

"And yours as well?"

"Let's say the court never even hears about ours."

"Default to status quo," she said. "But why would the claimant withdraw his claim?"

"Think poker," Treebone said.

"You're talking beyond my meager experience."

"If it's your bet and you have a straight flush but suddenly realize that your opponent has a royal flush, what's your next move?"

"Throw in my hand," she said. "Fold."

"There it is," Treebone said. "You fold."

The lawyer chewed a pencil eraser. "The whole thing about poker, I thought, was not to show your hand before you got the pot as high as you could."

"True," Service said, "but sometimes the hand is won long before the hands are shown. Good players going for high stakes can read other hands by how the betting goes. The good ones develop pretty remarkable instincts for judging the unseen."

"We're not talking poker," she tried to remind them.

"Everything is poker," Service said.

"Not a showdown of evidence; that's mine against yours, A versus B and the judge decides."

"Not if you make sure the other player sees your hand before the final bet."

"Isn't that cheating the rules?" the lawyer asked.

"The object is to win," Treebone said, "not to win pretty. And nobody ever said or wrote that showing the other side your hand is against any rules."

"A bluff that's not a bluff," Service explained. "You put your cards on the table and tell the other side, 'beat us if you can,' and then you remind them of the size of the bet and what they stand to forfeit, if they lose, beginning with criminal fraud charges."

"*Un jeu très haut risque*," the lawyer said. "*A periculo ludum*."

Service said, "You just made it very clear to us that for a variety of reasons, most of them psychological and having to do with timing, the judge may very well elect to rule for the claimant." He stopped talking and drew in a deep breath. "But *they* don't know that. Right now Kalleskevich and Bozian think they're in the catbird seat, but it doesn't matter what they think, it's the judge who will make the decision, and they can't really be certain he'll rule for them if they see documents that *show* theirs are fraudulent. When they see how weak their case is, they'll have no choice but to withdraw their claim. They'll think that because it will become paramount for their own security that we don't file officially."

"Their legal counsel may nevertheless urge them to stay in the game," O'Halloran said.

Treebone said, "Mouthpieces who haven't seen the evidence can't advise them of anything. So Grady takes them into a room with no lawyers either side and they play one hand of poker, yours against mine."

"Are all cops this crazy?" she asked.

"Only the great ones," Treebone said. "Which means the ones that always play to win."

"As a lawyer, I just don't know. I've never had a case quite like this. Hell, I've never even *imagined* anything like this!"

"Your field is underground natural resource rights," Service said. "Is that correct?"

"It's all this firm does, and we travel all around the country to do it."

"Here's the other factor," Service said, laying his new badge on the table.

She looked from the badge to his face. "Is that real?"

"Sworn in by the US Attorney in Marquette. It's entirely legal."

"Continue to make your point," she said. "I assume there is one."

"We have a meeting with no lawyers in the room, but we don't promise there won't be a US Deputy Marshal in there. As far as they know, I'm suspended, and by the time we get to a meeting, Bozian will have determined that I can't be a special federal deputy if I'm not on duty with the DNR. The US Attorney will not reveal to anyone that I've been deputized until I give them the say so."

"Good lord, you really do play dirty."

"No, he plays to win," Treebone corrected her. "Ain't no 'dirty' in winning when the other side lies through its teeth."

"But you will also be lying, by omission rather than commission," she said.

"It doesn't matter," Service told her. "If we have evidence that there's legal foul play, we can do pretty much whatever we choose to do to stop it and rectify the situation."

"To be quite candid," O'Halloran said, "I am getting outside my comfort zone. Why are we having this discussion?"

"Lori got you into this mess," Service reminded her.

"She did indeed."

"You've helped us sort this thing out, but as it turns out, we won't need a lot of legal services. All we need from you is to contact the other side and set up a confidential meeting and the ground rules."

"I'm to have no role?"

Service said, "You can help look at our documentation and help us think our way through how we should present all this. We'll want you to throw hand grenades at us, and play devil's advocate."

"I'm happy to do that. Who shall I say will attend from your side?"

"Allerdyce and me. For Kalleskevich, whoever he wants, but no practicing lawyer. Do you read military history?"

"Some, not a lot."

"Think 'forlorn hope.' To break the enemy and an impasse, you sometimes have no choice but to make a frontal assault."

"Aren't a lot of lives lost in that way?" she asked.

"Only two lives matter this time," Service said. "Limpy and me. We've been the point of attack for these assholes through this whole damn thing. Time to turn things around. This standoff ends now. We take them down or we don't."

"If you win, do you intend to press legal fraud charges?"

"That's not our call. The state's lawyers all report ultimately to the sitting governor, so it will land on his desk."

Treebone jumped in. "And word is he has his eye on the White House, so the last thing he needs is to be mired in a case of fraud perpetrated by a former governor from his own party, a fraud in which he has been an unwitting participant. Seems pretty unlikely he'll want to make an example of himself."

"They know you're a cop," the lawyer contended.

"I'm a game warden, and I'm sure they don't think of me as a real cop. Besides, they think I'm suspended and without credentials."

"Don't you have to assume they know about the US Attorney?"

"Did *you* know?" he countered.

O'Halloran shook her head slowly, a smile crossing her face. "Where do you want this meeting?"

"Let them pick the place, but tell them to bring their evidence."

"And if they refuse?"

"Make them understand that would be the dumbest decision since Bill Clinton decided to publicly deny having sexual relations with 'that woman.' But in truth, it doesn't matter if they bring theirs or not. The whole point is for them to see ours."

"Remind me to never gamble with you," O'Halloran said.

"Cops never gamble," Service said. "We only play sure things."

"Don't be so sure," O'Halloran said. "Bear in mind that until 2001 surface deeds had to be registered with the county and state register of deeds. But not so for mineral rights. This has now changed. In the past it was sometimes impossible to determine who owned the mineral rights. Now the state requires that said owners of said rights register said ownership within ten years."

"Ten years from when?" Service asked.

"I don't know the answer to that and will have to look it up," O'Halloran said.

Service played out the scenario. "If it's from the date one knows he owns something, then I have ten years from forty-eight hours ago to comply, is that right?"

"Presumably, yes, but I don't know."

"But if it's been ten years since the actual transaction, it's already unregistered and in the state's domain."

O'Halloran studied the table and said, "If there is a grandfathering clause, which is tied to the law's effective date, you've got two more years in which to comply. And if you fail, rights go over to the state."

She looked at him. "Has anyone ever told you that you have an inordinately, exceptionally complex mind?"

Treebone interrupted. "More times than I've been suspended."

A leering Allerdyce on Skype said, "Girlie dere gone come meetin' wit' us, Sonny?"

O'Halloran reached over and disconnected the Skype connection, no doubt leaving Allerdyce wondering what the hell had happened and complaining to Harmony to fix it.

Grady Service gathered up the paperwork for the cardboard box and looked again at the Dotz drawing. He closed his eyes and superimposed the flight lines on his mind's map, and after a few seconds he finally saw it. None of the flyover lines intersected over the caves. Everything was south, toward the Mosquito River, which meant artifacts had nothing to do with any of this. It was about diamonds.

CHAPTER 42

South of Laingsburg

SHIAWASSEE COUNTY

Ten days after his fall in the cave, Allerdyce had an air cast on his arm and a plaster cast on his leg and they were in a handicap-accessible lift van Service rented to haul them to the Kalleskevich meeting. O'Halloran had needed only one call to get them to agree to a meeting and two more to agree on a site.

As they drove south, Service left the old violator alone. Limpy had spent several days at Friday's house and had been the object of attention from Newf and Shigun. Allerdyce had spent most of every day cackling happily. Service thought ruefully, My old man had asked him to take the papers to the bank—one little favor and he'd screwed it up. Geez.

Since their meeting with O'Halloran, she had been busy. Her research had confirmed (1) that the lunch pail with the critical papers had been made by May Manufacturing of Sudbury, Ontario, (2) that Gibson Service had purchased a metal fourteen by five by nine lunch pail, (3) the date of that purchase, and (4) that the Escanaba jeweler Chrysocolla Koski had etched the metal nameplate.

She had also been able to establish that the deed to the mineral rights was not on current paper stock and that the paper stock used for the deed had been in heavier use in 1957 than any years before or after—until the paper line was discontinued in 1965.

The photograph of young Grady Service was from a Brownie Hawk-eye, which both Service and Allerdyce remembered the old man using all the time. The film developer had been in Marquette, but had gone out of business long ago and had given all the records to the Marquette County Historical Society, where O'Halloran had found the record of the sale, the order filled out in his father's nearly illegible scrawl. Everything she checked out proved to be accurate.

As no law at the time of sale required ownership of mineral rights to be filed, she came up short on this avenue of inquiry. She did find records that seemed to refer to the W. Stafinski property and a sale or property transfer to an E. Stafinski, but this lead died out quickly. Surface rights were sort of accounted for, at the state and county registers of deeds. The state had bought its property in the area of question from E. Stafinski. It was Molly Cloud who sold the surface rights to the state, and the mineral rights to Gibson Service before that.

The land was purchased by the state under the Michigan Wilderness Act in 1986, from E. Stafinski, aka Ellie Staff, subsequently Molly Cloud, who had lived in Marquette at the time, and who had been pre-deceased by her husband at their hunting camp, an eighty-acre parcel in what is now the Mosquito Wilderness Tract. E. Stafinski, aka Molly Cloud, had four eighties, which formed a square in portions of four sections in what became the Mosquito.

Having laid all this out, O'Halloran added, "There is no record of any company ever having owned the land claimed by Kalleskevich as property of one of his holdings."

Meanwhile, M's sources had traced D&D Hop Farms through multiple holding company stops until landing on one overarching holding company with a single owner, Kalleskevich.

"I really sorry dis happen," Allerdyce apologized as they drove south toward the rendezvous.

Wildingfelz was dressed in civvies and driving; Service sat shotgun. It had been her idea to drive so the two men could think about what they would be facing.

Starting in Indian River on Interstate 75, they began to encounter other COs in their black Silverados and Tahoes. The COs would run up beside the van, honk their horns, flip a salute, accelerate, and get off at the next exit. Wildingfelz always honked back, and this continued all the way through Flint and down Interstate 69 West.

Service guessed this to be a show of support arranged quietly by someone, most likely Chief Eddie Waco, except the chief did not know anything about this meeting or its agenda.

"Hey partner," he said.

Allerdyce said, "Yah?"

Service said, "Not you, her—my real partner."

"Yo," she said, grinning.

"All these trucks we're seeing. You set this up."

"No idea what you're talking about. Are you getting paranoid in your old age?"

"Go ahead and deny," he said.

"The tribe," Wildingfelz said from the corner of her mouth. "We may argue and irritate each other, but when it counts there's only one green and gray line."

"Shut up and drive," Service told her. "You . . . whippersnapper."

Allerdyce laughed. "I like dat, whiskersnakers."

"Good one, guys," Wildingfelz said, never breaking a smile.

*****

Below the Bridge was warm and humid, the sort of weather where it was spring one day and sweltering summer the next, with no transition. The meeting site was south of Laingsburg, the same place where Service had met Oheneff, the wayward wife of Kalleskevich. Seeing the place again, he worried that she had taped them and Kalleskevich was waiting with some kind of surprise, but there was nothing to be done about the past. He and Wildingfelz unloaded Allerdyce in his chair, went through the protocol with the security camera, heard the gate pop open, and made their way toward the lake and the hunting camp building. Wildingfelz immediately drove the van off to await a cell phone summons to pick them up.

Allerdyce got out of the van, squinted upward, and said, "Blue-balls sky."

As they walked, Service told Allerdyce, "Let me do the talking. Even if they ask you a question, I'll step in and repeat the question to you. But only if I do that will you actually talk to them, understood?"

The old man shrugged. "Don't worry, Sonny, I make dem t'ink I practice bein' gravestone."

"You damn near were."

"No more talkin'," Allerdyce said, and used his good hand to make a zipping motion across his mouth, cackling softly.

Crazy bastard is enjoying this.

Kalleskevich was waiting outside the camp building. He was the antithesis of King Kong. His hair was feral-gray like mildew, his shoulders rounded and slumped, and he was slightly bowlegged, which left him seeming to tilt to the right. Has he been drinking? Service wondered.

Their host helped Service pull Allerdyce into the camp building and led the visitors into the living area where the big window faced the lake. There in front of the window with the view sat Sam Bozian, his eyes dark, his skin the color of winter fog.

The Canadian lunch box was in Allerdyce's lap. There was no sign that the other side had brought a similar offering.

Kalleskevich said peremptorily, "No wires, no witnesses, straight talk only." He looked a frump, but had a surprisingly commanding voice that demanded both attention and obedience. Service had heard such voices before.

Bozian glared, and said nothing.

A moment of silence settled over them, broken by Allerdyce. "Youse boys are fucked," he said and began cackling.

God. Service put the lunch box on a table between Kalleskevich and Bozian and opened the latch.

Service said, "Our game, go ahead and take a look, Sam."

"You hired that bitch O'Halloran," Kalleskevich said, snorting.

"I beg your pardon?"

"You hired her," Kalleskevich said. "Frosty O'Halloran."

"Hired her to do what?"

Kalleskevich said, "*What* doesn't matter what. I hate that . . ." he didn't finish the sentence.

Nonsensical gibberish. The man's really uptight, Service thought.

"No idea what you're talking about, Mr. Kalleskevich, shall we press on? You claim that one of your companies owns the mineral rights to four eighty-acre parcels in the federally designated Mosquito Wilderness Tract."

"Fact, not claim," Kalleskevich said forcefully, but Service thought he detected weakness in the response, a slight hesitation maybe, the sort of thing you often felt in the split second before a fight went, like the point in an airplane before you feel lift assert itself.

"We have *proof*," Kalleskevich declared.

Service paused and said, "I don't know who you have handling your legal stuff, but you may want to slap an internal auditor on them. I think you guys are getting hosed."

Bozian remained quiet and did not look at the metal lunch box sitting in front of him.

Service flipped open the lunch box, took out the two documents, and set them on the tabletop.

Bozian leaned over and picked up the documents, read them, and impassively handed them to Kalleskevich.

Allerdyce spoke again, "How it feel get caught wit' youse's dicks in hand, boys?"

Service saw Kalleskevich exchange glances with Bozian. No words passed between them. Bozian stood up and walked out of the building. Kalleskevich followed.

Grady Service walked to the door and saw a Hummer back out of the garage and fly down the camp road. There were two heads in the vehicle.

Service reloaded the lunch box, put it back in Allerdyce's lap, called Wildingfelz, and started pushing the wheelchair back to where the van would be waiting. "T'ink we shuff lock up camp door for dose boys?" he said. "Got t'iefs ever'wheres dese days."

CHAPTER 43

Mosquito Wilderness Tract

"What's down in that cave belongs to all the people of the state," Wilding-felz said. They were standing just beyond where the cave entrance had once been, blocked now by a massive boulder Service had lowered into place five days ago. He had told his partner nothing about it, and she was seething.

"I'm not arguing that. But if we make this place known, the state will let archaeologists in and they'll bring students and write papers and pretty soon it will be crawling with all kinds of people. So I decided we needed to seal the entrance. It can always be uncovered sometime down the road, but for now it stays closed. I don't want people traipsing all over this place because sooner or later they will find the diamonds."

"God?" she said, looking over at him.

"Harmony, partner, listen to me. With diamonds near here, high gem-quality stones worth a lot of money, the reality is that the more people we have screwing around out here, the more likely someone is to stumble onto them. If that happens, this place will no longer be a wilderness. It will become a carnival for knuckleheads with treasure on their minds."

"God," she said again.

"This boulder solves our problem for now, but someday you may have to make a decision different than this. I'll no longer be around and then it will be all your baby," he told her. "And I do not envy you that decision or moment. This is a delicate, sweet, damn ugly place and I intend to keep it that way while I'm here."

Kalleskevich and Bozian had withdrawn the claim. The state attorney general had all the paperwork needed to determine what had gone down in the attempted fraud. It was up to them as to what happened next. Service was almost certain the whole thing would be ignored. Meanwhile, he was reinstated and awarded back pay, which came as a surprise.

"How did those boulders get there?" she asked.

"Same way we put moose up in the McCormick. A chopper."

"Won't Lansing want a reason for the expense?" she asked.

"Lansing? This isn't their budget and it's not their business. You and I take care of this place. We guard it, not them."

"Right," Wildingfelz said.

They both heard the sound of four-wheelers in the distance, and she looked at him excitedly and said, "Hear that?"

"I hear. You better book it if you're going to catch up to them. Yell if you need assistance. Go get 'em."

"You mean we, right?"

"No, I mean you. You're the one with the young legs and four-syllable eyes. I have thinking to do."

He watched the easy loping gait of his young partner. She runs with the silence of a wild thing, he thought. Yeah, we're gonna do just fine, her and me. And Allerdyce.

Author's Note

This is the eleventh Woods Cop novel, written over eighteen years of ride-alongs with Michigan Conservation Officers (COs) in the course of doing their duty.

It is a great privilege to be afforded this opportunity, and it has allowed me to see the job in practically every part of the state and to work in an astounding variety of conditions and situations. My problem is never what to put into a story, but what to leave out. Many of the things our COs encounter simply defy believability, even when one is right there watching it unfold.

My thanks to the officers and their families for all they do and contend with, and for putting up with the "white-haired old fart," as one citizen in Iron County once described me.

This book could not have been written without the expert advice, assistance. and guidance of Marvin Roberson, Forest Policy Specialist for the Sierra Club of Michigan. Marv is an outdoorsman, a conservationist, a wildland enthusiast, a dog lover, and a smart cookie who can simplify complex issues and make them more understandable for the likes of me. Our wildlands need more passionate advocates like Marv—especially in times when states desperately want outside investment and development.

If there are any errors in this story—in the law and any related matters—it is my sole responsibility.

I am a lucky man by all measures, and here's something to remember when you are out in Michigan's woods and on its waters: You may never see conservation officers, but they see you. Be safe out there.

What's next for Grady Service? We shall see.

Joseph Heywood
Michigan Technological University, Ford Campus
Alberta Village
Baraga County, Michigan
Eclipse Day, August 21, 2017